R.L. PEREZ

WILLOW & GRAVE

Willow Haven Press

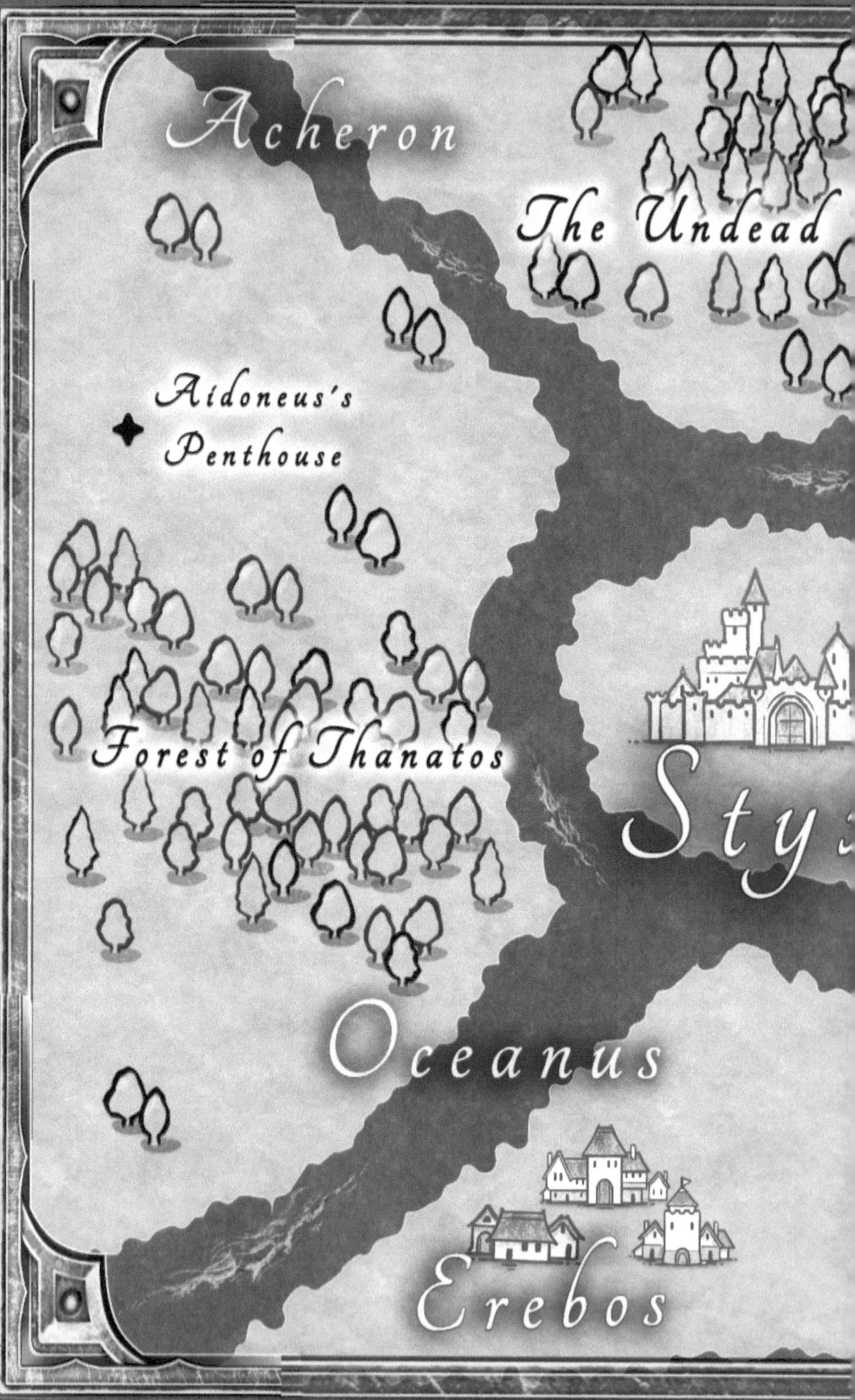

Acheron
The Undead
Aidoneus's Penthouse
Forest of Thanatos
Stys
Oceanus
Erebos

Cocytus
Portal to
Elysium
Tartarus
Pool of
Forgetfulness
Lethe
Gate to the
Mortal Realm
Realm of the Underworld

Askir Mountains
Faidon
Thanassian Empire
Voiceless Jungle
Sodara
Ruins of Rhea
Realm of Gaia

Emdale Mountains
Murane
Voula City
Salwaki Islands
Krenia
Manos Ocean

Ares Jungle
Fulcrum
Realm of Elysium

Portal
Amara
Portal

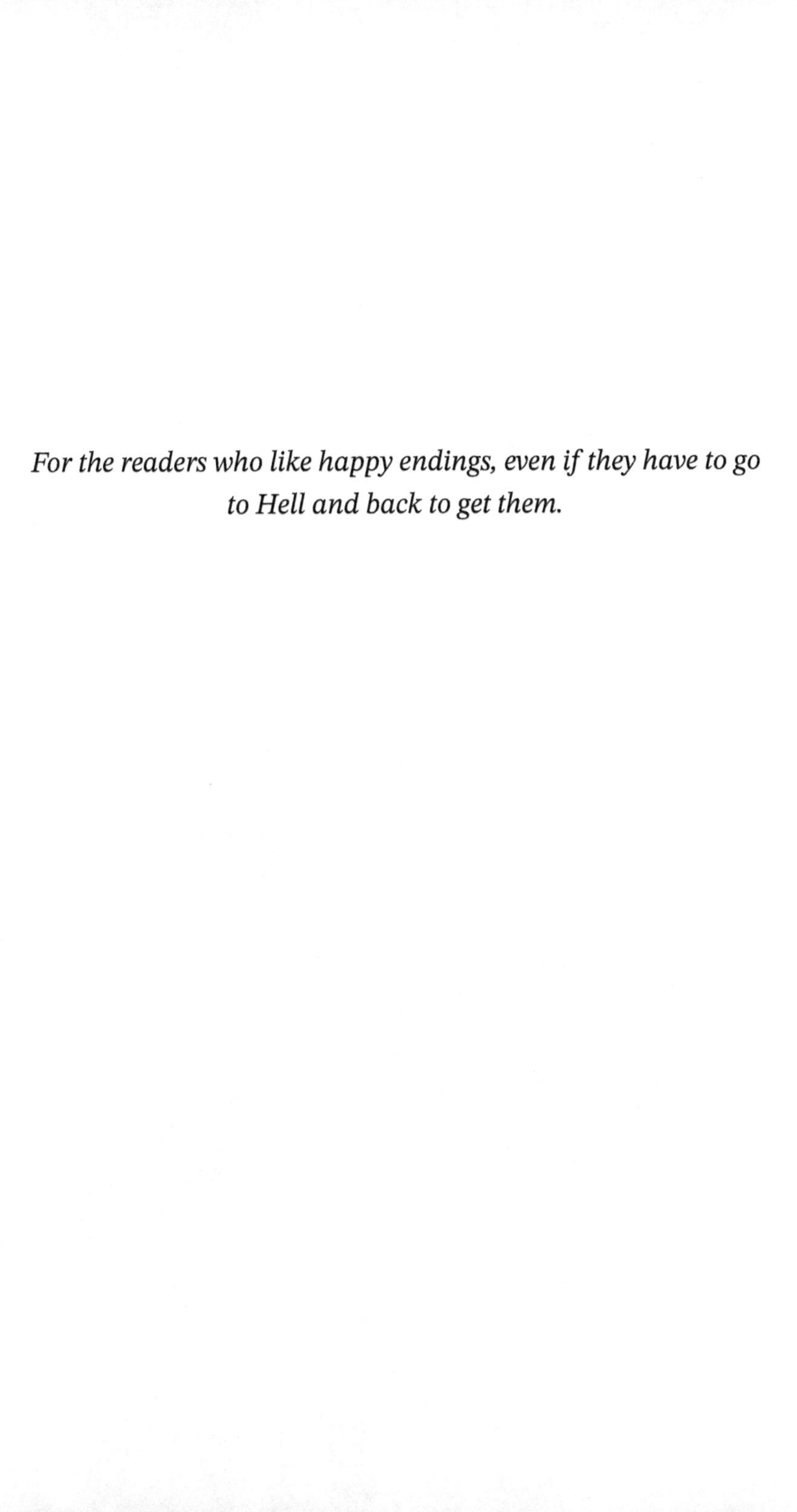

For the readers who like happy endings, even if they have to go to Hell and back to get them.

BROKEN
TRIVIA

SHE WAS NOTHING AND NO ONE.

All she knew was darkness.

Her mind drifted aimlessly among the cavernous void that surrounded her.

But there was another presence nearby. She could sense it.

Someone was watching her.

A tingling sensation swept over her, like a chill or a whispering wind. Only, she had no physical form. So how could she feel such things?

Echoes of screams and cruel laughter surrounded her—a taste of the horrors within Pandora's box. The screams of the victims, and the laughter of the darkness.

The most painful part of it all was that she still retained her memories. She still *knew* she was Pandora. Or Trivia. One of those two. She knew she had willingly sacrificed herself to seal up the box.

But the longer she floated in this infinite chasm, the less sane she felt. Were they memories at all? Or constructs of her imagination? Had she ever truly had a body of her own?

Of course she had. She remembered heat and longing and pleasure... A face with midnight blue eyes and golden hair.

Sometimes she could even hear Sol's voice whispering in her ear.

Other times, the details of his face and voice and laughter slipped through her mind like water droplets she was desperately trying to keep from running through her fingers.

Perhaps she had been trapped here for years. Or perhaps it was merely days.

Somewhere out there, Sol and Gaia were living their lives. Without her.

But she had chosen this. And she would do it all over again, if it meant saving them.

My debt is paid, she thought. *I have fully atoned now.*

She wanted this to bring her some semblance of peace. She wanted to move on. To leave this wretched place and cross over to the next world as a soul released from death.

But this hell would never release her. And she would never be free.

That was her sentence—an eternity trapped in Pandora's box.

Fitting, since it was her fault it was opened in the first place. She had no one to blame but herself.

A soft chuckle sounded nearby. This wasn't a faint echo, like all the other sounds in the darkness. This one felt *too* close, like the person stood only a breath away.

She wanted to speak, to ask who was there, but she had no voice. No mouth.

And even if she did, what could she say? The evil that lurked here was monstrous and vile, but it could not hurt her. She had nothing left for it to hurt.

She was already shattered. Broken. Fragments of a soul who had once been.

And this was how she would always be.

"Do you ever stop pitying yourself?" asked a voice.

That same shuddering chill swept over her mind. Who was speaking to her? Who was even coherent enough to do such a thing?

This place was a prison for all. Including her.

"Not for me," said the voice. "I alone am free."

This couldn't be true. *No one* was free in Pandora's box.

"Except for... its creator."

Oh gods, no. She wanted to vanish from existence, to hide from this presence that had haunted her for her entire life.

Of all the sins she wanted to escape, *this* was what she yearned to be rid of the most.

"You cannot hide from me, child. You never could. I am *always* with you. And now that we are in *my* domain, I have the power I have always craved."

A form shimmered into view, piercing through the darkness. Golden tan skin. A white dress draped over one shoulder. Raven black hair. And burning amber eyes.

Pandora. The true Pandora.

The goddess smirked, then flicked her wrist.

With a gasp, Trivia inhaled her first breath in what felt like eons. Her own body materialized, hovering directly in front of Pandora. Her skin was just a shade darker than Pandora's. Her hair looked like flames against the darkness. It floated behind her as if she were completely weightless.

Perhaps she was.

A cold sweat broke out on her skin—gods, it felt so strange to have *skin*. She blinked, her eyes dry and irritated. Her throat burned, and every inch of her ached with a bone-weary exhaustion that made her want to crawl into a hole and never come out.

"That would be too easy," Pandora crooned. "No, you must be *present* for this part, dear Trivia. I offered you freedom, and you threw it all away. To rest peacefully amidst the darkness would be too light of a punishment for you."

"I would hardly call this *peaceful*," Trivia snapped, her voice raspy from days—months? Years?—of silence.

Pandora planted a hand on her hip, one thin eyebrow raised. "Are you complaining? You *chose* this."

Trivia had no argument for that. Because it was true; she *had* chosen this.

But somehow, she hadn't realized it meant an eternity with *her*. Somehow, she had believed she'd finally been free of the goddess who tormented her.

How foolish of her.

"Mm, foolish indeed," Pandora agreed, smiling wide enough to show her teeth.

"Stop reading my mind," Trivia snapped, crossing her arms over her chest. She realized she was dressed in a burgundy tunic and brown trousers—the same clothes she'd been wearing when she and Sol had activated the failsafe in Elysium.

The last day she had seen Sol, she'd been wearing this.

When he'd screamed her name, begging her not to give herself up...

And she'd sobbed, pleading with him to save her mother instead of her...

"Gods, you're pathetic," Pandora sneered, waving her hand at the darkness that surrounded them.

In an instant, the world shifted, and a square of light appeared to Trivia's left. Through the square, she could see all manner of shapes and colors. They spun in a dizzying array, making her feel nauseous and disoriented. She shut her eyes, but Pandora tsked at her.

"None of that. I need you to see this."

An invisible force peeled back Trivia's eyelids, forcing her to watch. When her gaze fixed on the image in the square, her heart tumbled in her chest.

Sol.

He was standing next to the portal alongside Gaia. It looked like they were arguing, though Trivia couldn't hear anything. Sol gestured with his arms, his expression dark with anger.

So many times, that fury had been directed at *her*.

A lump formed in Trivia's throat at the sight of him. Gods, he was gorgeous.

"Mmm, isn't he?" Pandora purred.

"Stop doing that!" Trivia hissed. "Stay out of my head!"

"You don't get to command me anymore. This is *my* domain, child."

"I never commanded you," Trivia said. "You may not

have had a body, but you were *always* in control. Even when you led me to believe otherwise."

Pandora smirked, her face full of triumph. "It took you far too long to realize that, didn't it?"

Yes, Trivia thought. *Far too long indeed.*

Perhaps if she had known sooner, she could have changed things.

She could have saved the Underworld. Elysium. So many had perished because of her.

Pandora made a retching sound. "You think too much. How about we just watch instead?" She gestured to Sol and Gaia, her lips curling in satisfaction.

"Why are we watching this?" Much as she wanted to, Trivia couldn't tear her gaze away from Sol's beautiful form. Each moment she watched him, it felt like a blade was being wrenched through her chest. The sight of him, when she could no longer touch him, smell him, taste him... It was too much for her to bear.

"You'll see," Pandora crooned.

The tone of her voice made Trivia's skin prickle with dread. What was Pandora planning?

Then, she saw it. A tendril of black smoke inched its way toward Sol. It was so faint that Trivia would have missed it if she hadn't been looking.

Sol didn't notice. He continued shouting something at Gaia. Meanwhile, the darkness coiled around his calf, twining up his leg.

"Sol!" Trivia shrieked. "Sol, *watch out!*"

"He can't hear you, you fool," Pandora snapped, but her face was full of glee.

Another coil of shadows snaked up his other leg.

Trivia couldn't breathe, her eyes wide as she watched, helpless to stop it. Pandora flicked her fingers sharply, and the shadows suddenly tightened around Sol's legs, jerking him down to the ground. He buckled, gritting his teeth as he finally looked down to see that the darkness from Pandora's box had snatched him. On his knees, Sol sent a jet of sunlight directly into the shadows. But they held fast.

Gaia stretched her hands toward the darkness, murmuring an incantation Trivia couldn't hear. Vines and leaves sprang up from the ground, attacking the darkness.

Pandora made a frustrated sound. "Damn this earth magic."

To Trivia's surprise, one of the tendrils of smoke dissolved as Gaia's barbed vines severed it. Together, with Sol's magic, they managed to loosen the second shadow as well. Sol scrambled away from the shadows, his eyebrows lowering in rage. He shot more sunlight at the darkness, and it retreated, slithering away like a serpent.

A relieved breath whooshed from Trivia's chest. She closed her eyes briefly, thanking the gods that Sol had escaped.

But Pandora's chuckle had her eyes opening again and fixing on the goddess.

She still looked smug.

"That was only a taste of what I can do from here," she said. "Imagine if I unleashed it *all* on him. He would be powerless to stop it. You've seen the darkness yourself. You know how indestructible it is."

Trivia's chest seized with horror. "Why?" she croaked. "Why are you doing this?"

"Haven't I made myself clear?" Pandora drew closer, her amber eyes flashing. "This is all to punish you. We could have had freedom, child. We could have had *everything*. But you threw it all away for *them*." She pointed at Sol and Gaia with a disgusted sneer.

Trivia shook her head, her eyes hot with tears. "Please. Please don't..."

Pandora tilted her head and tapped her chin thoughtfully. "Perhaps I'll drag them down slowly, so they don't notice until it's too late." Her eyes lit up. "Or maybe I'll go after your sisters! That would be a fun challenge."

Tears spilled down Trivia's face. "*Please.* What do you want from me?"

"I want my life back," Pandora said. "I want what you promised me: *freedom.*"

"How am I supposed to give you any of those things when you have me trapped here?" Trivia shouted, her voice echoing in the vast space around them.

"*I* haven't trapped you. You did this yourself. My power only exists inside the darkness. I have no way out, just like you." She pointed a long-nailed finger at Trivia. "You find me a way out of this box, and I'll spare your little lover and your mother. I'll spare everyone you love. But only if you give me what I ask."

"*How?*" Trivia shrieked. She wanted to scream with frustration. "If you can't get out, how am I supposed to?"

"You are an earth goddess. You possess power I never

could access." She smirked. "You'll figure it out. Or else everyone you love will suffer."

"You can't—"

"I've had enough of your blathering." Pandora waved a hand, and in an instant, Trivia was back in that void of nothingness. Her body disappeared. Her voice vanished.

And she knew nothing but the agony swirling around her.

SCHEMES
CYRUS

CYRUS LANDED A PUNCH IN EVANDER'S GUT, AND HE pushed his advantage. He struck him again and again until his brother hunched over with a low moan. Victory pulsed through Cyrus, but it was short-lived. In a flash, Evander's ghostly wings shot outward. One of them knocked Cyrus sideways. He caught himself before he collapsed in the dirt.

Evander rammed his shoulder into Cyrus, then stomped on his toes. Cyrus howled in pain, gasping for breath. Evander's elbow rammed into his stomach, knocking the breath out of him. His fist connected with Cyrus's jaw. Cyrus tasted blood, and his body ached where his brother struck him.

But the ache was good. It was potent and strong and distracted him from the chaos of his thoughts.

From the agony of missing Prue.

Of being unable to help her. To find her.

With a growl, Cyrus attacked again, fists slamming into

Evander's bare chest. Evander bellowed in part rage, part anguish as he met Cyrus blow for blow. Both of them were covered in sweat and blood.

It was like this every day. Cyrus would meet with his council of advisors to brainstorm on how to locate the Titans. And when they came up short—as they always did—Cyrus and Evander would beat out their frustration on each other, looking for an outlet for their fury.

It would only last so long. Each day, the tension within Cyrus wound tighter and tighter, ready to burst. He wanted to tear the realms apart to find his wife without a care of who he killed along the way.

But he had a kingdom to think about.

The old Cyrus would have destroyed everyone and everything in his path to get Prue back.

But he wasn't that person anymore.

"Are you really just going to sit back and do nothing?" Evander hissed as he swung his fist and Cyrus blocked it.

"I'm doing everything I can," Cyrus grunted.

"Are you? That Titan said, '*When you are ready to negotiate for her freedom, you know how to reach us.*' What did he mean? If you have a way to contact them, why haven't you done it yet?"

Cyrus closed his eyes and pulled at his hair. "I don't know! Don't you think if I knew I would have done it already?"

"Have you checked the spell books? The Book of Eyes?"

Cyrus's blood chilled, and his nostrils flared. "You know how dangerous that book is."

"The Cyrus *I* know would have stopped at nothing to find Prue. Even if it meant diving into that godsforsaken book."

"Prue wouldn't want me to do that. Not for her."

"Who gives a damn what she wants? She isn't here!"

With a roar, Cyrus tackled Evander, pinning him to the ground and wrapping his hands around his throat. "You piece of shit," he growled, pressing his thumbs into Evander's throat. "You think this isn't killing me? You think I don't already feel helpless?"

Evander's hips bucked, jolting Cyrus enough that he loosened his grip on Evander's throat.

"You have... the power of... the Titans," Evander wheezed, shoving Cyrus off him and massaging his neck. "You're the... king of... the Underworld. And you're doing *nothing*."

"I'm trying to be smart about this," Cyrus said, wiping sweat from his brow. "If we go into another realm and start ripping apart villages in search of them, we'll be exposed. The Titans will know exactly where we are and they'll easily pick us apart. We will lose any advantage we have."

"And sitting here in the Underworld gives us the advantage?"

"It gives us the element of surprise. With me as king, I have the magic of the Underworld on my side. The Titans know that. It's why they didn't destroy us in the Undead Wilds as soon as Apollo died. But they also know we are scrambling and we are desperate. They are *expecting* us to do something foolish and reckless. Don't play into their hands, Evander."

Evander's throat bobbed as he swallowed hard, then dropped his gaze. There was a fire in him that Cyrus hadn't seen before. It was making him more unhinged every day.

"We *will* find them," Cyrus said, putting a hand on Evander's shoulder.

Evander jerked out of his grasp and bared his teeth. "Don't console me. I haven't been able to *breathe* since that day. They should be here with us. *She* should be here. I can't —I don't—" He broke off with a snarl, then ran a hand through his sweaty hair.

"Evander," Cyrus said gently, his brow furrowing. "It's all right. We can—"

"I said *don't console me*," Evander snarled.

Cyrus lifted his palms. "Fine. I won't. But you need to talk to me. Ever since Prue and Mona were taken, you've been... unwell."

"No shit," Evander snapped. "I wonder why."

"Brother, *talk to me*. You can't continue with this manic behavior. What happened to them was not your fault, and Mona wouldn't want you to think that way."

Evander shook his head violently, then spread his pearly wings. "I'm not doing this with you. Good luck with your useless schemes."

He shot upward into the air, his translucent wings beating furiously as he flew away from the castle and out of sight. Cyrus watched his brother leave, his chest tightening with unease.

It was like this every day. Evander was unwell, but whenever Cyrus tried to talk to him about it, his brother fled.

Cyrus knew how it felt to feel frustrated and panicked without the one he loved. But this ran deeper than that.

Evander blamed himself. Cyrus could see it in the haunted look on his brother's face.

But no amount of self-loathing would bring Prue and Mona back. If Evander was unwilling to think clearly, then Cyrus would have to be the levelheaded one.

How strange that their roles were now reversed. Ordinarily, Cyrus was more hotheaded and Evander was calm and collected.

But everything in the realms had changed. *Cyrus* had changed. And even if he could go back to who he was, he wasn't sure he wanted to.

"Cyrus," said a voice.

He turned to find Lagos standing at the entrance to the training yard. Cyrus strode toward him, hope and urgency pulsing within him. With the head of a bull, Lagos's expressions were impossible to read. But there was something about the stiff set of his shoulders that told Cyrus something had happened.

"What is it?" Cyrus asked, his chest thrumming with anticipation.

Lagos took a shaky breath. "We found it."

Lagos led Cyrus into the castle, up the stairs, and to the throne room. Cyrus let his gaze drift to the massive throne on the dais, his mind returning to that moment when he'd taken Prue right here in the throne room...

Despair twisted in his gut, but he forced it down. *She isn't dead. There is still hope.*

In the center of the throne room was a long table where two other demons sat—Theo, a dark-skinned demon with a long, serpentine tail, and Maleck, a massive demon with pale skin and a single blue eye. Sitting next to Maleck, his tongue lolling happily, was Cerberus the dog. Eons ago, Cyrus's father, Aidoneus had spread rumors of a terrifying three-headed beast, hoping to frighten enemies away from the realm. But in truth, Cerberus was just an ordinary black dog. Somehow, the canine had survived the destruction of the realm—likely because he possessed no magic and was therefore no threat to Pandora's darkness. The creature had taken a liking to the demons, particularly Maleck, who was scratching behind the dog's ears.

Lagos, Theo, and Maleck were the three most proactive demons on Cyrus's council. They had worked the hardest, sacrificing everything to track down clues for locating the Titans.

Cyrus could not have done this without them.

On the table sat the broken shards of a dish. As Cyrus gazed at the table, his heart sank with realization.

We found it, Lagos had said.

But he hadn't sounded pleased or triumphant.

He'd sounded dejected.

"Shit," Cyrus whispered as he drew closer to the table, running his fingers over one of the gray shards. These were the remains of the reflection bowl—an enchanted bowl of liquid that allowed one to see anywhere they wished in all the realms.

And it was broken.

"We found it on the outskirts of the Undead Wilds," Theo said softly. "Apollo must have smashed it before the challenge."

"Or one of the Titans," Lagos speculated.

It didn't matter who had broken it; whoever had done it knew that Cyrus would try to use it to locate the Titans.

And now he couldn't.

What game were the Titans playing? Why smash the bowl and then tell him if he wanted to negotiate, he knew how to reach them?

What was he supposed to do?

He brushed his fingers over each piece, mentally conjuring the image he remembered of the reflection bowl. How big had it been?

"Is this every piece?" Cyrus asked, glancing between the demons.

"Yes," said Maleck. "Every piece we could find."

"Can it be repaired?" Cyrus asked.

Silence met his words.

"I mean, as an ordinary bowl," he clarified. "If this were just a normal dish, could it be repaired?"

"Yes," Maleck said at once. "We can fuse the pieces together."

"Let's try that, then." Cyrus braced his hands on the table, struggling to maintain a calm persona. Inwardly, he was screaming and raging. This had been his one key to locating

Prue. The one thing he'd known would work. "How long would that take?"

"We can have it done by tomorrow," said Theo.

Cyrus nodded once. "Thank you. I appreciate all you have done."

The three demons glanced among themselves. Theo and Maleck wore looks of surprise and the hint of pride. Lagos, as usual, had an unreadable expression. Cerberus wagged his tail happily.

"Is there anything else?" Cyrus asked. "Anything you've found, or any concerns you have?"

The three demons exchanged another look, this one full of hidden meaning.

Unease prickled along Cyrus's skin. "What is it? You can speak plainly."

For a moment, the demons said nothing. Then, Lagos murmured, "The people are... agitated. Restless. Many of them have already begun to mourn the loss of the Queen of the Underworld."

Every muscle in Cyrus's body went rigid. "She is not dead," he bit out.

"I know," said Lagos. "But the people loved her. And it's been several days since the Titans took her. They... don't know what else to do."

Cyrus closed his eyes and ran a hand down his face. He was so tired. So godsdamned tired.

And all his efforts were just not enough.

When you are ready to negotiate for her freedom, you know how to reach us.

"Have you spoken to the people?" Theo asked Lagos.

"Yes. Many times. But it is hard to appease them when they saw firsthand how terrifying the Titans were."

Cyrus was only half-listening, his eyes still closed as he recalled the way that Titan had taunted him, as if he'd *known* how difficult it would be for Cyrus to find them.

"It didn't help that Apollo chose the Undead Wilds for the challenge," said Maleck. "That place is horrifying enough, even without those beastly Titans."

Cyrus's eyes snapped open with sudden awareness.

The Undead Wilds.

A chill skittered down Cyrus's spine as he thought of the ghostly wayward spirits of the Undead Wilds who had pledged their loyalty to him just after Prue and Mona had been taken.

For a moment, his mind returned to that scene. Right after the Titans' portal had vanished, the spirits had appeared. They had knelt before him as a sign of respect; a sign that he had become a king who was worthy of their loyalty.

"I swear a solemn vow to you that if you help me rescue Prue and Mona, I will see to it that you are finally freed," Cyrus had told them. "That your souls will find rest at last."

The souls had been silent for a moment as they considered his offer. Then, with one collective voice, they replied, "We accept."

But Cyrus's relief from their acceptance was short-lived.

"Do you know how to find Prue and Mona?" Cyrus had asked. "Where do we start?"

One of the souls had chuckled lightly. "It is not that simple, my king. First, we need payment from you."

Cyrus's eyes narrowed. "Payment? We already struck a bargain."

"Yes, and now we require a show of good faith. Give us a drop of your immortality to feed our starving souls. And we will tell you what we know."

Unease swirled in Cyrus's chest. A drop of his immortality?

His skin prickled, warning him of approaching danger.

"You pledged your loyalty to me," Cyrus argued. "Does that mean nothing? Will you not serve your king?"

The spirits' voices had raged, echoing loudly around him. "We are betraying our kind by revealing the mystic secrets of the past. Does *that* mean nothing to you? Will you not prove to us that your bargain was in earnest, and give us but a taste of freedom?"

Cyrus had gone perfectly still at that, his pulse thundering in his ears as he connected the pieces.

A drop of immortality.

A taste of freedom.

Gods above. The cost of freeing the Wild Spirits... was his own immortality. His very *life*.

They asked for one drop now, but they would keep asking for more until his immortal soul was gone.

He didn't even know if he *was* still immortal. The price might kill him instantly, and he would never see Prue again.

And who would rule his people? Who would care for the kingdom? If he died, no one could rescue Prue, and the realm would have no leader. No one to protect them. No one to oversee the rivers of souls or the magic of the land.

How could he even trust these spirits to fulfill their end

of the deal? They had been trapped in the Underworld for eons. How would they be able to locate someone in another realm?

"What is it?" Lagos asked, jolting Cyrus to the present. His dark eyes were fixed on Cyrus, missing nothing.

Cyrus quickly shook his head, ridding himself of that awful memory. The moment he knew he could never fulfill his promise to the spirits.

Not unless he wanted to die.

But... with the reflection bowl broken, what choice did he have? There were no other options.

"The Wild Spirits," Cyrus said slowly, his chest knotting with dread. "What do you know of them?"

Theo shuddered. "They are ancient," he said in a hushed voice. "They come from a time before dark magic. Before all of us. They come from an era that has long since been forgotten."

Cyrus stared at his hands, which gripped the edge of the table so tightly his knuckles turned white. Could he reason with the souls? If he explained his lack of immortality, perhaps they would be understanding.

He almost laughed at the idea.

"Perhaps the spirits know of an ancient magic you can use to contact the Titans," Maleck mused. Beside him, Cerberus whined softly and cocked his head to the side, likely noticing the tension in the room.

The Wild Spirits probably *did* know of all kinds of spells and magic that had been lost to time. What if they advised him to use a magic that would trap him in Tartarus forever?

Or what if they urged him to use the Book of Eyes, binding his soul to the mortal realm once more?

Could he even trust anything they said? As soon as they knew he had no immortality to give him, they could easily deceive him with false information.

Or refuse to help at all.

Theo hissed in a sharp breath and shook his head. "That is far too dangerous. Magic has changed so much since those spirits were alive. And you, my king, are not... yourself."

This was true. Cyrus was a human reborn, but infused with Titan magic. He had no idea what those ancient powers might do to him.

They could kill him.

Cyrus rubbed his chin, his thoughts spinning.

"Now it is your turn to speak plainly, Cyrus," Lagos said, his voice gentle. "What are you thinking?"

In another lifetime, Cyrus would have snapped at him, perhaps ordered him to leave the throne room. He might have even had him punished for speaking to him in such a cavalier way.

But those days were long gone. And what had once seemed like a weakness to him now gave him strength.

Lagos was here to support him. So were Theo and Maleck.

He was not alone.

He inhaled deeply and said, "The Wild Spirits require my immortality to be freed."

All three demons gasped, their eyes wide with fear.

"I have already sworn an oath to do what I can to free

them from whatever magic has trapped them here. I cannot go back on that."

"Cyrus, that will kill you," Lagos said softly. "The realm needs you."

Cyrus closed his eyes. He had been foolish to strike this bargain without considering the consequences. Without thinking it through.

But Prue's life was at stake. So was Mona's. How could he stand by and do nothing? Evander's accusations from earlier rang in his mind. *You're the king of the Underworld. And you're doing nothing.*

Cyrus took a deep breath. "The Wild Spirits *are* ancient. Which is exactly why I am wary of trusting them. We know nothing about them or where they came from. For all we know, they could be wayward souls from Tartarus that got trapped amidst an escape attempt.

"But... Apollo chose the Undead Wilds as the location of the challenge for a reason. What if Hyperion encouraged him to do it? What if the Titans have a connection to the Wild Spirits?"

Lagos inhaled deeply. "It is... certainly plausible. But if they have connections to the Titans, I don't think that is a good thing. What if they are allies of the Titans?"

"Regardless of any former alliances they might have held, they swore their loyalty to me," Cyrus said.

"And you believe them?" Lagos asked.

"I don't know," Cyrus said. "But I don't have any other options." Straightening, he said firmly, "I need to speak with them." He had half-turned to the door when Lagos gripped his arm.

"Cyrus..."

"I will not give up my immortality," Cyrus promised. "Not without consulting you three first. But, I must see what information they are willing to give before I offer the payment I promised."

Lagos nodded grimly. "Very well. But I'm coming with you."

Cyrus shook his head. "They need something from me. I don't believe they will hurt me. But I can't say the same for you, and I'm not willing to risk it." He looked at Lagos with a mixture of gratitude and regret.

He would actually feel much more comfortable if Lagos *did* accompany him. His stomach roiled with uncertainty at the thought of facing those spirits alone.

When they had pledged their loyalty to him, he'd felt powerful and exuberant, like he could conquer anything and anyone.

But since that moment, a part of him was terrified that he couldn't measure up to the ruler everyone expected him to be. What if he returned to his old ways? What if he made a horrible mistake? So many people were depending on him.

He had made so many missteps as king, so many grievous errors all for the sake of power. How could he be certain not to follow that same path once again? It had become instinct for him, and now he had to start anew.

For a god as old as he was, it was a daunting prospect.

For Prue, he reminded himself. *This is for Prue.*

He nodded once, resolve coursing through him. "I'll leave for the Wilds at once. Thank you for your counsel." He gestured to the shattered reflection bowl. "In the meantime, repair the bowl and let me know when it's finished. If the spirits can't provide us with any answers, that's the only lead we have."

The demons muttered their assent and began scooping up the broken pieces of the bowl. Cyrus turned and left the room, agitation burning inside him as he wondered if perhaps Evander had been right.

Perhaps he wasn't doing enough. Perhaps *none* of it would be enough to bring back his wife.

HOPELESS
PRUE

PRUE HAD TRAVELED THROUGH PORTALS BEFORE, BUT nothing like this.

The Titans' magic shifted and twisted around her, warping the air with something dark and unnatural that grated against the earth magic surging in her veins.

Wrong, wrong, wrong, the magic seemed to pulse.

Revulsion and nausea swept over her, and when the dark magic rippled, she thought she might vomit.

Mona's hand was clamped in hers. Her sister was trembling.

Prue had to be brave. For her.

She crammed her eyes shut, gritting her teeth and promising herself it would be over soon. Any second now, and the darkness would fade, and she would be able to *breathe.*

The air shifted again, and a whoosh of air filled her

lungs. An invisible force slammed into her, crashing into her store of magic and jarring her very bones.

She and Mona collapsed onto something rough and cracked, like stone or concrete. Blinking wearily, Prue glanced up at a murky gray sky. They were in a wasteland of decaying trees. A patch of square concrete was beneath her, and dust and sand surrounded her.

No flora in sight. But Prue was certain this was intentional.

The Titans were many things, but they were not stupid.

Prue pressed her fingers into the dry concrete, just to check. She summoned her magic and waited for it to surge forward, to plunge into the earth and seek out the energy around her.

But nothing happened.

Panic bloomed in her chest, and she tried again, drawing more from her well of power.

But the well... was empty.

Beside her, Mona was gasping, breathing in ragged and uneven breaths.

"No magic," Mona choked. "Prue, there's *no magic here.*"

Prue squeezed Mona's hand, searching for the right words to comfort her. But she, too, was spiraling.

What were they supposed to do without magic?

And what kind of place was this, that completely blocked their powers?

"Don't waste your energy," said a deep, familiar voice.

Prue shrank away from Hyperion's hulking form. The dark-skinned Titan loomed over them with a feral smile. She carefully edged herself so Mona was behind her.

"What do you mean?" Prue asked, portraying a confidence she did not feel. Without her magic, she felt weak and exhausted. If Hyperion attacked, there would be nothing she could do.

Hyperion's grin widened, his black eyes glinting. "There is no magic here. At least, not magic for *your* kind."

"Where is *here*?" Prue demanded.

Hyperion chuckled and shook his head at her. "All in good time, little goddess. We cannot share all our secrets with you. Follow me. I will show you to your room."

Hyperion turned and strode toward the dead trees.

Prue faltered and exchanged a bewildered look with Mona. Follow him *where*? What room? There was nothing visible for miles except dead trees and sand.

"Would you prefer to sleep out here on the concrete?" Hyperion called over his shoulder.

Prue was probably tired enough to do just that, but she stood and tugged on Mona's arm to help her up.

Mona's fingernails dug into Prue's arm as she hissed, "We can't follow him."

"But we can't stay out here, either," Prue said. "It's not safe. Not without our magic."

Mona chewed on her lip but made no argument.

This place could be in Elysium, but Prue suspected it was somewhere in the mortal realm. Especially since Elysium was allegedly being rebuilt by Pandora and Sol.

The Titans would not have taken them to their allies.

And the Realm of Gaia was the biggest realm of the three. From what Prue knew, there were plenty of dark spots where one could hide from unwanted witnesses.

Unfortunately, beyond the tiny island of Krenia, Prue didn't know much of the Realm of Gaia. She'd traveled through plenty of places with Cyrus, but none like this. The dry, dead landscape was very different from the icy mountain they had climbed together.

That felt like a lifetime ago.

Prue linked her arm with Mona's as they trudged after Hyperion. She cast a quick glance at the barren landscape around them, but it seemed that Hyperion was the only Titan with them. Where had the others gone? Had the portal deposited them somewhere else?

"Does any of this look familiar to you?" Prue whispered to Mona.

Mona's green eyes were wide with fear, but as she surveyed their surroundings, a familiar gleam of interest sparked in her gaze. Prue knew her sister needed something to draw her away from her all-consuming terror.

If anything could achieve that, it was Mona's love of research and facts.

"The dryness in the air reminds me of the Rhea Desert," Mona whispered back. "That's where Pandora and I met the fire witches. But this is... different." She shook her head. "I've read about magical voids where powers do not function properly. I'll have to think about where those spots are located and if any of them match this description."

Prue nodded, comforted by Mona's response. If anyone could figure out where they were right now, it was Mona.

Although Prue wasn't sure what good it would do. Even if they *did* discover where they were, they were helpless without magic.

Hyperion did not outright *say* that Titan magic functioned here. But it was too risky to try anything. Even if his magic was blocked like theirs, his brute strength alone would be enough to overpower them. And it was very likely the other Titans were lingering nearby and would appear at any moment.

But the real question was, why were they here? If the Titans wanted them dead, they could have killed them already.

No, Prue had a nasty feeling that the Titans had something sinister in mind for them.

She shuddered, drawing closer to Mona as they followed after Hyperion's long strides. When they reached the edge of the arid forest, Hyperion waved his hand in front of him. The air twisted with that same dark power, and Prue suppressed another shiver of disgust.

The barren forest shifted, and instead of an empty wasteland, Prue saw a large cottage made of decaying logs that looked rotten and on the brink of collapse.

Hyperion moved toward the cottage, and Prue and Mona followed. Apprehension and dread coiled in Prue's chest. It was clear that Hyperion's magic *did* work here.

Which meant whatever small hope they had of escaping had plummeted.

They had no chance at all of surviving whatever the Titans had in store for them.

Despair coiled tightly inside her, and she wanted to fall to the earth and sob, to scream at the injustice of it all.

But she couldn't. Mona needed her.

And she knew in her bones that Cyrus would tear the realms apart to find her.

Surely the Titans knew that. They were smart enough to discern how much Prue meant to Cyrus. They had known as much when they'd known to strike *her* instead of Cyrus.

Was this all an elaborate trap to lure Cyrus to a place with no magic?

He has Titan magic, Prue reminded herself. *He isn't powerless. He will come. Cyrus and Evander will both come for us.*

But the hopelessness crashed through her anew, because even if her husband *did* come for her, the Titans would kill him.

Cyrus and Evander were just two gods against five Titans. And their death magic would not work here.

No matter how powerful Cyrus was, he couldn't stop that many of them. Not when Prue, Mona, and Evander were powerless.

All the Titans had to do was hold a knife to one of their throats, and Cyrus would be helpless.

The wooden door to the cottage creaked open, and Hyperion stood by the threshold, gesturing for the sisters to enter. Prue gripped Mona's arm tighter as the two stepped inside.

The interior was dark and smelled of dust and mold. Prue wrinkled her nose, squinting against the darkness. A massive living room stood before her, filled with worn sofas and armchairs with ripped fabric. A staircase was to the left, and a ragged green rug lined the wooden floors.

Four large figures stood in the center of the room, their

forms outlined by the faint light filtering in through the windows.

Prue tensed, and Mona trembled beside her as the Titans straightened, their eyes narrowing on the two sisters.

"Be at ease," said Hyperion as he strode inside. The door slammed shut behind him. "They will not harm you. At least... not yet."

A few Titans chuckled at that, and Prue bit down on her tongue to keep from spitting at them.

They feasted on their fear. They *enjoyed* it.

"Why are we here?" Prue demanded. "What do you want from us?"

Hyperion spread his arms. "You are our guests here, little goddess. Not our prisoners."

Prue lifted her chin. "So we can come and go as we please?"

Hyperion's mouth curled into a smirk. "Of course. Although, only Titan magic can pierce through the shields surrounding the cottage. So, I'm afraid you'll be roaming in circles for quite a while."

The Titans laughed again, and Prue swallowed around a lump of anxiety in her throat.

Trapped. They were trapped here.

"That doesn't answer either of my questions," Prue said.

Hyperion moved closer until he towered over her. She resisted the urge to cringe away from him, knowing he was trying to intimidate her.

She refused to cower.

"You are here to bring about our freedom," Hyperion said in a low voice. "You are our bargaining chips. But rest assured we are not monsters. Your accommodations will be the best we can afford. You will not be chained or tied up during your stay."

Prue's eyes narrowed. "So we are just supposed to believe you won't hurt us?"

"We won't hurt you... unless we have to," said a purple-skinned Titan Prue recognized from the battle in the Undead Wilds. He had two ram horns and claws as long as Prue's forearm.

His statement was not reassuring in the slightest.

"We're bargaining chips for my husband, aren't we?" Prue asked. "What do you want from him? The throne to the Underworld?"

Hyperion tilted his head, assessing her. "Do you know where we came from, little goddess?"

Prue said nothing. In truth, she didn't know much about the history of the Titans.

"Elysium," Mona said softly. "You were the first rulers of Elysium."

Hyperion smiled, but there was no affection in the expression. "Yes. Until we were cut down by Jupiter, Uranus, and Neptune. They feared our power and thought we might use it to enslave the gods and goddesses."

"We killed our father, Uranus," said the purple-skinned Titan. "But the others managed to cage us in Tartarus. We have been there ever since."

"And now," Hyperion finished. "We have no home. We are free from Tartarus, and we will *not* go back. But Elysium is no longer ours to claim. Neither is the Underworld." He leaned closer, his black eyes boring into Prue's. "Where do you suggest we go? Do you think we should stay confined to this hellhole?" He spread his arms, gesturing to the cottage. "Do you think it's fair for us to be caged merely because we possess power that exceeds that of the gods and goddesses?"

"That's not true," Mona said, her voice gaining strength. "You weren't thrown in Tartarus because of your power. You were imprisoned because you rebelled against the gods." She stood straighter, her eyes blazing with defiance. "Don't try to feed us lies, Hyperion. It won't work."

Hyperion went perfectly still. Then, his eyes narrowed into slits. "You are smarter than I gave you credit for. And bolder. That will not serve you well here, little goddess. Watch yourself, or your sharp tongue might have to be cut out."

Prue felt Mona's arm shake alongside hers, but her sister held Hyperion's gaze, her nostrils flaring.

She was strong, and Prue admired her for that. Mona might be afraid, but she was still strong.

"Atlas, show them to their room," Hyperion said, his eyes still fixed on Mona.

The purple-skinned Titan drew closer, then spread one long, meaty arm toward the staircase. "After you, tiny goddesses." He chuckled, and a few other Titans joined in.

Prue shot him a glare before leading Mona up the staircase. The wooden boards creaked with every step.

This whole place seemed moments away from collapsing. And Prue felt like she was ready to collapse right along with it.

COMPANION
TRIVIA

THE EMPTY VOID CONSUMED TRIVIA'S ENTIRE BEING, night and day. She knew nothing but darkness. She felt nothing but despair.

Her thoughts floated in and out, sometimes coherent, sometimes not. When her mind was clear, she strained to come up with a plan to meet Pandora's demands.

But nothing she could think of would work.

And even if it could, she wasn't sure she could do it. She'd seen firsthand the destructive consequences of unleashing a goddess like Pandora. Trivia would never do that again.

But on the other hand, Pandora would make her watch while she tortured Sol and Gaia. They did not deserve that fate.

And Trivia didn't know if she could endure watching it, either.

It's my penance, she thought. *It's a fitting punishment.*

Her fleeting but passionate time with Sol was undeserving. She was lucky to have even that.

Oftentimes, when her thoughts were lucid enough, she returned to that perfect night where she and Sol had come together, their bodies merging in the most perfect way. They had made love all night and well into the morning, exploring and worshipping each other.

She would give anything to return to that night.

Her consciousness faded in and out. It was similar to sleep, but not nearly as peaceful. She did not dream. And time did not pass quicker when she faded.

She was still trapped in this chasm of loneliness, forever enduring her thoughts and the dread of when Pandora would return to torment her further.

She can read my thoughts, Trivia reminded herself. She had to be careful.

But what did it matter? Pandora already knew Trivia had no ideas for how to get her out of the box. That was no great secret.

And even if Trivia had some great plan of deception up her sleeve, she was far too weak and exhausted to carry it out. Her mind was sluggish and hazy. It seemed that, for every hour when she could think clearly, another three hours of foggy numbness claimed her.

How long before the darkness consumed her entirely? How long before she lost her mind and all sense of self?

How long before her body and soul simply became a part of the void?

A low hissing sound echoed around her, but Trivia ignored it. At this point, the horrifying sounds of the dark magic within the box were familiar to her, and it was quite easy to tune them out.

But the hissing sound persisted, until she realized it was someone's voice whispering, "*Psst!*"

Trivia's consciousness shifted. She tried to reach, to move her body, but she was nothing, and her body was not her own. She was just a collection of thoughts scattered in the darkness.

"Envision your body, one piece at a time," said a voice. "It will come to you."

No, Trivia wanted to say. *That will take too much effort. I just want to go to sleep.*

She prepared to drift away into that numbness that had become a sort of respite for her.

But the voice was persistent.

"If you let yourself fade, she'll win."

Awareness stirred in her mind again. There was so much she wanted to say to this new presence.

Shut up.

Who are you?

Why do you care?

Her thoughts strained to come together. She envisioned her toes, ankles, and feet, then her shins, knees, and calves. A solid weight filled her as her body took shape. She wanted to gasp in relief and surprise, but she couldn't breathe. A heavy weight was pressing on her lungs, cutting off her oxygen, suffocating her...

"Picture your lungs now or you'll asphyxiate," the voice said urgently. "*Now, Trivia!*"

Trivia obeyed, quickly envisioning her stomach and torso,

followed by her lungs and throat. A whoosh of air filled her lungs as she inhaled a rattling breath. She gasped deeply, the rush of oxygen almost painful to her now corporeal body. She envisioned her arms, elbows, wrists, and fingers. Then her shoulders, chin, nose, forehead, hair, and ears. One by one, she pictured each part of her body, then checked to ensure it had solidified. Her fingers wiggled. Her legs shifted. She raised her shoulders, then extended her arms.

"Am I here?" she croaked.

"Yes." A dark shape hovered in front of her, but she couldn't make out their face. The deep voice was vaguely familiar, though, like someone she had only encountered once or twice in her lifetime.

"How did you know how to do that?" Trivia asked, frowning as she squinted at the blurry shape before her. "Who are you?"

"A companion," said the voice. "Someone who has been sentenced to the same fate as you."

Trivia stiffened. Anyone who was here with her could not be trusted. All manner of dark magic existed in this place.

"Rest assured I am no friend of Pandora's," the voice said, disgust tainting their tone. "I wish to destroy her and escape this place. Will you work with me? If you do, I promise to bring you with me."

Trivia hesitated. She didn't trust this entity, whoever they were. And the deal seemed too easy. "What would I have to do?" she hedged. Years of being manipulated by Pandora taught her to be more cautious when accepting help from someone powerful.

"You will need to train your mind to shield from her," the

voice said. "Once you do that, we can plan. I have been here for a long time, and I have discovered how to reach the magic lurking inside the box."

A chill whispered over Trivia's skin, and she inched away from the stranger. "No. It's too dangerous. The darkness in here... It feasts on everything."

"I have found a way to weave wards around it," said the voice. "I've been here practicing for quite a while, Trivia. It *works.*"

Spell-weaving? Trivia's brow furrowed, and her skin prickled with awareness. She knew someone who could weave spells. Someone who was powerful and experimental with magic and...

Trivia jerked away, her eyes flaring wide as the figure took shape before her. The tanned skin and golden beard, the familiar kingly attire and black leather gloves.

"Midas," Trivia hissed, her nostrils flaring as fresh rage coursed through her.

But Midas only nodded. "Your anger is a good thing. Cling to that fury, Trivia. It will help keep you awake."

"Why should I listen to *anything* you say? It's your fault I'm even in here!"

"Ah, but from what I heard from your conversation with Pandora, it's *your* fault, isn't it? You blame yourself."

"Shut the hell up! I willingly gave myself up to save those I loved, but if it weren't for you, I *never* would have had to make that sacrifice."

"My point is, there are many layers to the truth. Nothing is one-dimensional, even in this vast space. What do you see right now?"

"Why the hell do you care? You betrayed me and my sisters. Leave me alone." Trivia closed her eyes, prepared to go back to the empty void, but the panic in Midas's voice stopped her.

"*Don't!* Trivia, if you leave now, Pandora will know."

Trivia opened one eye to glare at him. "What do you mean?"

"The void is *her* domain. What she doesn't want you to know is that you *do* have a modicum of control in this place. She wants you to think you are imprisoned and powerless. But you aren't. And I can prove it to you."

Trivia scowled at him. She didn't trust this bastard. Not for one moment. "Why should I believe you? For all I know, if I do what you say, it'll bring Pandora here and she'll punish me. You could even *be* Pandora in disguise. I have no way of knowing."

Midas's mouth pressed into a thin line as he considered this. "You can't trust me. There's no way to prove I'm being truthful. But... I can be forthcoming with you. And hopefully, that will help." He paused and took a deep breath. "I've been cursed for nearly a thousand years. Doomed to never touch another. To never *feel* anything against my skin. Do you know how miserable an existence like that is? Do you know the burden of carrying such an enchantment on your shoulders for so long?"

Trivia's entire body stilled at his words. She wasn't nearly as ancient as Midas was. But she *did* know the burden of carrying a curse she would do anything to be rid of.

"I was desperate," Midas said. "For years, I was mad with rage and depression. I lost my daughter. My wife. I was hunted for what everyone claimed was a gift. But it was only a curse. A wretched curse put on me by that bastard Apollo." He grit the words out, his teeth flashing with fury.

Yes, if there was anyone Trivia hated more than Midas, it was Apollo. Her *father.*

The word made her want to retch.

"Go on," she murmured. She still didn't trust him, but she wanted to hear the end of this.

Part of her was dreading it, though. She didn't want to know how similar they were.

She didn't want to entertain the idea that she was just as traitorous as Midas.

"When I heard that Gaia had arrived in my kingdom, I saw my opportunity," Midas said. "I made a plan, and I clung to it like a lifeline. It was all I had left. For nearly a decade, I had sought my own life. But the one thing my curse did not allow was for me to use it on myself. And even the blades of my opponents could not pierce my flesh. I bleed gold. Did you know that?"

Slowly, Trivia shook her head.

"Anyway, Gaia arrived. And I knew my nephew possessed sun magic. All I needed was to get you both to Elysium to channel the earth and sun magic into the fulcrum. Then, I would finally be free."

"And you felt no guilt over this?" Trivia asked in a hollow voice. She didn't have the energy to accuse him of duplicity.

After all, what right did she have? Midas deceived her for a few days. She had been deceiving everyone for years.

Perhaps they weren't that different after all.

"I felt immensely guilty," Midas said. "Guilt is something

else I carry every day. It is another burden associated with my curse. But hundreds of years of training my mind allows me to compartmentalize feelings like that. To prioritize more important things instead. To betray you and your sisters was a terrible thing. But it would have been even *more* terrible for me to continue enduring my curse. Even for one more year. One more month. One more day. It would have been too much for me. *That* was more important than anything."

He broke off, shaking his head sadly. "You are young, so you likely don't have as much experience. Your mind is fresh and you feel everything acutely. Your emotions rule you. But for me, I have had centuries of practice. That's why I'm able to exist like this." He gestured to his body, still floating in the dark void. "You and I have been in the box for the same amount of time, but I was able to weave my own wards almost instantly, granting myself freedom. The whole time I've been trapped here, I've been practicing control over my body and my magic."

Trivia could not argue with his reasoning. The rage of Pandora's soul as she'd lived inside Trivia's body had been unbearable. Because of that alone, Trivia had done her bidding—because she would have done *anything* to be rid of those violent emotions.

"You understand, don't you?" Midas asked softly.

"I am not your friend," Trivia snapped. "I am not your ally. You are not forgiven."

"That's not what I'm asking for. I'm asking you to trust me. Just in this one small thing so I can prove myself to you."

Trivia lifted her chin, her eyes narrowing as she assessed him. "If this works, and we get out, what will you do?"

Midas huffed a laugh as if this were a ridiculous question. "What *wouldn't* I do? Thanks to your mother and my nephew, my curse has been lifted. I would *live*. I would feast on all the foods I haven't been able to taste properly. I would lie with a dozen women and two dozen men. I would slit the throats of my enemies and relish the feel of their blood running down my fingers. I would experience *everything* I was robbed of when Apollo cursed me."

Trivia continued to watch him, still wary. It didn't feel right, to put her trust in a despicable man like Midas.

But her choices were limited. And it made sense that Midas despised Pandora as much as she did.

"I hold no vendetta against you, your sisters, or your mother," Midas insisted. "I only needed Gaia to break my curse. She can live a long and healthy life, for all I care. I might have a bone to pick with Apollo, so if you take issue with that, perhaps we will be at an impasse."

"Do what you want with Apollo," Trivia spat. "He is nothing to me."

Midas's lips curled into a slow smile. "There's that rage again."

Trivia closed her eyes as she was inexplicably reminded of the way Sol had described her fire and how he had yearned for it to consume him entirely.

Gods, she missed him. More than anything else, she longed for him.

If Midas was telling the truth, not only could Trivia spare Sol from Pandora's darkness... but she could be reunited with him again. She would get a second chance at happiness.

They could be together. They could create a life with one another.

The idea felt too good to be true. A paradise Trivia did not deserve.

This was another reason she didn't trust Midas. In her experience, if something *seemed* too good to be true, it was a trap.

"What is the worst thing that could happen if you choose to believe me?" Midas asked.

Trivia stared hard at him. "Pandora would find out, and she would punish me."

"How would she punish you?"

She shuddered. "She would torture Sol. My mother. My sisters."

"Doesn't she plan to do this to you anyway, if you don't provide her a means to escape?"

Trivia hesitated. This was true. She had nothing to lose.

She heaved a sigh. A kernel of hope bloomed in her chest, but she tried to ignore it. Hope was dangerous, especially in a place like this.

Instead, she looked at Midas with resignation, knowing he was her only way out.

And she was his.

With one stiff nod, she said, "Fine. I agree. Let's work together."

PAYMENT
EVANDER

EVANDER WAS UNSTABLE. HIS MIND WAS FRACTURED, and his body no longer felt like it belonged to him.

Ever since he had lost Typhon, he'd felt... *off.*

But now, without Mona, he didn't even know who he was anymore. He had no purpose. No drive. No sense of awareness or belonging.

He was lost. Broken. Irreparable. Even if he did get Mona back, he still didn't know if he would ever feel whole again.

His pearly wings spread wider, carrying him through the sky. Every passing day brought more light and vibrance in the air, making the sky feel more real. The murky fog was slowly dissipating. Evander suspected it was because Cyrus had been chosen as the rightful king of the realm, and now the land was healing itself through that bond.

Cyrus had truly come into his own power. He was the king the people deserved. He knew his place. He *belonged* here.

Evander envied that. His wings beat harder, the wind whipping at his face as he soared over the rubble-filled lands. This place still had a lot of healing to do, after enduring the horrors of Pandora's box. It would take ages before it could be restored to its former glory.

But this was a start. Grass was beginning to sprout. Silvery water trickled along the rivers, a promise of more to come. Soon, the souls would have a stream to carry them from one path to the next.

Soon, the realm would be fully mended.

Evander wanted to feel relief. He really did. This place was his home. He understood the dangerous repercussions of a broken Underworld.

But he felt... nothing.

Hollow.

When Romanos had absorbed his magic and Evander had seen Mona—held her, touched her—he had felt nothing but joy. Nothing but the comfort of knowing she was there with him and they could be together.

But each moment made him feel more and more unsettled. As if, every day, another crack formed in his armor, hacking away at the pieces of himself.

His wings pumped harder, and he gritted his teeth as exhaustion filled his bones. He was almost spent. Soon, his ghostly wings and tail and horns would vanish, and he would just be... Evander once more.

But he didn't even know who that was. Someone without magic. Without a purpose.

Someone powerless.

With a growl of frustration, he arced low, circling the

Undead Wilds. He often came here, forcing himself to relive the moment Mona had been taken through the Titans' portal.

If he hadn't lost Typhon, he would have been able to save her. He was certain of it.

He'd failed her. He'd failed Prue, too.

He'd failed *everyone*.

The strength of his wings failed, and he felt them wither away as the ghostly presence of Typhon withdrew. He found himself missing that monstrous voice in his head.

Now, he felt nothing but emptiness.

He landed hard on the ground, dirt and roots scraping his hands and knees. The pain sent a spark of awareness through his body, bringing clarity and focus to his mind.

It was fleeting. Soon, he would withdraw, just like Typhon did. He would fade away to an empty shell. He would cease to exist.

He rolled until his back was against the hard ground as he glared up at the sky. He hated this. All he felt was rage and helplessness. The frantic anxiety coursing through him made him desperate and panicked. He had to *do* something. He couldn't just sit around like Cyrus.

He had to take action.

Evander sat up and ran a hand down his face. His eyes closed, and he heaved a weary sigh.

Then, he heard voices.

They were nothing more than whispers, soft but insistent, like hissing snakes.

His eyes opened, and he looked around. The Undead Wilds were nearby. It was likely only the wayward spirits.

Even so, he was deeply curious. And if Cyrus wouldn't do anything, then perhaps it was up to Evander.

He could talk to the spirits. He could negotiate with them.

He clambered to his feet, brushing leaves and twigs from his body as he made his way to the forest. The whispers grew louder with each step he took. His skin pebbled, and his body prickled with awareness.

The magic here was powerful—powerful enough for him to sense it. He had no magic, but he could *feel* the energies in the air.

The canopy of trees partially blocked the light of the sky, shrouding Evander in darkness. But still he pressed onward, embracing the murmurs and allowing them to drift over him like soft caresses.

"God of death," one of them whispered to him. "What brings you to our domain?"

Evander looked around, but he saw nothing. The voices had no bodies. He had seen them materialize before Cyrus. For whatever reason, they had decided not to do so for him.

That was fine. He did not need to see their faces to speak with them.

"You vowed to help Cyrus get Mona and Prue back," Evander said, his voice firm and unwavering. "I was there when you asked for a drop of his immortality. I know the price you seek, and... I am here to pay it."

The air filled with frustrated hisses, as if the spirits were upset. "Why does the king not come to us himself?"

"He is seeking other paths first."

The voices stilled at that. Then, one of them said quietly, "He does not trust us?"

No, Evander wanted to say. But he didn't want to cause trouble between Cyrus and the spirits. So, instead, Evander said, "He intends to enlist your help once he formulates a plan. But I cannot wait that long."

The voices purred around him, making the hair on the back of his neck stand on end. "Impatience. So unbecoming of a young god such as yourself."

"I don't care," Evander snarled. "I will not let Mona suffer. I will not stand idly by while she is in danger."

"Is that what you think the king is doing? Being idle?"

"No. But—"

"Does he appreciate your subordination?"

"I am his older brother," Evander snapped. "He does not command me."

The words felt vile on his lips. He had never defied Cyrus before. He had always been content to abide by Cyrus's laws and keep to himself.

But perhaps it was time to change that. He did not agree with Cyrus's methods. And he would not risk Mona's life.

"We have no bargain with *you,*" one of the voices crooned.

"Then, let's strike one," Evander said without thinking. "Let *me* make the payment in Cyrus's place."

Once more, the spirits fell silent, and the air seemed to pulse with excited energy.

Shit, Evander thought. *What have I done?*

But he couldn't take the words back. And, if the spirits managed to find Mona for him, he would not regret it.

Of that he was certain.

"You would give your immortality to us?" asked a voice, tinged with disbelief.

Evander swallowed hard. Would he?

If they demanded his life, he would give it, so long as Mona could be safe.

There was *nothing* he would not give to save her.

"Yes," he said, his voice firm and unwavering.

The spirits chuckled as if they could sense his desperation. His willingness. His heart drummed erratically inside his chest, a pounding rhythm warning him of going too far.

He ignored the warning.

"Prove your willingness to bargain with us," said the voices, speaking together as one. It sounded like a hundred spirits were murmuring at once. "Give us a drop of your immortality."

Evander went rigid, his chest cinching painfully as he realized this was truly happening. There was no turning back after he crossed this line.

He wasn't ready. Not yet. To buy himself more time, he asked, "Why do you need my immortality anyway? You are already dead."

The spirits laughed again. "Yes, but with the immortality of a *death god,* we can live again. We can have a taste of the mortal lives we have craved for millennia. One immortal lifespan from you will feed all of us a morsel of the land of the living."

Evander held perfectly still. Inside, his pulse thundered even louder. *Don't, don't, don't,* it seemed to say.

"Will this bargain kill me?" he asked. The logical side of

him screamed to see reason, to stop before he made a grave mistake.

But the more dominant side of him shushed this voice. Logic was not in control here. It hadn't been for a long time.

"Silly god," the spirits taunted. "It will not kill you. You will simply be as a mortal. Weak and fragile. Your existence will be temporary, but you will still live."

Evander's mouth went dry. This sounded like a trick. Deception. Could these spirits lie to him?

"How do I know you won't simply steal my immortality from me right now and go back on your word?" he asked.

"We will not take it from you until the two earth goddesses are returned," the spirits vowed. "As a sign of good faith."

Good faith. Those were the same words the spirits had used with Cyrus, to urge him to offer a drop of his immortality. Evander couldn't ignore the amusement layered within the voices, as if this entire ordeal were a joke to them.

They thought him a fool. An easy mark. Someone to manipulate.

But... what if they were telling the truth? They might believe him foolish, to offer up something as precious as his immortality. But he had no need of it anymore. His life was empty without Typhon or his magic. He was as good as mortal anyway.

Not much would change for him. He would lose the ghost of Typhon, yes. But it would be a relief to be free of that constant reminder of what he had lost.

And... he would have Mona back.

"One drop of your blood," the voices whispered. "That's all we need for now. We will collect the rest of your immortality after the goddesses are safe."

Before he could second guess his decision, Evander said loudly, "I'll do it."

The spirits swarmed around him, a cacophony of murmurs and chants. A breeze whispered against his skin, tousling his hair. Energy churned in the forest, coiling tighter and tighter. The woods were so thick with magic that Evander almost couldn't breathe.

A single luminescent form materialized before him. He recognized it from the day the spirits had sworn fealty to Cyrus. This was a woman, her hair long and flowing down her back as she smiled mischievously at him.

"Give me your hand, death god," she said.

Evander stretched out his palm to her, then held perfectly still. Unease roared within him, but he ignored it. This was the right path. It had to be.

The soul drew closer, then slashed something across his palm.

Evander winced. It was so fast, he hadn't expected the pain. What had she cut him with? And how had she done it, if she was only a spirit?

But she only smiled at him, her teeth gleaming as a droplet of silver blood pooled along the cut on his palm. The spirit held out her hand underneath his, catching the drop before it fell to the earth.

She inhaled deeply, her eyes closing. "Ah... That sweet nectar of immortality. So vibrant. So pure. There is nothing quite like it." She brought her fingers to her lips and licked Evander's blood, then made a low humming noise. Around her, the other spirits chanted excitedly.

Evander suppressed a shiver and dropped his arm, then straightened. "How do I find the goddesses?"

"The way to the Titans is simple, death god," the spirit said. "You must find the one place without magic. The one place where the blood of the gods is useless."

Evander blinked, not understanding. "Where is that?"

The woman's smile widened, as if she thoroughly enjoyed his confusion. "It is in the mortal realm. Unseen by prying eyes, and hidden from mortal minds."

Evander shook his head. "Speak plainly, please!"

The woman laughed, the sound echoing around him. Her form began to fade.

"Wait!" Evander stepped toward her, panic flooding his chest. "Please! I cannot give you my immortality until I find her."

The woman's form brightened, and she tilted her head at him, considering this. "The mortal realm is much changed since I last saw it. But I believe the name of the land you seek is called *Rhea*."

Before Evander could reply, the spirit vanished, and the echoes of the voices around him faded. After a moment, nothing but dead silence surrounded him, the stillness so jarring it made his insides churn.

He was panting as if he'd been sprinting, his chest heaving and his mind spinning. He turned to leave—prepared to travel through the portal to get to the Realm of

Gaia—when he noticed a figure standing by a large oak tree, his face pale and his jaw slack.

"Evander," Cyrus said weakly. "What the hell have you done?"

PLANNING
PRUE

THE COTTAGE HAD TWO BEDROOMS UPSTAIRS. ATLAS showed them to the one on the left, which consisted of two dirty and stained cots and a table in between. The shutters over the window were cracked, and the air smelled like mold.

Atlas offered a cold smile before shutting the door with his departure. Prue checked the handle—no locks.

That would have been far too easy. Already, she was shocked the Titans were giving them privacy.

Assuming their magic couldn't enable them to listen in on the sisters' conversations.

We'll have to risk it, Prue thought, turning to Mona and taking her hands. "What do you know about this place?" She kept her voice low, just in case.

Mona bit her lip as she glanced around the dismal bedroom.

"I know," Prue said, squeezing her sister's hands. "It's bleak. Better than a prison cell, though."

Mona nodded, then closed her eyes, her brows knitting together in a look of concentration. "In all the books I've read, there were only two places described to be voids for the magic of the gods. One of them is the Manos Ocean."

Prue's heart lurched. "You mean the whirlpool you jumped into to get to the Underworld?"

Mona's mouth quirked up in a half smile. Instead of making her blanch, the memory only seemed to empower her, as if reminding her of the courage she was capable of. "Yes. That one. The other void is located in the Rhea Desert. There are said to be ancient ruins there where raiders slaughtered a family beloved by the gods. As punishment, the gods removed all magic from the area and cursed it with an endless drought. To this day, no flora or magic can thrive there." She paused and swallowed hard. "I think that's where we are."

The Ruins of Rhea. Prue had seen the landmark on a map once, back when she and Cyrus were attempting to sail across the sea to get to the tiny village of Faidon.

"The fire witch coven is somewhere in the desert," Mona went on. "But I don't know how far. The desert spans over fifty miles, so they could be anywhere."

"And the place is warded by Titan magic, so it's not as if we can sneak out and track them down," Prue said grimly. She sighed. "I suppose our options are limited. We have to keep our heads down until Cyrus reaches out to negotiate." Her chest twisted at the thought. What would Cyrus offer in exchange for her and Mona?

She wasn't sure what she feared more—that Cyrus would give up his entire kingdom, or that he would refuse the Titans' demands.

The Cyrus she had known would have torn apart every realm to get her back. But he had since changed. He had been reborn as a human, then become infused with Titan magic. He had won the right to his throne, and she knew in her heart that this time, things would be different.

He was not the king he once was. And she knew that he would be mindful of the needs of his people.

It only made her love him more.

But it also made her afraid for what she and Mona would have to endure.

"Perhaps not," Mona said slowly, jerking Prue from her dismal thoughts. That familiar calculating look shone in her eyes.

Prue's pulse quickened. "What do you mean?"

"*God* magic might not work here. But what about witch magic?"

Prue sucked in a breath. "Runes?"

Mona offered a smile and nodded.

"Damn." Prue exhaled in a short burst, then huffed a laugh. "I can't believe I didn't think of that. Runes are what saved me in that prison cell in the Thanassian Empire."

Mona's expression turned smug. "I know."

Prue whacked her arm. "What rune are you thinking of?"

Mona's face went blank, her eyes distant. Prue could tell her sister was mentally sifting through all the runes she had studied. Her lips moved wordlessly, as if she were whispering to herself.

Prue folded her arms over her chest as she waited. Eventually, Mona's mouthing turned to muttering. "The *unlock* rune wouldn't be much help here. I don't think dislodging a person's spirit would help, either, since they are Titans and I have no idea if their souls are even accessible... It will likely only enrage them." She started pacing the length of the tiny room, arms crossed as she chewed on her thumbnail.

"Commune with the dead," Mona whispered, then shook her head. "Healing rune..." She froze, then straightened, her expression brightening. "I've got it! A fire rune."

Prue arched an eyebrow. "A fire rune?"

"Yes. We send it straight up in the air. If it's infused with enough witch magic, it should alert the fire witches."

Prue didn't like the word *should*. What if it didn't work? What if the Titans caught them? "Don't you think the Titans will be able to sense the magic?"

"Not witch magic," Mona said. She sounded so confident that Prue almost believed her. "The only issue is... I have no idea how powerful the Titans' wards are. If it's a simple ward spell, it will only deflect sight and sound, and magic will be able to pierce through it."

"I doubt it's a simple ward," Prue said with a grimace.

"So do I." Mona tapped her chin in thought. "I wonder if there's a rune that can destabilize a ward." When Prue made a noise of protest, Mona added, "Only for a moment, I mean."

Prue snorted. "You think they won't notice if it's *only for a moment*?"

Mona winced. "You're right. It's too risky."

Prue frowned, then lifted one finger. "Hold on." She

glanced at the door, half expecting to see Atlas leering in the doorway, listening to their entire conversation.

But the door was still shut.

Prue drew closer to Mona and whispered, "There's only five of them. If you can think of a rune that can dismantle their wards for long enough for us to send fire into the sky, then I can come up with a distraction that will draw the Titans' attention. They won't notice the wards coming down."

Mona's eyes grew wide. "Prue, you can't be serious."

Prue nodded slowly. "Can you do it?"

Mona's face paled. That same far-off look appeared on her face. After a moment, she muttered, "Yes. There's one rune powerful enough to do it—the spell-breaker rune. But it'll drain me."

"Shit. Can you still send the fire signal?"

Mona's hesitation was answer enough.

"Dammit." Prue sank to the edge of the nearest cot and rested her head in her hands. They were so close to coming up with a plausible plan.

"I can do it... if you give me some of *your* blood," said Mona.

Prue's head snapped up, her eyebrows lifting. "Really?"

"I think so. If I have your blood available, I can cast the rune spell as if it's coming from you. You can distract them. Then I'll use my own blood for the fire rune."

"How much blood do you need?"

"For the spell-breaker?" Mona hesitated. "A full cup."

Prue's stomach flipped. "An entire *cup* of my blood? Mona, how the hell are we supposed to manage that?" She spread her hands, gesturing to the bare room around them. No sharp objects. No containers for collecting blood.

This plan was doomed from the start.

All Prue could think of was the many things that could go wrong. Mona not getting enough blood, or passing out from exhaustion after the first rune. Prue's diversion going wrong, or the Titans discovering what she was up to. The fire signal not alerting the fire witches.

It was Mona's turn to take her sister's hands. Prue didn't realize she was trembling until Mona held her.

"Prue." Mona's voice was firm. "Do you trust me?"

Prue nodded, finding comfort in her sister's confidence. Mona was often ruled by fear, but right now, she was perfectly calm.

"Then trust that this will work. We just have to time everything perfectly."

Prue chuckled nervously. "Easy, right?"

"We can do this. Are you with me?"

"Of course." She had complete faith in her sister. Mona was the smartest woman she knew.

If anyone could come up with a way to accomplish this, it was her.

Mona smiled, and the sight loosened something in Prue's chest. "Good. Then, let's start planning."

BROTHERS
CYRUS

CYRUS HAD CERTAINLY MADE HIS FAIR SHARE OF reckless decisions. Hell, he had even given up a piece of his own soul to save Prue's life.

If anyone could understand the need for a dangerous and impromptu solution, it was him.

Even so, he couldn't believe Evander had bargained his own immortality to save Mona.

There was a time when Cyrus would have made the exchange in a heartbeat. In fact, he *had* made such an exchange—when he had brought Prue back from the dead. He had fully expected to die to pay that price.

But he hadn't. And now he knew that not all exchanges were so simple.

With his title as king restored, he had more than just Prue relying on him. He could not make careless decisions like that anymore.

Evander did what you could not, said a small voice in his

head. *You were unable to save Prue... but Evander could. He did what was necessary. But you couldn't.*

The thought filled his mouth with a foul, sour taste. His anger, his shame, his panic all felt more potent from that one singular thought.

"What the *hell* were you thinking?" he demanded, shoving Evander in the chest so hard that his brother stumbled backward. "How could you be so foolish?"

"I was doing what needed to be done!" Evander shouted. "Unlike *you.*"

Cyrus had never seen him like this before. Evander had always been calm and level-headed. The most even-tempered of all his brothers, except maybe Romanos.

"Mona wouldn't have wanted this," Cyrus said. "She would be horrified. What will happen when you rescue her, and she realizes she only has one mortal lifetime with you? Then, you'll die, and she'll continue living for hundreds, maybe even thousands of years."

Despair flashed across Evander's features, but his expression hardened as a mask of icy fury settled into place. "She's made plenty of careless decisions without my input. For one, she sacrificed all of her memories to return to the Underworld. She sacrificed *me.* I think she would understand my decision. Especially if it means her sister gets home safely. That's all she cares about."

Bitterness laced his words, and Cyrus stared at Evander. Hurt and anguish and devastation filled his silver eyes.

Evander was in pain.

That same cool mask returned, and Evander's lip curled. "Don't look at me like that. I don't want your pity."

Cyrus scowled. "Don't tell me what to do. I have to clean up your shit now, so I'll look at you however the hell I want to."

"Clean up?" Evander let out a harsh laugh. "I *saved* your ass. I know where the Titans are. Do you want to know, or do you want to keep fighting with me?"

Cyrus froze. "The spirits told you?"

"Yes. They knew. This whole time, they knew, and you were too much of a coward to ask them."

"I didn't want to ask them because I knew they would extract payment from me! Just like they did to you."

"Well, at least *one* of us had the balls to get things done."

Cyrus's rage boiled over, and he took a step toward Evander, teeth bared. "Watch yourself, brother. I'm still the king of this realm, and you'll show me some damn respect."

"I'll show you respect when you earn it."

Cyrus shoved Evander again, but this time, his brother retaliated with a swinging fist. A heavy force collided with Cyrus's jaw, sending him flying. He crashed into the earthy ground with a deep groan.

Evander advanced, but Cyrus was ready. As he climbed to his feet, he summoned his Titan power. Lightning streaked across the sky, and the ground rumbled. White-hot power danced along Cyrus's arms.

Evander stilled, his eyes growing wide.

"Want to try calling me a coward again?" Cyrus bellowed. He slammed a bolt of electricity straight into Evander's chest. Charred flesh filled the air, and Evander soared backward, then collided with a thick oak tree. A deafening *crack* filled the air as the tree split in two. Branches and leaves crashed to the ground, making the earth tremble again.

Evander slumped over, his head lolling. Silver blood oozed from the back of his head, staining the forest floor.

"Shit," Cyrus hissed, withdrawing his magic as he sprinted toward his brother.

Smoke rose from Evander's form, and an ashy black mark stained his chest. Cyrus ripped open Evander's shirt, but no injuries marred his pale flesh.

Thank the gods for that.

Evander coughed, his eyelids fluttering open as he gazed at Cyrus in confusion. "Bastard," he muttered.

Cyrus couldn't help but snort. "You started it. Can you stand up?"

Evander let out a grunt and pushed away Cyrus's extended hand. Slowly, Evander stood. He teetered slightly, but after blinking a few times, clarity returned to his gaze.

"You'd better be careful," Cyrus said. "Once we've rescued Prue and Mona, you might not be able to walk away from an injury like that." His tone was half teasing, but in all honesty, it was a solid warning.

Evander would not be as indestructible for much longer.

The statement sobered Evander, who looked at Cyrus with a grim and almost haunted expression. There were certainly inner demons at work here, and they were tormenting Evander to no end.

Cyrus wished he could do something to help. But he had a feeling that the only one who could vanquish those demons was Evander himself.

"No matter what," Cyrus said softly. "You're still my

brother. You know that, right?" He placed a hand on Evander's shoulder.

Evander's lips grew thin, and his eyes swelled with emotion. He offered one stiff nod and started walking. He had a slight limp, but Cyrus knew it would heal quickly, thanks to their god blood.

God blood that Evander wouldn't possess for much longer.

Lagos, Theo, and Maleck helped unearth several different maps buried in the castle vault. Cyrus had heard of Rhea before, and Evander confirmed that it was the same desert where the fire witches lived.

"Unfortunately, it's huge," Evander said as they pored over the maps on the throne room table. "I have no idea how to locate a spot without magic in a desert so vast."

"Perhaps the fire witches can help?" Theo suggested. "They are powerful enough to assist in a fight against the Titans."

Cyrus shook his head. "We can't risk it. And they would be foolish to pick a fight with the Titans. It would mean war for their people. But they might be able to point us in the right direction."

"They would likely know of a place where the Titans could be hiding," Maleck mused, rubbing his chin. "If they've lived there for a long time, I'm sure they know the ins and outs of the desert."

Cyrus nodded. "Yes, that's what I'm counting on." He cast a glance at Lagos. "Has the portal been repaired?"

"Yes," said Lagos. "It just needs a dose of magic to power it."

"We also repaired the reflection bowl, as you requested," Theo said. He bent over to retrieve something under the table. When he resurfaced, he was holding the mended bowl. The cracks from the broken pieces were still stark, but they had been welded together.

Cyrus stared at it. "Have you tested it?"

Theo shook his head, then set the bowl down on the table. Lagos grabbed a pitcher of water from a servant in the hall, then poured it into the bowl. Cyrus expected the bowl to leak, but it held the contents perfectly.

Swallowing hard, Cyrus felt every pair of eyes watching him as he braced his hands on either side of the bowl. "Show me Prue," he commanded.

The water rippled and swirled. To his surprise, an image appeared within the bowl. It was... *Prue.*

Gods above. The sight of her made his stomach lurch, and fresh longing coursed through him. His heart twisted painfully in his chest, and for a moment, he couldn't breathe. The world seemed to stop for a full moment as he stared at her.

Prue sat on a small cot alongside Mona. They were speaking with one another, their expressions serious and their heads bent together. It looked as if they were in a small room of some sort.

At least it wasn't a cave or a dungeon.

"Where are they?" Evander murmured, leaning closer.

"I—I can't tell," Cyrus said. "Show me the Titans."

The water rippled again, and a new image appeared. Two of the Titans—one of which was Hyperion—sat on a ragged sofa in a room similar to where Prue and Mona were. They seemed... comfortable. Unbothered.

The sight was unsettling. They clearly had no reservations about Cyrus attacking them. The thought made Cyrus feel part offended, and part nervous.

If they weren't worried, then they obviously had a plan in place for when Cyrus came for Prue.

And he had no idea what that plan was.

"Show me Atlas," Cyrus said.

The water rippled again, and the purple-skinned Titan appeared. He was standing in a forest of dead trees, alongside another Titan Cyrus recognized as Oceanus. Cyrus squinted, trying to make out other details. But all he could see was a decaying field and a vast array of dust and dirt.

It looked like they were in the middle of nowhere.

With a growl, Cyrus pushed the bowl away and rubbed his forehead. Once more, he felt the others watching him, waiting for him to decide what to do.

Even Evander was silent, though Cyrus waited for him to say, *I told you so.*

Because he'd been right. The reflection bowl didn't hold the answers.

The Wild Spirits did.

Cyrus rubbed a hand down his face with a long sigh. "All right. Evander and I will cross through the portal to the fire witch clan. Hopefully, the witches will be able to tell us about any hiding spots located within the Rhea Desert where we can search."

"I'll come, too," Lagos said. "I worked in Tartarus for a long time. I'll be able to smell Titan magic from afar."

Cyrus looked at Lagos, his brow furrowing. "You want to go to the mortal realm? Are you sure?"

"You aren't the only one who would go to great lengths to save Prue." Lagos's voice was full of an emotion that surprised Cyrus. He knew the demon was fond of Prue, but he didn't realize how much.

The thought made his chest cinch even tighter, because he knew Prue would do the same for Lagos.

He turned to Theo and Maleck. "Can you manage the council in our absence?"

They both nodded. Maleck added, "I'll address the people once more and assure them a solid plan is in place to bring back their queen."

"Thank you." Cyrus glanced at Evander, whose expression was stony as he stared at the reflection bowl. "Are you ready?"

Evander's eyes flashed. "I've been ready for a long time, brother."

"Good. Let's get Prue and Mona back."

MENTOR
TRIVIA

MIDAS WAS THE LAST PERSON IN ALL THE REALMS Trivia expected to be her key to escaping Pandora's box.

But from what she knew about him, he was skilled in magical training. He was an alchemist and magesmith, and one of the few male witches in existence.

He knew much about power and how to train one's mind.

But that didn't mean Trivia had to like him.

"Clear your mind again," Midas ordered for the tenth time.

Trivia let out a low growl. "I *am*."

"No, you aren't. I can still sense your rage. It's flowing carelessly around you."

"I wonder why," Trivia grumbled, then closed her eyes. The same murky darkness from before still surrounded them, but her feet were on the ground, and her hair was no longer floating around her. For hours, she and Midas had been training together, and she felt solid enough to stand on her own two feet.

She considered that proof that he was telling the truth. At least partially.

In her mind, she pictured the sea. The rolling waves. The sand sparkling in the sun. The warmth against her skin. She inhaled deeply, and released all the tension in her muscles and thoughts. With a long, slow, exhale, she emptied her mind of everything. She only focused on those waves surging in and out. In and out.

In. And out.

Her breathing slowed. Calmness settled into her bones.

"Good," came Midas's soft voice. "Now, project that blank slate to your surroundings. Spread that awareness farther than just your body."

Trivia's brows knitted together, but she forced herself to focus on the waves. This was the part that always snapped her out of her focus. When she had to empty her mind but also think about her next task, it was almost impossible to move forward.

During her last three attempts, she had gritted her teeth and concentrated so hard that she got frustrated and lashed out at Midas.

This time, she would go about it differently. Instead of thinking about her next move, she focused on the ocean's waves for a few more beats.

One.

Two.

Three.

Then, slowly, she envisioned the tide coming in. The

water lapped over the sand, inching closer to the grassy hill just beyond the shore. Inch by inch, the waves moved in. The sand slowly vanished underneath the swell. The cerulean waters sparkled in the sunlight, easing Trivia's nerves and cooling her temper.

She felt nothing but peace. She merely watched the sea surge higher and higher until it reached the bottom of the hill, covering the sand completely.

"Gods above," Midas murmured.

Trivia's eyes fluttered open, and she stifled a yelp.

She stood on a veranda overlooking the very sea she'd been picturing. What had once been nothing more than her imagination was now a reality before her. But it wasn't quite the same. There was no grassy hill. And these waves were more turquoise than bright blue. Gleaming white pillars supported a dome-shaped ceiling that towered over her. The walls were adorned with gold geometric patterns that gleamed in the sunlight.

Trivia swallowed hard, trying not to panic at this change in scenery. "What—What is this place?"

"It's Pandora's construct within the box," Midas explained. "This is the home she built for herself."

Realization struck Trivia, and her eyes widened. This looked just like Elysium. In fact, she was almost certain she'd been on a similar veranda in the palace during her stay there.

The minute differences could be attributed to how much time had passed since Pandora lived in Elysium. The ocean and beach were nothing more than an illusion. It was likely the enchantment had changed over the years.

A sharp sting of sorrow pierced Trivia's heart as she

considered how long it had been since Pandora had been *home*. She probably missed it terribly.

Trivia knew firsthand how potent that feeling was. She had lived with it her entire life. Not just from Pandora's memories, but her own.

Trivia had never had a home before. Not truly.

Not until she'd met Sol.

"Whatever you did that time is the key," Midas said, startling Trivia from her thoughts "Focus on that every time."

A lump formed in Trivia's throat, and a sour taste filled her mouth. She hated thinking of the beach.

It always reminded her of Sol. Gods, she missed him.

"All right." Her voice shook slightly. "What now?"

Midas crossed his arms. "You've pushed yourself a lot today, Trivia."

Today. Trivia nearly snorted at the word. There was no concept of time in this place. How could Midas possibly know how long they'd been training?

But he was right. Her bones were weary, and her head throbbed with fatigue. She needed to keep her mental shields up for when Pandora sought her out again, and her mind was getting weaker with each passing moment.

"I can handle it," she insisted, knowing she would need to work harder if she hoped to succeed.

"Very well. Shields up," Midas warned, and then his awareness pressed forward, creeping toward her like a snake.

Trivia's eyes closed, and she pictured a stone wall settling into place between herself and Midas. He pushed against it, and the stone cracked and crumbled. With a grunt, she imagined a brick wall in front of the stone. Piece by piece, she assembled the wall, layering more and more bricks to keep him out. Midas kept pushing, and the wall trembled.

But it held. He could not get through.

"Very good," said Midas, and Trivia let out a long breath, her heart racing in her chest. When her eyes opened, the veranda had disappeared, and the black void surrounded her once more.

Despair twisted in her chest. She hadn't realized how much she loathed the darkness until she had escaped it.

Midas seemed to notice her crestfallen expression. "It's difficult to concentrate on two things at once. Especially when you're inexperienced. You'll get there, Trivia. For now, accept the victory that you were able to access Pandora's construct *and* shield your mind against my attack."

Trivia nodded, but her brow was furrowed. How much longer would this take? If she had no idea how much time was passing, then there was no guarantee she would get out of Pandora's box in a week, a month, even a year. What if Sol wasn't there when she returned? What if he'd died? What if he'd moved on with someone else?

What if there was nothing left for her to return to?

"How do you do it?" Her voice sounded hollow.

Midas blinked at her. "Do what?"

"Live on and on, beyond those you love, beyond everything and everyone? How do you leave it all behind?"

Midas's expression dimmed. His eyes shuttered, and his face hardened into something firm and unyielding. "I told you before—priorities. I could waste away, losing my mind to sorrow and regret. Or... I could move on and *live*. When I gave myself the choice, it was easy. I chose survival."

Trivia shook her head. It wasn't that simple. She had willingly given herself up to let Sol live. Her will to survive was gone because she had expected to stop living.

But she hadn't truly died. In a way, this fate was worse than death. She had to live with her decisions and her anguish. She had to accept what could never be.

She had to keep living... even when she didn't want to.

Midas's expression softened. "I recognize that look. You want to end it all. But there's no way to do it." He sighed. "I wish I could say I've never been there, but I have. Many times. You have something I never did, though. A *choice*. If you don't want to return—if you don't want to *live*—then I won't force you to. We can stop. I can find my own way out of here."

Trivia met his gaze, her heart feeling so heavy that it dragged her down. She wanted to let it pull her under, to carry her into oblivion. To a place where she didn't have to think or feel.

She realized Midas was waiting for a response, so she shook her head slowly. All she could think about was Sol's look of utter devastation when she gave herself over to the darkness.

Even if he wasn't waiting for her. Even if there was nothing left. Trivia had to at least try. She needed that second chance, if only to prove that she could lead another life. That she could do things right this time.

"I'm just tired," she said at last. "You're right. I need a break. But I want to keep going."

Midas nodded slowly, his eyes full of pity.

The sight made Trivia want to retch. Her anger rekindled, and she turned away from him.

It didn't matter that this man was her mentor. He was still horrible, and she despised him.

She hated this situation. She hated that she was relying on *him*, of all people, to escape. Any other person in existence—except for maybe Apollo—would have been preferable.

But, for now, Midas was her only hope. Her only chance.

And he understood what she was going through.

She hated that, too—how similar they were. She had betrayed everyone; she was no better than Midas.

Trivia's eyes closed, and she pictured the ocean once more. Not to empty her mind, but to escape. She let her body float away on those waves, imagining her fears and regrets drifting off into a sea of nothingness.

She would try again soon. She would get better and better until she was strong enough to face Pandora and break through her magical construct.

But for now, there was nothing but her and the sea.

RUNES

MONA

THROUGHOUT THEIR PLANNING, MONA MAINTAINED an air of confidence and calmness. She trusted in her knowledge of runes and in her ability to cast spells. She knew the runes would work.

The sisters had discovered a cracked lantern in the closet, which they had broken apart to use the base as a cup to hold Prue's blood. Mona had found a loose floorboard and managed to wriggle free a nail to carve into Prue's arm. They made sure to draw the blood near her shoulder, in a place that wouldn't easily be visible to the Titans.

It wasn't easy, collecting the amount of blood they needed. Mona had to dig the nail deep into Prue's flesh, carving a wider gash to allow the blood to flow. And after it was finished, Mona insisted on waiting to properly bandage it with a strip of cloth torn from her tunic before they continued with their plan.

Through it all, Mona was determined. She felt capable and steady. She knew this would work.

But uncertainty clouded her mind as soon as Prue rose from the cot, smoothed her palms over her skirt, and announced, "All right. I'm ready."

Panic and terror welled up in Mona's chest at the thought of her sister offering herself as bait to the Titans.

Oh Goddess, Mona thought. *I can't do this. It's not going to work. It isn't going to be enough, and the Titans are going to kill Prue.*

She jumped to her feet. "You can't."

Prue's brows knitted together and she faced Mona. "I have to. Their magic is strong here, Mona. They'll know what we're doing... unless they have something to distract them."

Mona gripped Prue's arm tightly. In a whisper, she said, "They don't need *both* of us as leverage. If you anger them, Prue... I'm afraid they'll kill you."

Prue's eyes softened and she gathered Mona in her arms, crushing her in a tight embrace. "They need me," she murmured, "because I'm Cyrus's wife. I'll be fine. I promise."

Prue's grip loosened, but Mona clung to her even more tightly, trying to prolong their embrace. She didn't want to let go.

But she had to.

At long last, she released Prue and offered a sure nod. Before Prue left the room, Mona grabbed her hand. "Be careful, Prue. Don't do anything stupid."

Prue snorted. "When have I ever?"

Mona could only roll her eyes at that.

Prue eased the door open and crept down the stairs. Mona moved to the door, intending to close it, but she couldn't help but linger at the doorway, listening. Prue's voice drifted up from below.

"I need to speak with Hyperion."

Mona winced, knowing the Titans would not like what came next.

Prue intended to confront Hyperion—to tell him off for what he did to her in the Underworld and during Cyrus's challenge.

She intended to pick a fight with him.

And if the other Titans wouldn't let her see him, she would fight *them* instead.

Either way, it would not be pretty.

So Mona had to hurry.

Her palms began to sweat as shut the door and carefully set the bowl of Prue's blood on the small table by the window. With the nail from the floorboard, she pried one of the window panes loose. She and Prue had practiced this earlier to ensure they would have a way to shoot fire into the sky.

Mona's hands shook as she gently eased the window pane onto the cot, careful not to drop it. That was just what she needed—for a loud shattering sound to alert the Titans. A cool breeze wafted into the room, but it was full of rot and decay and lacked the familiar earthy scent Mona had grown to love. She wrinkled her nose, then focused on the cup of blood.

She had to get this exactly right.

But Goddess, so much was on the line. When Mona

studied spells and runes for her own pursuits, it was easy to memorize and absorb information. But here and now, with Prue's life at stake...

Her hands shook even harder. Her heart pounded so loudly she couldn't breathe.

Focus, Mona, she told herself. *You are not a coward. You can do this. Prue trusts you.*

Mona only wished she trusted herself as much as Prue did.

Clearing her throat, Mona waved her hand over Prue's blood and whispered, "*Excito.*"

The air hummed, but the sound was stilted and strained. A mere whisper of the power she was accustomed to. Unease swirled in her chest, but she shoved it down deep. She knew this would be different. She had to push through and trust the magic.

Closing her eyes, Mona murmured the incantation. "*Muros finire. Et magicae gratis.*" She flexed both hands over the blood, her fingers curling into a shape that resembled elongated claws.

Magic hissed around her, but when she opened her eyes, the pool of blood remained unchanged.

"Shit," she whispered. The energy in this place was so stagnant that even her ordinary witch magic couldn't get through without a struggle.

As if this spell weren't complicated enough.

Mona cupped the broken lantern between her palms and screwed her eyes shut once more. Digging deep into the power source of her entire being, she said the words in a low, ethereal voice. "*Muros finire. Et magicae gratis!*"

Her voice rose with each syllable, the words ringing around her. The glass in her hand heated, making her skin hot. She chanted the words over and over, pushing through the pain as the heat of Prue's blood scorched her skin.

From downstairs, Prue's shriek echoed. Mona's voice faltered, and the cup of blood cooled.

Dammit. She closed her eyes and refocused, then repeated the words of the spell once more. Despite every ounce of fear within her, every facet of terror at the thought of what Prue was doing to buy her time, Mona homed in on the singular task of spell-casting.

Say the words.

Offer the blood.

Let the Triple Goddess do the rest.

"Muros finire. Et magicae gratis."

The words poured from her lips. The air buzzed and crackled with electricity. The walls began to shake.

Someone shouted from downstairs. It wasn't Prue.

Prue's voice followed, a shrill shout.

Something shattered. Heavy thumps followed.

Sweat dripped down Mona's brow. She spoke the words faster, more urgently. A violent churning encircled the small room, whipping at her hair and tickling her skin. Her third eye opened, and Goddess above, it was the most peculiar sensation. What had once been second nature to her now was foreign and unfamiliar. She had relied so much on her goddess powers that she had forgotten how it felt to sense magic with her third eye.

With a gasp, Mona's back arched, magic coursing through her. Something cracked in the air, and a burst of energy whooshed around her like a tornado. She inhaled a rattling breath, and for the first time since she'd arrived here, she finally felt as if she could breathe normally.

There was magic here once more. *True* magic.

A slow smile spread across her face. She set down the broken lantern, which was now empty, and lifted one hand in front of her face. A tendril of thorny vines appeared, wrapping around her palm and encircling her fingers like an embrace. It was as easy as breathing.

More crashing from downstairs instantly sobered her. Mona stumbled over to the open window, then used a broken shard from the lantern to slice into her palm. With blood running down her hand, she whispered, *"Accendo."* She flexed her fingers toward the sky, and a coil of flame sliced through the air like an arrow. When it reached the clouds, it exploded like fireworks, shooting in different directions.

Pop.

Pop.

Bang!

One by one, the sparks burst in the air, growing louder in succession.

Shit. Mona's heart dropped to her stomach like a stone. She hadn't meant to put that much power into the spell. She'd become accustomed to the stale magic in the air that she hadn't held back anything.

It had been too much. Too visible. Too *loud.*

She prayed to the Goddess the fire witches would see that and come quickly.

Because the Titans certainly would have noticed. Not

even the most violent distraction from Prue could have prevented them from seeing that explosive display.

Sure enough, thundering footsteps sounded on the stairs.

Mona uttered a squeak of alarm before darting across the room, flattening herself against the wall behind the door. In her chest, her heart thundered madly.

The air suddenly crackled and went still. A stifling, crowded feeling suffocated her throat and chest, making it hard to breathe. Fatigue spread through her, making her form droop. Her head felt cloudy and incoherent.

The Titans' wards were back in place. Which meant her powers were gone.

And the amount of energy it had taken to cast those two runes was dragging her down, down, down...

Fresh panic bloomed inside her, making her dizzy. Dread and despair coiled around her like serpents, freezing her in place.

Then the door burst open.

DIVERSION
PRUE

PRUE'S HEART SKITTERED AS SHE MADE HER WAY downstairs. The deep voices of the Titans drifted up to her, too muffled for her to make out any words.

She lifted her chin. She could do this.

They wouldn't kill her. They needed her alive to negotiate with Cyrus.

With this reminder fresh in her mind, Prue descended the final steps and rounded the corner.

The murmuring stopped at once, and four pairs of dark eyes fixed on her.

Four. One Titan wasn't here.

Damn. If the last Titan was keeping watch somewhere, it was likely they would notice when the wards came down. Prue's gaze flicked over each Titan before landing on Hyperion, who lounged in an armchair, his eyes narrowing.

"I need to speak with Hyperion," she said in a clipped tone.

"Is that so? Well, I'm afraid I'm busy at the moment." Hyperion turned to speak with Atlas on his left. A clear dismissal.

Prue stomped toward him, her hands curling into fists. It wasn't hard to project the rage she felt toward this Titan. He had siphoned magic from her and tried to kill her. He had intervened during Cyrus's challenge, nearly killing him, too.

He had worked alongside Apollo to steal the throne of the Underworld.

"I need to speak with you," Prue repeated, her tone harsh and unyielding. "*Now.*"

Hyperion's face slowly turned to fix an icy stare on her. The chair creaked as he stood, and Prue's mouth went dry as she realized just how much he towered over her. Crackling power rippled off him, charging the air with electricity.

"You hear that?" Hyperion called to the Titans surrounding him. "The little goddess wants to throw a temper tantrum."

A few of the Titans chuckled and guffawed at that.

"What is your problem with me?" Prue demanded. "I did nothing to you. To *any* of you." She made a sweeping motion with her hand to indicate the room at large. "I have no quarrel with you. But you've tried to kill me twice."

"No quarrel?" Hyperion leaned closer, his foul stench stinging her nostrils. "You're the daughter of Gaia. You are married to Aidoneus's son. Both of them worked tirelessly to cage us in Tartarus. I would hardly call you innocent, little goddess."

"I just want to protect the people of the Underworld!" Prue shouted. "Why are you standing in the way of that?"

"We only want to be free," Hyperion said. "Why are *you* standing in the way of that?"

"What does your freedom entail? Do you intend to slaughter the gods and goddesses who defied you? To slaughter their innocent children? Do you intend to honor and respect the souls of the Underworld? If you do, I'll gladly step aside and let you roam the realm as you wish."

She waited, but Hyperion only smirked at her. The other Titans snickered again.

"Such a naïve little girl," Atlas sneered from the sofa. "Should we tell her, Hyperion?"

"Tell me what?" Prue demanded. Her pulse quickened. She didn't like the looks of smug satisfaction that passed between the Titans.

"Aidoneus and his precious sons wanted to use *demons* to fuel the rivers of souls. Did you know that?"

Prue's stomach twisted with dread. A sour taste filled her mouth.

"The rivers are alive. Aidoneus needed to fuel the rivers from *somewhere*. So, he sought to use the population of demons—to drain their souls and draw power for the rivers."

Oh god. Prue was going to be sick. Hyperion drew closer until she was backed against a wall. Still, he leered over her, revealing his fangs.

"Aidoneus didn't want to sacrifice any of the death gods to power the rivers," Hyperion hissed. "No, they were far too valuable for that. Instead, he sought a source that was dispensable. A source no one would miss."

Prue shook her head, her eyes squeezing shut. "No."

"These are the people you are standing by," Hyperion

spat. "They are monsters. More monstrous than we are. Wake up and face the truth, girl."

Magic churned in the air, and Hyperion's brow furrowed. He sniffed, as if trying to scent out whatever power was circling the cottage.

Prue's heart lurched as she realized Mona must have cast the spell. With a sharp gasp, Prue shoved at Hyperion's shoulders, but he didn't even budge. "You're *lying!*" she screamed.

Hyperion bared his teeth, looking every bit the predator he was. "I am not."

"You said Aidoneus *wanted* to use demons to fuel the rivers," Prue said, her voice rising with her fury. "But he didn't, did he?"

Hyperion went perfectly still.

"I know for a fact that the rivers are fueled by the death gods themselves," Prue said, her voice gaining volume. "Because when Cyrus was called to the mortal realm, his river dried up from being disconnected from its source."

Hyperion's nostrils flared, and a muscle twitched in his jaw. He was caught in his lie, and he knew it.

Prue jabbed a finger straight into Hyperion's chest. "You *are* a liar. So don't try to turn me against them, you sick bastard. You're a brute, and I refuse to be intimidated."

Rage contorted Hyperion's features, and he slammed his forearm into her throat, pinning her to the wall and making her cry out. "Is that why you came downstairs? To fling accusations at me? Bold of you, considering your life is in my hands."

Prue's throat burned, but she managed to choke out, "You... can't... kill me."

Hyperion's nostrils flared. "Maybe not. But I can suck that soul of yours dry. Leave Cyrus with nothing but an empty husk for a wife. How will it feel to return to your home as a withering wisp of a human? You think your doting husband will still love you?"

Prue gritted her teeth, clawing at Hyperion's arm as her lungs strained for air. Sharp pain lanced through her throat. She tried to inhale, but nothing came in. Black spots danced in her vision.

She managed to jerk one of her knees upward, ramming it between Hyperion's legs. He grunted, his grip loosening just enough for her to shove his arm off her. She ducked, her vision foggy, and crashed into a side table. A vase shattered, littering the floor with tiny shards.

The other Titans were on their feet in an instant, eyes blazing.

But then, Prue felt it. Heat and energy coursed through the air, filling her with vibrance and clarity. She straightened and inhaled deeply. Magic crackled in her veins, alive and ready to do her bidding.

It had worked. The wards were down.

Goddess, it was a relief, to feel her power flowing through her once more. All she wanted to do was choke the life out of each of these Titans.

But she couldn't. Mona had said the wards would only be dismantled for a moment. As soon as they were back up, the Titans would overpower her. And they would know what Mona had done.

She had to pretend she was still powerless.

With a groan, Prue hunched over as if injured, massaging her throat and staggering away from the approaching Titans.

"She doesn't need all her limbs," said one, licking his lips hungrily. "Perhaps she could lose a few fingers. Or even a hand. Cyrus wouldn't mind, would he?"

Prue didn't have to pretend to shudder. But she adopted a horrified expression, cowering away from the Titans.

Hyperion chuckled. "As long as her heart still beats, I don't care what you do with her."

"The left hand is mine," said Atlas with a grin.

"I'll saw off her pretty little feet," said another.

The Titan closest to her lunged, and Prue dropped the pretense and kicked him hard in the face. He cried out, stumbling backward. Another Titan reached for her, but she scrambled out of the way, rolling along the floor. She hit something hard—a table perhaps—and overturned it, not caring when it hit the floor with a loud *crash*.

Her goddess blood granted her strength and agility, and she had to use that to her advantage. At least until Mona had completed the spell.

After that, she was in deep shit.

One step at a time, she told herself, ducking to avoid Atlas's swinging fist. She lifted a wooden stool to block his next strike. With a roar, he jerked the stool out of her grasp and flung it against the wall. The wood splintered and cracked, leaving the stool broken.

Something heavy slammed into the back of her head, and she screamed, darkness momentarily clouding her mind as she threatened to black out.

Then a Titan grabbed Prue from behind, one meaty arm covering her chest. She wriggled, trying to break free, but his arm was so thick and large it covered both of hers. She stomped on his toes, and he groaned, but his grip remained firm.

The other Titans cackled as they drew closer, a dark and hungry look gleaming in their eyes.

"I think you've caused us enough trouble, little goddess," said Hyperion. He lifted a jagged blade from the counter behind him and drew closer to her. "Maybe we should start with cutting out that tongue of yours. I think we'd all appreciate the silence, wouldn't we?"

The Titans laughed. Prue's stomach churned as she struggled anew, her legs flailing uselessly.

Shit, this was not good.

A deafening *boom* sounded from outside, and everyone went still, eyes going to the door.

Crack. Crack. Crack.

One after another, explosions split through the air, crackling like thunder.

Prue's heart seized in her chest. What *was* that?

"Prometheus," Hyperion said, "Go and see—"

His words cut off as another Titan burst through the front door, panting. "Fire," he gasped. "There's fire in the sky."

Cold horror washed over Prue. *No.* Mona's spell wasn't supposed to be like this. The Titans weren't supposed to know.

Slowly, Hyperion fixed a murderous gaze on Prue, his

eyes narrowing into slits. "Go and check on the other little goddess, would you, Prometheus?"

The Titan who had threatened to saw off Prue's feet lumbered toward the stairs, his heavy footfalls echoing. Hyperion, still wielding the knife, drew closer to Prue.

In a low voice, he said, "Now, you're going to tell me exactly what you two have been up to." He pressed the blade against her cheek. "Or I'll slice off your tongue and force it down your throat."

IMPASSE
CYRUS

THE WORLD SHIFTED, MORPHING AND CHANGING AS Cyrus, Lagos, and Evander stepped through the portal. They emerged in darkness, the air musty and damp. Cyrus wrinkled his nose. He'd forgotten how stale the air smelled in the Realm of Gaia.

Beside him, Lagos wobbled, his legs unsteady. Cyrus grabbed his arm to keep him from falling over.

"Gods," Lagos muttered, shaking his head. His hands were trembling. "That was... disorienting." He inhaled deeply, then made a grunt of displeasure. "What's that horrible smell?"

"The human realm," Cyrus said grimly. "You'll get used to it."

"It's not just that," Evander said, looking around. "We're in a cavern. There isn't much fresh air here."

Cyrus frowned, blinking in the darkness. He couldn't make out anything except the moist rock wall beside them, barely illuminated by the lingering glow of the portal. It felt strange that Cyrus hadn't been here before but Evander had.

The last time Cyrus had been in this realm, he'd been with Prue.

A bolt of yearning split through him, sharp and merciless. Gods above, he missed his wife.

Soon, he told himself. *You'll have her back soon.*

He didn't want to think about what state she'd be in when he found her. Or what horrors she'd endured at the hands of the Titans.

No. For right now, all he needed to think about was the next step: locating the fire witches.

"So, where do we go from here?" Cyrus asked his brother.

Evander hesitated, glancing back and forth between the rock wall and the portal. "I'm... not sure. I wasn't entirely conscious when I came through last time."

Cyrus sighed, inching forward with his hand outstretched. His fingers met the moist surface of the cavern wall. He stepped forward, his feet crunching on rocks.

This wouldn't work. He would trip and fall, likely breaking his neck and killing himself before he could even get to Prue.

"To hell with this," he muttered before spreading his hands and summoning his Titan power.

"Cyrus, don't—" Evander warned, but it was too late.

Energy crackled through him, and he summoned the smallest kernel of magic. White light sizzled along his fingertips, bathing the cavern in a brilliant glow that revealed a narrow tunnel built into the rock wall. He never would have found that without a light source.

"This way," Cyrus said with a satisfied smile, stepping toward the tunnel.

Before he could, however, shouts rang out, echoing and bouncing off the cave wall. A soft amber glow appeared on the other side of the tunnel, followed by heavy footfalls.

"Shit," Evander muttered. "They sensed your magic."

Cyrus dropped his hands, and the electric power coursing through him vanished. In an instant, several figures appeared at the mouth of the tunnel, each wielding a ball of fire in her palm.

"Who are you?" barked the woman in front. She had dark skin and gleaming golden eyes that blazed with fury.

Cyrus opened his mouth to speak, but Evander grabbed his arm to stop him.

"Farah," Evander said, stepping forward with his palms outstretched. "It's good to see you again. This is my brother, Cyrus, and our friend Lagos." He gestured to Cyrus and Lagos in turn.

Farah's eyes narrowed as she focused on Cyrus. "Osiris? God of the dead?"

Cyrus straightened. He wasn't sure he liked the threat in the woman's voice. "Yes. That's me."

Her nostrils flared. "You are not welcome here, death god."

Of course he wasn't. Cyrus barely refrained from rolling his eyes.

"Please," Evander begged. "Mona and her sister Prue were captured and brought somewhere in the Rhea Desert. We could use your help in finding them."

Farah stepped forward, her movements slow and

measured. Her gaze never strayed from Cyrus. The flames in her hand rippled as she walked. "What unholy magic have you brought to my coven, God of the Underworld?" Her voice was soft and lethal.

Cyrus swallowed. How could he explain this in a way that wouldn't mark him as an enemy? With a steady breath, he said carefully, "I was struck by a Titan in a duel. I managed to absorb a modicum of his power, and now it flows through my body."

"Impossible," Farah said at once.

Cyrus shrugged his shoulders. "What's your explanation, then? I am clearly not a Titan."

"We have dealt with deities before who dabbled in Titan magic, death god. It did not end well for them."

Cyrus stiffened, thinking of Pandora. "I did not willingly acquire this power. I can assure you, I have not meddled in the magic of the Titans. I am here to destroy them."

Farah's flames flickered, and something like recognition stirred in her eyes. "You know the Titans are here?"

Cyrus nodded. "Can you tell me where they are?"

"We do not know. We felt the earth tremble when they came into the realm. Wherever they are, it is close enough to send power rippling through our caves. One of our tunnels collapsed from the force of it."

Cyrus's chest tightened. The Titans were here. They were so close... *Prue* was so close...

"Will you let us pass through?" Evander asked, his voice laced with urgency.

"I cannot possibly allow Titan magic to fester among my sisters," Farah snapped. "It is far too dangerous and volatile. It would likely cause another of our tunnels to collapse. You must return through the portal and find another way."

"Farah *please*—" Evander begged, but Cyrus was done negotiating.

He spread his hands, summoning his power again. Lightning flashed, igniting the cavern. Several witches gasped as he struck the cavern wall next to him. Rocks trickled from the ceiling and crashed to the ground.

"My brother asked kindly," Cyrus growled, "but I will do no such thing. You will let us pass, or I will tear this cavern apart piece by piece. The choice is yours."

Farah let out a low hiss, her eyes flashing. For a moment, her pupils narrowed into snake-like slits. The fire in her hand intensified, spearing toward the ceiling until a pillar of flames appeared beside her. "Go ahead and try, death god. You will not get far."

But Cyrus only cocked his head and smiled. "Perhaps not. But how many of your beloved witches do you think I'll take down before you manage to stop me? How many lives are worth losing over this petty argument? Simply let us pass, and no one will get hurt."

Farah hesitated, her expression conflicted. But she did not vanquish her fire. Behind her, the other witches summoned more flames as well, until a wall of amber fury stood between Cyrus and the exit.

This was about to get messy.

But Cyrus bared his teeth, unafraid of the challenge. If he had to kill these witches to get to Prue, he would do it without a second thought.

He was no longer in the Underworld. These people were not his to protect.

They were dispensable.

Evander hurried forward, hands outstretched as he placed himself between the witches and Cyrus. "Please. *Please.* Farah, you know me. I would never intentionally put you or your coven in danger. You know the Titans must be stopped. And Cyrus is the only one who can do it. He's the only one with enough power. *Please* let us pass so we can put an end to this. Would you prefer they remain in your realm, wreaking havoc and destruction?"

Farah shrank back a step, her brows knitting together. The flames next to her shrank until they were nothing more than a ball in her hand.

"Is Romanos here?" Evander asked.

"No. He is in the Thanassian Empire with the Gorgon sisters."

Cyrus's chest hollowed. Damn. Clearly the fire witches weren't on their side. And with Romanos gone, he wouldn't be able to help, either.

From his left, Lagos cleared his throat and stepped forward. Cyrus withdrew his power, momentarily forgetting the demon was with them.

"If I may," Lagos said politely. "The sisters we are here to rescue are quite precious to us. There is nothing we would not do to save them. Please understand that we have no intention of going back through the portal. Not when Prue and Mona are so close to us. This is the only way, fire witch. And the three of us are willing to die for this cause."

Cyrus blinked, emotion stirring in his chest at the fervor

in Lagos's words. It touched him in ways he'd never known before.

The demon was as committed to this as Cyrus was. If Prue were watching, she would be welling up with tears.

Farah dropped her hands, her fire vanishing as she gaped at Lagos. It seemed she, too, had not realized the demon was there. "You—You are a demon."

Lagos inclined his head. "Yes."

Farah's face paled. Behind her, the witches began whispering and murmuring to one another. Farah's mouth opened and closed a few times before she stammered, "I—Demons... should not be here. They do not belong in our realm."

"Well, clearly this one is an exception," Cyrus said.

Farah shook her head. "Forgive me. I just—I have never met a demon who is so... civilized."

Lagos bristled, clearly offended by this.

"I mean to say," Farah said quickly, "the only demons we have encountered are the monsters from Pandora's box. Before the box was opened, demons could not travel to this realm." Her gaze shifted to Cyrus, and a strange sense of awe filled her expression. "You are friends with this demon?"

"I am," said Cyrus. "I trust him with my life."

Farah inhaled a soft gasp, then looked over her shoulder at the witches behind her. She nodded, and they doused their flames as well, save for one, who raised her arm as a sort of torch to light the way.

"Perhaps I misjudged you, death god," Farah said, drawing closer and bowing her head to him. "A king who can befriend a demon is certainly someone worthy of my respect."

Cyrus blinked, startled by this abrupt change in the witch's behavior. He exchanged an uncertain glance with Evander, who shrugged.

"I—uh—thank you," Cyrus muttered, bowing his head in return. "I appreciate that."

"You are not like your father," Farah said with a small smile. "That is for certain."

"Good," Cyrus said, his voice coming out as a growl. "Then I'm doing something right."

Farah jerked her head toward the tunnel behind her. "Follow us. We will escort you through the caves."

Relief spread through Cyrus's chest as Farah and the witches turned to stride through the narrow tunnel. Before following, Cyrus put a hand on Lagos's shoulder.

"Thank you for that," he murmured. "This might have turned into a nasty fight if you hadn't said something."

Lagos only grunted, and Cyrus couldn't tell if it was meant to be a laugh or a scoff. Together, the three of them set off after the witches.

PROJECTION
TRIVIA

IF TRIVIA MEASURED HER DAYS BY HOW OFTEN SHE rested, she and Midas worked for five days on clearing her mind and strengthening her shields. Five days of mental strain. Five days of throbbing headaches.

On the sixth day, Trivia was so tired that she was tempted to give up—to take Midas up on his offer and just... stop.

But when he greeted her for their next training session, what he said surprised her.

"I want you to try to project your construct into my mind."

Trivia blinked at Midas, intrigued by this. The two of them no longer floated in the infinite void; they stood alongside one another, with Pandora's construct floating in and out of focus. If Trivia concentrated enough, the veranda overlooking the beach would become crystal clear. But Trivia wanted to save her energy for whatever task Midas asked of her.

"Project a construct to *you*?" she repeated. "I've already done that."

Midas shook his head. "No, not this." He waved his arms at their blurry surroundings. "I want you to send an image into my mind—and my mind alone. Make me see it, even if it's not there."

Trivia frowned. "I can't do that."

"Yes, you can. Your powers have grown since we began. You have managed to shield while simultaneously maintaining your own mental construct. Now, I want you to shield *and* project that construct into my mind. Make me feel like I am there."

"I *can't do that*," Trivia gritted out. "*You* haven't even been able to project anything into my mind. What makes you think I can do it?"

Midas leaned closer, his eyes intense. "Because you are linked to Pandora's soul."

Trivia could only stare at him, her thoughts too muddled for her to keep up.

"Your personas may have split when her box absorbed you," Midas went on. "But your souls are still connected. I can sense the tether between you two. She wants to get out because that will sever your bond completely. It will lock you in while giving her freedom. As long as you two reside in the same atmosphere, you are connected."

Trivia shook her head. "You're wrong. *She* has the power here. It's her box! She can control what I see. She can use the darkness against Gaia and Sol. I can't do any of that."

"Because you haven't practiced. She is centuries old. She has far more experience than you do. And this box is made from her own magic. *Of course* she's better at it than you. But I promise you, the potential to access her powers is still there. You just have to reach it."

Trivia's mouth twisted as she stared at Midas, full of doubt. He couldn't possibly be serious. If Trivia held as much power as Pandora, why did she feel so helpless? Why was she a prisoner here?

It didn't make any sense.

"Go ahead and try," Midas urged. "See what happens. You've already made great improvements over just a few days."

She couldn't argue with that. Though each day wore on her brain, drilling into her skull with relentless fury, she had far more freedom than those early days of floating in the dark void.

With a sigh, Trivia closed her eyes, picturing that same beach. A grassy hill overlooked the sparkling sand and the cerulean waves. The rushing water was a soothing rhythm to her ears.

If she concentrated enough, she could hear Sol's laughter as he splashed water at her face.

Her throat tightened with emotion, and she suddenly found she couldn't breathe.

Something prickled along her defenses, and Trivia instantly shielded her mind. Brick by brick, her wall slid into place, and she fortified it with another. Midas's magic slammed into her. Bricks crumbled, but she rebuilt them over and over. A wall of stone appeared on top of it. Then steel. Then marble. She envisioned every hard surface she could think of and threw it up before Midas could intrude on her private thoughts.

These are mine, she thought. *Sol is mine. No one else's. You don't get to see this. It's only for me.*

Fire burned in her chest, melting away the hopelessness that had dragged her down for so long.

"Excellent," Midas said softly. "Now, project your construct to me. Spread your awareness."

Trivia faltered. She had been so focused on closing off her thoughts, and now Midas wanted her to open up to him?

She strained against her instinct, which was to keep fortifying. Keep shielding.

"Don't let me in," Midas said quickly as if reading her thoughts. "*Project.* You are still in control. You choose what I see. That's the difference here."

Trivia licked her lips, her mind struggling to keep up her defenses *and* figure out how to project. Shielding and clearing her mind had become second nature. She knew exactly how to do those things, like stretching a familiar muscle.

But this was foreign to her. She wasn't sure what to do first.

She recalled how it had felt when she'd first spread her awareness—when she had pictured the tide coming in, inch by inch.

It had been the first time she'd accessed Pandora's construct.

So, how could Trivia make it her own? How could she show Midas what was in her mind?

I can do this, she thought. *I am powerful. I have strength.*

Her brow furrowed, and her breathing turned sharp. She pictured her mind stretching and spearing toward Midas. The ocean stayed with her, floating in her thoughts as she reached for him.

Trivia envisioned grasping Midas's wrist, her fingernails digging into his skin. And with that grip, she channeled her mental construct into his mind. She urged her magic forward, probing into his thoughts.

Midas sucked in a sharp breath, but Trivia kept pushing. She flooded images of the sea, the current, the beach, the field... She poured it all into his mind, holding nothing back. With a cry, she felt herself buckle, collapsing to the floor, but she couldn't stop. She heard his low groan, felt his pain.

But she couldn't shut it off. She didn't know how.

Agony split through her head as if her skull were being cleaved in two. Images flashed across her mind. Water. Sol. Sunshine. Leaves. Sand. Sol. Seaweed. Grass. Sol.

Sol, Sol, Sol...

Trivia screamed, throwing her head back as she slammed the door on her mental construct. Her shields, her thoughts, her vision all vanished, leaving nothing but quivering pain in their wake. She hunched on all fours, nausea coursing through her until she felt she might retch.

With a hoarse cough, she looked up, then let out a yelp of alarm, scrambling away.

Midas was unconscious, floating in the air in front of her. His golden hair fanned out before him, his arms outstretched as he lay there, suspended.

He... was in the dark void.

And *she* had put him there.

"Midas?" Trivia asked hesitantly.

He didn't respond.

"Shit," she hissed, inching toward him. She shook him by the shoulder. "*Midas!*"

Still no response.

What had she done to him? How could she reverse it?

Thinking fast, Trivia closed her eyes and mentally reached for Midas once more, this time with no construct or shields in place.

An onyx wall slammed into her, sending her reeling. She staggered back, barely catching herself before she landed on her ass.

Panting, she sat up, gaping at Midas's form. How had he done that? How were his walls so strong, even when he was in the void?

Then, a low laugh echoed around her, and her blood ran cold.

No, no, no...

Footsteps echoed, and before she turned, Trivia knew it was Pandora.

"Did you really think I wouldn't notice?" the goddess crooned.

Trivia's stomach hollowed, and she closed her eyes, willing Pandora to leave. This was just a nightmare. It wasn't real. Perhaps Midas was projecting this very image into Trivia's mind. Any moment now, he would withdraw and laugh at her for falling for his trick.

"I know *everything* that goes on here," Pandora said, her voice growing closer.

Trivia finally whirled to face her, not wanting the goddess

to come any closer. Feigning a confidence she did not feel, Trivia lifted her chin. "If that's true, then why let us carry on for so long? Why not stop it right away?"

"Because I enjoy toying with my prey before striking." Pandora's mouth stretched into a wide smile.

Trivia's eyes narrowed. There was something... off about Pandora. The darkness in her eyes wasn't as potent or lethal. There was something hidden in their depths. Something she did not want Trivia to see.

"That was you?" Trivia asked, gesturing to Midas's floating form.

"Yes." Pandora sniffed. "I grew bored."

"So, are you here to punish me then?" Trivia asked. "If so, what are you waiting for? Do it."

Pandora's nostrils flared. "You do not command me, child. Watch your tongue."

But as Trivia stared at the goddess, she did not feel fear. A strange curiosity overtook her. Pandora was hiding something. And Trivia intended to find out what it was.

"Have you found a way to free me?" Pandora asked, clasping her hands in front of her as if she were some demure princess. "If not, I'm afraid my darkness will have to play with that charming sun god again..."

Cold horror spread through Trivia's chest, but she shoved it down. Something told her Pandora was bluffing.

Have you found a way to free me? The words clanged in Trivia's mind, echoing over and over.

Pandora needed *her*. She needed Trivia to free her.

Because she couldn't do it herself.

Midas had been right. Trivia *did* hold power. More power than Pandora.

Trivia cast a glance at Midas's unconscious figure floating in the darkness. Pandora hadn't done that to him. *Trivia* had. Midas was strong enough to ward against Pandora's attacks.

But he hadn't expected Trivia's to be so powerful.

"You try my patience, child," Pandora hissed. "Answer, or I will unleash my shadows on your precious sun god."

Trivia said nothing, her sluggish mind working frantically to keep up with what she had discovered.

Pandora had sensed Trivia's power when she'd projected to Midas. It had drawn the goddess here. And when Pandora had appeared, she'd claimed it was *her* doing.

She wanted Trivia to think herself weak.

"No," Trivia said softly.

Pandora stiffened. "What?" she bit out.

Trivia thought of the vision Pandora had forced on her, of the tendrils of darkness creeping toward Sol and Gaia. Gaia's earth magic had managed to dissolve one of Pandora's shadows.

Damn this earth magic, Pandora had said.

That same earth magic flowed through Trivia's veins.

And Pandora needed it to escape.

"I said *no*," Trivia snarled, squaring her shoulders and glaring at Pandora. "I will not free you. And I will not let you threaten Sol any longer."

Pandora's face paled, and Trivia's chest swelled with triumph. She'd won. She'd caught Pandora in her farce.

The goddess had control over her no longer.

Then, to her surprise, Pandora began to laugh. She threw

her head back and cackled, the sound resonating and echoing around them.

Trivia went still, her skin prickling with unease. Why was Pandora laughing?

Pandora clapped her hands together with glee, her laughter subsiding as she gave Trivia a wide grin. "Oh, this is just *delightful,* isn't it? You've discovered your powers. Ah, what a relief it is to finally have a worthy opponent." She spread her arms, and darkness descended, swallowing up Trivia completely. Midas vanished, and Pandora melted into the shadows.

Trivia could see nothing. Not even her own hand in front of her face.

Then Pandora's voice was at her ear. "This is going to be fun."

BEACON
CYRUS

Cyrus's blood was still humming from the adrenaline coursing through his veins. His Titan magic flowed through him, sizzling with electricity that longed to be unleashed.

He had been ready to do battle, right there in that cave. A strange, savage part of him *yearned* to do it. To attack. To let loose all the pent-up rage and frustration that had been building since Prue was taken.

Now that the moment had ended, the energy pulsing within him had no outlet. No hope of release. It churned violently within him, gnawing and roaring, tired of being caged.

As he followed the witches through the tunnel, he curled and uncurled his fingers into tight, trembling fists. His breathing was erratic and shaky, and he focused on deep inhales.

This did nothing to calm his raging pulse. Gods, he felt ready to burst at any moment.

"How long have Romanos and Marina been gone?" Evander asked, his soft voice echoing off the cavern walls.

Cyrus wiped sweat from his brow and shook his head, trying to clear his thoughts and focus on what Farah was saying.

"A few weeks," she replied. "And you should not refer to her as *Marina* here. She is known as a Gorgon sister, or Hestia's chosen vessel."

Cyrus's brows knitted together. Who was this Marina, and why was she with Romanos? Were they romantically involved?

He shouldn't have been surprised by this. After all, he and Evander had bound themselves to powerful earth goddesses. It only made sense that Romanos would also be drawn to a powerful woman.

"Do they know about the Titans?" Evander asked.

Farah was silent for a moment before responding. The flame from her hand cast half her face in a soft golden light, illuminating the frown lines that marred her expression. "They were not here when we sensed the Titans' presence. But I am sure the Gorgon sisters are aware of it. A disturbance of that magnitude is difficult to overlook, especially by those with great power."

Great power. Well, damn. It was a shame that these Gorgon sisters weren't available to assist them against the Titans.

Before he could think better of it, Cyrus asked, "If these Gorgons are so powerful, do they have a plan for eradicating the Titans? Or Pandora's box? Surely there's something they can do."

He felt Evander stiffen beside him. He had probably crossed a line with his questioning. But he didn't care. The fury pounding within him made him reckless.

Farah's lips grew thin, and her eyes flashed with irritation. She kept her gaze fixed forward as she continued moving through the tunnel. "This may come as a shock to you, death god, but the Gorgon sisters have matters to deal with all over the realm. They are not merely weapons waiting to be wielded as you see fit."

Cyrus rolled his eyes, knowing she wouldn't be able to see it. "I never said such a thing. If the Titans' presence is as monumental as you say, then surely the Gorgons intend to do something about it. I am merely curious."

Farah huffed a wry laugh. "Curious to know if the Gorgons can be summoned to your aid, you mean."

Cyrus did not deny it. It was no secret that he and Evander sought help in rescuing Prue and Mona.

"I do not know of their plans," Farah admitted. "They answer to a higher power than I am worthy of. But I know they care a great deal about this realm and its inhabitants. They were tracking down a pack of violent chimeras that had been terrorizing the human villages. I am sure that, once they return, they will develop a plan for the Titan... situation." She heaved a sigh, then added, "But there is a limit even to their magic, death god."

That wasn't nearly as reassuring as Cyrus had hoped.

Evander nudged Cyrus's elbow, then shook his head slightly. *Let it go,* he seemed to say.

Cyrus raised his palms in mock surrender. Fine, he would drop it. Clearly the Gorgons and these witches would be of no help to them.

That was fine. Cyrus was eager to take down the Titans all on his own anyway. His magic was ready for it.

The tunnel opened up to a massive cavern about the size of the throne room in the Underworld. Several witches in tan robes meandered about. There was a fire pit in the center, upon which rested a bubbling cauldron. Shelves had been built into the cavern walls, stocked with various jars and vials.

Farah spread her arm, indicating a tunnel across the cavern. "That will lead you out into the desert. But be warned, the dry heat can be quite brutal. We can supply you with waterskins for your journey."

"Thank you," Cyrus said, inclining his head to her. "Do you happen to have an idea of where in the desert the Titans might be hiding? Or where we should start looking? You are far more knowledgeable of this realm than we are, and we could use your expertise."

Farah's lips quirked in a knowing smirk. "Flattery is a much better strategy for you, death god, but it does not work on me. Unfortunately, the Rhea Desert spans over a hundred miles, and I have no idea where the Titans might be hiding. There are likely various cave networks underground that we haven't yet discovered, similar to this one. That is where I would start searching."

Cyrus frowned. "With their explosive magic, I don't think they would settle somewhere underground. The risk of tunnels collapsing would be too great." He rubbed his chin, considering.

"It would be a place without magic," Evander said. "A place where the blood of the gods is considered useless. Unseen by prying eyes and hidden from mortal minds."

Cyrus's head whipped toward his brother, his eyes narrowing. Those did not sound like Evander's words at all.

Had he gotten this information from the Wild Spirits?

Farah's brow furrowed, her gleaming eyes flicking from Evander to Cyrus and back again. This witch missed nothing.

After a moment, she said, "If it's a magical void you seek, try the Ruins of Rhea. It was once a thriving city that was destroyed by the gods eons ago. Now, it holds no magic."

Cyrus straightened, hope blooming in his chest. "That sounds like the place. Where is it?"

"Originally, it was ten miles south of Sodara. But since the gods cursed the village, it is... altered."

Cyrus's chest twisted with dread. "Altered how?"

"It changes and moves, depending on the magic around it. If the area nearby contains too much magic, the ruins will vanish and reappear in a place less saturated with energy."

Cyrus let his hands fall against his thighs in exasperation. "How the hell are we supposed to find this place if it's always moving?"

Farah's nostrils flared, her eyes turning sharp. "Watch yourself, death god. I am not your enemy here. I am helping you as best I can."

Cyrus closed his eyes and suppressed a groan. "You're right. Forgive me. I am... merely agitated."

"I can see that." Humor laced her tone.

"How far do the ruins usually shift?" Lagos asked.

Farah paused, considering. "From what I understand, it is usually within a five-mile radius. But I could be wrong. We do not track these things."

Lagos nodded, then turned to Cyrus. "If we can get close enough, I believe I can scent the Titan magic."

"How close would we need to get?" Cyrus asked.

"A few miles, perhaps."

Cyrus nodded. It might take them some time, but it was the best plan they had. "Which direction is Sodara?" he asked Farah.

"Northwest. Once you cross the dunes, you'll see the city. Or, what's left of it." Her eyes turned grim. "The darkness from Pandora's box has destroyed much of this realm."

"I'm sorry for your loss," Cyrus said, and he meant it. He had seen that darkness firsthand. He wouldn't wish it on anyone.

"Farah, is there anything you can give us?" Evander asked, a pleading note in his voice. "A tracking spell? Some kind of potion or concoction? Anything you can offer would be greatly appreciated."

Farah offered a sad smile. "Unfortunately, most of our spells can only be used by those who possess witch blood. But... if you are traveling to a land without magic, there are some elixirs we can give you that provide a short burst of power. Mind you, it is brief and not very strong. But it may give you the upper hand if the Titans are expecting to over-power you."

Cyrus's eyebrows lifted. "That's quite impressive."

"Your surprise is a touch patronizing, death god," Farah

said with a chuckle. She waved down a blonde witch who stood by the shelves. The witch approached, and Farah murmured something to her in soft undertones. The blonde witch nodded, then returned to the shelves, gathering various vials in her arms.

Before she could return, a panicked shout erupted in the cavern, echoing against the walls. Three witches appeared at the tunnel leading to the desert, their faces pale and stricken.

Farah straightened. "What is it?"

"A beacon," said one of the witches, breathless from her sprinting. "From the west. Fire magic."

Cyrus's blood chilled. The Titans?

Or... Prue?

"It was not one of ours," said another witch. "I did not recognize the magic. But it was definitely a witch. Runic magic, maybe."

"Mona," Evander whispered, his eyes widening.

"It's a call for help," Farah said, exchanging solemn looks with Cyrus and Evander.

"Will you answer?" Cyrus asked. "Not for me—but for your fellow witches?"

Farah's eyebrows flattened. "We do not interfere with the matters of Titans. It is too dangerous for my coven. We will point you in the direction of the beacon, but that is all. After that, you are on your own."

Cyrus nodded. This wasn't all that surprising. But he couldn't pass up one last opportunity to try to sway her.

The blonde witch returned, then thrust several vials full of purple liquid into Evander and Cyrus's hands. "Shatter these, and they will provide you with a brief burst of power where you can access your magic," she said, her voice faint compared to Farah's firm timbre. "But anyone nearby will also be able to summon magic as well, so be wary."

"Thank you," Evander said, shoving the vials in his pockets. Cyrus did the same, then accepted three waterskins from Farah.

"Show them where the beacon came from," Farah instructed the still breathless witches. To Cyrus's surprise, the coven leader put a hand on his shoulder and squeezed. "May the Goddess bless you in your quest, death god. I sincerely hope you are able to free your wife and her sister."

Cyrus offered a half smile that didn't feel very genuine. "Thank you for your assistance. I... apologize for my behavior. And my threats. I am not at my best today."

Farah hummed with amusement. "I have dealt with your kind before, death god. Behavior like that is not surprising. But an acknowledgment and an apology *is*. So, for that, I am appreciative of you. And I wish you well."

"Same to you."

Cyrus, Evander, and Lagos followed the three witches toward the exit. A few steps later, Cyrus frowned and muttered to Evander, "Did you tell Farah that Prue was my wife?"

"No. Why?"

Cyrus glanced over his shoulder at Farah, who lifted her hand in farewell, her eyes glinting with amusement and an otherworldly look that made him believe she saw far more than he gave her credit for.

Cyrus shook his head and faced forward again. "No matter. Let's focus on saving our goddesses."

For the first time in days, they actually had a lead. And the prospect of being reunited with his wife was so real, so attainable, that Cyrus could almost feel her rushing into his arms.

Soon, my love, he thought. *Soon, you will be free. Just hold on for a bit longer.*

WITS

MONA

Mona huddled behind the door as the Titan stormed into her room. He hadn't noticed her yet, but he would soon.

Her mind was still clouded, churning, and muddled. She couldn't think straight. And Goddess, she felt *so weak.*

He was here to kill her. Prue was right—they didn't need *both* of them alive.

Mona would never be able to fight him off. Not without magic.

Magic...

Mona glanced down at her still bleeding hand. Her heart pounded madly against her rib cage. Dizziness crept into her mind, threatening to drown her.

Without another thought, she shoved the door forward, making the Titan stumble. While he was down, Mona flexed her bleeding hand toward him and shouted, *"Disjungo!"* She shoved all her remaining energy into summoning the rune.

The magic gathered around her, but it was slow, like molasses. The air here was so arid that it took a long moment for her rune to take effect.

During that moment, the Titan staggered to his feet, rage brimming in his dark gaze.

Mona let out a squeak of terror, backing away from him.

He took a menacing step, the floorboard creaking from his movement, then halted. A choked sound rose up his throat. His eyes bulged. He gripped his neck as if she were strangling him with an invisible rope.

Mona could only watch, wide-eyed, as the Titan's face drained of color. He slumped to his knees, his body convulsing. Mona sidestepped before his massive form could crush her toes. She darted around him, hand at her chest, trying to control her breathing.

But a part of her was curious about how this rune affected a Titan. It was meant to dislodge a person's soul from their body, but Titans weren't entirely human...

Even so, it was clear her rune had done *something* to him. And she didn't want to wait around for him to awaken.

She raced toward the open door but hesitated at the top of the staircase. The sounds of scuffling reached her ears, followed by a sound that chilled her to the bone.

Prue's anguished whimper. Mona had *never* heard her sister utter that sound before.

Prue was always the strong one. Fearless and confident, even when facing the deadliest of horrors.

She made another sound, this one a tortured moan.

Then came Hyperion's voice. "That's it. Make her bleed."

Oh, Goddess. Mona was going to be sick. She was going to vomit all over the stairs.

They were torturing Prue.

They were *torturing* her sister. Her brave, beautiful sister.

Fear iced over Mona's body, freezing her in place. But as Prue made another desperate sound—a plea mingled with a sob—something else rose up inside Mona.

Rage.

She gritted her teeth. Her vision tinted red as she thought of what those vile monsters were doing to her beloved sister. She had literally gone through Hell and back to save Prue, and she wasn't about to stand by and do nothing while those beasts mutilated her.

But she had to be smart. To rush in without a plan would be something Prue would do.

Mona needed Prue's strength right now... but she still had to keep her wits about her. She was vastly outnumbered, with little access to magic. She could cast another rune, but she was so drained that she wasn't sure she could manage anything too powerful without fainting from exhaustion. Each one took so much of her energy because of how barren the air was.

But a lesser rune—that was something she could manage.

What she needed was a way to draw the Titans away from Prue. Something to divert their attention.

She almost laughed at the irony. Prue had volunteered for this very task—something Mona had been too terrified to do herself.

But, here she was.

Letting her rage fuel her, Mona dug her fingernail into the bleeding cut on her arm, drawing more droplets of blood. She hissed from the pain, but the sharp intensity of it sent a bolt of clarity in her mind. She crept back into her bedroom, checking to ensure the Titan was still down. His body twitched, but he was otherwise motionless.

With careful steps, Mona reached the open window, then slid her bleeding hand through the gap. Closing her eyes, she murmured, "*Sono.*"

Her skin prickled, and energy swirled around her. A tendril of magic flowed from her fingers, shooting toward the sky. But unlike the fire spell, this one was almost translucent against the murky gray surroundings.

After counting to ten, Mona opened her mouth and let out a shrill, piercing scream. The rune projected her voice somewhere above the cottage, circling the sky. Her shout rang out, reverberating through the forest as if she were floating high in the air.

Downstairs, the Titans shouted in alarm. Heavy footfalls indicated they were searching for the source of it. Mona's scream increased in pitch and volume, allowing her anger and panic to flood her. She channeled all her emotions into that singular sound until it resembled a screeching, dying animal.

The Titans' shouts turned into petrified yelps. Mona heard the front door open, and a few Titans exited. She noticed them sprinting toward the forest—toward her scream—as if to uncover who was making that noise.

The magic was fading. Any moment now, her rune would wear off and her voice would return to her body. She ended on one final, powerful note before she fell silent, her throat raw. Swallowing hard, she inched toward the staircase again, pausing to listen for any sounds.

Nothing. Then, a low, wet rasping sound.

Goddess above... *Prue.*

Mona was about to fly down the stairs before she heard someone move. Someone who was much heavier than Prue.

Dammit. Of course the Titans wouldn't send everyone out to investigate Mona's scream. Desperate for another diversion, Mona scanned her surroundings, finding nothing of use at the top of the stairs. Then, her gaze fell to her grubby shoes.

It would have to do.

She snatched one of her worn shoes off her feet, then launched it as far down the stairs as she could manage. It landed near the kitchen, and a clatter rang out. A Titan grunted, then lumbered off in the direction of where her shoe had fallen.

Then, Mona was moving, flying down the stairs. She didn't pause to take in her surroundings or look for the Titans. All she focused on was the trembling form in the middle of the floor, covered in blood.

Prue.

The entire left side of her face was covered in blood, her hair sticky and matted. Her skin was far too pale, and her lower lip was split and bleeding. Mona raced over to her, her heart twisting so painfully in her chest she thought she might collapse right alongside her sister. Hot anger burned behind her eyes, but she didn't have a moment to cry or rage over Prue's condition. She had only seconds before the Titan realized she was there.

As delicately as possible, Mona thrust her hands under Prue's arms and tried to haul her to her feet. Prue let out a groan of pain, and Mona froze.

From the kitchen, the Titan let out a roar.

Shit. Mona could either stay with Prue, or avoid this Titan's wrath.

"I am *not* leaving you," she told Prue through gritted teeth.

She was not a coward.

With fury in her gaze, she glared at the approaching Titan—Atlas, the purple-skinned demon with ram horns. He stomped toward her, fangs bared and clawed fingers flexing toward her. When he was only steps away, Mona lifted her hand and whispered, "*Disjungo.*"

The air hummed, then fell silent.

Nothing happened.

"*Dammit!*" Mona hissed.

Atlas only grinned, drawing closer.

"My... blood," Prue croaked.

"What?" Mona hissed.

"Use it!" Her raspy voice was insistent.

Atlas lunged, and Mona pressed her hand to the fresh blood coating the left side of Prue's face. "*Disjungo!*" she cried.

Just like the other Titan, Atlas went rigid, then sank to his knees. His shoulders shook, and tremors overtook his entire body. Prue slumped against Mona, no doubt drained from the cost of fueling a rune with her blood.

"I've got you," Mona whispered. She scanned the cottage, noting every doorway. Was there a back door? If she and Prue hobbled out the front entrance, the other Titans would notice.

"Window," Prue wheezed, blood dribbling from her lips.

"Shh," Mona said softly. "Don't strain yourself, Prue. I said I've got you. I'll get you out of here, I promise." Her eyes latched onto the massive window in the back of the kitchen. Damn, Prue was a genius.

Mona gently eased Prue on the floor, then raced over to the window. After realizing it was bolted shut, she snatched a rusted candlestick from the table and used it to shatter the glass. She dragged the candlestick over the edges of the pane to ensure no shards remained, then returned to Prue. Hoisting her up, Mona slid Prue onto one of the dining chairs. "I need you to go through first, in case one of them comes back. Can you climb?"

Prue mumbled something incoherent, but Mona interpreted that as a *yes*. Mona lifted her sister, arms quivering. Sweat pooled down her neck and face. Prue struggled, then her weight eased as she no doubt found purchase on the other side. With one last shove, Mona managed to get her all the way through the window.

Something crashed upstairs. The other Titan must have awakened.

With a gasp, Mona scrambled through the window. Prue was crouched on the other side, one hand outstretched toward Mona. Mona took it, and the two collapsed in the dry weeds just outside the window.

Lightning burst in the sky—the Titan's rage, no doubt.

Around them, the Titans were shouting something to one another. Mona wasn't sure if they were still trying to locate the source of her scream, or if something else had spooked them. Either way, she was grateful for the distraction.

"Come on." Mona wrapped Prue's arm over her shoulders, then helped her to her feet. More lightning forked through the sky. Together, they edged around the cottage, away from the shouts, until something made Mona go perfectly still.

"...those damned death gods," a Titan was saying.

Prue gripped Mona's tunic, her hand surprisingly strong. She, too, had gone rigid.

"Both of them?" another Titan said.

"No. It's just the one. The king."

Prue and Mona exchanged a look of surprise and relief.

"Cyrus is here," Prue whispered.

RUN

PRUE

Hyperion had sliced into Prue's lips with his blade before she finally admitted what she and Mona had done.

And after that, he had cut off her left ear, claiming she could keep her tongue but still deserved punishment for what she'd done.

The pain was so all-consuming that she couldn't think. She couldn't see straight. The ache on the side of her head pounded with a throb that seemed to have its own pulse. Every sound, every movement, only exacerbated the feeling.

Goddess, she just wanted to die. Just to take away the pain.

She had managed to rip a large chunk of her tunic, then held it against her ear to staunch the blood flow. But even that was too much effort, and she wound up curling up on the floor, pressing her head against the wad of fabric.

The chaos of the following events passed by in a haze. Screams and shouts. Thundering footsteps. Mona was there, her hands on Prue, trying to lift her. Prue wanted to help, to stand on her own feet, but she was so damn *weak*. The agony splitting through her was unbearable.

Mona urged her to move, and Prue's feet shuffled forward. With each step, her strength seemed to rekindle. Her head still throbbed, but her legs were fine. She *could* walk.

By the time they reached the window, Prue felt well enough to wriggle through—at least, with Mona's help.

And when she heard the Titans talking and realized Cyrus had come for her, hope crept into her chest.

Followed immediately by dread.

"What is he doing?" Prue hissed to Mona. "He's going to get himself killed."

Mona's eyes were distant, and Prue could tell she was thinking hard. "Evander must be with him. He wouldn't have let Cyrus go alone." She looked around, as if Evander would magically appear beside them.

"A diversion?" Prue asked, horror leeching into her thoughts. Just like her, Cyrus was offering himself up as bait.

Prue's plan had gone to shit. She didn't want to think about what would happen if Cyrus's plan failed, too.

Lightning ignited in the sky. Prue glanced up, realizing the strikes were from Cyrus, not the Titans.

"We have to do something." Prue shifted, trying to step forward, but a burst of pain sliced through her. She groaned, raising a hand to the wound in the side of her head. Thankfully, the bleeding had stopped, but the injury felt like it was on fire.

Mona gripped her arm tightly and shook her head. "We aren't doing anything. If they catch us, it's over. The best thing we can do for Cyrus and Evander is to stay hidden. Otherwise the Titans will have leverage over them."

The shout of a Titan made Mona and Prue jump.

"Where is he?" the Titan roared. Prue recognized Hyperion's voice, and she closed her eyes, nausea roiling through her. She recalled his wicked grin as he carved the knife through her flesh.

Mona's hands were on Prue's shoulders, squeezing her to awaken her from the nightmare. Prue shook her head and took a long, shaky breath.

"I see his lightning strikes," said the other Titan. Oceanus maybe? Prue couldn't tell. "I can smell him. But I don't know where he is."

"Idiots," Hyperion seethed. "*Find him.* He can't hide from all of us."

Prue met Mona's gaze and widened her eyes. What did this mean? How was Cyrus staying out of sight?

A voice roared nearby, one Prue knew in her bones. Her very soul quaked from the intensity of it, and her body yearned to draw closer to him.

"I am here!" Cyrus bellowed, his voice deep and powerful. "Shall we negotiate? Or are you too frightened to face me?"

What the hell is he doing? Prue thought, her heart racing. As if expecting her to bolt, Mona pinched her arm and shook her head.

"I see him," Hyperion said. "There. At the edge of the wood. Go, *now*."

Heavy footfalls indicated the other Titan had lumbered off. But Prue remained perfectly still, knowing Hyperion was still close by.

She heard him sniff deeply. Then, he chuckled.

"I can *smell* your blood, little goddess," he murmured. "You cannot hide from me."

Shit. *Shit.*

Mona tugged on Prue's hand, and the two of them crouched low to the ground, inching backward as quickly and quietly as possible. They rounded the corner of the cottage, then huddled close to the wall.

Hyperion's footsteps followed. "You think this changes anything? You are still my prisoner. My plaything. And I'll show that wretched death god exactly how much of your pretty face I can carve up."

Prue shut her eyes, her stomach churning with vicious intensity. The scrape of his blade. The sharp sting of her blood. The burning, scorching pain. Her broken screams.

Mona's fingernails dug into Prue's arm. With a gasp, Prue's eyes flew open, and she found her sister's eyes were blazing with fury.

"You are stronger than this," Mona whispered. "Do not let him win."

Prue sucked in breath after breath, but the oxygen wouldn't come. Her lungs strained. Her throat closed. Goddess, she was suffocating. She couldn't *breathe.*

Mona's lips thinned, her gaze filling with despair. "I love you," she breathed.

Before Prue could stop her, Mona stood, stepping into Hyperion's path. In a firm, confident voice, Mona said, "It's not Prue. It's me."

Prue pressed a hand to her mouth, shaking her head as if she could undo Mona's decision to face the Titan. Goddess, what was she doing? She would get herself killed!

I love you, she'd said.

Perhaps that was precisely what Mona intended to do.

"I smell *her,*" Hyperion sneered. "Not you. Your attempt at trickery is feeble."

"Her blood is on my clothes. That's what you smell. I told her to run."

Hyperion hesitated, as if he almost believed Mona's words.

Prue's pulse thundered loudly, and she feared it would give her away. She remained crouched there like a fool, a *coward,* letting her sister fight this battle for her.

Get up! she screamed at herself. *Mona is right. Do not let him win!*

"Perhaps you're right," Hyperion mused. "But you can still be of use to me. After all, you haven't been acquainted with my blade just yet. We should remedy the situation."

Panic flooded Prue's veins, sending sharp clarity to her mind. She scanned the dead grass around her, searching for a weapon, for something she could use against Hyperion.

She was too weak to cast a runic spell. But perhaps there was something else.

Her eyes landed on a shard of glass from when Mona had shattered the window. Prue snatched it up, then flattened herself against the wall, trying to steady her breathing.

"If you touch me..." Mona said.

"What will you do?" Hyperion chuckled. "Your lover isn't here to save you. It's just the king. And we both know who he'll choose."

Mona took a shuddering breath, and the sound wrenched through Prue's chest. She gritted her teeth, loathing the Titan with every fiber of her being.

She would not let this monster hurt her sister. She would not allow him to spill any more blood.

Rage flowed through her, powerful and violent. Before she could overthink it, Prue darted out from behind the building. Hyperion leered over Mona, mere inches away from her, his bloody blade raised. His eyes shifted to Prue and widened slightly.

But she didn't stop. With a shriek, she lunged for him, colliding with his broad chest. She slammed into him so hard that her head jolted and her skull rattled from the impact. Pain shot through her, and the space where her ear had been now pulsed with agony.

The force of her strike sent them both tumbling to the ground. Mona cried out her name. Prue slashed the shard of glass, drawing blood from Hyperion's shoulder. He growled, then swung his dagger. Prue managed to roll off him before he could stab her.

Then Mona was there, a feral cry pouring from her lips. She pinned down Hyperion's hand with both of hers, then wrestled the dagger free from his grasp. Hyperion grunted, shoving at Mona with one meaty arm. His thrust sent her sprawling in the grass. With a crack, her head struck a rock, and she collapsed.

Prue wanted to run to Mona's side, but her sister had given her an opportunity, and she couldn't waste it. Without bothering to climb to her feet, Prue slammed the jagged piece of glass into Hyperion's thigh, then twisted it deep. Rivulets of black blood gushed from the wound.

Hyperion howled, the sound piercing the air.

Prue withdrew the glass, then rammed it into his gut. Blood bubbled from his lips as he reached for her, fingers flexing.

Something shattered nearby, and purple smoke drifted in the air. It smelled like… saffron. Prue frowned, then glanced around, her body tense as she expected another fight.

"End him!" shouted a familiar voice. "Prue, end him now!"

Prue gasped as she made out Lagos's figure amidst the magenta fog. "*Lagos*? But how—"

"Use your magic!" he urged. "Quickly!"

Prue drew in a breath, only then noticing how *free* the air felt. Energy crackled through her as her magic soared to life.

It felt just like when Mona had broken through the wards. Prue's earth magic was back.

With a sigh of relief, she summoned her roots and vines. They rose from the ground and twisted around Hyperion. He opened his mouth, no doubt ready to inhale her power as he'd done before. But Prue slashed the glass across his throat, cutting off his breath. He choked, blood seeping into the dead grass around him. His eyes grew wide, and his skin turned ashen.

Prue summoned more of her magic, drawing vines and thorns that tangled around Hyperion's limbs, anchoring him to the earth. He sputtered and wheezed, trying and failing to draw breath. Prue only glared at him with cold fury as he bled out, her brambles chaining him, preventing him from escaping.

She forced herself to watch until he went perfectly still. Until his eyes rolled back and his body shuddered once before dying.

Even then, she continued to stare at him, just to be certain he was dead.

Hyperion did not move. He did not breathe.

He was dead.

Prue released a long, trembling breath, then dropped the glass. Lagos rushed to her side, tugging on her hands to help her stand. Prue threw her arms around him, sobbing into his shoulder. "Goddess, Lagos! How did you get here? How—What was that smoke?"

"An elixir, courtesy of the fire witches," Lagos explained. "Come, we don't have much time. Evander and Cyrus are providing diversions so I can get you out."

"Evander's here?" Mona croaked. She was on the ground, struggling to rise. One side of her forehead was coated in blood from when Hyperion had thrown her.

"Of course he is." Lagos blinked at Mona as if it made little sense that Evander *wouldn't* come for her. "Cyrus was able to tear a hole through the wards with his Titan magic. But I don't know if it will hold. We must move, quickly."

"What about Cyrus and Evander?" Prue asked. "We can't just leave them. They'll be killed!"

"This is the plan, Prue," Lagos said grimly. "They can't

withdraw until they know you're safely outside the wards. We have to go. *Now.*"

Prue exchanged a panicked look with Mona, who nodded grimly.

"You agree with him?" Prue asked incredulously.

"If we want to save them, we have to get out of here first," Mona insisted. "If we're outside the wards, we'll have our magic back. We can use it to tear this place apart from the outside."

A knot formed in Prue's throat. Shouts echoed around her. They were getting closer. She swallowed down the protest climbing up her throat and gave a stiff nod.

Lagos took her hand and started running. Prue's steps were sluggish as the strength from her magic wore off. It seemed the witches' elixir was only temporary. The three of them ran around the back side of the cottage, pausing when two Titans raced past.

"He's over here!" one of them cried. "I saw him flying!"

"Evander," Mona breathed, her eyes sparking with hope.

Prue was panting, a stitch forming in her side. Hot blood dripped from the side of her head. Her wound had reopened.

She wouldn't last much longer.

"It's just past that tree," Lagos murmured, pointing to a jagged stump of a tree that marked the beginning of the dead forest.

"If we move from here, we'll be exposed," Mona said. "They'll see us."

Lagos pulled a glass vial from his pocket. It was filled with a liquid the same color as the smoke from earlier. "I have one left. We can use it now, but it won't last long." He glanced at Prue, then made a gruff noise of concern.

Prue shook her head. "I... can't," she wheezed. "Nothing... left."

"I can do it," Mona said. "Break the glass, and I'll hold them off."

"Mona," Prue rasped. "*Don't.*"

"I have no intention of dying today," she said firmly. "I'll be right behind you. I swear it."

Prue nodded, somewhat appeased by this. Too often, her sister sacrificed herself to save others. She couldn't bear to watch it happen again.

"All right," Lagos whispered, glancing at them both. "Prepare yourselves."

He hurled the glass to the ground.

And the three of them sprinted toward the trees.

Prue focused on her steps, one foot in front of the other, as she pushed as hard as she could. *Move,* she urged. *Faster. Run!* Her breaths seemed to tear through her chest. Pain lanced through her head, streaking across her brain like a line of fire.

The ground rumbled as Mona's power surged to life. Cracks appeared, and thorny vines sprang forth.

Titans shouted from behind them. One of them cried out, but his voice was cut off. Prue envisioned one of Mona's brambles strangling him.

They were so close now. Just a few more steps.

Mona screamed. Prue faltered, then released her hold on Lagos's hand.

Atlas had Mona by the throat. His dark eyes bored into

Prue's as he squeezed. Mona's body convulsed. She clawed at his hand, trying to loosen his grip.

"*No!*" Prue roared, barreling forward. She didn't care that her energy was gone. She didn't care if she had no strength left.

She *would not lose* her sister. Not today. Not ever.

Before she could crash into the Titan, Lagos surpassed her. With his head bowed, he launched himself straight into Atlas's chest, horns out. A sickening crunch echoed around them as Lagos's horns impaled the Titan. But Lagos kept pushing, driving deeper into Atlas's flesh. The Titan shrieked, the sound piercing the air.

Atlas released Mona, who fell to the ground in a heap, gasping for air. Prue was at her side in an instant, helping her to her feet. Mona blinked at her, dazed, but still alive.

Thank the Goddess.

"Lagos!" Prue shrieked. Atlas's arms were flailing as he tried to pull Lagos's horns free. But the demon was relentless, shoving harder, his roars of fury feral and unhinged.

"Prue, I see it!" Mona cried, pointing toward the tree.

Prue followed her gaze and found a small rip gleaming through the tree bark. If she squinted, she could barely make out Cyrus's face on the other side.

"Prue!" he shouted. His voice called to her soul, beckoning her, drawing her closer. She yearned to run to him.

But she couldn't leave Lagos.

Mona tugged on her arm. "Prue."

"No," Prue wrenched her arm free and raced toward her friend. "Lagos!"

Atlas managed to wrench free, his chest soaked in blood. He shoved Lagos off him, then grasped the demon's throat with both hands.

A scream ripped from Prue's throat as Atlas met her gaze, then twisted hard.

The crack of Lagos's broken neck resounded in the wood, ringing through Prue's ears. She would never forget that sound. It seared into her brain, making her go cold with undeniable horror.

No. *No*—

"Prue, it's closing!" Mona yelled. "We have to move!"

Prue could do nothing but stare in horror as Lagos's body collapsed like a doll. He crumpled, falling to the earth. He did not move.

Atlas stalked toward them, his eyes dark with hunger.

"Forgive me, Prue," Mona whispered. She summoned more vines, and they wrapped around Prue's body, pinning her arms and legs together.

"No... No, *Mona*!" Prue thrashed against the restraints, but they held firm. "Mona, please! I can—I can bring him back. *Please*! We can still save him!"

Tears streamed down Mona's face as she jerked Prue forward. "I'm so sorry," she sobbed before shoving Prue through the rip in the tree stump.

Prue fell forward, tumbling and rolling until strong arms caught her. Cyrus's face swam into view, but Prue could barely see through the tears that blurred her vision.

Lagos. *Lagos*—

"Cyrus," she said, shivering in his grasp. "Lagos. I can

save him. We can save him. Bring him back. Earth magic. Life. We can—We can…"

"She's in shock," someone said. Evander perhaps?

"Close the rip!" Mona said. "*Now!* Atlas is coming."

Lightning flashed, momentarily blinding Prue. She couldn't stop muttering, her body cold. So cold.

"Lagos. Earth magic. Life. Bring him back. Back. Back…"

The snap of Lagos's neck rang through her mind as Prue's head slumped, and she succumbed to darkness.

MOTIVE
TRIVIA

TRIVIA TRIED TO FREE HERSELF FROM THE DARKNESS, but Pandora's magic was stronger. The goddess's laugh sounded in her ear, and Trivia closed her eyes, picturing her tranquil beach. She saw the rolling ocean waves, the glittering sand...

And then, Pandora's face appeared, blocking her view of the coast.

Trivia yelped, her eyes opening as darkness consumed her once more.

"Silly child," Pandora crooned. "Your mind belongs to *me*. Nowhere is safe for you."

Trivia gritted her teeth, remembering what Midas had told her. *I am more powerful than I think,* she told herself.

She imagined her construct again, more detailed than before. The briny scent of the sea. The wind whipping against her face. The heat of the sun beating down on her. Sol's laughter amongst the waves.

For a moment, Trivia was there, her bare toes wiggling in the sand as she drew in a breath that tasted of saltwater and sunshine.

She was *here.* She focused on the acute sensations of her body in the construct, then projected them forward. The tide rolled in, covering her feet with cool water. It rolled over more and more sand, drifting closer to the hills beyond the shore.

More, she urged. *More.*

Trivia envisioned Pandora on the beach with her. She pictured the waves crashing over the goddess's form.

A grunt sounded nearby, and Trivia's eyes flew open. Pandora was on her knees in the sand next to her, the waves rolling toward her.

"*No!*" Pandora seethed.

In an instant, the vision changed, returning to darkness once more.

"Two can play at this game, girl," Pandora spat, her voice dripping with venom. "Now, it's my turn."

The darkness bled away to something new: the ruins of a broken city. The white chunks of marble and shattered blue shingles told her exactly where this was—Amara, the human village in Elysium.

What was left of it.

A lump formed in her throat, and Trivia inhaled a shuddering breath. If Pandora was trying to torment her with these visions, it wouldn't work.

Voices drifted closer, and Trivia went rigid. She recognized the male voice immediately.

Sol.

No, please no, Trivia thought, slamming her eyes shut before she had to look at him. The yearning already coursing through her was so painful it was unbearable.

"I'm not leaving," Sol was saying. "If she comes back—"

"She is not coming back," said another voice. This belonged to Gaia. "The sacrifice she made was permanent. It cannot be undone."

"Can't you just... bring her back? You're the goddess of life!"

"It isn't that simple. She *can* be brought back, but only under certain conditions. For one thing, she is not dead. She still lives. I cannot resurrect someone who hasn't died."

Pandora's chuckle echoed around Trivia. "You see why letting you wither away and die would be far too dangerous? No, you must *live,* child. Live with your consequences. Live with your guilt and regrets. Suffer as I suffered—chained to an existence you would give anything to be free from."

A tear spilled down Trivia's cheek as she opened her eyes at last, her gaze locking onto Sol. He stood in front of Gaia, his arms rigid and his expression hard as stone. Gaia's arms were crossed, her eyebrows drawn together.

Sol was fighting for *Trivia.* He was waiting for her.

"This war is bigger than us, Sol," Gaia said. "There are others who need our help."

"No one needs me as much as she does," Sol said, a muscle flexing in his jaw. "You can leave if you must. But I'm not going anywhere."

"Yes, little god," Pandora taunted, her voice full of savage delight. She was standing next to Trivia, her eyes glinting as she watched the scene before them. "Stay here in this broken realm. Urge Gaia to leave you. Then, you will be free for the taking. Defenseless. Powerless. No one will save you."

Panic pulsed in Trivia's chest. "*No. Pandora, don't—*"

"I told you what would happen if you disobeyed me," Pandora hissed. "This is *your* doing."

"No!" Trivia shouted. She tried to picture her construct again, but Sol spoke, his voice drawing her back in.

"I know you have other daughters who need you." Sol's voice was gentle. "You can go to them. I will remain here. It would be better if someone looked after the realm."

Gaia's lips thinned, but her gaze was hesitant. She was considering his suggestion for her to leave.

Don't do it, Mother, Trivia pleaded, begging the goddess to hear her. *Please don't leave him. Without your earth magic, he can't fight off Pandora. Please!*

"Very well," Gaia said at last. "I will travel through the portal. But if you sense the darkness from her box coming for you, you *must* leave. Trivia wouldn't want you to get yourself killed because of her. You must live, otherwise her sacrifice will have been for nothing."

Sol's nostrils flared, and his eyes sparked with rage. But Trivia knew him well enough to sense the despair etched into his expression. He was in pain.

She had caused that pain.

"Sol," Trivia whispered, desperate for him to hear her. But she was only a spectator in this vision. She wasn't really here at all.

No matter how much she yearned to be.

"Ah, you miss him, don't you?" Pandora's tone was mocking. "Let's reach out to him, shall we?"

She flexed her finger, and tendrils of shadow crept along the ground toward Sol's foot.

"Don't!" Trivia shrieked, grabbing Pandora's wrist.

But the goddess only smirked as the shadows receded. "I'm not stupid enough to snatch him right in front of Gaia. But... how about just a taste?" With her other hand, she curled two fingers inward. The shadows reached for Sol, brushing the back of his calf.

Sol stiffened, then glanced behind him. But Pandora's shadows had vanished. Sol's brow furrowed, and he frowned slightly before facing Gaia again.

Do something, Trivia ordered herself. *Do not let this happen!*

But gods above, it was so damn hard to pull herself away from Sol. She could watch him for hours, drinking in his form, his eyes, his voice... She missed everything about him.

Focus! she screamed at herself. *You are stronger than this. You can overcome this.*

Trivia pictured her construct again. The gleaming waves. The white sand. The blazing sun.

The vision of her beach appeared, drowning out Sol and Gaia. But the image flickered, then vanished.

Trivia's construct wasn't strong enough.

She let out a stifled shriek of rage and frustration, while Pandora merely laughed.

"Don't you wish you were as strong as me, child?" Pandora teased. "I'll admit, I did think you would last longer than this."

Trivia's hands curled into fists as she watched Gaia stride toward the portal. *No, no, no...*

How could Trivia overcome this if Pandora's magic was so much more powerful?

With a gasp, she suddenly recalled what Midas had told her: *Your personas may have split when her box absorbed you. But your souls are still connected. I can sense the tether between you two.*

Did that mean that Trivia had access to *Pandora's* magic, too? If Trivia could reach the arsenal of power flooding from the goddess, she could use it against her.

Trivia took a deep breath and closed her eyes again. Instead of picturing her own construct, Trivia summoned Pandora's. The veranda appeared, the white curtains drifting in the wind, the turquoise waters rippling beneath the sun.

Then, just as Midas had coached her, Trivia projected the vision forward. She focused on her pain, her anguish, her longing for Sol. She channeled those torturous thoughts she often shied away from. Her instinct was to cringe, to hide, to bury herself from the emotions that were so potent and so cutting. But she didn't. She pulled on them, drawing them to the surface.

Pandora appeared on the veranda beside her, her eyes wide with alarm. "What are you doing?"

Trivia didn't answer. She kept digging, summoning more grief, more misery, more heartache. Her chest twisted, and she hunched over from the force of the emotions barreling through her. Gods, it was so much. She couldn't breathe...

Beside her, Pandora groaned in pain, clearly weighed down by the same thing.

Their souls *were* connected. Trivia's pain was Pandora's pain.

"Bitch," Pandora seethed. "You can't win this. I am… stronger."

Trivia gasped for breath, her lungs struggling to draw in enough air. But a bolt of satisfaction flashed through her. She *could* win.

But she would have to give up everything. There would be no escaping this.

If their souls were still connected, then the only way for Pandora to truly die… was for Trivia to die, too.

Gaia can bring me back, Trivia thought, clinging to that hope. *I know she can.*

But a small fear crept into her mind. What if Gaia didn't *know?* What if Trivia died, but her mother never found out? If she didn't realize Trivia needed to be brought back, then Gaia would do nothing.

Besides, Gaia mentioned there were certain *conditions.* And Trivia would bet she didn't meet those conditions. She was not selfless like Mona and Prue. She did not deserve a second chance.

That's all right, she thought, feeling a modicum of peace as she accepted her fate. *If it brings down this wretched goddess and the darkness of her box, then I will do it.*

So, Trivia kept pushing. She tugged on those memories, the sights and sounds she missed so much. Sol's laughter. His moans of pleasure. His barbed insults.

She conjured more, digging into the far recesses of her mind. The affectionate look in Gaia's eyes. Prue's smile. The way Mona had forgiven her, standing by her side no matter the horrid things she'd done.

"Gods, stop it, *stop it!*" Pandora screamed.

Trivia fell to her knees. Hot liquid dripped down her face, and she realized her nose was bleeding. But she pushed on. She would not stop.

She would give it all up.

"If you don't stop," Pandora rasped, "then he dies."

Trivia blinked, her vision blurry, as she raised her head. Pandora was on her knees, too, but Midas lay next to her. Pandora's hand was wrapped around his throat.

Trivia went perfectly still. "You don't... have the strength... to kill him," she gasped.

"Are you willing to bet his life on that?" Pandora's face was pale, but her arms did not shake like Trivia's did. A small smile lit the goddess's face.

Trivia swallowed hard, her body spasming from the intensity of her emotions. "He's dead anyway," she said. "Once you die... so does everything... in the box."

Pandora's smile widened, and she shook her head. "You're wrong. Midas is an exception. He has power. Wards. Enough to protect himself when the box shatters."

Trivia blinked. She was lying. She had to be.

But... it made sense. If anyone could shield himself from the fallout of the box's destruction, it was Midas. He was certainly smart enough to figure out a way.

And he did have power. Trivia had seen it firsthand.

Trivia's arms shook, and she collapsed, face-first onto the ground. Her breathing was shallow and harsh. She wouldn't last much longer.

She couldn't do it. She couldn't save him.

"Such a shame," Pandora whispered. "He worked and

fought *so hard* to be free of his curse. I suppose he'll never know what an uncursed life is like."

A choked gurgling sound made Trivia lift her head, staring in horror as Pandora began to choke Midas. His face turned red. Then blue.

Trivia didn't think. A sudden burst of strength coursed through her. With a roar of anger, she lunged for Pandora. They collided. Pandora's grip loosened on Midas's throat. Trivia rolled, taking the goddess with her. Her fingernails clawed at Pandora's face. Pandora's fist connected with Trivia's jaw.

But Trivia had something more powerful. She had her magic. And she had Pandora's, too.

With one last push, Trivia managed to shove Pandora into the concrete floor of the veranda, her hands pressing into her face. Pandora struggled fruitlessly, arms waving, hands scrambling.

Trivia called on her pain, projecting it onto Pandora until the goddess went limp.

Then, she summoned her earth magic.

The concrete floor cracked. Vines snaked forward, wrapping around Pandora's wrists like chains.

Pandora screamed. "No! Stop it. *No!*"

Trivia tasted blood in her mouth. Her ears were also bleeding. Her heart seized in her chest, squeezing and squeezing. She felt faint. Darkness crept into her vision.

She was dying.

But she didn't care. The goddess would die with her.

With one last shout, Trivia gave up everything, shoving

her power into Pandora. She held the goddess still, ensuring she felt the full force of the blow.

An earth-shattering blast shook the walls. The construct vanished. The ground rumbled. Power exploded around them, ricocheting and bouncing as the darkness trapped inside the box swarmed. It was as if the magic had a soul, a mind... and it knew the end was coming.

Screams echoed in Trivia's ears, mingling with her own. A funnel cloud of magic appeared, barreling toward her. The storm raged. The wind whipped at her.

But Trivia only smiled, because she had won.

She poured every ounce of her strength into the destruction of Pandora and her darkness. Drip by drip, the essence of her soul—of Pandora's soul—vanished.

The darkness let out a shrill, broken cry. The funnel cloud faded. The wind died.

And as the last dregs of life bled out from her, Trivia slumped over, finally giving in.

She had won.

It was over.

She gave herself up to the darkness.

SHELTER
CYRUS

Lagos had managed to sniff out the Titans' magic after they had traveled in the direction the fire witches had indicated. From there, it had taken Cyrus several tries to manage a faint wisp of his power to crack open a tear through the Titans' wards. He was so used to explosive bursts of power that it took more finesse to hone his magic into a singular, precise strike.

Evander and Lagos had had to coach him through the process of projecting bolts of lightning into the sky. Neither of them were experts on the matter, and it had taken the better part of an hour for Cyrus to conjure lightning in the sky without looking at his target.

It was paramount that the Titans be unable to see him. If they discovered his location, they could destroy him on the spot.

But he needed to distract them from one side, while

Evander took the other, flying in the air to avoid the Titans' strikes.

When Cyrus revealed himself, he had faced Oceanus. He had demanded to speak face-to-face with Hyperion and Atlas. His goal was to gather as many Titans as he could. If they were negotiating with *him*, they wouldn't be focused on Prue and Mona.

The moment he'd seen his wife's face half covered in blood, a riot of emotions overcame him. Rage at the sight of the wounds that marred her perfect body. Pure, overwhelming relief that she was alive. That she was only steps away from him...

And then—Lagos.

Cyrus still couldn't believe it. He'd watched Atlas twist Lagos's neck. And in that moment, he had known it was too late. Prue was screaming, reaching for her friend, but if they returned for him, the Titans would capture them all.

Cyrus had to close the tear in the wards. They couldn't retrieve Lagos's body.

They could not revive him.

Prue continued to sob and scream until her body was overcome with tremors. Cyrus held her tightly, swallowing down his own grief and despair. He hadn't realized how close a friend Lagos had become until the demon had died.

Now, Cyrus's insides twisted and his chest cracked in two.

His friend was gone. His strong, courageous friend was *gone.*

Eventually, Prue lost consciousness, but Cyrus refused to set her down. He marched alongside Evander and Mona, trudging through the sandy desert as they made their way back toward the fire witch coven. His steps were slow and clumsy, especially with Prue's weight in his arms.

Even when Evander offered to carry her—even when his arms and legs screamed in protest—Cyrus pressed forward.

The pain distracted him from his devastation.

And a heavy part of him felt he deserved it. He deserved far worse. Lagos had been there to help *him*. It had been *Cyrus's* plan.

Cyrus had been the one to close the tear. To abandon Lagos to his fate.

It was his fault. The burden of that loss would rest on his shoulders for the rest of eternity.

Cyrus would never be able to escape it.

Mona and Evander remained silent during their journey. Tears streamed down Mona's face, and Evander's mouth was set in a grim line, his hand clutched tightly in hers. Cyrus wondered if his brother was thinking of Lagos, or the bargain he now had to fulfill with the Wild Spirits.

When Cyrus's face and lips were caked with sand, and his legs throbbed so painfully he thought they might snap in two, he finally recognized the entrance to the fire witch coven. Wind whipped around them, flinging sand particles into their eyes. Evander descended first, climbing between rocks until he found the hidden cavern underneath. With a hand on his arm, Mona guided Cyrus down, ensuring he didn't fall while carrying Prue.

As soon as they entered the cave, darkness and cool air greeted them, a blessed respite from the heat and sand of the desert. The fire witches surrounded them, peppering them with questions. Thankfully, Mona answered most of them. Cyrus could only stand there, holding Prue, his body numb and unresponsive. Now that he'd made it here, he wasn't sure what to do with himself. He didn't want to think about the next step.

The Titans were still out there. Two had perished from the attack, but that still left three—Atlas, Oceanus, and Prometheus. They were few in number, but they were still powerful. Dangerous. Hell-bent on exacting revenge on Cyrus for tricking them.

There was nothing more deadly than a vengeful Titan.

"Cyrus!" shouted a voice.

Cyrus blinked, realizing Farah stood in front of him and had likely said his name several times. He blinked slowly at her. "What?"

Farah gestured to Prue, still lying limply in his arms. "Would you like our healer to tend to her?"

Cyrus's gut response was *no*. He didn't want to part from Prue. He wanted to keep holding her, touching her, proving to himself that she was real and she was alive.

But her body was covered in blood. He had no idea how much of it was hers. Her eyes were sunken and her skin pale. She had clearly been through an ordeal.

Reluctantly, Cyrus nodded, the motion stiff. Farah sent for the coven healer, and Cyrus insisted on remaining by Prue's side the entire time. The healer used poultices and elixirs, murmured incantations, and spread a balm along Prue's split lip and the jagged gash on the side of her head. Only when the healer had cleaned away the blood did Cyrus realized what had happened.

Prue's ear had been sliced off.

White-hot fury raged through him. He wanted to ram his fist into the wall. He wanted to flip over the table and smash the bottles on the shelves.

He wanted to gut those Titans one at a time, making them suffer for what they had done to Prue.

When the healer was finished with Prue—who still hadn't woken—she asked to inspect Cyrus for injuries. He waved her away. Oceanus had managed to strike him in the abdomen, but the blow had only grazed him. The trek through the desert had exacerbated the wound, but it was the least of his concerns.

"Mona," Cyrus said, gesturing to the earth goddess who was speaking in hushed tones with Farah. Evander lingered nearby, and Cyrus wondered if he felt the same desperate need to be alongside the one he loved, just to ensure she wouldn't disappear. "Please see to Mona's injuries."

The healer nodded and shuffled away, leaving Cyrus to sit on the bench next to Prue's prostrate form. He looked at her, then gently tucked a few loose curls behind her ear.

Her only remaining ear.

Hot tears stung Cyrus's eyes, and he quickly blinked them away. Gods, this was his fault. *His damn fault.* The Titans had taken Prue because of *him.* It had all been about negotiating with *him.*

If Prue wasn't his wife, this never would have happened. She never would have been caught up in this war.

She would have been *safe.*

"Gods, Prue," Cyrus said thickly, running his thumb

down her jaw. "You would have been better off if you had just stayed on that island."

Prue did not respond. Her chest barely moved with her shallow breaths. Cyrus kept checking often to ensure her pulse was steady. He was so terrified she would simply wither away in her sleep.

At some point, he leaned his head against the rocky wall and fell asleep. When a hand came down on his shoulder, he jerked awake with a sharp gasp.

Farah raised her palms and backed up a step, her eyes full of concern. "I have spoken with Mona. She relayed the events of your battle to me. I am so sorry for your loss."

Cyrus could only nod. His throat was so tight he couldn't speak.

"The Titans will seek retribution," Farah said grimly. "I doubt they have enough power to travel to a different realm. We must expect their retaliation here in the Realm of Gaia."

Cyrus nodded again. He had considered this. As much as he yearned to bring Prue back to the Underworld, he could not leave the fire witches and all the mortals here to the whims of the Titans. Whatever they had planned could not be good.

"If you'll allow me to leave Prue with you, I can find my own way to the village for shelter," Cyrus said in a hollow voice. "I will not impose."

Farah's lips thinned. She sighed, then crossed her arms. "You and your wife may stay with us."

Cyrus looked up at her in surprise. "But my magic—"

"You managed to rescue two fellow witches from the

clutches of the Titans. I think it's safe to say you can be trusted amongst my sisters."

A sour taste filled his mouth. He couldn't be trusted at all. His choices and consequences brought nothing but tragedy. Lagos was dead because of him. And Farah thought she could *trust* him?

It was absurd.

But Cyrus would not argue. If it allowed him to remain with Prue, he would let Farah believe this lie.

"Your brother has insisted he must return," Farah continued.

Cyrus followed her gaze. Evander stood on the opposite end of the cavern, his hand casually resting on the small of Mona's back while they conversed with two other witches.

"Yes, I'm sure he did," Cyrus said in a low voice. Evander had debts to pay. Had he already told Mona?

"In exchange for providing you shelter, we only request one thing," Farah said, her voice solemn. "We ask that when the Gorgon sisters return, you confer with them about the Titans."

Cyrus met her gaze. "I vow to do everything in my power to eliminate them from the realms. It's my fault they are here, and I will not rest until I fix the mess I've made."

Farah's eyes shone with something akin to respect. A small smile quirked her lips. "You are certainly not like what I imagined, death god."

Cyrus frowned. "What did you imagine?"

"Someone arrogant, believing himself to be all-powerful and untouchable. Someone who answers to no one but himself."

Cyrus snorted. "Yes, that's still me."

Farah chuckled. "Perhaps so." She waved a hand to a curly-haired witch standing behind Cyrus. "Wren will show you to the more secluded caves we use for sleeping. You and your wife are welcome to stay there."

"Thank you, Farah." Cyrus poured as much respect and earnestness into his voice as he could muster. Words could not convey how grateful he was to these witches for providing hospitality and refuge. Were it not for their elixirs, Cyrus wasn't sure if they would have made it out alive.

He cringed inwardly as he realized not all of them *had* made it out alive.

Gods, he still couldn't fully grasp that Lagos was gone.

The curly-haired witch stepped forward, her gold eyes shrewd as she surveyed Cyrus. He assumed this was Wren. "You're quite different from Rom." Her voice was blunt, and Cyrus imagined she spoke her opinion often and unapologetically.

He quirked an eyebrow at her. "Yes, well, Romanos has more experience in the mortal realm than I do."

Wren pointed to Prue. "Do you need help carrying her?"

"No." The word was clipped. Cyrus rose, then reached for Prue. The moment his fingers wrapped around her wrist, she gasped, her eyes flying open.

Cyrus's heart leapt into his throat, his pulse racing. He knelt to the floor and crouched beside her, clutching her hand in his. Had he imagined it? Or had she truly awoken?

She gasped, the sound loud and rattling. Her eyelids fluttered, and a flush rose up her cheeks. She wet her lips, then looked around, her eyes dazed. "I—Cyrus?"

"Yes, I'm here, love," Cyrus whispered, pressing her hand to his lips. Gods, he was so damn relieved she was awake. His eyes burned with tears for the second time, and he didn't bother stifling them.

Prue tried sitting up, then winced. "*Shit.*" Slowly, she raised a hand to the jagged scar where her ear had been. "That—" Her mouth fell open, and her face paled. "Oh, Goddess." Her hand started shaking as she slowly turned to look at Cyrus. "It wasn't a dream, was it? That... that was all *real?*"

Cyrus sucked in a breath. Her fingers felt cold in his grasp. Gods, was he going to lose her again? Would the shock of it all pull her under once more?

Instead of replying, Cyrus drew closer, pulling her to his chest and holding her. His hands traced circles along her back as she shuddered against him.

"It's all right," he whispered. "It's going to be all right."

"Please," Prue breathed. "*Please* tell me it's not true. Please tell me he isn't gone."

Cyrus squeezed her tightly, pouring as much affection and comfort as he could in the embrace. He needed her to feel his warmth, his strength. He needed her to know she wasn't alone.

Prue's fingernails bit into Cyrus's arm. "Cyrus, answer me."

With a sigh, he withdrew and cupped her face in his hands. "Look at me, Prue."

Her lavender eyes met his, and there was more strength and clarity in her gaze than he had expected.

His wife was strong. She would weather this like she had every storm of her life.

"It's real," Cyrus said softly. "It's all real. And Lagos... Lagos is dead."

It was the first time he'd uttered the words aloud, and now he hated himself for it. Now it was *real.* There was no taking it back. There was no reversing the situation.

Lagos was truly dead.

Prue's face crumpled, and tears streamed down her face. She shook her head, her lower lip wobbling. "No. *No.*"

"I—I'm so sorry, Prue." Cyrus's voice cracked, just like his heart. Seeing his wife like this was breaking something inside him. Something he worried could never be repaired again.

He wanted to hold her again. But the guilt, the gnawing pit in his stomach, made him realize he was the last person who should be comforting her right now.

Because all of this was his fault.

A hard lump formed in his throat, making it difficult to swallow. "Should I get Mona?"

Prue blinked rapidly. "Mona's here? Is she all right?" She gazed around the cavern, hope brightening her eyes.

Cyrus stood. "I'll fetch her."

Prue snatched his hand, her grip firm. "Cyrus, don't go."

He stared at their entwined hands, unable to look her in the eye.

"Cyrus," she said again, her voice gentle. "Stay with me. Please."

He nodded tersely. "If that's what you want."

Prue's brows drew together, and he knew she could tell something was off. But the last thing he wanted to do was lay out *his* burdens for her to bear. She had enough to deal with.

"Should I show you the privacy caves now, or wait?" Wren asked awkwardly.

Cyrus had completely forgotten the witch was there. He ran his thumb along the inside of Prue's wrist and looked at his wife expectantly. "What do you need right now, Prue? Do you want to stay here with Mona, or go rest in the caves?"

Prue stared at him, a dozen emotions warring in her gaze. He tried to look as reassuring as possible, to let her know it was all right if she would prefer to be with Mona right now.

Prue opened her mouth, then hesitated.

"You are welcome to return to the communal space at any time," Wren offered. "I just need to show you the route to take so you don't get lost in the tunnels."

Prue glanced at Wren, then back at Cyrus. "Let's go to the privacy caves," she said at last. "I—I should probably rest."

Cyrus's eyebrows lifted in surprise. But when she gave him a meaningful look, he realized what she meant.

We need to talk, her eyes said.

Anxiety wriggled in his stomach, but he shoved it away. This conversation needed to happen.

Prue needed to know the part he had played in Lagos's death.

"All right." Cyrus helped Prue to her feet. She teetered slightly, but once she found her balance, she took a few solid steps.

Wren turned and led them toward the cave on the left

side of the rock wall. With his arm laced through Prue's, Cyrus followed, dreading the upcoming conversation—and the looming possibility of losing his wife's trust forever.

DEBTS
EVANDER

Evander refused to leave Mona's side, even for a moment. He had thought that rescuing her from the Titans would fill him with relief, that this unsettling *wrongness* inside him would be cured... but it wasn't.

His chest still roiled with uncertainty. His stomach still knotted with unease.

Nothing was right. Not even with the woman he loved at his side.

He could tell Mona sensed his discomfort, judging by the frequent concerned looks she shot his way as they mingled among the fire witches. Mona had lots of questions, particularly about the handy elixir they had used when infiltrating the Titans' hideout. Not to mention Mona was clearly fond of many of the witches here from her last visit. She greeted them as if they were her own sisters.

Seeing her eyes light up, her face brightening with a

genuine smile, was almost enough to unravel the tension and turmoil coursing through Evander.

Almost.

He needed to tell her. He needed her to know the bargain he had struck with the Wild Spirits.

But there wasn't a moment to tell her. There were so many witches around them, and he needed a private moment to speak with her.

It wasn't the right time. It would have to wait.

His body was restless, itching to move, to run, to *fly*. But he could do nothing but stand by Mona, his hand on her back.

After another witch Mona had been speaking with walked away, Mona turned to look at him, her eyes narrowing with suspicion. "What's wrong with you, Evander? Tell me."

Evander closed his eyes. His head throbbed, and his blood hummed with a low pulse that seemed to chant a reminder to return to the Undead Wilds.

Go back. Go back. You must go back.

"I... I have not been myself as of late," he said softly. This was technically not a lie.

Mona's expression softened. "Because of Typhon?"

Evander flinched. Gods, Mona knew him too well.

She drew closer and placed her hand on his cheek. Her skin was warm and smooth, and he leaned into her touch, his eyes closing. Her scent of parchment and saltwater filled his nose, and he sighed with contentment.

In this moment, they were simply Mona and Evander. Nothing more, nothing less. He could pretend that all was well. He could pretend that they were just two souls who had fallen in love by the river in the Underworld.

A knot formed in Evander's throat as the pleasant vision shattered. Because he *had* to tell her. She would never forgive him if he didn't.

She might not forgive him anyway. But he had to risk it. She deserved nothing less than the truth.

He opened his eyes and found hers filled with worry and despair. He wasn't sure what she was thinking, but her expression was so utterly devastated that he knew she was afraid for him. She was likely envisioning all manner of horrifying scenarios.

He took a deep breath, his gaze dropping so he wouldn't have to look at her when he spoke. "I must leave for the Underworld."

Mona was silent for a moment. "Right now? But... the witches need our help. The Titans are still out there."

Evander withdrew from her, and she dropped her hand. His cheek instantly cooled, and he yearned for her touch once more. He shook his head. "I cannot stay here. I have... debts to pay."

Her brows knitted together. "What does that mean?"

"There was a price required in order for us to find where the Titans were hiding. Now, I have to go and fulfill what is owed."

Mona drew closer to him, then gripped his hands in hers. "Evander, speak plainly. Just *tell* me what it is. I can handle it."

"I offered my immortality," Evander said, his voice barely above a whisper. "I made a bargain with the spirits of the

Undead Wilds. In exchange for their help, I promised to give them my immortality. And now I must go back and fulfill my end of the deal."

Mona's face paled, and her head reared back. Her mouth fell open as she stared at him. "Evander, you *didn't*..."

He tightened his hold on her wrists and looked at her with a fierce expression. "There is *nothing* I would not do for you, Mona. Surely you understand that."

Her eyes filled with tears. "But you have so much more than just *me*, Evander. So much more of your life to live. You have a brother. A home. A duty to your kingdom and your people."

Evander scoffed. "They mean nothing to me." He said the words without thinking.

Mona took a step back, her eyes wide. "You don't mean that."

"*You* are all I need." He wanted to reach for her, but that *wrongness* in his chest tightened, making it difficult to breathe. He rubbed his forehead. "Please try to understand, Mona. I couldn't just let you die. *You* gave up your life to save your village. And then you jumped into a deadly whirlpool to save Prue. How is this any different?"

She tilted her head at him, those otherworldly emerald eyes seeming to see straight through him. "But *why* did you do it, Evander?"

"To save you!" How could she not see it? How could she not see that he would give up *everything* for her? Did she not understand the depth of his love for her? "Mona, I love you. I need you. We should be together."

Mona's eyes moistened, and she took a shuddering

breath. "I love you, too. But... I fear you only saved me so you could save yourself."

It felt like she had struck him. His chest seemed to split open from her words, and he stared at her in horror. "How can you say that?"

"You don't know who you are, Evander." The sorrow in her voice pierced straight through his heart, making him feel emotions he didn't want to face. "And you need *me* in order to feel like yourself again."

His nostrils flared, and he shook his head. "So, this is the thanks I get for my sacrifice? You lecture me on my motivations? Should I have left you to die by the hands of the Titans, then? Is that what you would have preferred?"

"Of course not!" she cried. "But Evander, you are lost! And clinging to me is not going to help you. Taking needless risks is not going to give you the answers you seek."

Then what is? he wanted to ask. There were only two things that had ever made him feel alive: Typhon and Mona.

Now, he was on the brink of losing both.

He was on the brink of losing *himself.*

Gods, he couldn't bear it. His soul was ripping in two. His inner turmoil was slowly tearing himself apart. He wouldn't be able to bear this much longer. Heat burned behind his eyes, and he blinked rapidly before he started to weep.

He straightened, projecting a confidence he did not feel. In a strained voice, he said, "So, will you come with me, or not?"

Are you with me, or not?

Am I going to lose you, or not?

Is this the end... or not?

A million questions raced through his thoughts, circling faster and faster, making him feel nauseous and desperate, panicked and afraid.

A tear raced down Mona's cheek. She closed the distance between them and placed her hand on his cheek. His own tear met her fingertip, and she caught it before brushing it away. He couldn't stop the moisture from pooling and coursing down his face, much like his very soul was plummeting. Down, down, down, so far into the abyss that he could no longer reach it.

"Pay your debts, Evander," Mona whispered. "Find yourself. Find a purpose that gives you life. Something that takes your breath away. Something that isn't *me*. When you've found it, I'll be waiting for you."

Evander closed his eyes as the pain cut through him anew, digging deeper into his chest. He was being carved open, sliced in two with merciless brutality.

Mona was slowly destroying him, one word at a time.

He would never recover from this.

"Mona," he rasped, unable to speak without leaking more tears. "What if I never find it?"

She lifted her arms, wrapping them around him and bringing his body against hers. He leaned his head on her shoulder, weeping freely. She clung to him, gripping him tightly as her own frame shook with sobs.

"I will *always* be there for you, Evander. Always. From here to eternity, my soul will always find yours."

His heart seized from those words. He had uttered them to her in the Underworld after they had made love. She had saved his life then. Gods, it felt like eons ago.

How Evander wished to go back to that moment, when he knew exactly what he wanted and what his life should be like.

"If you leave me and are unable to find yourself, to find anything else worth living for, I will remain by your side," Mona said. "No matter how broken you might feel or how lost you are, I will be with you. But... please try. Will you try?"

She pulled back to look into his eyes, her hands still cupping his face as if he were something precious. As if he were worth anything at all. "Please try, my darling. For me. I —I cannot lose you. *Please.*" She sniffed, her face streaming with tears.

His throat was so tight with emotion that he couldn't breathe. He couldn't speak. He leaned his forehead against hers and just *felt* her. Held her. Touched her.

Mona was right. He was clinging to her because she was all he had left. His river was gone. His realm was broken. And now, his immortality would soon be lost, leaving him with nothing but a fragile mortal existence.

He would be frail and breakable after this. He wouldn't be able to take any more risks.

One misstep, and he could die. The terror on Mona's face told him she was thinking this, too.

He was out of second chances. This was it. And she was right—if he couldn't find himself or find something else worth living for, he would waste away. He would throw himself off a cliff just to *feel* something, and then his life would be over.

Their love—their story—would be over.

"You know I would give anything, right?" Evander whispered. "I would give *anything* to feel whole again. To live a life with you, content and unbothered."

Perhaps such a fantasy didn't exist. Perhaps he would spend the rest of his life yearning for something that could never be.

What kind of life would that give Mona?

She offered him a watery smile. "Yes, I know. I know you didn't choose this. And I know it's not your fault or your doing. Sometimes our souls long for something we cannot recognize until we find it. And Goddess, I hope you find it, Evander. I hope you find it soon."

She stood on her tiptoes and kissed him. Her lips were salty with her tears, but Evander captured her mouth fully as if he had never tasted anything more delicious in all his life. His fingers tightened along her waist, drawing her closer. She angled her head, her tongue sweeping over his mouth and parting his lips. His hands pressed into her back. One hand inched upward, his fingers threading through her long black hair.

Gods, she tasted divine. She tasted like *home.*

A hollow ache built in his chest, an echo of the beast who had once lived inside him. The creature who loved Mona just as he did.

He and Typhon had been one, both drawn to Mona, soothed by her presence. Now, a part of him had died.

He would be seeking for that other half of himself forever. Seeking, seeking, seeking... but never finding.

When they finally broke apart, gasping for breath, Evander murmured against her lips, "Live your life, Mona.

Don't wait for me. If I'm able, I'll find you again. But if I don't..." He trailed off, unable to utter the words.

If he didn't find her again, it either meant he had fully lost himself... or he had died.

Mona blinked rapidly, her eyes glistening. "Evander—"

"If our roles were reversed, what would you have me do?"

Her mouth clamped shut at that, and he knew the answer. Hell, she had given herself up to the darkest magic so that Prue could live her life and be happy.

She would do it all over again. For him, for Prue, for anyone she loved. He knew that much.

"*Live*, Mona," he urged her. "And I will try to do the same. I swear it."

Evander pressed one last kiss to her lips, this one much more tender. Her lips were soft and smooth, and he wanted to taste them one last time.

Then he released her and stepped away. If he continued to touch her, to hold her, he knew he would never let her go. His eyes lifted, glancing behind her to see the entire cavern of witches watching them, unabashed.

Evander's eyebrows drew together. He knew he should feel embarrassed that so many people had witnessed his fight with Mona. But he couldn't bring himself to care—not when this might be the last time he ever saw her.

He looked at her then, drinking her in fully. Everything from her long and disheveled hair, her dirty and blood-stained tunic and trousers, and her tear-stained cheeks. He wanted to memorize every feature, every blemish and mark on her body.

He nodded at her, trying to convey everything he felt in that singular look.

Then, he turned and left, striding down the tunnel toward the portal that would take him to his future.

Or his doom.

PUNISHMENT
PRUE

THE PRIVACY CAVES CONSISTED OF ONE LONG TUNNEL that resembled a hallway, with several rows of small, closet-sized caves on each side. Piles of pillows and blankets took up the floor space in each hollow, providing a soft cushion for sleeping. Snores echoed throughout the tunnel, indicating other witches were taking advantage of the makeshift sleeping quarters. There were no doors, but it was far better than trying to sleep on the rocky ground in the main cavern, surrounded by other people.

Prue and Cyrus followed Wren down to the very end of the tunnel. The last niche was farther from the others, allowing at least a modicum of privacy. Prue was certain if she shouted or screamed, the others in the tunnel would hear. But no one would overhear a conversation in hushed tones.

Cyrus was rigid beside her, unease rippling off his body in waves. It put her on edge to see him like this. He was haunted. Tormented. She could see it in the darkness of his eyes, the set of his jaw, the downturn of his lips.

He was not himself.

But then again... she wasn't, either. The moment Lagos's neck snapped kept replaying in her mind, over and over.

Crack.

The twist of Atlas's hands.

The way Lagos's body crumpled.

The feral grin on the Titan's face, as if he *knew* how much Lagos's death would break her.

He hadn't done it in self-defense. He had done it to wound her.

"Supper will be served in an hour," Wren said, jerking Prue from her anguished thoughts. "Just shout if you get lost. Someone will find you." She offered a wry smile, then turned and walked back up the tunnel, leaving Prue and Cyrus to stand awkwardly in their privacy cave.

Prue stared at the pale blue comforter and cream-colored pillows that lined the floor. She should feel exhausted—her body still ached from her injuries, and a dull throb pulsed through her skull. Her head felt foggy as she adjusted to the sounds around her being much duller, since she only had one ear now.

But her mind was racing, her thoughts frantic and unhinged. She would certainly not be resting.

Cyrus inhaled deeply and turned to face her, his expression guarded. "What do you need? What can I do for you?"

Prue looked at him, but he wouldn't meet her gaze. He stared at her chin, that same hollow look on his face.

"Cyrus," she whispered, drawing closer to him.

He took a step back. "Stop."

She froze. "Stop what?"

"Whatever *this* is..." He gestured between them vaguely. "Stop it. I don't deserve it."

Prue frowned. "You don't even know what I was going to say."

"You were going to ask me what's wrong. Or you were going to comfort me. But neither is appropriate right now. So please just stop."

Her brows drew together. "What the hell are you talking about? We just went through a terrible ordeal. Of course they would be appropriate right now."

Cyrus shook his head, then took her hands in his. His fingers were cold and trembling. "Just... just tell me what *I* can do for *you*. Please. Let me be useful. Somehow."

"You can be useful by being my husband and answering my damn questions. *Talk* to me, Cyrus. Is it Lagos?"

He flinched, indicating she'd hit her mark. Goddess, she hadn't realized how fond he'd become of the demon. They must have truly connected in her absence.

The thought drove a dagger straight through her heart. She would have loved to see their friendship grow, just as hers had from the beginning. Lagos had been her first ally, her first true friend in the Underworld. And it both warmed and shattered her heart to know that Cyrus had experienced the same camaraderie with him.

"I'm grieving, too," Prue said in a soft voice. "Lagos was—"

Cyrus suddenly pulled away from her, running a hand through his hair. "It's not just *grief*, Prue. It's—It's... guilt, shame, *horror.* I don't deserve to feel anything or to be comforted because it's *my fault.* Lagos's death is on my hands, and you should utterly despise me for it."

She sucked in a gasp at the harshness of his words. "Cyrus, that's not true!"

"Yes, it is! *I* brought him there. *I* came up with the plan. *I* assigned him to track you down while I distracted the Titans. Lagos was following *my* orders. All of this rests on me, Prue. So please spare me your pitying glances and your false sense of concern. It is wasted on someone like me."

Frustration rose up inside her. Goddess above, she didn't have the patience for Cyrus's assumptions and orders right now. "Is that what you want?" she snapped. "You want me to hate you? To shout at you? To *blame* you?"

"Yes!" he shouted.

Prue's head reared back as she stared at Cyrus. Was he serious?

Somewhere down the tunnel, someone hollered at them to be quiet, but they ignored the outburst. Cyrus stared at Prue, his eyes blazing with fire. He closed the distance between them, his expression full of rage. "Hate me. Strike me. Punish me. Do it all, Prue. I want your hatred and your fury. Take it out on me until I am on my knees begging you for mercy."

She shook her head as something boiled within her. Everything inside her was so intense and volatile that she couldn't hold it back much longer. "You don't get to tell me what to do, Cyrus. I'm not your subject. I'm not a puppet to be controlled. And I will not simply shout at you because it's what your masochistic mind craves. Go punish yourself. Leave me out of it."

She turned away from him. A snarl ripped from his throat, and he grabbed her wrist, jerking her back toward him.

Without thinking, Prue slapped him hard across the face. The sound echoed in the cavern, and his head swiveled from the force of it.

Prue gasped and staggered backward. Shit. She hadn't meant to do that.

Cyrus slowly turned to stare at her, his eyes wide and his cheek red from where she struck him. His mouth fell open.

"I—I'm sorry," she said at once. "I didn't—"

"Do it again."

She stiffened. "What?"

"Hit me again."

"Cyrus—"

"Dammit, *hit me,* Prue!"

She made a frustrated sound and whacked him on the other cheek, just to shut him up. This time, he deserved it. She was sick of him telling her what to do.

He stumbled back, shaking his head violently. Now both his cheeks were red, and his eyes were wide and wild. "Gods, I needed that."

"You're insane, Cyrus."

"I'm *poisonous,*" he said. "Can't you see that? Everything I touch dies. No matter how hard I try to be good, everything crumbles around me. The moment I fell in love with you, Vasileios stabbed you. Then, when I got you back, Kronos took over my body. You gave up your godsdamn life to save me from Tartarus caving in. And then the Titans abducted you and *cut off your ear.* My most loyal subject died on my watch. I—I can't do this anymore, Prue. It's nothing but pain and more pain, and the guilt and exhaustion from bearing these burdens is *too much* for me."

Prue took in his words, her heart racing and her chest cinching. The despair pouring from his lips, the tortured agony etched into his face, was too much for her. Goddess, she wished she could take it all away for him.

But it weighed on *her,* too. He was not alone in this. How could she make him see that?

He needed something to jar him from this before he spiraled. He was too consumed by the raw and festering emotions, and she needed to wake him up somehow.

The slap had seemed to do the trick.

Maybe he needed more.

Before she could reconsider, Prue shoved him hard.

Cyrus stumbled again, nearly falling to the floor. When he righted himself, she dug the heels of her hands into his chest, pushing him until he fell against the cavern wall. With a grunt, he stared at her in bewilderment. "Prue—"

"You want pain?" she asked, prowling toward him. "You want punishment? Fine. I'll give it to you." She slapped him again.

He groaned, a protest rising from his lips. She struck his other side before he could speak.

"You're right, Cyrus." She kicked him in the shin, and his knees buckled. "How dare you? How dare you give up everything for the woman you love? How dare you win your people's loyalty by earning the crown and sparing them from a rule of tyranny at Apollo's hand? You could have marched an army of demons to the Titans' hideout, risking lives, commanding them to do your bidding. But you didn't. I'm willing to bet my life that Lagos *volunteered* to come with you. Because I know him. He wouldn't have let you go without him. His death is not on you."

She pushed him into the wall, pinning him there with her hands, then drew her face close to his. "How dare you be the king your people need? How dare you be a loving husband who seeks only to serve his wife? And above all, *how dare* you be a king who *feels* things? Who endures the emotions and the guilt that comes with having a conscience?"

His nostrils flared, and he was gasping for breath. His face was red, and a thin line of blood trickled from his nose.

"Do you feel something yet?" Prue whispered. "Have I punished you enough?"

Cyrus grabbed her shoulders, and his mouth crashed into hers. Adrenaline still coursed through her body, and she shoved hard against him, pinning him to the wall with her body. Her hips rolled, and he groaned against her lips. His tongue ravaged her, gliding along her mouth. She bit down on his lower lip, and he let out a low growl.

In a swift movement, he spun her around, pressing her back into the wall, caging her with his arms. "You'll be my ruin," he murmured before his mouth claimed hers. "My destruction." Another fierce kiss. "My undoing." His mouth moved to her throat, where he sucked and nipped. Prue leaned her head back against the rocky wall, her eyes closing as pleasure rocketed through her.

Fabric ripped as Cyrus tore open her tunic, baring her breasts to him. She let out a hoarse cry as his hand cupped her breast. His other hand clamped over her mouth, cutting her off.

"Shh," he hissed in her ear. "You don't want the witches to yell at us again, do you?"

She made a noise somewhere between a laugh and a scoff. "I can't promise to be quiet about this, Cyrus."

He smirked. "Perhaps not. But we can certainly try." His hands grabbed her ass, and he hitched her upward. She wrapped her legs around his middle, feeling his hardness rubbing between her legs. Goddess, the friction of him against her core was enough to undo her completely.

Holding her against him, Cyrus turned, then carefully lay her against the blankets on the floor. More fabric ripped, and a cool breeze nipped at her bare thighs as Cyrus tugged open her trousers. "Let me worship you, my queen."

His fingers danced along her inner thigh, and she bit down on her lip to keep from moaning. With his other hand, Cyrus ran his thumb down her cheek, then tugged at her bottom lip, prying her mouth open. "Bite me if you need to," he said, his voice low and sultry. "Bite as hard as you need."

Fire coursed through her veins at the seductive heat in his words. Obediently, she caught his thumb in her mouth, letting her tongue circle his fingertip.

A grumbling noise of satisfaction poured from his mouth. "Gods, that tongue of yours..."

She captured his thumb between her teeth, then dragged them up and down.

He hissed out a sharp breath, his eyes darkening with

lust. "If that's how you want to play…" He inserted a finger between her legs.

Her hips bucked, and she uttered a strangled sound. He pressed his thumb deeper into her mouth.

Another finger curled inside her. She ground against him, demanding more. Those two fingers pumped in and out, the motion slow and torturous. Her blood boiled, the tension coiling tightly inside her. So much pain and anguish roiled and churned, fit to burst. *Goddess* did she want to release it all. To unleash everything.

Cyrus's fingers pushed deeper. Moisture pooled within her, the heat almost unbearable. His thumb pressed against her tongue, and she bit down again to keep from shouting his name.

"That's it," he murmured. "Take as much of me as you need, Prue."

I need all of you, she wanted to say. *Give me all of you.* But she was too overcome with the violent sensations firing through her. His fingers moved faster, the rhythm pounding through her with relentless force. Her hips rolled as she rode his fingers, driving him deeper, harder, further. Her thoughts spiraled, her mind emptying of everything except one singular thought: *more.*

Cyrus seemed to read her mind. His fingers curled, brushing against her inner walls, and she almost went mad with need. She moaned against his thumb, her teeth digging into his flesh. But he didn't seem to notice. He was panting and grunting as if it were his cock inside her and not just his fingers. Sweat trickled down her brow, pooling along her throat. Cyrus leaned over and licked her neck, lapping up those beads of sweat as it if were the nectar of the gods.

"Give in to me, Prue," he rasped. His tongue glided down her collarbone until he reached her breasts. He took her nipple between his lips and sucked hard.

She cried out, barely containing her scream. When he clamped his teeth around her nipple, she unraveled completely. Release barreled through her. An explosion of pleasure washed over her, dousing her in fire until the flames consumed her entirely.

"Cyrus—*Cyrus*—" Her voice was strangled and muffled by his fingers. She tasted his blood on her tongue and knew she'd bitten too hard. But Goddess, the fire still rolled over her, unending and eternal. She kept riding his hand, and he plunged his fingers even deeper as she continued to drown in that wave of pleasure. It crashed over her, dragging her under, and she gladly let it. She wanted to be fully engulfed in this feeling, in the way his touch set her aflame. All the tension and emotions that had wound up inside her burst free in a violent explosion. Cyrus coaxed it out of her, drawing every drop of rage and regret, sorrow and grief... He pulled it from her, letting it seep out of her.

Gradually, she relaxed, her body limp against the blanket. She wasn't entirely sure they'd managed to be quiet enough, but thankfully, the other witches in the tunnel either didn't notice or didn't care enough to complain.

To be honest, Prue didn't care either way. In that heated moment, she would have screamed until her throat was raw, not caring who heard.

When Cyrus withdrew both hands, he collapsed next to

her, panting almost as hard as she was. She offered an exhausted laugh.

"Did my pleasure weaken you, my king?" she teased.

He rolled on his side, his eyes sleepy but full of pride. "'Tis hard work, worshipping my queen."

She propped her head up on her elbow. "And what about you? Surely you are in need of service as well." She reached for his trousers, which strained from the hardness of his cock. Oh yes, he was certainly ready.

But he caught her wrist and shook his head. "No. Not—Not right now, Prue. Just let me serve you. For now, it's only you."

She raised her eyebrows. "Do you need me to punish you some more?"

He snorted. "As arousing as that was, I think I'm all right." When she opened her mouth to protest, he repeated, "For now."

She sobered and nodded, understanding his state of mind a bit better now. He needed a purpose. He needed to serve her without getting anything in return. Her punishment had been therapeutic for him, as had his ministrations of her body.

If he could give her what she needed, she could do the same.

"Do you want to be alone?" she asked.

He shook his head, drawing one arm around her and pulling her into his chest. "No. I just need to enjoy the warmth of my wife lying next to me while I rest. That's all."

She closed her eyes, burying her face in his chest and inhaling his delicious scent. "I can do that."

PURPOSE
TRIVIA

"YOU CAN BRING HER BACK, CAN'T YOU?"

"I—I don't know."

"Why not? Dammit, *do something!*"

The voices floated around her, distant and hazy. Trivia was certain she was dead. She waited for her soul to cross over, for clarity to brighten in her mind. What awaited her on the other side?

Tartarus, no doubt. But... Tartarus had been destroyed. So, what else was there? A numbing void, like within Pandora's box?

Oh, gods—Pandora! Where was she? Had she been defeated?

Had Midas died? Or had Trivia managed to stop the goddess from killing him?

Gods, her head hurt... Why was she in so much pain, if she was already dead? Something wasn't right.

"There *has* to be a way," said one of the voices. This one was deep and vaguely familiar. A man. "I don't care what you have to do, just do it!"

"Ordering me about is not helping," snapped the second voice. This one was a woman. "Her blood is different. This isn't just another mortal or another goddess. There are certain conditions to bringing back a vessel like hers."

"What the hell are you talking about? There isn't time for this!"

"She is a child of Janus!" shouted the woman. "She holds the magic of the Triple Goddess within her! Only when the three sisters are reborn can their powers be unlocked. But their death must be an act of selflessness. A sacrifice. It's the only way."

Silence followed her words. Then, the first voice said, "How can we tell? We don't know what happened to her."

"I know." A third voice joined the conversation, this one more grim than the other two.

Trivia's concentration ebbed, and the voices faded. Ah, at last she was moving on. Surely the pain would subside now.

But no, it only intensified, drilling into her skull with brutal intensity. She wanted to swat at the pain, to bat it away like a pesky insect. *Leave me alone!* she wanted to scream. *I'm finished. I've paid my dues. Let me rest now.*

But the pain only seemed to laugh at her, burrowing deeper. Yes, it was certainly like an insect, digging into her flesh, so far in that she could no longer pluck it out. It would fester inside her for an eternity.

"Trivia, please," whispered the first voice.

Something within her stirred at the sound of that voice—the sound of her name.

I love you, Trivia. The echo of that voice resonated inside her, awakening her soul. Gods, she wanted to drown in that voice. The way it aroused her and soothed her. The way it made her bones tremble and her blood sing.

It *called* to her. And amidst the pain and darkness and confusion, she emerged, following the sound.

"Gods above," he murmured. "*Look.*"

The woman gasped. "Yes. Yes, my darling, come back to us." A warm hand pressed into her chest, and power seeped into her. The pain ebbed, leaving a comforting heat in its place. It spread through her, coursing through her veins and filling her with life. Sounds became clearer—she could make out the distinct sound of rushing waters and the smell of saltwater. A breeze tickled her skin. She tried to move, but she still couldn't reach those parts of her body.

But she could *feel* now.

She was alive.

"Trivia, I need you to live. I need you to breathe."

Sol, she thought. It was Sol calling to her. She would follow the sound of that voice anywhere in all the realms.

Even the jaws of death could not stop her from coming to him.

Her eyes flickered open, her lids crusty and heavy. She yearned to close them once more, but the tether connecting her to Sol was far stronger.

I have to go to him, she thought. *I have to see his face. To touch his skin.*

Her lips were cracked and dry, but she managed to

wheeze out his name. "Sol." Her voice sounded like sandpaper.

"By the gods." Sol let out a laugh of disbelief. Hands pressed into her shoulders, her cheeks, sending more warmth through her body. Slowly, inch by inch, she was awakening. A faint throbbing still echoed in her skull, but it was diminished compared to the anguish of before. More power flooded her, filling her with energy and strength. It felt so... *foreign.* It was earth magic, but different from her own. More pure. More vibrant. It called to memories buried deep. Memories she didn't even know she had.

"Sol," she said again, her voice clearer now. But her throat was so dry, her tongue sticky. She smacked her lips, and something cool and wet touched her mouth.

"Drink," Sol urged, and Trivia obeyed as he carefully poured water into her mouth. Her vision was so hazy. Even with her eyes open, she could only make out vague shapes around her. Two figures stood above her, and she knew one of them was Sol. Judging by the sound of the waters around her, she was either by a river or the ocean.

Could she be in Elysium? Was she on the very beach she had envisioned while in Pandora's box?

It seemed like a dream. Too good to be true. A fantasy that could never be. Something she did not deserve.

"Is she alive?" This third voice was almost unfamiliar. It tugged at something within Trivia's mind.

When recognition finally dawned, something jolted within her. "*Midas?*" she asked in bewilderment.

Her vision sharpened suddenly, the shift so intense that it sent another spiral of pain through her head. Something soft tickled her ears and cheeks. She was lying in the grass with a canopy of trees hanging over her. Sol knelt by her side, his face pale and his midnight blue eyes filled with worry. On his left was Gaia, her eyes closed and her brows drawn together in concentration. One of her hands was pressed to Trivia's chest. Then Trivia realized Gaia was using her magic to give her strength.

Her mother had brought her back to life.

Behind Gaia and Sol stood Midas. He hovered a safe distance away, as if he was afraid to get too close. He wrung his hands together, his mouth twisted in unease.

Trivia's gaze snagged on his hands. They were gloveless.

Her head lifted, but Sol gently eased her back down. "Careful. Let Gaia finish."

Trivia shook her head. "I—I don't understand. What happened? Why is Midas here? His gloves—Pandora—The box—"

Sol pressed a finger to her lips, silencing her. "It's all right, love. We'll explain everything. Just let your mother finish."

Mother. Gods above, Trivia still couldn't believe it.

Gaia had brought her back. Gaia had saved her.

Her mother had saved her.

Tears stung her eyes. The concept was unfathomable, the idea that someone loved her enough to bring her back. But here were Sol and Gaia, so desperate to keep her alive, desperate to save her...

Yes, this certainly had to be a dream, for she did not deserve this at all. Not one bit.

"Can you talk to me while she works?" Trivia begged. "Please, I have to know. Is Pandora still alive?"

"No," said Midas. "She's dead. Her box was destroyed."

"Impossible," Trivia said at once. "She was too powerful. The darkness was too strong."

"You were stronger." There was pride in Midas's voice.

She closed her eyes. No, he didn't understand. Surely he was mistaken. "I don't—I can't—I'm not strong enough to defeat her! There's no way."

"Midas told us you gave it all up," Sol said, brushing the loose hair away from her face.

Midas nodded in agreement. "Trivia, you used up so much power that you killed yourself. Pandora was not willing to do the same. In the end, your strength outmatched hers because you gave *everything*. Something she never had the courage to do."

Trivia blinked rapidly, trying to keep the tears from spilling over as she stared at Midas. But she failed. The moisture tracked down her cheeks. "She was going to kill you. I—I—"

Gaia let out a long, slow breath, then opened her icy blue eyes to gaze at Trivia. "You gave up your life for him, didn't you?" Slowly, she turned to shoot an accusing stare at Midas.

He raised his palms. "I didn't know she was going to do that. I—I had no idea." He took a slow breath. "Gods, Trivia, I—Why? Why would you do that for *me*, of all people?"

Trivia swallowed hard, the memories from before sliding into place. Her fight with Pandora. The darkness creeping closer to Sol. Pandora threatening Midas's life.

"I don't know," Trivia admitted. "I didn't think, I just acted. You had endured so much. I figured if I couldn't live an uncursed life, then I wanted you to do it in my place. You and I are the same, Midas. Both cursed. Both willing to betray everyone we love to be free. I wanted to believe in second chances, and if that meant you lived and I didn't, then so be it."

Midas's lips parted, his face slack with shock.

To Trivia's surprise, Sol barked out a laugh, then turned to glance at Midas. "She's got bigger balls than you do, uncle."

Gaia snorted, then covered her mouth. Her expression cleared, but her lips twitched, betraying her amusement.

Trivia wanted to laugh, but her chest felt too tight, as if she couldn't get enough air. Her body was... *off*. Like another person's organs were inside her. Like her skin wasn't the right size for her skeleton.

"How do you know Pandora's box was destroyed?" she asked. "How do you know the darkness didn't just flee somewhere else?"

Midas drew closer and withdrew a small object from his pocket. Trivia felt the blood drain from her face as she recognized the small black box. Unease and dread filled her.

"Oh my gods," she breathed. She wanted to wriggle away from the cursed thing before it consumed them all.

But she felt no power emanating from it. It was... just an ordinary box now.

Still, she stared at it, waiting for something to happen. Waiting for the darkness and destruction to burst from it.

Nothing happened.

"I—I can't believe it," she whispered. "She's really gone?"

"See for yourself," Gaia said, gesturing to Trivia's chest. "Can you sense her?"

Trivia swallowed hard. She hadn't dared to try and reach the goddess that had inhabited her body for so long. She was too afraid of what she would find.

But she could avoid it no longer. With a deep breath, she closed her eyes and searched within herself. She prodded that deep part of her soul where the goddess had once resided.

There was no answer.

She tried summoning her rage that often fueled Pandora's fire.

Still no response.

Trivia's eyes flew open. "She's not there." Her gaze flicked from Gaia to Sol and then to Midas as she searched for confirmation.

Neither of them looked at her with fear or pity or sorrow. There was nothing but relief and pride.

Pandora was gone.

This time, Trivia *did* laugh. It burst from her, and once it started, she couldn't stop it. The chuckles cascaded from her, building and building until her eyes were streaming, her stomach contracting with such deep laughter that her shoulders shook and her abdomen ached. Sol laughed with her, and Gaia grinned widely. Even Midas managed a small smile.

Trivia couldn't stop herself. She reached up and tugged on Sol's collar, dragging him on top of her and kissing him fully on the mouth. He let out a small yelp, his arms flying out to catch himself before he crushed her.

But she didn't care if he collided with her. She didn't care if he knocked the breath out of her and smashed her to pieces.

She was alive.

Pandora was dead.

The box was empty.

And for the first time in her entire existence, Trivia felt whole.

She kissed Sol, clinging to him, relishing the feel of his skin against hers. Gods, she had yearned for this. She had truly believed she would never experience it again.

For several moments, they held each other, making up for lost time.

Trivia could have continued forever, memorizing his lips, tasting him again and again... but before long, Gaia cleared her throat.

"I'm grateful to you, daughter," she said quietly as Sol and Trivia broke apart. "Thank you for your sacrifice, and for showing me what true selflessness is like."

Trivia shifted in the grass, uncomfortable from her words. "I'm not selfless. I never have been."

Gaia smiled. "We can all change. And it's clear to me that you have. No one is perfect, of course, but you are becoming someone new. Someone admirable. And I'm so proud of you."

Trivia's face flushed, and she glanced down, unsure of how to respond to such praise. She didn't feel worthy of it, but to contradict the kind words felt rude.

Gaia stood, smoothing her hands on her skirts. "What you do next is up to you. But you should know, the

Titans have invaded my realm. And I can ignore it no longer."

Trivia's heart lurched, and she jumped to her feet. Dizziness rushed over her, and she teetered. Sol was in front of her in an instant, his hands on her shoulders to keep her steady.

"What?" she asked. "How? When?"

"I don't know the particular details," Gaia admitted. "All I know is that while you and I were trying to rebuild Elysium, Apollo was in the Underworld raising the Titans."

At the sound of her wretched father's name, Trivia's blood boiled, and her hands curled into fists. "*Apollo,*" she seethed. "I want to choke the life from that bastard and watch the light leave his eyes."

"Don't we all," Midas said darkly.

"But we can't," Gaia said solemnly. "Apollo is dead."

"What?" Midas and Trivia said together.

"How do you know?" Sol asked.

"When your soul is as tethered to someone as mine was to his, you can sense these things," Gaia said, her tone filled with part sorrow, part disgust. "If I had to wager a guess, I would say one of the Titans he summoned killed him. Apollo was always one who preferred giving orders rather than following them, and I'll bet the Titans didn't like that." She gave a cruel smile. "He got what was coming to him."

"No, he didn't," Midas snarled. "Apollo deserved a slow and vicious death."

"Perhaps you're right," Gaia said. "But he's gone, and that's all that matters to me. My daughters are safe from his wrath for good." Her eyes softened as she looked at Trivia.

A lump formed in Trivia's throat, but she nodded. Once,

her heart thirsted for revenge, and nothing was more important than making Apollo suffer.

But now, with Sol's hands on her shoulders and her mother standing before her, she realized there *were* more important things than revenge. And they were right here in front of her.

Except... there were a few things missing.

"Prue and Mona," Trivia said urgently. "Where are they?"

"The mortal realm," Gaia said. "I need to go to them and do what I can to stop the Titans."

Trivia exchanged a glance with Sol, and he nodded. "We'll come with you," Trivia said. "Just tell us how we can help."

Gaia's lips lifted with pride. "I figured you would want to, but I thought it best to give you a choice. Something you have not had much of in your life."

Trivia's heart constricted so much it was almost painful. Gods, it felt so unexpected, to be loved like this. She still felt undeserving—and perhaps that feeling would never leave— but it also filled her with a sense of purpose, a sense of fulfillment.

She wanted this feeling to last forever.

Trivia took Sol's hand and laced her fingers in his. She looked at Midas, who was staring at his hands.

"Is it gone?" she asked him. "Your curse?"

"Yes." He kept his gaze fixed on his fingers as he wiggled them. "I've touched all manner of things. Not a glimmer of gold." He looked up at her, his eyes full of joy and wonder. "It's... truly gone."

"What will you do now?" she asked. "Will you fight with us? Or will you go on to live a free life?"

Midas's face fell, his expression suddenly somber. His eyes turned distant as he considered her words.

She expected him to say farewell. He had sacrificed so much for freedom. It was what she would have done, once upon a time. Before Sol, before Pandora's box... she would have taken that freedom in a heartbeat because she had fought so hard for it. If she didn't take advantage of it, then everything she had sacrificed would have been for nothing.

But things were different now. She found something else to fight for. Something more important.

She just wasn't sure if Midas felt the same way.

"I—I don't know," Midas admitted. "I'm a mortal now. I could die before I've even lived."

Trivia nodded. She understood that fear, too.

How often had she longed for a second chance she did not deserve? And now that she had it, she was willing to risk it all for those she loved.

"Well, then we wish you well," Trivia said.

Sol stepped forward and extended his hand to Midas. Something within Trivia's chest lurched at the sight. She wanted to scream, to jerk Sol away from Midas.

But when the king gripped Sol's hand, nothing happened. They shook hands and exchanged smiles. Midas clapped Sol's shoulder, then patted his cheek.

Gaia only glanced at Midas, her expression unreadable. She inclined her head but said nothing before turning away. Trivia could tell the earth goddess was not too fond of Midas, and she couldn't blame her. Midas had betrayed everyone. In fact, Trivia had every right to hate him, too.

But she couldn't. Were it not for him, she never would have accessed her true powers and defeated Pandora. In her eyes, Midas was forgiven.

They were even.

With one last smile at Midas, Trivia followed after Gaia and made her way toward the portal with Sol at her side.

Her story was not over yet. She had a battle to face.

And she was not afraid.

ATTACK

MONA

HER HEART WAS BREAKING, BUT MONA CONTINUED TO work. Ignoring the shattered remains of her soul, she busied herself by making preparations with the fire witches. They had hoped to wait for the Gorgon sisters to return before tracking down the Titans, but there had been no word from them. Farah hadn't admitted her concerns, but it was clear in the tight draw of her eyebrows and the dip of her frown as she worked.

She was worried.

Mona didn't know the Gorgon sisters as well as Farah did, but she was worried, too. Together, their powers were supposed to be unparalleled. Unmatched. Unrivaled. Mona had heard the tale of how the Gorgons had defeated Neptune, one of the strongest deities of all.

If something had happened to the Gorgons, then Mona feared the realm had no chance at all.

Her fingers trembled as she tied off poultices and

prepared vials of elixir. She filled canteens and wrapped bedrolls for the journey.

But in her mind, all she saw was Evander's broken expression when she told him she would not be coming with him.

Mona paused before corking another vial, her fingers shaking so violently that she couldn't continue. Her chest shuddered with a rattling breath, and her eyes burned hot.

What if I've made a terrible mistake? she wondered.

What if Evander died... because she hadn't been there to help him?

She shook her head roughly and took a slow, steadying breath. She had made the right decision. If she had gone with him, she would have been fretting over Prue and Cyrus and the battle with the Titans. She would have worried over the fate of the fire witches.

If she had returned to the Underworld, she would have been abandoning her fellow witches. And she never would have been able to live with herself.

"Where do you suppose they are?" a voice asked.

Mona looked up to find Wren sitting a few paces away, grinding willow leaves for a healing elixir.

"Who?" Mona asked, distracted. She had to set the cork down to wipe the sweat from her palms before trying again.

"The Titans. Where do you think they are hiding?"

Mona considered this. When she wasn't thinking of Evander, her mind was whirring with possibilities. Where *would* the remaining Titans go? From what she had read, they were exceptionally powerful—even more powerful than Apollo and the kings who had come before him.

Hiding didn't seem like something they would do.

"I think they are planning something," Mona said softly. "Something big. And if we don't find them soon, they will strike us with a blow powerful enough to destroy everything we've ever known."

Wren was silent for a moment. Then, she chuckled. "Wow. You're so good at keeping my spirits up, Mona."

Mona sighed. "I'm sorry. My mind is scrambled right now."

Wren nodded sympathetically. "Evander will be all right. He's endured far worse."

"I know," Mona said, although she wasn't reassured. She caught Wren glancing toward the entrance tunnel, her eyes full of worry.

Mona wanted to say something to comfort her, but the words were lost to her. How could Mona offer hope when it seemed there was none?

Wren suddenly uttered a sharp gasp and jumped to her feet. Her hand pressed to her chest, her eyes wide as she murmured, "By the Goddess!"

Several other witches were on their feet as well. Mona followed suit, frowning as she glanced around the cavern. "What's going on?"

Without responding, Wren took off toward the entrance tunnel.

That was when Mona sensed it. A swell of heat coiled around her, tickling her skin and awakening her magic. She drew in a breath, inhaling the familiar scent of ashes and woodsmoke.

Only once had she smelled this before: in the Voiceless Jungle when she had met the Gorgon sisters.

Relief spread through her, warming her body and numbing the pain of Evander's departure. The Gorgons were here. This was exactly the joyous news she needed right now.

A scream pierced the air, echoing in the cavern and bouncing off the walls. Mona froze at that sound, her blood chilling. A crowd of witches stood by the entrance tunnel. One of them was on her knees, sobbing.

Mona's heart dropped to her stomach.

Hurried footsteps sounded behind her. Mona turned to find Prue gasping for breath as she made her way toward the crowd, her tunic rumpled and her hair disheveled. "What's happened? I sensed something powerful nearby. Is everyone okay?"

Mona's mouth was so dry she couldn't respond. Her eyes were pinned to the commotion at the entrance. She couldn't bring herself to move closer to see what had happened.

She dreaded what she would find.

"Mona?" Prue asked, her voice tinged with worry. She grasped Mona's wrist.

A tense moment passed. Mona's eyes were glued to the witches, who were murmuring to one another in hushed voices. Several of them were weeping openly.

Prue laced her fingers through Mona's. "Come on." She tugged on Mona's arm, drawing her forward. Mona's feet shuffled of their own accord, bringing some awareness into her cold body.

A rush of appreciation filled her as Prue guided her forward. Mona wasn't sure what she would do without her sister. Prue seemed to sense Mona was in no state to make decisions or give explanations. She needed action to snap her out of her haze.

Prue always knew exactly what she needed.

As they approached the crowd, Mona made out words that made her shiver.

Killed.

Dead.

Slaughtered.

"This means war," whispered a witch.

"What can we do?" said another. "She is dead. The Gorgons cannot help us now."

Slowly, Prue and Mona weaved through the crowd, making their way to the mouth of the cave. There sat four figures, bruised and blood-stained. Mona immediately recognized them: the three Gorgon sisters and Romanos, Evander's brother.

Except... something was wrong. One of the sisters—Lilith, if Mona could recall correctly—was lying on Marina's lap, her eyes closed. Her chest wasn't moving, and her face was deathly pale.

Oh no, Mona thought, feeling sick with dread. *No, no, no.*

Marina was sobbing, hunched over as she smoothed Lilith's hair away from her face. On one side was Romanos, his arm around Marina and his head on her shoulder. He was bleeding from a deep gash above his eyebrow.

On Marina's other side was the third sister, Vivian. She was staring with wide eyes at the ground, unseeing and unresponsive. Wren moved toward her and sank to her knees. Without a word, the two women embraced one another.

Wren's arms wrapped around her, holding her close. She stroked her hair, whispering, "I've got you, my darling. I've got you." Vivian's shoulders shook as she, too, began to sob.

That's who Wren was so worried about, Mona realized, her chest aching at the sight of the two witches.

Prue's fingers tightened around Mona's as she, too, took in the scene before them. Neither of them said a word. The air was potent with grief and despair.

Nothing could be said. Because it was clear that Lilith, a Gorgon sister, someone who was meant to be powerful and unstoppable, was dead.

Romanos's eyes fixed on Mona, and he straightened. "Mona," he said.

She went to his side, taking Prue with her. Together, they crouched next to him, and Mona took his free hand in hers and squeezed it. "What happened?" she asked gently. Marina and Vivian were too consumed with grief to speak, but perhaps Romanos could explain.

The death god's silver-streaked hair was matted with blood and dirt. His eyes were bloodshot and red-rimmed as if he, too, had been crying. He blinked several times before he spoke.

"We were meeting with the Thanassian delegation," he said quietly. "Things were going well. We were set to return the following day. But... there was a massive earthquake. The ground split in two. And from below emerged this... horrible creature." He inhaled a shuddering breath, his expression so haunted that it stirred something in Mona's soul.

This was a god who had worked in Tartarus for eons. He had witnessed the vilest of souls and the darkest of prisons.

If something had spooked him, Mona knew it had to have been something utterly horrifying.

"It was a Cyclops," Marina said suddenly. Tears still streamed down her face, but her eyebrows were lowered, and the set of her jaw betrayed her fury. "But it was something *else*. It was coated in death magic that we could not penetrate. It was *massive*." She shook her head slowly. "In all my years, I have never seen anything like it. It was wholly unnatural."

Unnatural. That could only mean one thing...

"The Titans," Mona whispered. "They must have created it."

Romanos nodded grimly. "It destroyed the Thanassian castle and the entire delegation. We held it off as long as we could to get the people out of the city. But... it was too big. Too powerful." He closed his eyes, his face turning ashen. "Never before have I encountered magic like that in this realm. Cyclopes are creatures of death magic. Creatures of *Tartarus*. They shouldn't even be allowed here."

"No, they shouldn't," said another voice.

Mona looked up to find Cyrus standing behind Prue, his arms crossed and his face full of fury. "The Titans drew from a power that was not theirs to take." His gaze shifted to Prue, and sorrow filled his blue eyes. "It was Lagos."

Prue stiffened beside Mona. "What are you talking about?" Her voice shook.

"Besides my brothers and me, Lagos was the only other one here who held the keys to Tartarus. Unless the Titans returned to the Underworld themselves, that's the only explanation for how they accessed such magic and created these beings."

"But... Lagos died," Mona whispered. Prue was trembling so violently that Mona wrapped her arms around her, trying to keep her calm.

"His soul hadn't passed on yet," Cyrus said. "Magic is tethered to the soul, and the Titans are powerful enough to pull on that essence before it reaches the Underworld."

Mona's chest felt hollow. Goddess above, he was right. She of all people knew how sacred the bond between a soul and a person's magic was. She felt sick at the thought of the Titans using Lagos's fallen body like that.

Prue groaned, her body caving inward as her eyes closed. Her brows pulled together, and her mouth twisted in a horrified grimace. "Goddess, this can't be true. How can they—I can't—"

Mona tightened her embrace, clutching her sister to her chest. Cyrus's face crumpled, and he looked as if he yearned to carry Prue away from here. Mona nodded at him, indicating she understood.

Both of them would do anything to shield Prue from this.

But there was no hiding from this. Not anymore.

The Titans had made their move. This was a declaration of war.

LIVE

EVANDER

As Evander crossed through the portal to the Underworld, Mona's words echoed in his mind: *Sometimes our souls long for something we cannot recognize until we find it. And Goddess, I hope you find it, Evander. I hope you find it soon.*

Gods, he was so lost.

The air shimmered, and power cascaded over his body. In an instant, he had been transported from the desert cavern to the foggy expanse of the Underworld. It took a moment for his eyes to adjust, but once they did, he froze.

A crowd of demons stood in front of the portal, with Theo and Maleck in the front. Their eyes were anxious, their faces taut with apprehension.

Oh, shit.

They were waiting for their king and queen to return. For their beloved Lagos.

They were waiting for good news. Because gods knew they needed some.

"My lord," Theo said breathlessly, wringing his hands together. He peered around Evander as if expecting more figures to follow after. When he realized it was only Evander, his face paled and his eyes went wide.

"All is well!" Evander said quickly, raising his hands. "Prue and Mona have been rescued. They dwell with the fire witches in anticipation of the Titans' retaliation. They would have come here, but they feared drawing the Titans' wrath to this realm. For now, it looks like the battle will occur in the Realm of Gaia."

Whispers and gasps rippled over the crowd.

Maleck drew closer, his brows knitting together in concern. "And what of Lagos? Is he with them as well?"

Evander faltered. Oh, gods. *He* was the one who had to tell them. He couldn't possibly... This was *Cyrus's* responsibility.

He swallowed hard, suddenly feeling ill.

"My lord?" Maleck asked hesitantly.

Evander's throat was so dry he couldn't speak. He had spent eons shepherding the souls of the river Cocytus, explaining to them that they were dead and had moved on to the next plane of existence. He was accustomed to delivering bad news. Some souls had wailed and shrieked like banshees. Others had merely wept quietly. Some had been in utter denial and yelled in his face about how wrong he was. A few had even laughed, assuming it was a joke or a dream.

So why did this feel so different, to deliver such news to the demons? Was it because they were alive, of flesh and blood, standing before him? Or was it because he actually knew them, and had known Lagos, too?

He drew in a breath and envisioned himself standing on the bank of Cocytus. In his mind, a soul had just arrived.

He immediately pictured Mona, but then shoved the thought away. Instead he pictured the soul he had encountered before her, an older man with wispy white hair.

"I am sorry," Evander said gently. "But... Lagos was killed defending your queen. He knew the sacrifice he was making, and he made it bravely."

More gasps filled the air, this time more hushed and full of horror. A few demons covered their mouths. Others' eyes were full of tears.

"No," Maleck whispered, pressing a hand to his chest. "No, it cannot be!"

"I—I am so terribly sorry," Evander said, and he needed these demons to understand how much he meant it. He had not known Lagos as well as Prue and Cyrus had, but he still felt that death acutely. It was a loss that could have been prevented. Perhaps if he had wielded his magic differently or conserved the ghost of Typhon, he could have been there in time to save Lagos.

Perhaps if he had managed to fell more Titans, like Atlas, then Lagos would not have died.

But what then? What if a Titan had gotten hold of Mona or Prue or Cyrus? The sisters were goddesses, but they were not invincible. Even a goddess could be killed.

And Cyrus... he was mortal now, as far as they knew. All Atlas would have had to do was twist his neck, just like he'd done to Lagos, and the King of the Underworld would be dead.

Something stirred in Evander's chest at the thought, slithering and writhing and coiling like a serpent.

He didn't like this feeling one bit, so he buried it deep before it consumed him.

Theo approached, tears streaming down his face. He took Evander's hands in both of his and bowed deeply. "Thank you, my lord, for bringing us this news. I know it must have been difficult for you."

That *thing* twisted in Evander's chest again, cutting off his breath and rendering him incapable of speech.

Theo was *thanking* him for announcing his dear friend had died? This was so unexpected. Even in his years overseeing Cocytus, a soul had never *thanked* him for delivering the news of their death.

It was not glad tidings to be shared with others.

Evander finally found his breath, but it was shaky and uncontrollable. In a strained voice, he repeated, "I am... sorry." He needed Theo to understand that Evander was *not* someone to be thanking right now. He was someone to yell and shout at. Someone to take out their frustrations and grief on.

But the demons did no such thing. Some embraced one another, sobbing. Others stood there, unmoving as they stared in the distance and processed the news. Maleck drew closer to Theo and wrapped his arm around him. All the while, Theo continued to hold Evander's hands... as if he were comforting him.

In a flash, Evander yanked his hands free from Theo's

grasp. No. This wasn't right. Evander did not deserve comfort or compassion. He was not worthy of any of this.

"I'm terribly sorry," Evander said again. It seemed it was the only thing he knew how to say. "I... I must leave you now."

His throat closed, cutting off any words. Even if he *could* speak, he wouldn't know what to say.

All he knew was he had to leave this area immediately before the sight of these demons completely destroyed him.

As Evander approached the Undead Wilds, that feeling of eerie emptiness surrounded him. And, strangely, he felt more at ease. More at home.

How odd that this haunted place would feel like a comfort to him.

Something is very wrong with me, he thought.

Whispers and murmurs floated around him like a hissing breeze. A chill raced down his spine, and he suppressed a shudder.

"You have returned," breathed a voice.

Evander froze, his feet coming to a halt on the ground. Leaves swirled in the air around him. He glanced around the trees, but no figures appeared.

Even so, they were there. He could sense them.

"Yes," Evander said. "I have."

A silvery form appeared before him—the same woman from before. Her long hair flowed down her back, the strands floating in the wind. "And were you successful?" she asked.

A lump formed in his throat as he thought of the demons' grief over losing their friend. He could hardly call it a *success* when Lagos had lost his life.

"The goddesses were rescued," Evander said. "Thank you for your help."

The woman smiled, but there was no warmth in it. "It was not given freely. You owe us payment, death god."

"I know. I am here to pay my debt. Just tell me what I must do."

The woman tilted her head at him, her gaze sweeping over him slowly. "I am afraid the process is... unpleasant." She didn't sound at all unhappy about this; if anything, she sounded *eager.*

Unease rippled over Evander, but he could hardly turn away. He had agreed to this. "I understand."

"Aren't you curious? Don't you want to know how painful it will be?" She seemed positively gleeful.

"It doesn't matter. Whether it's painful or not, it is inevitable. I cannot run from it."

The woman's eyes narrowed slightly. "Brave words, even for a death god. But they all try to run from it in the end."

Evander's brow furrowed. Who was she referring to?

Had other people made similar bargains with these souls?

Something tugged at Evander's wrist. He yelped, turning to find one of the souls tying a thin cord around his arm. Another soul appeared and did the same thing to his other wrist.

"I—What—" Evander's protests were cut off as the

female soul shoved his chest hard enough to knock him flat on his back. The air whooshed from him, and pain split through the back of his skull.

The restraints on his wrists tightened. More cords were tied on his ankles. He shifted, trying to move, but the tethers must have been anchored into the ground. He was stuck.

"I... I offer myself *willingly*," he insisted. "You don't have to tie me down!"

The woman hovered over him, her pearly form translucent enough to reveal the canopy of trees behind her. "There is great need for this, death god. For when we bleed every drop of that precious god blood from your body, you *will* fight. And we can't have that."

Evander's stomach hollowed. *Every drop of blood....*

Gods above, what had he gotten himself into?

"I don't understand," he whispered. "I thought—I thought you were just going to take my immortality."

The woman smiled widely. "And how do you think we do that? Your immortality lives in that silver blood of yours. Once every drop is gone, your immortality will belong to us. This is how it's done, death god. There is no other way."

Evander was gasping for breath now, the panic rising in his chest with such strength that he thought he might faint.

A silver blade gleamed in the woman's hand. It was slightly transparent, just like her body, but Evander had no doubt it could still cut his flesh. They had taken a drop of his blood before.

Now, they were going to take *all* of it.

The soul drew closer to him.

Gods no. Gods no.

From within him, a voice that had long since been silenced screamed out in rage and terror.

I want to live!

Over and over the voice shrieked, bellowing into the endless void, the chasm that had become his soul.

I want to live. I want to live. I want to live.

The words brought fire and life into his very being when there had been nothing but despair and emptiness.

He needed life. More than he needed Mona, more than he needed Typhon... *He needed to live.*

Evander roared with fury, thrashing against his restraints. The earth moved underneath him as his ghostly wings spread wide. Something snapped, and suddenly he could move his left wrist.

The woman gasped and drew back, her eyes wide and fixed on his wings.

With his free hand, Evander tugged at the cord on his other hand, fingers clawing.

Live, he ordered himself. *You must live, Evander.*

Shimmering forms swarmed around him as the other souls closed in, no doubt to stop him from escaping. He bared his teeth, fury and desperation fueling him. His heart raced and his blood thrummed. Never before had he felt so alive.

"Stop!" the woman screeched, raising her hand. Evander snarled at her, but then he realized... she wasn't speaking to him.

She was speaking to the souls.

At the sight of her raised fist, the other spirits froze,

creating a rippling crowd of silver in front of Evander, like an ethereal mist.

The woman was still staring at Evander's wings, her mouth open in horror and shock. "Where—Where did you get those?"

Evander only bared his teeth at her. He was not about to sit and answer questions when they were planning to bleed him. His other hand was free now, and he was frantically undoing the knots at his ankles. Soon he'd be free. Soon...

"Answer me!" the woman screamed. Her shrill voice pierced the air, ringing against Evander's ears. The note of terror in her voice was what made him freeze.

He slowly looked up at her, his teeth still bared and his body still rigid. "They once belonged to the demon inside me."

She uttered a hollow, trembling gasp. Evander stiffened, his eyes narrowing as he scrutinized the spirit. One hand was covering her mouth, and her shoulders were shaking.

"His name," she sobbed. "Tell me this demon's name. Please."

Unease spread through Evander's chest. The fire from before still raged, desperate for release. His blood thrummed with the need to destroy, to fight his way to survival. He couldn't convince his mind or his body that the threat was gone.

But... something was off. Something had happened, and his muddled mind was struggling to keep up.

"Typhon," he said at last. "The demon's name was Typhon."

The woman sank to her knees and released a keening

wail, like the mournful howl of a wolf. Behind her, the other spirits cried out, echoing the sound of her grief.

Evander tried to scramble backward, alarmed at this reaction, but his ankles were still tied down. He wrenched the cords free, his fingers shaking. When they were loose, he looked up and found the woman's tear-stained face mere inches from his.

With a yelp, he fell backward, shuffling away from her.

"Stay back," he warned, though what could he do against these spirits? They were already dead.

Then the woman's fingers met the talon of his left wing, and he went perfectly still. He could... *feel* her touch. It was as warm and solid as if she stood before him in the flesh.

His mouth fell open, his blood chilling as he stared at her, uncomprehending."What..." He couldn't even form the question. "I—I don't understand."

"Typhon was one of us," the woman whispered. "He was once a Wild Spirit. And he has been missing for a millennia."

TOGETHER
TRIVIA

THE MOMENT TRIVIA, SOL, AND GAIA STEPPED through the portal and entered the mortal realm, Gaia groaned and sank to one knee, pressing a hand to her heart.

It didn't take Trivia long to discover why. The very air reeked of death. The wind whispering against her skin smelled of ash and decay.

It smelled like Tartarus.

She glanced upward at the night sky, squinting against the breeze that burned her eyes. It took her a moment to orient herself, to figure out where exactly they were.

Sol recognized it at the same time. "By the gods," he whispered in horror.

Trivia's skin prickled, her heart racing as she took in her surroundings. Beneath the saturated layer of death magic, she could make out the faint hint of earth. This place had once been rich with Gaia's magic.

Now, it was nothing more than a tomb.

The three of them stood in the remains of Midas's mighty underground castle. The ceiling had caved in, exposing the midnight sky. Cracked roots and broken rocks surrounded them. Jagged holes lined the walls, broken through by roots and thorns.

And the air was deathly still. Not a sound stirred, aside from the hissing wind that tickled Trivia's skin.

When they'd last been here, the castle had been magnificent, and a thriving coven of earth witches had lived here. Trivia remembered traveling through the Voiceless Jungle and how silent but *alive* everything had felt. Saffron, the mysterious witch who resembled a shadowed silhouette, had led them to Midas. A hydra had attacked, but the earth witches had easily rebuilt the walls and ceiling, leaving it as impressive as before.

But Saffron and the witches were gone. So was the castle. So was the magic.

Gaia sucked in a sharp breath, grunting with effort. Her eyes closed, and her brows drew together, her face taut with tension. "May the Triple Goddess bring you peace," she whispered, pressing her fingers to her lips and then to the ground. "May your deaths be avenged tenfold."

A knot formed in Trivia's throat as she looked around once more. She hadn't wanted to believe it... but of course her mother could sense it.

The earth witches who had lived here were all dead.

"What could have done this?" Sol asked softly, brushing his fingers against a broken tree root. "This could not have been the work of Titans."

"It's not," Trivia said at once. "This is something... *else.*"

She thought of the hydra that had attacked this place. "Something dark was drawn here." She looked at her mother, waiting for some kind of explanation.

But Gaia shook her head, her frown deepening. "It's no magic I'm familiar with. It's something new, something tainted with Titan magic. Whatever it is, it was created by them."

Trivia's stomach hollowed at the thought of the Titans *creating* a new creature. A new monster.

"Is it still here?" Sol asked. He drew closer to Trivia, his arm sliding behind her as he looked around warily. She wasn't sure he realized he had moved. He must have done so on instinct. The thought sent her a modicum of comfort, but it was fleeting.

Gaia peered up toward the sky. After a moment, she said, "No. But I can tell which direction it's traveling. It's likely we'll encounter it on our journey."

"Where are we going?" Trivia asked. "Do you know where the Titans are?"

"No," Gaia admitted, lifting her skirts as she stepped over a smashed log. "But I know where my daughters are. We'll head in that direction."

Trivia exchanged a look with Sol. A muscle feathered in his jaw, but his eyes were soft as he gazed down at her. Wordlessly, he took her hand, his fingers lacing with hers. His warm palm strengthened her resolve.

She nodded at Gaia. "Lead the way, Mother."

With every step they took in the Voiceless Jungle, Trivia's heart weighed heavier and heavier. The stench of death only grew more potent, and the startling silence around her seemed to weep with grief. When she had first traveled through these woods, the lack of sound had seemed rooted in magic, as if the air were so potent with energy that nothing could penetrate it. Not the snapping of a twig or the chirping of a bird.

But this... this was so very different.

Now, the jungle was silent in acknowledgment of the lives lost. It was a silence of mourning. An aching song of lamentation and despair.

The very trees seemed to pulse with agony. They cried out in rage and sorrow against the crimes that had been committed here.

Tears spilled down Trivia's face, and she didn't bother to try to stifle them. The witches who had lived here deserved to be remembered. To be wept over.

Sol's hand was still in hers, and she clung to his strength, reminding herself that he was still here. So was Gaia.

The war was not over. They could still end this before more innocent lives were lost.

Though they did not have the benefit of the fire witches' magic to guide their way, Gaia had no trouble seeing in the dark. The earth shifted beneath their feet, parting for the earth goddess. The forest itself seemed to bow in her presence, obeying her whim and laying a path before her.

Even with the earth witches gone, the woods still recognized their magic.

May you find rest in the next life, Trivia thought. *May your souls cross over with ease. May you reunite with your ancestors.*

She had never been one to pray. It felt silly, with a goddess walking beside her. But she had to. In her bones, she needed to send something to the other realms, even if it was only her pleading thoughts. Anything to help those lost souls find peace.

"What will happen to them?" Trivia asked, her voice hoarse from the long silence. They had finally emerged from the jungle, and although the magic-wielders were gone, it still felt appropriate to honor the stillness of the woods. "The Underworld is still..." She trailed off. She had been about to say *in shambles,* but all she could think of was how it was her fault.

Gods above, was it *her fault* that the souls of those witches wouldn't have any rivers to cross? Had Trivia single-handedly ensured an afterlife full of torment for them?

She inhaled a shuddering gasp, suddenly finding it difficult to get oxygen into her lungs. She crouched to the ground, dizziness clouding her mind.

Gaia took her hand, jolting her from her panic. Her blue eyes were full of intensity and fire.

"The souls are fine," she assured Trivia. "I know it. I *sense* it. While the rivers of the Underworld have been recovering, souls have been gathering between worlds. There is a place for them, even if it's temporary. Do not fret, my darling."

Trivia nodded, closing her eyes. She was so tired. So very tired. The heavy emotions of the day weighed down on her, dragging her into darkness.

Gaia stood, then removed her cloak and handed it to

Trivia. "Use this for warmth. The wood here is sacred. I'm going to search for firewood that is separate from the jungle."

Trivia stood, a protest already on her lips.

Gaia raised a hand to stop her. "I'm fine. The earth recognizes me. I'll be able to find wood faster than either of you. Besides, you need rest." She glanced at Sol.

Trivia followed her gaze and found the sun god sitting with his arms propped on his knees. His head was bowed, and Trivia wondered if he, too, was praying.

"I won't be long," Gaia said before striding away. Within seconds, the darkness swallowed her whole.

Trivia shuddered, the air suddenly icy in her absence. She sank to the ground next to Sol, wrapping Gaia's cloak tightly around herself.

She and Sol sat in silence for what felt like hours. Trivia eventually rested her head on his shoulder, her eyes closing. She was certainly tired enough for sleep, but her heart was so heavy that she couldn't find rest.

After a long while, Sol's soft voice made her open her eyes.

"There is... so much more I could have done."

Trivia lifted her head to look at him. He was staring in the distance, but it was clear his attention was elsewhere. There was a firm set to his mouth and jaw that indicated his frustration.

"What do you mean?" she asked.

"You often berated me for it, but I lived a life of frivolity and carelessness. I was so consumed by my need to distance myself from emotion that I didn't think... didn't think about the consequences for *others*. All I knew was how to survive without losing myself. But I never once considered other people. Other souls. Perhaps if I had, I could have... could have..." He trailed off with an anguished sigh.

Trivia linked her arm with his, burrowing herself into his warmth. "If we are laying out our regrets and grievances, I'm certainly the victor here. I have done the most damage to all the realms. If I hadn't destroyed the Underworld, Apollo never would have tried to take the throne. He never would have brought the Titans back."

"But you were *fighting*." Sol turned to look at her, his eyes haunted. It reminded her of that night she'd seen him gazing at the moon in Elysium, battling with a grief she had known nothing about at the time. "Your motives were misguided, but you spent your entire life fighting injustice. What did I do? I lounged about and painted idyllic scenes while others were suffering. I did *nothing*."

"Sol—" Trivia gripped his arm tighter.

"Don't," he growled. "Don't comfort me, Trivia. I—I can't..."

"I wasn't going to," she argued.

He snorted at that. "Right."

"I wasn't!"

He gave her a flat look. "Fine. Then, what *were* you going to say?"

She dropped the cloak and climbed onto his lap, her legs wrapping around him. She held his face in both her hands, forcing him to meet her gaze.

"We are both terrible people, Sol," she said firmly.

He winced, then let out a hollow laugh. "Thanks."

"Will you let me finish?"

"By all means. Please insult me further."

She smirked. "We've both done terrible things. Whether by actively tearing things down, or by doing nothing to stop the destruction. But one thing I learned while in Pandora's box... is that the choices of yesterday don't matter as much as the choices of today and tomorrow. You can mourn the person you've been, but don't let it keep you from becoming someone better. Every decision you make can shape you into someone new. Someone *good*." She pressed her palm against his chest, feeling his heartbeat. The pounding rhythm soothed the tension in her body. "You can choose differently, Sol. No one is forcing you to continue the life you've led. All it takes is one shift, one small decision to put you on a different path." She tucked a lock of his golden hair behind his ear. "Make that choice right now. And, little by little, you'll become someone worthy. Someone decent."

Sol's lips parted as he gazed at her with wonder and awe. His eyes seemed to sparkle in the moonlight.

When he said nothing, Trivia shifted on his lap, suddenly uncomfortable. Why wasn't he saying anything? He was looking at her like she was a goddess.

She didn't deserve that look.

"I don't know from experience," she went on, finding herself rambling. "I'm only a few choices into my new life. So I really have no idea if I'll become someone worthy or not. It's just... something I believe in."

"Gods, Trivia," Sol breathed, a slow smile spreading across his face. "When did you become so... *wise*?"

Trivia blinked at him. "I'm not."

He laughed. "You are. That was the wisest thing I've heard in a hundred years."

Trivia whacked his shoulder. "Liar."

It was his turn to capture her face in his hands. His fingers caged her, framing her delicately as if she were something precious that he didn't want to break. She was startled to find his eyes were moist.

"I only know two things right now," he said softly, his breath tickling her lips. "I know I want to fight. And I know I want you by my side."

He kissed her, his lips desperate and hungry. His mouth was hot against hers, mingling with the salt of his tears. He angled her head to better devour her, and she found herself melting in his grasp.

He pulled away with a tortured groan, resting his forehead against hers and breathing heavily. "It's too much," he whispered. "Gods, this grief, this—this *misery*… is too damn much." He swallowed hard. "This was why I buried myself for so long. So I wouldn't feel this."

Trivia brought his mouth back to hers, her lips fervent. She had to make him see. To make him understand. His arms circled around her, drawing her closer.

"I know," Trivia murmured between kisses, "that I'm alive… and you are, too…" She pressed her mouth to his again, tasting him thoroughly, her tongue sweeping along his. Her hand pressed against his chest once more, feeling for his pulse. "Your heart beats." Another kiss. "And so does mine."

She pushed against him until he was lying on the ground with her hovering above him. His hands cupped her rear, and she rolled her hips. "Right now, that's all that matters. You and I are here. Our story isn't finished yet. We will take this grief and make something new out of it. Something to cherish. Something that will thrive."

She pressed her lips to the corner of his mouth, then his chin, his jaw, and his nose. She paused at the hollow of his throat, watching it bob as he swallowed again. "I want to feel everything, Sol," she whispered. "The good and the bad. I want all of it." She withdrew to gaze down at him. "Don't you?"

He stared at her, his fingers tightening, digging into her skin. "Yes," he rasped. "Yes. I want it all."

Trivia blinked tears from her eyes, struggling to draw breath. The emotion brimming in Sol's eyes was so fierce that it burrowed deep into her soul, peeling back layers of herself she didn't know existed. He was raw and vulnerable now, exposing everything to her.

If he was laid bare before her, she would do the same.

"I'm scared," she admitted in a broken voice. Tears streamed down her face. "There's so much death and destruction. We could be next. Whatever monster did this could be lurking around the corner, waiting to destroy us." She closed her eyes, her face crumpling. "But gods above, if that's what awaits me, I will accept that fate... as long as it means I get to be here with you. Tonight. Right now."

"I thought—I thought I'd lost you for good," he whispered. "I thought I'd never get to touch you again. To feel you. To taste you. I don't want to waste another moment, Trivia."

He leaned in and dragged his tongue along her throat. A

violent shiver of pleasure rippled over her. Gods, how she'd yearned for this. In the darkness of Pandora's box, when she'd believed she had nothing left but her memories of Sol... even those didn't do him justice.

She tugged at his trousers, sliding her hand underneath until she gripped his cock in her fingers. He jerked against her with a low groan.

They didn't have much time. Gaia could return at any moment. The idea of Gaia catching her making love to Sol was mortifying, but Trivia didn't care. They both needed this. They were headed to a war they might not survive. And Trivia would be damned if she wasted this precious time with him.

She tugged her own trousers free, wriggling until they slid off her legs. The wind danced over her bare skin, making her shudder. But the smoldering heat in Sol's gaze was enough to warm her.

"Give yourself to me tonight, Sol," she said, pulling his cock free. It was hard and firm and ready for her. "Nothing else but us. If we accept the good and the bad, then let us savor the good. Right now."

She spread her legs and sank onto him. They both groaned as he filled her, gliding into her as if their bodies were always meant to fit this way. She angled herself so he could drive deeper, and his eyes closed as he let out a sharp gasp.

"*Gods,* Trivia." He thrust harder.

"Yes," she whispered, her hands digging into the earth on either side of him. "*Yes,* Sol." Her hips writhed, dragging an anguished sound from him.

His fingers dug into her thighs as he moved again, withdrawing only to slide into her once more. Her breathing was ragged as she took him in, every glorious inch of him. His pace intensified. In and out he thrust, setting a rhythm that made her see stars. Her blood turned molten, her veins lighting on fire. More tears pricked her eyes, but she let them fall, let all her emotions go.

She wanted it all. The good and the bad.

Sol lifted his hips, pounding into her with feral intensity. His gasps turned into moans. He cried out her name. She buried her face in his neck, struggling to hold on when all she wanted to do was splinter apart, to shatter into a thousand pieces. Within her, that tension coiled tighter, prepared to burst. And gods, she wanted it to.

Harder and harder. Sol's grunting was animalistic, like he had unleashed a demon. Trivia licked his sweat-slicked neck, then bit down on him.

He cried out and shuddered, finding release with one final powerful thrust. Trivia followed after, her body spasming around him, drawing every last breath, every last drop of him.

She shattered.

She fractured.

She let it all go.

Gasping for breath, she rested her head against his chest, her mind emptying of everything but the exhaustion settling into her bones. She focused on his heartbeat, much quicker now than it had been before. But steady and reassuring.

He was alive.

So was she.

And together, they would fight.

"You're mine, Sol," Trivia said breathlessly, tracing circles along the fabric of his tunic. "Whether we live through this or not, your soul belongs to me. Don't forget that."

Sol took a few shallow breaths before he murmured, "Never." He kissed the top of her head. "Now and forever, my soul is yours."

Trivia settled against him, curling into his warmth. He draped the cloak around her naked legs, sheltering her from the cold.

Together, they would weather every storm. They would face every threat as one.

No matter how bleak or hopeless their situation, they would keep fighting each day.

Fighting for hope and fear. Love and death. Joy and misery.

They would fight for the chance to experience it all.

Together.

CALL

CYRUS

THE ATMOSPHERE IN THE CAVES WAS A MIXTURE OF wrath and despair. Half of the witches were thirsty for vengeance, eager to dive into battle for retribution of their fallen goddess. The others were mournful, uttering prayers and performing séances in an attempt to communicate with Lilith from beyond the veil.

Marina had shifted to her serpent form almost immediately upon arrival. Several other witches had followed suit, including the other Gorgon sister. Cyrus leaned against the cavern wall, watching the serpents glide across the ground. He got the sense that the witches were more comfortable in their snake forms, and perhaps more detached from their emotions.

He couldn't blame them. If something ever happened to Evander...

He shook his head. He couldn't go down that path.

Because it was very likely to come true, given Evander's bargain with the Wild Spirits.

Once he was mortal, Evander could easily die. Cyrus wasn't even sure if Evander would survive the transition.

A hard lump formed in his throat. Cyrus had spent much of his life putting distance between himself and his brothers, mostly to avoid conflict. Many of them had been conniving and power-hungry—much like himself—and he knew that getting close to them would only expose his weaknesses.

But the brothers he was most wary of were dead now. Only Romanos and Evander remained.

And Cyrus couldn't stomach the thought of losing either of them.

"I'm ready," Prue said, appearing by Cyrus's side and jerking him from his dismal thoughts. His wife shouldered a small pack, her expression grim but determined.

Cyrus nodded. Neither of them had bothered trying to convince the other to remain behind. Cyrus knew her well enough by now. She would not hide from a fight.

And Prue understood how much blame and responsibility Cyrus felt over the situation. The Titans had sought negotiations with *him.* Clearly, they wanted some hold on the Underworld.

Their attack on the Gorgons was Cyrus's fault. He had incited this by making a mockery of them. He had pretended to negotiate as a ruse to get Prue and Mona out.

Now, the Titans were seeking retribution.

This was bigger than just his realm now. The entire Realm of Gaia was at stake. The witch clans. The mortals.

Everyone on this plane of existence was in jeopardy because of his actions.

He'd made the wrong call, infiltrating the Titans' hideout like that. Now Lagos was dead, and more would follow.

He should never have left without ensuring the Titans were all dead. He should have made a frontal assault when he'd had the chance.

"I've already spoken with Farah," Cyrus said. "She and the other witches won't be far behind." The fire witches had taken the death of the Gorgon quite personally. It hadn't been their fight before, but it certainly was now.

Prue's eyes shifted to the white snake curling in on itself in the corner of the cave. Marina, even in her serpent form, hadn't moved much. Cyrus sensed she was grieving—that even in her animal form, she couldn't escape it.

"What about Marina and Romanos?" Prue asked softly.

"We can't wait for them." Cyrus's voice was solemn. "The Titans will keep killing people until I face them."

"I know." Prue squeezed his hand. "I just wish we had more numbers on our side."

Cyrus had considered traveling to the Underworld and gathering armies. But there wasn't time for that now. Besides, how could he allow more blood to be spilled on his account?

He needed to try to face the Titans in earnest this time. If they had started creating unholy creatures, then it wouldn't be long before the entire realm was overrun with them.

"You didn't think you could leave without me, did you?" asked a voice.

Prue and Cyrus turned to find Mona, also carrying a small sack, her eyebrows raised expectantly.

Prue's lips flattened as if she had, in fact, hoped to sneak out without Mona noticing. "Evander's still not back?"

"No," Mona said tightly, her eyes dimming. "But I can't stand by and do nothing. I wasn't close to Lilith, so it doesn't feel right to share in the witches' grief right now. But I can do *something*. You and I are goddesses now, Prue. We have enough power to fight."

Cyrus's stomach knotted at her words. Yes, Prue and Mona were powerful.

But the Titans were even more so. They had felled far stronger deities than the two sisters.

He thought of Prue and the gash in the side of her head that had only barely finished healing. There was a scar there, and her ear would not grow back. She was forever altered from the torture they had inflicted on her.

The idea of the Titans causing his wife even more pain made Cyrus want to roar, to smash through walls and burn down buildings. He couldn't stand it.

Prue nudged his arm. "Do you have the map?" Her voice was gentle, and he wondered if she only asked because she knew his thoughts were spiraling.

Regardless of her motives, he welcomed the distraction. Clearing his throat, he checked his pockets for the folded map Farah had given him. "It's here." He glanced at Mona. "Do you remember the way through the Voiceless Jungle?" When Mona nodded, he said, "Good. If you can get us through there, I think I can navigate our way to the Thanassian Empire."

"It's been a while, hasn't it?" Prue asked, her eyes softening.

Something warmed in Cyrus's chest as he looked at her. "Yes, it has."

The last time they had been in the Thanassian Empire, they had been reluctantly traveling together to close the gates of the Underworld. In the small village of Faidon, they had finally admitted their love to one another, sealing their bond in a heated night of passion.

He would never forget that night.

Cyrus let out a steady breath. "All right. Let's go."

The three of them made their way to the exit, pausing occasionally to bid farewell to some witches along the way. When they reached the cavern entrance, they found Farah and four other witches waiting, each of them dressed in copper armor.

Cyrus straightened at the sight of them, his brows knitting together. "Farah, what's going on?"

"The four of us are prepared to fight alongside you," Farah announced, lifting her chin. Her amber eyes gleamed with fierce intensity, and she looked every bit the warrior Cyrus knew her to be.

"I thought your coven would follow after us," Cyrus said.

"I thought so, too," Farah said. "But we decided we simply cannot wait. Not all of my sisters are able to fight. And I will not ask them to in their time of grief. Wren will head the coven in my absence and prepare those for battle if and when they are ready. But for now, the five of us cannot stand by and do nothing. I'm sure you share the same sentiment."

Slowly, Cyrus nodded. His heart stirred at the sight of these women, bravely willing to step into battle. "Farah, you will likely die. You all will. I need you to understand that."

"Death has already struck our people," said the witch next to Farah. Cyrus vaguely recalled her name was Nadia. "It will strike again whether we are prepared for it or not. We want to act now, while we still have the choice to do so."

The other witches murmured their agreement, squaring their shoulders with defiance blazing in their eyes. Cyrus gazed at each of them, admiring their fearlessness. There was no hesitation on any of their faces. They were ready, even if it meant facing death.

He inclined his head as a sign of respect. "Then, I am proud to consider you my allies in this battle."

Farah offered a small smile.

"And I will be grateful to have a navigator who knows these lands better than I do," Cyrus added in a mutter.

Farah chuckled. "I'm sure you are. Come. We'll lead the way."

After exchanging glances with Prue and Mona, Cyrus followed the armored witches through the tunnel that would lead them out into the desert.

Cyrus had to admire the witches' finesse. Even in their battle armor, they still glided gracefully through the desert, their steps far more lithe and nimble than his, Prue's, and Mona's. The witches were patient and often paused to allow the three of them to catch up. The wind bit at Cyrus's face and stung his eyes, burning his skin with the incessant grains of sand that seemed forever embedded in his flesh.

Gods, he hated the desert. This miserable terrain only made him yearn for his home in the Underworld. Even with the enchantment partially broken from the destruction of Pandora's box, the Underworld was still preferable to this.

At long last, they reached the ruins of Sodara, and the witches stopped, removing parts of their armor and sitting on chunks of concrete and debris to rest. Cyrus was somewhat mollified to see the witches panting and covered in sweat—proof that the trek had been grueling for them as well, even if they hadn't shown it.

They passed around waterskins and rested in silence, all of them too fatigued to speak. Cyrus squinted in the distance, knowing the Voiceless Jungle was close by.

He was both eager to end the journey, and dreading what he would find on the other side.

"We can't be the only ones who have noticed," Mona said softly, still breathing heavily. "Surely other witches, other deities, have realized the Titans are dabbling in powers that could destroy the realm." She glanced at her sister. "Surely we can't be the *only* ones seeking to end this?" Her voice sounded hopeful and uncertain at the same time.

"You forget that our sister has done an exceptional job at destroying two of the three realms," Prue said in a dry voice after taking a long gulp of water. "Whatever gods remain are busy picking up the pieces of their lives. Whoever might be able to help us is either dead or too afraid to show their face."

"Trivia is not to blame," Mona said, her voice surprisingly

sharp. "She's been manipulated by the goddess Pandora for her entire life, and she's strived tirelessly to make amends for her wrongdoings."

Prue blinked, and the other witches fell silent at Mona's outburst. After a long, awkward moment, Prue said softly, "I—I didn't know."

"I know." Mona sighed. "I'm sorry. I suppose I have a soft spot for tortured souls possessed by a dark presence." Her voice turned bitter, and her eyes grew distant. It wasn't difficult to understand she was thinking of Evander.

Prue touched Mona's hand. "Perhaps it's better that he isn't here. Perhaps this means he'll be kept safe and survive all this."

Cyrus swallowed hard, realizing Prue was implying the eight of them would *not* survive.

"Perhaps," Mona said doubtfully, chewing on her lip. "I also wonder about our mother. I don't believe she would abandon her own realm."

Prue's brows knitted together, her expression tightening. Cyrus intertwined his fingers with hers and offered a gentle squeeze.

With a shaky breath, Prue said, "It's possible Gaia has her own matters to deal with. I haven't seen her since I sent her to find Pandora—er, Trivia."

"They both left to rebuild Elysium with Sol the sun god," Mona supplied. "I haven't heard from any of them since then."

"Pandora's darkness is still out there," Cyrus said grimly. "And if Trivia is trying to distance herself from the vengeful goddess, then it's likely those dark forces have targeted her."

When Mona and Prue looked at each other with equally worried expressions, Cyrus knew this conversation wasn't going anywhere helpful. With one last sip of water, he turned to the witches. "Are you ready to continue?"

Before they could respond, the ground began to quake. Cracks formed in the dirt, spearing in every direction. Concrete split, and glass shattered.

Cyrus grabbed Prue and pulled her to the ground, shielding her with his arms. Dust and dirt filled the air. The quaking intensified, roaring so loudly that Cyrus's ears throbbed.

Screams pierced the air, and Prue shouted, "Mona!" She tried to move, but Cyrus tightened his grip around her, holding her in place.

When the air stilled and the dust settled, Cyrus slowly lifted his head, blinking against the hazy fog that surrounded them. A few witches coughed. Some had shifted to their serpent forms in self-defense.

Cyrus coughed and waved the dust out of his face. As soon as he released her, Prue darted forward in search of her sister. Mona was on the ground, partially concealed by a mountain of ash. Prue helped her sister up, dusting her off and wiping the ash from her eyes.

"What was that?" Mona choked, brushing the soot from her body.

Cyrus went perfectly still as the air seemed to whisper around him. The hairs on his arms stood on end. The back of his neck prickled with the sensation that someone was watching him.

Then, as he squinted through the haze of dust and ash,

he made out the jagged edges of a massive fissure that had split through the broken city. Cracks covered the ground, but his eyes were drawn to a gaping pit that yawned before them, ready to devour them whole.

It looked like Tartarus. The very air seemed to thrum with the same energy as the place he detested most in all the realms. Unease and nausea spread through him, making his skin clammy as he recalled just how horrifying that place was. The visions he had seen... The terrifying array of emotions he had experienced...

Mona suddenly stiffened and stepped forward, her eyes wide. "Evander?" Her voice was filled with part shock, part relief. A wide smile spread across her face. "It's Evander! I can hear him!"

She tried to surge forward, but Prue clamped down on her wrist, holding her in place. Cyrus strained to hear, but there was nothing but eerie silence.

"What are you doing?" Mona snapped, jerking her arm out of Prue's grip. "Let me go to him!"

This time, Cyrus grabbed her hand. "Mona. No one is calling."

Mona shook her head. "No, I can *hear* him. Our souls call to one another. Even when no one else can hear our melody, *I can.* I know what he sounds like, and he needs me!"

Something wasn't right. Fear wriggled through Cyrus's chest, and he exchanged a worried look with Prue. Wordlessly, they nodded to one another.

They could not allow Mona to leave. Whoever was calling to her was *not* Evander.

"Cyrus," whispered a voice.

Cyrus went rigid, his spine straightening. He swallowed hard. "Who's there?"

Prue sucked in a sharp breath beside him.

"Cyrus, it's me," said the voice. "I'm alive."

Cyrus's breath hitched, and his heart seized in his chest. "L-Lagos?"

Lagos huffed, the sound so familiar and yet so foreign because Cyrus had thought he would never hear it again. "Of course it's me. My death was only a ruse to trick the Titans. But I am well. I just need your help climbing out of this crater."

Cyrus's heart soared. Lagos was alive! His death was not on Cyrus's hands. He could fix everything that had gone wrong that day. He could make things right again.

He stepped forward, but Prue's fingernails dug into his arm. "Cyrus, stop," she hissed. "It's not real."

"It's Lagos," Cyrus said, his eyes moist with tears. "Prue, he's alive. He's all right."

Prue's expression was grim as she shook her head slowly. "It's *not real*. Remember Tartarus. Remember how we resisted those visions."

Confusion and fear bled through the joy lifting Cyrus's heart. He didn't want to lose this relief that was spreading through him, warming his body and making his blood sing. He didn't want to return to the reality where Lagos was dead.

"Goddess above," Mona whispered, shaking her head violently. Her eyes screwed shut, her brow furrowing as tension crossed her features. "Oh, it hurts. It *hurts*!" With her free hand, she pressed it to her temple, her face contorted with pain. She made an incoherent sound of frustration. "Prue! It's—It's—"

A deafening screech filled the air, making Cyrus's ears throb. He froze, his blood chilling as something *whooshed* nearby, causing a breeze to ripple through his hair. Feathers brushed against his arms. He cringed away from them, drawing closer to Prue and Mona. As he glanced around, he realized the witches were nowhere to be found.

"Farah?" he called out. "Nadia? Where are you?"

No answer.

A cold sense of foreboding filled his chest. *Oh, gods.* What was happening?

"Their call lures men to their deaths," Mona was reciting, her gaze distant and slightly manic. "They sing songs of deepest desire and promises of wishes fulfilled. Their call is resisted by no one, not even the gods themselves." She was shaking now as she met Prue's gaze with wide, stunned eyes.

Cyrus's heart dropped to his stomach. He knew exactly what creatures were hunting them.

Sirens.

Talons and feathers brushed past Prue. Something sharp scraped against her arm, dragging a path of fire along her flesh. She cringed away from the onslaught of sirens, scanning the skies for them. But the air was still so clouded with dust that she couldn't see them.

She squinted, realizing it wasn't dust, but *fog*. A dense fog poured out from the fissure in the earth, obscuring their surroundings. She clung to Cyrus and Mona, desperate to keep them close. The panic within her flared, and she feared one of them would get snatched by the creatures.

"Prue," murmured a voice.

Prue froze, then crammed her eyes shut. *It's not real. It's not real.*

"Prue, I can help you! Just come to me, and we can face this threat together."

Her mother's voice washed over her, and oh, how Prue

yearned to run to her. To dive into her arms and cling to her. With Gaia on their side, they could not lose.

"Prue!" Cyrus called out. He grunted, then barked out a curse.

Prue's eyes snapped open as she focused on her husband. He was nursing a deep gash in his shoulder, gritting his teeth as he tried to stifle the flow of blood.

In an instant, everything came into focus. She hadn't realized until that moment how foggy her senses had become. Sight and sound had been blocked out, drowned by the soothing call of her mother's voice.

"Damn sirens," Prue hissed, reaching for Cyrus to inspect his wound. The blood was already starting to clot, the flow of liquid slowing. Thankfully, it didn't look too severe.

The sirens screeched louder, diving for them. Prue tugged Cyrus out of the way, narrowly avoiding getting skewered. But the sirens were relentless, pecking at them, talons extended. It seemed that once they knew their calls were being ignored, they attempted a different tactic.

And it was working.

Prue cried out as another talon gouged her cheek, drawing blood.

Cyrus made a noise of frustration. "I can't strike them if I can't see them!" A faint bolt of lightning blazed to life behind the fog, but it was fleeting, and the sirens dodged it easily.

Prue gritted her teeth, then crouched to the ground, pressing her fingers into the dirt. She closed her eyes, drawing power from deep within her. The ground trembled, and roots sprang from the cracks in the earth. She summoned more, pulling energy, soaring higher and higher. The roots gathered around her, Mona, and Cyrus, growing in height until a web of branches and vines surrounded them like a protective wall. Sweat poured down her face and neck, and she was panting, the power draining her.

Mona took her free hand, lacing their fingers together and chanting words Prue couldn't understand. The ground hummed, and a burst of energy filled Prue's body—Mona's magic had joined her own.

The branches thickened, forming a dome around them to shield them from the sirens' attacks. Light filtered through the gaps, and the branches creaked when the beasts collided with it.

It wouldn't hold forever.

"Mona," Prue said urgently. "Tell me you have a plan. How can we stop them?"

Mona shook her head, her face pale. "Resisting their song is supposed to kill them. These are nothing like the sirens I've read about. They're... different."

"Because they're fueled by Titan magic," Cyrus growled.

From outside the dome, the sirens screeched and shrieked. A creature slammed into the branches, making them quiver. Leaves fell from the impact.

Prue frowned and shook her head. "That doesn't make any sense. Romanos described a *Cyclops.* Why would the Titans send sirens after us?"

Cyrus's eyes grew wide. "It's a diversion. They don't want to kill us, they want to *delay* us."

"Delay us from what?" Prue asked.

"From reaching the Thanassian Empire?" Mona suggested. "Perhaps to keep us preoccupied while the Cyclops does their bidding."

Cyrus's expression turned dark. "I don't know what plans they have for the Thanassian Empire, but it can't be good."

A branch cracked and split away from the dome, falling between Prue and Cyrus. She flinched as chunks of tree bark fell around them, then drew more of her magic to fill the gap. "It doesn't matter *what* they're doing in the Thanassian Empire if we can't get out of here. With the fog in the air, we can't do anything!"

Mona lifted a finger, her eyes sparking with realization. "Hold on. Sirens travel in packs. They are bonded to one another. What if we can use that bond against them and *lure* them to us? Use their own powers against them. Then, we can kill them."

"How do we do that?" Prue asked.

"We have to catch one. We have to let them come close enough to be captured."

"They keep flying away too quickly," Cyrus said.

"If we can injure their wings, we can keep them grounded." Mona met Prue's gaze. "I think it's time for that fire rune again."

With Prue's arm already bleeding from when a siren's beak gouged her, it was easy to pour droplets into Mona's empty canteen. With her eyes closed and her expression tight with concentration, Mona whispered the incantation.

"*Accendo eduro.*"

Flames appeared in her palm, but instead of a single

strike in the sky like in the cabin, it lingered in her hand like a forever-burning fire.

A small smile appeared on Mona's face. "If you can get one close enough to me, I'll burn it."

Cyrus offered a savage grin. "Not a problem." He turned to Prue. "Whenever you're ready."

Prue nodded and took a deep breath, then withdrew her magic. The dome of branches vanished, and the sirens' screeches intensified, as if they were calling to one another, alerting them to the exposure of their prey.

Feathers tickled Prue's arms, and she yelped, jerking away instinctively. Beside her, Cyrus tensed, his body poised like a predator. His nostrils flared, and his eyes sharpened.

Another siren dived for them, and Cyrus lunged. He grunted as he tackled the creature to the ground, wrestling with its dark feathers.

Prue sucked in a breath at the sight of the creature. It had the face of an old woman, wrinkled and ancient, with a large, black beak and all-black eyes. The rest of its body resembled that of a giant vulture: raven-black wings and long, sharp talons.

It writhed and shrieked, trying to wriggle out of Cyrus's grip. But he held fast.

"Now, Mona!" he bellowed.

Mona appeared by his side, and the fire in her palm swelled. She pressed it into the siren's wing.

The piercing scream that echoed around them was deafening, making Prue's ear throb and her bones tremble. The keening wail reverberated and seemed to multiply, as if the other sirens were suffering along with it.

"Get ready, Cyrus!" Mona warned.

A cacophony of high-pitched roars and cries filled the air, swarming around Prue, Mona, and Cyrus. Frantic flapping of wings sounded nearby. Prue's body was rigid, prepared for an onslaught of attacks from the sirens. The damn fog was obscuring everything. If she could only *see...*

In a flash, three sirens slammed into the ground before them, twitching and convulsing as if in tremendous pain. Cyrus wasted no time; lightning crackled from his fingertips and scorched the beasts, leaving nothing more than charred husks behind.

The cries grew more angry. More anguished.

"They feel each other's pain," Prue whispered.

A dozen sirens fell to the ground, writhing in agony. Cyrus summoned his lightning, igniting the sirens until they were no longer moving.

Prue's heart stuttered in her chest as she stared at the smoking remains of the creatures.

This wasn't right.

A swarm of sirens fell before them, bodies twisting in unnatural angles, their faces stricken with pain and fear. Cyrus lifted his hand—

"Stop!" Prue cried, grabbing his arm to hold him still.

Cyrus froze, staring at her with wide eyes.

A hard lump formed in Prue's throat. She couldn't speak. All she could manage was a single shake of her head. Slowly, she lowered Cyrus's hand and approached the nearest siren. Its wings were folded inward as if it could cocoon itself and hide from the devastation of losing members of its pack.

"Prue," Cyrus warned.

"This is *wrong*," Prue said over her shoulder. "This is what they want! Mona and I are goddesses of earth—of *life*. To destroy creatures like this is exactly what the Titans want. But the sirens are not our enemy. If they are only here to divert us, then they don't deserve to be destroyed for it."

"They were created with Titan magic," Cyrus objected. "Their very existence goes against the laws of the gods."

"They cannot be *unmade*," Mona said thoughtfully. "Once created, you can't undo it. Even if they are killed, it doesn't erase the fact that they existed. Nothing can."

"You two aren't seriously suggesting we keep them alive?" Cyrus's voice was incredulous. "We won't be able to get past them without being pecked to death!"

Prue gave him a sharp look. "If there's one thing I've learned from being Queen of the Underworld, it's that even the most monstrous of creatures deserve to be cared for. You yourself possess Titan magic. Should you also be destroyed for it?"

Cyrus's mouth snapped shut at that.

"Let me *try*," she pleaded. "If it doesn't work, we'll do it your way."

After a moment, Cyrus offered a stiff nod.

Relief spread through Prue's chest, and she looked at Mona. "Will you help me?"

"Of course," Mona said.

Together, they drew closer to the siren. Wet, rasping sounds poured from its beak, and Prue's heart shattered. "Goddess, what have we done?" she whispered.

Mona's fingers slid through hers and gave a tight squeeze. They both knelt by the siren's side. It was too wounded to even glance at them. Its dark eyes blinked, staring into the distance. Prue wondered if it was so close to death that it couldn't register their closeness.

Mona gently pressed her hands into the siren's feathers, then murmured, "*Sano.*"

Nothing happened.

Mona's brows drew together in frustration. Her voice was firmer as she said, "*Sano.*"

Prue placed her hand on top of Mona's, drawing from her own well of power. Their voices rang out as they said together, "*Sano!*"

Wind billowed around them. Heat burned underneath their joined hands. The siren's body jerked violently from the force of their magic. Its head whipped up, and it squawked loudly at them, almost indignantly.

Prue gasped, her head rearing back in surprise. Her whole body tingled with energy, her blood simmering and her heart racing.

The siren snapped its beak, and Prue and Mona scrambled away before getting pecked at.

"We're sorry," Prue said, extending her palms. "Please forgive us. We only want to help."

The siren cocked its head at them, assessing. Then, its beak opened, and a soothing melody poured out.

Prue stiffened, waiting for the siren song to overwhelm her body, to draw her in and lure her to her death.

But it didn't.

The siren continued to sing, the melody soothing and beautiful. It sounded both lovely and sad, like a tale of lovers torn apart. Beside her, Mona sniffed, her eyes welling with tears.

"It's—It's the song of their kind," Mona whispered. "A song of death and destruction. But also freedom and flight."

Prue swallowed hard, sorrow tightening in her chest.

When the song was finished, Prue found her own cheeks wet with tears. She wiped her nose and gazed at the siren in wonder. She had never imagined that such dangerous creatures could also be... beautiful.

The siren's beak opened once more, and this time, Evander's voice spoke to them. "Thank you. Your healing has freed us."

Mona's breath hitched. Prue couldn't imagine how awkward it must feel to hear this siren speak with the voice of the man she loved.

"We were enslaved," the siren continued in Evander's gentle voice. "But the pain of our bondage was swallowed up in the magic you gifted us. We are indebted to you."

Prue blinked, her lips parting in wonder. *Indebted.*

On impulse, she blurted out, "Will you fight with us?"

The siren cocked its head again. "Fight?"

"We are trying to take down the Titans. Destroy them before they take over the realms. Will you help us?"

The siren said nothing for a long moment. Prue waited, holding her breath, daring to hope...

"Yes," the siren said at last. "We seek to take down the masters who have caged us. But not all of our pack will follow."

Prue frowned. "What do you mean?"

"To face the Titans means to do battle against one of our own."

Prue shook her head, but beside her, Mona went still as death, her eyes wide. "What are you talking about?" Prue asked.

The siren's voice was somber. "One of the Titans has used dark magic to alter his body. He has taken the form of a siren."

ABOMINATION
TRIVIA

"Do you hear that?"

Trivia blinked sleepily as she curled into Sol's warm chest. Her eyes were closed, and she wanted to fall back into the beauty of unconsciousness.

But then, she heard it, too.

A distant rumbling, like a volcano.

Her eyes flew open, and she sat up. Gaia's cloak was still wrapped around her. The early rays of dawn peeked over the horizon, but they were masked by a strange fog that had settled over the ground.

Gaia was nowhere to be found.

Sol was sitting up, too, his brows furrowed as he stared at something in the distance.

"What do you think it is?" Trivia asked.

Sol shook his head, frowning. "There was something... off about the sun as it rose. It didn't feel natural." He cast a worried glance at her. "I think someone is meddling with powers they shouldn't."

"The Titans?"

Sol's grim silence was answer enough.

Trivia stood, then pulled on her trousers and fastened Gaia's cloak around her front. "My mother still hasn't returned. Something is definitely wrong." She bit her lip, considering. If something was powerful enough to deter the Goddess of Earth, then what chance did Sol and Trivia have?

A resounding *boom* shook the earth, making the ground tremble. Trivia yelped, thrown off balance. Sol caught her before she fell, keeping her steady. The two of them crouched to the ground, huddling close together. The quaking intensified. Cracks split the earth, opening wide. Trivia and Sol staggered backward, narrowly avoiding getting swallowed up by a massive crevice. It seemed as if the very earth were slicing in two.

Trivia ducked her head, and Sol braced his arms around her, shielding her. She crammed her eyes shut, holding her breath as she waited for death to consume her...

Then, it stopped. The air stilled. Panting, Trivia hesitantly peered around Sol's arms to find the air thick with dust that mingled with fog. Jagged fissures covered the once smooth ground, some thin and others large enough for Trivia to fall into.

Trivia was clinging to Sol's tunic, her whole body shaking. "Do—Do you think it's the same creature that destroyed the witch coven?"

Sol said nothing. A muscle feathered in his jaw, and his

nostrils flared as he squinted in the distance. Trivia followed his gaze, noting that the fog seemed the most dense about a mile to the east.

The crevices also seemed to widen in that direction as well.

Sol and Trivia exchanged a significant look. It was clear what direction they needed to go.

"Should we wait for Gaia?" Sol asked quietly.

Trivia shook her head. "She would have been back by now. I'd wager that something took her. And it's waiting for us down there." She pointed to the swirling mist that seemed to coil in the air as if it were alive.

Sol helped her to her feet. Hand-in-hand, they strode toward the fog, dodging craters and fissures along their way.

When a high-pitched screech pierced the air, they both stiffened.

Trivia squeezed Sol's hand. "What do you—" She froze as she heard her mother's voice echoing.

"Trivia! Daughter, help me. Please!"

"*Mother!*" Trivia cried, releasing Sol's hand and sprinting forward. Sol shouted something at her, but she didn't listen.

Gaia's voice was full of panic and fear. Trivia had never heard her mother sound like that before.

"You must hurry!" Gaia yelled. "They are getting closer. I don't have much time!"

"I'm coming!" Trivia called, sidestepping more cracks and holes as she followed the sound of her mother's voice.

"*Trivia!*" Sol bellowed, freezing her in her tracks. She turned and looked over her shoulder, but all she could see was fog and dust.

Sol cried out again, the sound laced with pain.

Shit. Trivia glanced back and forth, conflicted as to which direction she should go. Gaia, or Sol? Both of them needed her help...

"Trivia, it's a *trick*! It's not really Gaia!" Sol's voice was urgent and firm.

Trivia sucked in a sharp breath, looking once more toward the direction where she'd heard her mother's voice.

"Come back!" Sol pleaded. "Trivia, where are you?"

"I'm here!" Trivia answered, turning back toward Sol's echoing shouts. "Follow my voice!"

"I think I can see you." Sol sounded closer now. Trivia squinted as she made out a figure in the fog.

Relief spread through her, and she smiled as she hurried toward him.

But as the fog cleared, the figure before her materialized.

It wasn't Sol.

With a loud screech, a large creature slammed into her, pinning her to the ground. Trivia screamed and wrestled with the beast, but its talons cut into her flesh, pinning her. Inky black eyes bored into hers, surrounded by a wrinkled female face and a dark beak.

"Oh, shit," Trivia wheezed, struggling in vain to free herself.

The siren leaned closer, its eyes hungry.

Hungry for *her.*

Its beak opened wide.

Trivia pressed her fingers into the dirt beside her and summoned her power. Roots sprang forth, and vines wrapped around the siren's wings. It cawed loudly, batting a wing at the vines. Its talons loosened their hold on Trivia for a brief moment. But it was all she needed.

She shoved at the siren, then rolled away from it, her arms bleeding from the sharp cut of its talons. The siren screeched and flew toward her. Trivia conjured a branch, then used it as a club to whack at the creature.

The siren screamed. Wings beat nearby, and several other figures appeared.

More sirens.

"Oh gods," Trivia whispered, backing away as the sirens surrounded her. They cawed and screeched angrily, flitting closer, their wings outstretched.

One of them spoke to her with Sol's voice. "I told you it was a trick, darling."

Trivia shuddered at the sound of her lover's voice pouring from that wretched beak. She gripped the branch in her hands tightly, prepared to beat as many of those damned birds as she needed to in order to survive.

As one, the mass of sirens rushed toward her. She roared in fury, striking one siren, then another. A third sliced her with its beak. She went down, then dug her free hand into the earth and conjured more vines. They wrapped around three sirens, pinning them to the ground.

But there were too many of them. Six more flapped toward her, beaks cutting, talons scraping. Blood poured from her wounds. The pain seared through her, white-hot and all-consuming. She swung blindly, trying to free herself. But gods, her body was throbbing. Her skin was on fire.

She couldn't fight. She couldn't—

A flash of brilliant white light burst in the air, burning against her eyes. She turned away from it, hissing. The sirens let out several shrill cries, using their wings to shield their eyes. The light only intensified, more brilliant than the sun itself.

"Sol," Trivia breathed, recognizing his magic. She shut her eyes, barely strong enough to summon a canopy of leaves to cover her face before Sol's magic scorched her.

The smell of burning flesh reached her nose. The sirens shrieked and screamed, then took to the skies. The beating of wings grew more and more distant before vanishing entirely.

After a moment, the light slowly faded. Trivia's protective leaves disappeared, and Sol's worried face appeared before her.

"Gods above, Trivia," he murmured, tearing off strips of fabric from his tunic to bind the worst of her wounds. "I can't leave you alone for a moment, can I?"

Trivia managed a hoarse laugh, her body still wracked with pain. "Seems you didn't escape completely unscathed, either." She gestured to a bleeding cut on his cheek, then another on his leg. She groaned when Sol tied the cloth around a particularly deep gash on her forearm. "How are we supposed to move forward with Gaia missing and sirens surrounding us?"

Sol flashed her a grin. "The sirens have always loathed sun magic. That's how Apollo banished them the first time. Just stay with me, and you'll be fine. Don't go wandering off again." He winked, as if she had merely made a clumsy misstep, not gotten herself nearly pecked to death.

"Are you powerful enough to send them back?" Trivia asked quietly.

Sol's expression sobered. Doubt clouded his expression, and Trivia knew his answer.

Only Apollo was strong enough to eliminate the sirens.

And he was dead.

Trivia took a deep breath. "Help me up."

Sol extended his hand and hoisted her to her feet. She wobbled slightly, and his arms came around her.

"Don't you dare carry me," she barked.

Sol snorted. "Wouldn't dream of it."

Trivia took a few moments to inhale and exhale, long and slow, trying to steady herself. After a moment, her legs felt strong enough, and she nodded wordlessly at Sol. He kept one arm wrapped around her waist and the other outstretched, a beam of sunlight pouring from his palm.

Their trek was slow at first. One of the sirens had torn into Trivia's thigh, and each step sent needles of pain shooting through her. After several paces, she paused, then channeled her magic toward that specific wound. She closed her eyes, envisioning the healing earth magic sweeping through her, mending her, knitting her body back together...

She was gasping by the time her magic responded. But after testing her leg, she realized the wound was healed.

Sol raised his eyebrows. "Impressive."

"Don't ask me to do it again," she panted, wiping sweat from her brow. "That took a lot out of me."

"You're still adjusting to your strengthened powers. It takes time."

"Time we don't have," Trivia said bitterly.

Sol said nothing as they continued onward, their pace quicker with Trivia's leg healed. It cost her, though—exhaustion pulled at every muscle and limb, threatening to drag her down into the crevices waiting for her.

But she pushed herself. She had to keep moving. For Gaia. For Prue. For Mona.

For Sol.

And for herself.

The occasional siren flew toward them, squawking loudly. Sol was quick to blast them with his sun magic, making them flee. Gaia's voice echoed frequently through the mist, as the sirens no doubt learned not to get too close to the sun god. It was clear they were trying once more to lure Trivia in with their siren call.

Every time her mother's voice called out to her, Sol's grip tightened on Trivia's waist.

"Can you hear it, too?" Trivia whispered.

Sol shook his head. "No. But every time they speak to you, you draw in a sharp breath, your eyes sparking with hope and longing."

Trivia glanced at him and the sorrow in his eyes. It made her heart twist painfully in her chest.

"I know how it feels to yearn for your mother," he said.

Trivia squeezed his arm, her eyes closing for a moment. Gods, she was so full of regret and shame. The agony of her mistakes, her choices that had cost so many lives... It was too much to bear.

"I'm so sorry," she whispered. "Your mother would still be alive if it weren't for me."

Sol said nothing for a long moment. And after a while,

Trivia expected he wouldn't respond. Perhaps they had reopened a wound that hadn't fully healed yet. She wouldn't blame him if he still hadn't forgiven her.

"My mother was always haunted by Gaia's banishment," Sol said suddenly, his tone thoughtful. "I think she blamed herself for not defending her friend. When the opportunity to defy Apollo presented itself, my mother didn't hesitate. I think she was waiting for her moment. I think she always knew she would die opposing Apollo. In fact, she *welcomed* it. She had always been a warrior, and there is no greater shame than living a long life as a coward. She would have preferred to die this way, I think."

Trivia wasn't sure how to respond to this. From what little she knew of Hestia, this made sense. But it still didn't erase what Trivia had done, nor did it absolve her of any guilt.

And that's okay, she told herself. *This isn't about you—it's about Sol and what he needs. Forget yourself for a moment and focus on him.*

"I know you didn't have the closest relationship with her," Trivia said quietly. "But I'm glad you knew her well enough to understand her like that."

Sol looked at her, expression contemplative. "You'll come to know Gaia in the same way. I'm sure of it."

Trivia offered him a weak smile, but it didn't lessen the sharp pang of fear that sliced through her at the thought of Gaia dying somewhere alone, with no one to help or comfort her.

A sudden bolt of lightning streaked across the sky, muted

by the dense fog around them. Trivia jumped, eyes widening. "What was that?"

Sol didn't answer. He went completely still beside her.

Then, they heard it.

The shrill, piercing screams of sirens.

Another flash of lightning. Then another. The screams grew more anguished. More desperate.

Trivia's breath hitched. "What—What's happening?"

"I don't know. Something is attacking them."

"It can't be a Titan—can it?"

Before Sol could respond, everything fell silent. The lightning ceased. The screams subsided. Nothing but an eerie stillness settled around them.

Trivia didn't like it one bit. She tightened her hold on Sol's arm, unable to shake the sense that they needed to run. To flee. To *hide*.

The ground trembled. Trivia ducked, crouching low, expecting more cracks to form in the earth.

But this was... different. The ground continued to quake and quiver, but it wasn't as violent as before. And there was a strange rhythm to it.

"Trivia," Sol said sharply.

She stood, drawing closer to him. Only then did she realize the shaking was coming from a loud, distant thumping.

Footsteps. *Enormous* footsteps.

"Oh, gods," Trivia whispered. She frantically looked around, searching for a place to take cover. But they stood in a wasteland, surrounded by cracks and mist. Perhaps if they lay on the ground, whoever was coming wouldn't see them?

"I know that smell," Sol muttered. "*Shit.*"

"What is it?"

The thunderous footsteps were almost upon them. Each step was so loud it drowned out all sounds.

"Cyclops," Sol said in between the pounding.

"Not just any Cyclops," said a cold, sinister voice. It echoed all around them, deep and resonant, like the voices of ten men. The sound made Trivia's skin pebble, and a chill swept over her.

A massive figure took shape through the mist, towering over them. It stood as tall as the castle of Elysium, and Trivia had to crane her neck to stare at it in horror.

It wasn't just a Cyclops, but a *giant.* Thick, meaty legs stood before them. Trivia only came up to its shins. As she gazed up and up and *up*, she found a one-eyed gray-skinned demon leering down at her. It wore nothing but loose leather trousers, its muscular chest left bare. Its singular eye was white and all-seeing. Jagged teeth spread into a wide, feral grin.

From what Trivia knew of them, Cyclopes were large, but not *this* big. And they certainly didn't have demon flesh.

She swallowed hard, trying not to tremble as she stared up at this beast who could easily squash them with a single step. "What are you?" she called to it.

"I am called *Atlas*," the Cyclops said smugly.

Sol was shaking his head. "Impossible. Atlas is a Titan. And Titan magic can't produce something like this."

Leather shifted as the Cyclops leaned forward to closer inspect Sol. A droplet of saliva dribbled from his lips, large enough to splatter over them both and drench them completely.

"Ah, little sun god," Atlas crooned. "It is quite possible indeed. You see, Titan magic, when combined with death magic, can produce *all manner* of abominations. And we've summoned them all as a welcome gift just for you and your little witch goddesses."

FREE

EVANDER

"I DON'T UNDERSTAND," SAID EVANDER, TRYING TO control the wild thumping of his heart. He glanced at the woman before him, noting how *human* she looked. "Typhon was a demon. He had horns and wings and..."

His voice trailed off as the woman's form began to change before his eyes. Her head and torso stayed the same, but the rest of her body elongated to form that of a massive serpent. Her long tail wriggled behind her, just as translucent as the rest of her.

"I am Echidna," she said. "And Typhon was my mate."

Evander's mouth fell open, and he shook his head. He still couldn't comprehend this. It didn't make *sense*.

Behind Echidna, several other forms materialized. Some had wings like Typhon. Others had multiple heads or extra arms. Some had the head of a lion or a bull.

There were all manner of demons and beasts here. They had only taken the appearance of mortal souls.

"Where—Where did you all come from?" Evander breathed, awestruck by this revelation. "And how did Typhon possess me?"

"Typhon and I birthed many creatures," Echidna explained, gesturing behind her. "The Wild Spirits are our family. But one day, Jupiter determined we were too dangerous to roam freely. He wanted to destroy our kind. Typhon resisted, challenging Jupiter for the throne. When they battled, Typhon was defeated and caged underneath a volcano for thousands of years. The rest of us were doomed to an eternity without peace. Without rest."

"That doesn't explain how Typhon found me," Evander said.

"I do not know this, either," Echidna said thoughtfully. "I have been trapped here ever since. When did you first notice his presence?"

"A witch cursed me in the mortal realm," Evander said. "When I returned, he had taken over my body."

Echidna cocked her head at him in consideration. "What was this witch's name?"

"Clotho," Evander said. "She had two sisters, but I never met them."

Echidna went rigid, her eyes wide. "You speak of the Fates."

Evander's brow furrowed. "The *Fates*? No. They—They wouldn't... They *couldn't*... How were they in the mortal realm?"

"When Apollo sought power, he summoned the Fates to show him his destiny," Echidna said. "He didn't like what he saw, so he cursed them to live out the rest of eternity in the mortal realm, cut off from Elysium.

"In retribution, the Fates made bargains with those who had been similarly punished. They could not help themselves—but they *could* help others." She sucked in a rattling breath. "I thought my Typhon had perished under the volcano. But... if his soul lived on, and Clotho found him... it's possible that she infused his soul into your body to help him escape."

A knot formed in Evander's throat. This entire time, he assumed the witch who had cursed him had merely tricked him, using him for her own amusement.

But she had been trying to free Typhon. She had been trying to free so many others who had suffered because of power-hungry gods like Apollo and Jupiter.

Evander stared at Echidna, his heart wrenching at the look of hope on her face. "I'm sorry," he said quietly. "But Typhon is gone."

Echidna's face fell, her brows drawing together in confusion. "I saw you summon him earlier. He is still a part of you."

"It's temporary. When I was taken to Elysium, the part of my soul that he inhabits was dying. My brother siphoned Typhon's magic out of me, and I have not been able to bring him back since. Not fully."

Echidna fell silent. Behind her, the other Wild Spirits murmured with one another, their whispers echoing in the woods.

"He lingers," Echidna mused, her voice distant. "He waits for me. For *us*." When Evander shook his head, not following her line of thought, she went on, "Typhon and I are still bound. Even through his banishment and his connection with you, he is still bound to his family here. It's why his wings appear ghost-like." She gestured to her own body. "Just like us. He is waiting for us before he finds peace."

"But how can you be freed?" Evander asked. "My immortality—"

"Your immortality would have done nothing for us except grant us one moment of freedom," Echidna said sadly. "There is nothing in all the realms powerful enough to undo Jupiter's curse. Unless..." She faltered, then frowned. "Our curse was linked to Typhon's entrapment. I assumed that, with him dead, we were doomed to an eternity of roaming these woods. But... if he still lives—if he can be freed— perhaps we can, too."

"I don't know how to free him," Evander admitted.

Echidna slithered closer to him, coiling lower to the ground so she could look him in the eye. "You already did. Or, you started to. When you unleashed those wings, that was Typhon trying to get out."

"I release him all the time," Evander said. "It never lasts very long. Perhaps an hour or two, depending on how much energy I'm using. Then, he vanishes."

"Have you ever released him here in the Wilds?"

"Yes. During Apollo's challenge with my brother."

Echidna gasped, then turned to the souls behind her. "How—How did we not know?" Then, her eyes widened. "The Titans. Their magic is potent enough to hide Typhon's essence from us."

"And we remained hidden during that battle," said a soul

behind her with six arms. "We did not want to be discovered, if you recall."

Echidna nodded. She turned to Evander. "Can you try to release him now? Perhaps if I touch him..." She extended a hand to Evander, who instinctively scrambled away from her touch.

Echidna froze, her eyes narrowing.

"You tried to kill me," Evander said. "I haven't forgotten."

"Don't be a fool," Echidna hissed. "Everything has changed now! Can't you see?"

"And what will you do, once Typhon is freed? Will you simply let me go?"

"Of course," she said at once.

Evander huffed a dry laugh. "I don't believe you. You also claimed that losing my immortality would be painless. That I would be nothing more than a mortal. You lied."

Echidna's nostrils flared. "Don't you *want* to free Typhon? I thought he meant something to you."

"He did. But I value my life now—more than I ever did before. I want to *live*. And if freeing Typhon endangers my life, then I won't do it."

"We could just kill you, death god," Echidna snarled. "Nothing is stopping us. We could tie you down and finish what we started."

"You could," Evander agreed. "But if you do, Typhon will never be freed. And you'll never know if you and your family can find peace."

Echidna froze at that, her body rigid. Her lips curled back, baring her teeth. "What do you want, death god? Name your price."

"Swear by your blood," Evander said. "Swear that you will not harm or kill me. And, if by freeing Typhon I am able to set your souls free, I need you to help me and my brother before you cross over."

"Help you?" Echidna laughed harshly. "We would never help the gods. Not after what we have suffered."

"It's a small price to pay for your freedom," Evander said. "You have proven you can still touch, even as ghosts." He gestured to her hand, which still clutched the translucent dagger from before. "You can wield a weapon."

"It takes immense concentration to do this," Echidna argued. "We cannot maintain this for long."

"I don't need you to. We only need the element of surprise. If you are free to come with me to the Realm of Gaia, I need you to help us against the Titans. Just for a moment. For long enough for my brother to overpower them. Please."

Echidna was shaking her head. "You ask too much of us, death god." Behind her, the spirits began to fade.

Evander stood up quickly. "Wait!"

Echidna watched him, eyebrows raised.

"What if I swore to try to free those who were unfairly punished by the gods? To continue Clotho's work?"

"You would offer such a thing to us monsters?"

"You aren't monsters," Evander said softly. "I knew Typhon for a long time. He was vicious and demonic. But he was not a monster. He saved me many times. He saved the woman I love. I would do *anything* for him. And if there are others out there who were dealt unjust fates, then I want to free them as well."

Echidna tilted her head thoughtfully. "This would require you to travel to the mortal realm."

"I understand."

Echidna glanced over her shoulder at the few souls who lingered. They exchanged whispers with one another. Evander strained to listen, but he couldn't make out any words.

At long last, she turned to face him once more, her chin lifting. "Very well, death god. If you also agree to swear in blood, then we will do the same." She lifted the dagger, then dragged it across her other hand. Pearly droplets fell to the ground, sizzling when they met the earth.

It wasn't real blood—Evander knew this. But it was still her essence. Her soul. She was offering it freely to him.

Evander stood, then offered his own hand. With one sharp movement, Echidna sliced into his palm. His own silver blood oozed and dribbled to the ground.

"You first, death god," Echidna said, her eyes flashing with a warning. The threat on her face was evident: if he refused to speak first, the deal was off.

Evander swallowed hard, hoping he was making the right choice. "I, Evander, death god of the Underworld, swear by my blood and soul to exert every effort to free Typhon and his family, provided it does not endanger my own life. I also swear that, if the Wild Spirits are freed and they fulfill their end of the bargain, I will dedicate the rest of my life to freeing those who have been unfairly punished by the gods."

Echidna nodded stiffly to demonstrate her approval. Then, she said, "I, Echidna, Wild Spirit and mate of Typhon, swear by the essence of my soul that neither I, nor my kin, shall harm or kill Evander the death god. I swear that, if we are freed, we shall do battle against the Titans in the mortal realm. And, once our bargain is fulfilled, we vow never to harm Evander or his kin."

Evander's eyes widened at her last sentence. He hadn't demanded this, but it was generous of her to include it. It hadn't occurred to him that, once the spirits were free, they could easily swarm Evander and Cyrus and destroy them.

Echidna offered a faint smile. She was acting in good faith.

And he appreciated her efforts.

"The bargain is struck," he murmured.

"The bargain is struck," she echoed.

Heat exploded in his palm, scorching his skin and burning through his flesh. He hissed, cradling his hand as the agony sliced into him, coursing through his veins. Echidna groaned as well, no doubt experiencing a similar pain.

Evander crashed to his knees, the white-hot fire sizzling along his flesh and bones, melting him, devouring him from the inside out. Gods, it was unbearable. He was going to die...

Just as suddenly as it appeared, the pain vanished. He was gasping on all fours as he struggled to inhale and exhale. Sweat poured down his face. He could still feel an echo of the pain lingering along his skin. When he held up his hand, the cut from their bargain was gone.

Slowly, he rose to his feet, finding Echidna watching him expectantly. "Are you ready, death god?"

Evander nodded, then closed his eyes. He called upon

that fleeting presence of Typhon's ghost. In an instant, he felt his wings form behind him. His fingernails elongated into talons. The weight of his horns settled on his head.

Echidna's eyes grew wide with wonder as she drew closer. "Magnificent," she whispered, reaching a hand to touch him.

This time, Evander did not shrink away. He held still as Echidna ran her finger along the edge of his wing. He shuddered, and a rumbling sound vibrated through him.

Mine, Typhon murmured.

Evander stiffened. "Typhon?"

Echidna froze, but Evander quickly said, "No, keep going. He recognizes you."

Something stirred within Evander—something he had thought was gone forever.

For the first time since he was in Elysium, he felt Typhon rise. Echidna's fingers continued gentle sweeping motions over his wing, and a roar of yearning filled Evander's chest.

Evander closed his eyes with a groan. The strength burning within him was both familiar and foreign all at once. He had forgotten how *powerful* Typhon's presence was.

A shudder rippled over him, and he fell to his knees. Echidna gasped, but Evander shook his head, eyes closing against the intensity of Typhon's emotions. "It's all right," Evander grunted. "It's just... so much."

So much pain.

So much longing.

So much grief.

Mine! Typhon bellowed.

The ground shook, and a resounding cry rattled the trees.

Every single spirit went utterly and perfectly still, including Echidna. A stunned silence followed, broken only by Evander's broken breaths.

Then, after several tense moments, Typhon whispered, *Echidna.*

The word echoed around the forest, and only then did Evander realize the name had burst from his own lips.

But it wasn't his voice—it was Typhon's.

Echidna uttered a sound that was a half laugh, half sob. "Yes, my love. I am here." She drew closer to Evander, running both her hands along his wings now. The acute sensation of her gentle touch sent tremors rippling over Evander's body. Gods, the force of Typhon's desire for her was overwhelming... It almost made *Evander* see Echidna in such a way—her beautiful, shimmering eyes, the lust and longing brimming in her own gaze...

Evander shook his head with another anguished groan. What was wrong with him?

A sudden thought occurred to him, and he huffed a wheezing laugh. "Is this how it was... when you felt what I did for Mona?"

Typhon growled in answer. And Evander had to laugh again.

"I am sorry, old friend, for putting you through that," Evander murmured. He had to close his eyes once more. If he looked at Echidna again, he worried that same maddening lust would overwhelm him.

It was disorienting. Unsettling. *Jarring.*

But he couldn't blame Typhon. The lovers had been separated for a millennia.

"Be free," Evander urged him. "Be with her again, my friend."

Typhon hummed as Echidna continued to stroke him. Her fingers had moved to the small horns atop Evander's head. Evander couldn't stop the low moan from rumbling through him.

"Please," Evander pleaded. "Please, Typhon. Go to her. *Please.*"

"Come to me, my love," Echidna breathed, her soft voice gentle and coaxing.

Typhon seemed to thrash against the restraints of Evander's body. Evander frowned, feeling helpless. Perhaps it was something *he* could do. If *he* was in control of his body right now… could he somehow unlock whatever door Typhon was trapped behind?

Could he let Typhon take over?

Evander recalled that moment from so long ago when he and Typhon had finally merged together. He had no longer seen the demon within him as an adversary or something to fight. He saw Typhon as an equal—another side of himself. A side he had fully accepted and embraced.

Evander didn't realize he was gritting his teeth until he forced himself to relax. He let go. His form sagged as he released all the tension and stiffness in his body.

Be free. He said the words to himself and to Typhon.

Evander could be free.

Typhon could be free.

They could both be released from their chains and bindings. They could both finally *soar.*

A resonant cry tore from Evander's mouth. His back

arched as his voice poured from him, echoing in the vast space and spiraling around him. His arms were rigid, spread on either side of him. Something heavy tugged at his chest, and his cry sharpened in pain. His body jerked wildly as a massive energy violently *ripped* through his chest, tearing through muscle and flesh. His bones shattered. His rib cage cracked. His body was breaking, breaking, breaking... Howling screams filled the woods, sounding more like a feral wolf than his own voice.

His vision blurred, then went black. He fell into nothingness as darkness swallowed him.

He was dead. He had to be. The pain of Typhon tearing through him was too much for his body to bear.

"Wake, prince of death," said a soothing voice.

Evander inhaled a rattling gasp that felt like his first breath of air in days. He sucked in gulps full of it, swallowing greedily, his throat raw and cracked.

Echidna hovered over him, her eyes shining. Her long serpent's tail curled behind her. Dozens of pearly forms lingered beside her, their eyes wide and fixed on something next to Evander.

With a jolt, Evander touched his chest, expecting to find it carved open, to find blood and intestines all over his body.

But there was nothing there. He was unharmed.

And yet... there was something *different* about him. Something empty and yet whole. Something settled and yet unfamiliar.

"Evander," said a deep voice.

Evander tensed, his body rigid as he slowly turned to face the figure next to him.

Gods, it couldn't be...

Towering over him, his wings stretched wide and his massive muscular arms at his sides, was Typhon. He was much taller than Evander, and he had long hair that fell down his back in dark waves. His forehead was elongated, and large tusks protruded from his mouth.

He was every bit the beast Evander envisioned. But... he was *familiar*. Evander knew him almost better than he knew himself.

A stunned laugh burst from Evander's lips. Tears brimmed in his eyes, and he choked on a sob as he beheld Typhon for the first time.

He couldn't believe it. Typhon was free. Typhon was *here*.

Evander stepped toward him—whether to clap him on the back or embrace him, he wasn't sure—but then he stopped, his expression falling.

Typhon had the same shimmering silver form as Echidna and the rest of the spirits.

He was dead.

"You—You—" Evander's voice broke, and he couldn't speak around the lump in his throat.

Typhon's mouth twitched in what appeared to be a smile. It was difficult to tell around his massive tusks. "I am well, brother. I am *home*."

Gods, that deep, resonant voice was so easily recognizable. It felt like Evander was speaking to himself.

Echidna slithered forward, her arm sliding around Typhon's waist and pulling him closer. He towered over her, but as he gazed down at her, the soft, tender glow on his face was unmistakable.

Evander's chest swelled with something akin to relief. Yes, he could tell by the look of contentment and peace on Typhon's face that he was truly home now.

"We owe you a debt, death prince," Echidna said, tearing her gaze away from her lover to cast a grateful look at Evander. She inclined her head deeply, a sign of respect which Evander returned.

"A debt we intend to pay in full," Typhon added.

Evander blinked, tears still leaking from his eyes. "Can you?" His voice was barely a breath. He didn't dare hope, didn't dare believe that Jupiter's curse had truly been broken.

"Can't you feel it?" Typhon asked. His left arm was wrapped around Echidna, but his right stretched outward, gesturing to the surrounding forest.

Evander's brow furrowed as he looked around. The spirits were there, just as they had been before.

Then, he realized—the woods were silent and still. There were no whispers or murmurs. No haunted sounds flitting around the wood.

The spirits before him were no longer wayward. They had found their home. The path before them was finally clear, and they could know rest.

They stayed... for *him.*

To repay their debt.

Evander's chest swelled, and he grinned at Typhon. Echidna burrowed closer to her lover, her eyes closed and a small smile on her face. Typhon laughed, the sound deep and vibrant as it carried through the forest.

"Lead the way, old friend," Typhon said. "Today, we fight as brothers in arms. One last time."

ENTRANCED

CYRUS

HE HAS TAKEN THE FORM OF A SIREN.

The words echoed in Cyrus's mind, making him go numb with horror and dread. He was just about to ask which Titan had done this when several deep, thundering blasts shook the ground.

Cyrus instinctively grabbed Prue, his hands on her arms as he pulled her against him. The rumbling continued, and Cyrus looked around, eyes narrowing as he tried to identify the new threat.

"It's footsteps," Mona whispered, crouching close to the ground, no doubt so she could avoid toppling over from the earthquake.

"Yes," murmured the siren beside them, still using Evander's voice to speak. "More than one Titan has altered himself."

Cyrus's blood ran cold. "Speak plainly," he said impatiently. "Tell us what has happened."

"Of the three Titans," said the siren, "one has become a siren. Another, a Cyclops. And the third, a chimera."

"Good gods," Cyrus breathed in horror, his flesh tingling from unease. It was unnatural. It was shocking.

And... *impossible.* How had the Titans managed this?

"Did they acquire more magic to do this?" Mona mused, clearly wondering the same thing. She seemed more curious than horrified, and Cyrus wondered if the revelation hadn't fully registered for her yet. Beside him, Prue's face had turned ashen, her mouth twisting into a grimace.

"I am not sure," the siren admitted. "We sirens cannot sense magic on other creatures."

"Are you bonded to one of them?" Prue asked. "The Titan who is a siren—if we hurt him, will you be hurt as well?"

"No. Not even Titan magic can forge a bond between sirens. He is *not* one of us." The siren spoke with venom, warping Evander's voice into something unrecognizable.

Prue exhaled, her eyes closing for a moment before she met Cyrus's gaze. He saw relief on her face, and he knew she was hesitant to attack a Titan if she knew it would hurt the entire pack of sirens.

But Cyrus would not have hesitated. Regardless of his wife's sympathy toward the creatures, he would not have batted an eye at the casualties lost if it meant he could erase the Titans from existence.

Prue seemed to notice the hardness etched on his face. Her expression turned stony, and she looked away. The thundering footsteps continued, drawing closer.

Mona looked up toward the sky, her brows drawing

together."This is one of them," she murmured. "I can smell his magic from here."

Cyrus inhaled deeply, and there it was. The pungent aroma of Titan magic. He hadn't noticed it before—perhaps because he often smelled it on himself, thanks to his Titan powers.

"He approaches," the siren warned, rising so it stood on its talons. It tilted its head toward the sky, black eyes flashing. "The one who poses as my kind."

Prue frowned. "The *siren* is—" She broke off as another loud *boom* interrupted her. "It's making *those* sounds?"

Cyrus shared her confusion. How could a siren be massive enough to cause the ground to shake?

The siren in front of them uttered a loud squawk and suddenly bolted for the sky, disappearing in a haze of smoke.

"Wait!" Prue called, stretching her hand as if she could call the creature back.

"Mona," Cyrus said stiffly, his gaze narrowing toward the sky. "Can you conjure that dome of branches again?"

In answer, a cocoon of vines and leaves formed around them, shrouding them from the mist and muffling the echoing booms that were growing closer.

It wouldn't do much. But perhaps it could conceal them from view for long enough for them to get their bearings.

Cyrus still had no idea what was coming. And clearly, it was fearsome enough to frighten away the sirens.

He peered through the leaves, holding his breath as he waited. The heavy footsteps drew closer. The ground shuddered with each sound. The mist began to clear, parting for whatever approached.

Prue suddenly uttered a sharp gasp, then covered her mouth. Her body was trembling, and her eyes filled with tears.

"What is it?" Cyrus turned to her. She was peering through the leaves on the opposite side, away from him. She shook her head, tears spilling down her face.

Cyrus followed her gaze, his fingers brushing leaves out of the way, and his heart dropped to his stomach.

Five bodies were strewn on the ground, limbs jutting out at odd angles. Scorch marks covered their faces, making them almost unrecognizable. Each one wore a familiar suit of armor.

It was the fire witches. They lay on the ground, eyes wide and motionless, staring into nothing.

All five of them were dead. And they had only been steps away, concealed by the mist.

"No," Mona breathed, her face as pale as death. "H-How?"

"Their bodies are burned," Cyrus said solemnly. "If I had to guess, I would say the sirens convinced them to destroy each other." A hard lump formed in his throat, and he suddenly found it difficult to breathe. "They—They never stood a chance. We possess god blood, and it made us strong enough to withstand their call. But the witches..." He trailed off, his eyes closing. Rage and regret swarmed in his chest, threatening to suffocate him.

He understood the sirens had been acting on the Titans' orders. But suddenly, he wanted to wring each of those damned birds' necks for retribution. Farah was dead. The *coven leader* who had trusted Cyrus enough to fight alongside him was dead.

And he hadn't been able to stop it. He had done nothing.

Images of Lagos's broken body flashed in his mind. Once more, the lives of good people had been lost because of *him*. He was not a brave enough or strong enough leader to protect them. Prue and Mona would likely die, too.

What was he even doing here? How could he win this battle?

"Cyrus." Prue's warm hands were on his face, forcing him to meet her gaze. "Stay with me. We can do this. We—We knew there would be casualties." Her voice broke on the words, and her eyes sparkled with tears. But her expression was fierce as she looked at him. "*Do not leave me.* Stay and fight with me." She pressed a hard kiss to his lips. A faint tendril of heat coiled in his chest from the commanding way she claimed his mouth with her own.

When she withdrew, her gaze was pleading, begging him to stay alert. To breathe. To fight.

He had to fight. For her. For his people.

Cyrus brought his forehead to hers and focused on her breaths. In and out. In and out. After a moment, his panicked breathing leveled, matching the rhythm of her inhales and exhales.

He pulled away to look her in the eyes. Before he could speak, something crashed into their dome of branches. Leaves and twigs went flying. Cyrus, Prue, and Mona collapsed in a heap of vines and foliage.

A deep, guttural roar pierced the air, making Cyrus's ears rattle and his skull throb. He rolled, wincing when a sharp thorn pierced his skin. He found Prue's hand and clutched it in his, relieved to feel her squeezing back.

A massive dark shape hovered over them, far bigger than the sirens they had just faced. This one was three times as tall, its inky wings spread wide. Its talons alone were nearly as long as Cyrus was tall. Instead of the face of a woman, this creature wore a face that was all too familiar. Green skin. Malicious black eyes. And a pair of white horns.

Oceanus.

Cyrus started at the creature, utterly confused. While Oceanus's appearance was horrifying, his body wasn't large enough to make such thundering footsteps. And even if it was... it would have just *flown* to them instead of walked.

So, what giant creature had made such booming footsteps? What else was out there?

Before Cyrus could think on it any longer, Oceanus spoke.

"*Come to me,*" he crooned. His booming voice resonated around them, brushing against Cyrus's skin and warming his blood. He found himself shifting through the leaves, desperate to draw nearer to the magnificent beast before him. Prue and Mona did the same, scrambling over one another to get closer.

Oceanus laughed at their response. "Such feeble, malleable minds," he taunted. "This will be far too easy."

Cyrus blinked, shaking his head violently to clear the fog in his mind. Oceanus's siren call was far stronger than the others. Cyrus grabbed Prue and Mona by the arms, halting them before they dived for Oceanus. Their eyes were vacant and hazy, drawn in by the lure of the siren call.

"*Bow before me,*" Oceanus commanded.

Cyrus's back bowed obediently, his body responding without his permission. He gritted his teeth, trying to resist, but it felt like an invisible hand was pushing on his spine, forcing him to bow.

He grunted, warring with himself, trying to gain control. "You... *coward*," he spat, gasping for breath.

Oceanus's dark eyes glittered. "Coward? I think not. I'm stronger than *any* of you pathetic little gods."

"Prove it," Cyrus snarled. "Stop hiding behind your siren lure. Make this a fair fight, and let's see how strong you are."

Oceanus hesitated, his eyes narrowing. Suddenly, he hissed, launching forward and pinning Mona to the ground with his talons. Only then did Cyrus notice the vines that had been snaking toward the Titan in an attempt to wrap around him.

Mona had been trying to attack him from behind with her magic.

She yelped and struggled, shoving against Oceanus. But her attempts were futile. His massive form crushed her, and his talons dug into her flesh. Mona's scream filled the air.

"Mona!" Prue surged forward, but Oceanus's head snapped up, his eyes flaring.

"*Kill him,*" he hissed with his siren call. "*The death god did this to your sister. Kill him now.*"

Prue stiffened, her body freezing in place. Her arms locked at her sides, and her back was rigid. Slowly, she turned to glare at Cyrus, her lavender eyes milky and unfocused.

"Prue," Cyrus said slowly, raising his hands. "Listen to me..."

Prue bared her teeth, then spread her arms wide. The earth cracked, and thorny brambles shot forward, wrapping around Cyrus's legs.

"No!" he bellowed before crashing to his knees. He severed the vines with his lightning but halted when Prue drew closer. He didn't want to strike her.

Her face was contorted with fury, making her unrecognizable. She had never looked at him like this before.

"Prue," he begged. "It's *me*. You can fight this. I know you're strong enough."

Prue kicked him in the chest, sending him sprawling. She aimed to kick him again, but he grabbed her ankle and twisted. With a yelp, she fell to the ground. Cyrus jumped to his feet, climbing atop her and pinning her with his knees. He grabbed her wrists before she could strike him again.

"Look at me!" he cried. "Prue, fight it!"

She snarled and hissed like a feral animal, her eyes still clouded from Oceanus's influence.

She was fully entranced. There was no reaching her. This was not his wife. This was someone else—a vessel of Oceanus.

With a roar, Cyrus reached toward Oceanus, flinging a bolt of lightning straight into the Titan. Oceanus shrieked, toppling from the force of it. The smell of burned feathers filled the air.

But Prue took advantage of Cyrus's distraction. One of her branches lashed his arm, drawing blood. Vines coiled around his arms, tugging him violently until he crashed to the earth, his head slamming into the hard ground. Stars danced in his vision, and darkness crept toward him, threatening to drag him to unconsciousness.

Prue stalked toward him, her face as impassive as ever. More vines encircled Cyrus, tethering his wrists and ankles to the ground. He tugged fruitlessly against them, struggling in vain to free himself.

"Prue," he rasped. "Please."

Prue said nothing as she hovered over him. In her hand, she conjured a long, jagged branch with a tip as sharp as a spear.

Cyrus felt the blood drain from his face. Oh, gods. She was going to kill him. "Prue!" he bellowed.

A scream echoed, and Prue froze, tilting her head slightly toward the sound.

It was Mona. Oceanus had embedded one of his talons straight through her thigh.

Prue's nostrils flared, her eyes burning with clarity. "M-Mona?"

"*Finish him!*" Oceanus hissed. "*Kill the death god!*"

Prue's breath hitched, her eyes going milky once more. Her body jerked and twitched unnaturally. She raised the branch in her hands, aiming for Cyrus's chest.

A brilliant blast of white light filled the air, momentarily blinding Cyrus. He turned his head, eyes closing against the force of it.

Then, dozens—no, *hundreds*—of voices echoed around him, reverberating as if he stood in a massive cavern.

Oceanus screamed, and then came the sound of a blade slicing into flesh.

Prue groaned and fell to her knees, gasping for breath. Her vines loosened, and Cyrus tore them away, rushing to her side. She was coughing up blood, her face pale and her eyes haunted.

But they were *her* eyes. Brilliant lavender. They stared at him with stark clarity.

Cyrus's hands were shaking as he clutched her shoulders. "Thank the gods." He pulled her against his chest, massaging her back and stroking her curls. She clung to him weakly, still reeling from Oceanus's violent control over her body.

Cyrus looked over her shoulder, his gaze fixed on the sky, trying to make sense of what he was seeing. Thousands of white blurry shapes danced in the air, flitting about with such speed that Cyrus couldn't make out any details. Somewhere close by, Oceanus was screeching. The sounds of flesh tearing and ripping still filled the air.

Someone—*something*—was attacking the Titan.

Then, a figure appeared who Cyrus would recognize anywhere. He stood out amongst the white lights around him, his dark clothes a sharp contrast against the luminescent chaos.

His face taut with concern, Evander hovered over Mona's prone figure. He bound the bleeding wound in her thigh, then gathered her into his arms, his eyes burning with fury.

Then, he met Cyrus's gaze and hurried toward him, still carrying Mona.

"You—You aren't real," Cyrus said in a strained voice. Surely, this had to be a trick from Oceanus. Or perhaps one of the other sirens.

Evander offered a grim smile. "I'm afraid I am, brother.

And I'm not alone." He glanced up at the sky, then frowned. "Are those..." He trailed off as several loud squawks and screeches echoed nearby.

Cyrus squinted upward, then noticed the frantic beating of black wings darting between the pearly forms in the sky. A savage smile spread across his face. "The sirens. They're fighting back."

Evander looked at him in confusion. "*Sirens*?"

"Evander," Mona croaked, gripping his arm, her eyes weak. "What—What have you done?"

Evander brushed sweaty strands of hair away from her face. "I'm here, my love. And I've brought an army with me." He looked at Cyrus with determination and pride on his face. "I have freed the Wild Spirits, and they are here to fight for us."

SEPARATE
TRIVIA

THE SIGHT OF THE GIANT CYCLOPS TOWERING OVER Sol—large enough to crush the sun god in his massive fist—should have struck Trivia with fear. She should have been cowering from the monster before her.

But instead, she felt nothing but rage, raw and untethered.

Pandora had dabbled in these same dark powers, conjuring all manner of foul creatures and beasts, intent on unleashing chaos on the three realms and watching everything burn. And even after Pandora had been silenced, her soul still lived on—along with the dark forces of her box.

And Trivia was done with it. She was *finished* with these deities who believed they could wield powers beyond their capabilities. She was fed up with those who sought to control others, who created monstrous nightmares just for the sake of power.

She was sick of people trying to use her as a puppet, as a pawn in their game.

Atlas thought himself to be the puppet master, pulling strings and organizing chaos over the realms, just like Pandora.

And, just like Pandora, Trivia would destroy him, too.

While Atlas leered at Sol—clearly relishing the way the sun god's face paled, his eyes wide with fear—Trivia closed her eyes and summoned her mental construct. Just like Midas had taught, she envisioned the beach in Elysium where she and Sol had gone swimming. The waves lapping. The sun beating down on her. The warm sand between her toes.

Within the safety of her mental construct, Trivia drew on her power. It burst forth, eager and ready. She spread her hands, and vines coiled around her wrists and forearms, climbing up her body. The ground trembled, and roots and branches sprang forth. She pulled more power, more energy from the earth, calling on every drop of magic. Bushes and shrubs appeared. Thick and sturdy tree trunks rose, climbing higher and higher until they provided a canopy of shade above her. Their branches stretched on and on.

When Trivia was surrounded by a lush jungle, the evidence of her power, she blinked, bringing herself back to reality. Atlas turned to face her, clearly sensing the magic emanating from her. Her hands glowed white, and with a shout, she thrust them toward the Titan.

Power slammed into him, sending him careening backward. The ground trembled when he fell, but Trivia didn't stop there. She conjured vines as thick as ropes that slithered around Atlas like snakes. They coiled tightly around his wrists and ankles.

He roared, thrashing against the restraints. They snapped easily, but Trivia was relentless. Vine after vine encircled him. When one broke, three more tightened around him.

Atlas's single eye was blazing with fury as he snarled. A jet of gold light speared directly into his face, blinding him. Atlas howled, his eye closing, tears leaking from it.

Trivia glanced at Sol, who stood next to her, wielding his own magic. He nodded at her, his jaw tense and his face determined. He was still pale, the fear in his eyes evident. But he was here with her, and he was fighting.

Just like they promised.

"We don't stop," Trivia vowed to him. "Not until this is over."

"Together," he agreed.

They closed in on Atlas, assaulting him with their magic. His shrieks of pain rang in the air, echoing around them. Trivia pushed and pushed, drawing more of her power. The ground split. Roots climbed forward. One of them impaled Atlas's shoulder, the tree growing straight through his body. Black blood oozed, spilling onto the ground like ink.

Trivia gritted her teeth, feeling the strain of pushing too far. She wasn't accustomed to so much magic flooding through her so quickly. She was going to burn out soon.

But it wasn't enough. Atlas needed to *die.* This wouldn't be over until he was destroyed.

"Do you have enough power to fully blind him?" Trivia asked Sol, pausing to wipe sweat from her brow.

"I—I don't know," he panted. "Hold him down, I'll get closer."

"Be careful!" she called as he inched around the massive body tied to the ground, still struggling against the vines.

He was too strong. And Trivia couldn't keep conjuring vines forever.

Atlas shifted, making the ground tremble. Sol cried out, and Trivia's heart seized in her chest. She flexed her hands, calling on more power, thickening the vines and wrapping several around Atlas's throat.

"Sol?" she called, squinting through the fog that lingered in the air. Atlas's body was so large that she couldn't see his head. After a moment, she made out Sol's brilliant magic, piercing through the fog.

"I'm all right," Sol answered, voice echoing. "The bastard tried to bite me." More light flooded through, and Atlas roared. "Trivia, shut your eyes."

Trivia obeyed, turning to bury her face into her shoulder. Streams of light shot through the air, burning against her skin. She groaned as the heat scorched her, causing sweat to pour down her body in rivulets.

Atlas's scream was devastating. It filled the air, shrill and resonant, making Trivia's ears numb. The sound rattled through her, making her bones quiver. It seemed to ring forever, an endless echo of torment. She wouldn't be surprised if it even reached Elysium and the Underworld.

It was never-ending. She would hear that sound for the rest of her existence.

With a groan, Trivia sank to her knees, slamming her hands over her ears. Gods, she would never hear again after this. Atlas might be blind, but she was deaf. Even after his scream faded, her own ears continued ringing with the sound. It haunted her, forever imprinting on her brain.

Warm hands grasped her arms, and she shrieked, the sound muffled as she struggled against her assailant. When her eyes opened, she found Sol before her, saying something she couldn't understand. It sounded like he was underwater, his voice mangled and distorted.

She shook her head, not understanding. Sol jerked his thumb toward Atlas, then covered his own eyes. "Blind," he mouthed with a sure nod.

Trivia managed a grin, despite her still ringing ears.

Something heavy slammed into her, sending her flying. Her stomach dropped, her body weightless for a moment before she crashed to the ground, arms scraping and shoulder colliding with the hard earth. Her head struck rocks, making her vision darken. She slumped over, pain ricocheting through her body in sickening waves. She tried to move, to shake her head and climb to her feet, but her body was broken. Her foot was jutting at an odd angle, and when she tried to move it, fresh pain shot up her leg.

"Trivia!" Sol bellowed, his voice distant. Gods, how far had she fallen? And what had struck her?

In answer, Atlas's rasping laugh boomed. His foot sank to the ground with a deafening *crash.*

He had managed to kick Trivia.

"You fools," he snarled. The ground trembled as he moved, no longer restrained by Trivia's vines. "You think blinding me changed anything?"

Trivia was gasping, struggling to draw air. She needed to

move. But something pressed on her chest, cutting off her breaths. Hot liquid ran down her side—blood.

Sol's sun magic burst in the air, igniting the sky. The ground shook, and Sol cried out.

"No!" Trivia screamed, blood bubbling from her lips. "Come *on!*" she growled at herself. She managed to roll, her shoulder throbbing and agony making her limbs quiver. When she was on her stomach, she tried drawing her legs up to rise on all fours. But gods, her *leg...* It was surely broken. She couldn't even stand, let alone walk.

She couldn't get to Sol.

Tears streamed down her face. "*Sol!*"

She waited for him to answer, to assure her he was still alive. But there was nothing but silence. Until—

Another scream echoed, but it wasn't Sol or Atlas. It was a woman, and her voice was familiar.

Trivia stilled, her eyes growing wide. She *knew* that voice.

It was her sister, Mona.

"Mona?" Trivia called. Then, louder, "*Mona!*"

Atlas moved, and the earth quivered, making Trivia slide sideways. Her head lolled, and she couldn't stop herself from shifting in the dirt. Her head met something hard, and she groaned as that same darkness threatened to take over, to pull her under.

Stay awake, she commanded. *Stay awake!*

"Be silent, witch goddess," Atlas snarled, his voice closer than before. His foul breath stung her nostrils, and she knew his head was close by. Maybe she could grab a branch and shove it down his throat.

Then, his words sank in. *Be silent.*

He didn't want her calling out for Mona. But... why?

Trivia spat blood onto the ground, then barked, "Where are your other Titan friends? Fighting you is too easy, and I need a challenge."

Atlas growled, the sound rumbling through her. Oh yes, he was definitely close now. Even blind, he could easily follow the sound of her jeering voice and crush her.

But she had to keep going. She had to know...

"Well?" Trivia challenged. "Where are they? Or are they already dead? I wouldn't be surprised."

"I am not alone!" Atlas bellowed. "My brothers are here. But I am strong enough to defeat you on my own."

"Liar," Trivia said with a wheezing laugh. She spit out more blood, then crooned, "Where are you, Titans? Show yourself before I cut off Atlas's head!"

A crash echoed, and cracks spread from the ground. Atlas had slammed something heavy into the earth—his fist, perhaps?

"I do not need them!" Atlas shouted. "Besides, they have better things to do than argue with a dying goddess."

"I don't believe you!" Trivia said. "I bet my sisters killed them."

"No!" Atlas roared. "It's impossible. Without you—" He stopped abruptly, but a triumphant smile spread across Trivia's face.

That was it. The Titans were keeping her apart from her sisters.

Gods above, Trivia realized. *The power of the Triple Goddess...*

It could only be accessed after the three sisters died and

then returned. Mona's words echoed in her mind: *The three of us were bound by a powerful enchantment that kept us locked in our mortal bodies. Only upon death can our true powers be freed.*

The Titans wanted to stop them from reuniting. With Trivia brought back from death, nothing was stopping them from joining their powers... except the space separating them.

Trivia tried to push up with her arms, but all it achieved was more excruciating pain. *Dammit*! She couldn't move. She couldn't get to Mona.

Healing powers, she thought. *I did it before. I can do it again.* Her arm trembling, Trivia lifted a hand and summoned her power. A feeble white glow resonated from her palm. She drew more, picturing her mental construct, thinking of those shimmering waters...

"Come on," she urged. Heat burned in her hand as she brought it to her chest, pressing down. She urged more power into her own body, willing it to heal her, to knit her skin and bones back together. "*Heal!*" she commanded.

Warmth flooded her body, but it was fleeting. It flared, then diminished, as if that one singular burst was all the strength she had.

She groaned, dropping her arm by her side. Then, she froze. Her ankle still throbbed, but... her wounds were no longer bleeding. She lifted her head tentatively.

No pain. She was weak, but *some* of her wounds had been healed.

She could work with this.

"Are you still alive?" Trivia called, pretending she was too wounded to do anything but tease Atlas. "Or did my cutting words finally end your pitiful existence?"

She managed to climb on all fours. Panting, she used her good leg to boost herself upright. She tested the weight on her injured leg, then immediately buckled.

No. That wouldn't do.

But if she had one good leg, then she could limp. Or at least hop.

She could *move*. This was progress.

"Sol, where are you?" Trivia whispered, her throat burning with emotions she didn't want to think about. He had to be nearby. Surely he was just unconscious. Atlas must have knocked him out. That was all. He would rise soon.

She kept telling herself this, unwilling to consider the alternative.

"If the other Titans are *really* still alive," Trivia said loudly, shuffling forward, hobbling on her good leg. "Then, how many of you are left? It can't be more than two, right?"

One for her, one for Prue and Mona, who were likely together. The perfect distractions, keeping the three sisters apart.

It was a brilliant plan. Atlas was so massive that it would be easy for him to serve as a literal barrier between the sisters.

But if Trivia could inch past him... He was blind, after all.

She just had to do it as quietly as possible.

Atlas said nothing, and Trivia huffed a laugh. "I'm right, aren't I? It's just two of you!"

"Wrong," hissed a voice. It wasn't Atlas.

Several figures appeared through the mist, making Trivia go still, her insides twisting with dread.

No, she thought in horror. *No, it can't be this many...*

A lion's head appeared first, teeth bared and eyes dark with rage. It inched closer, followed by... a *goat?*

Trivia sucked in a sharp breath. This was a chimera. Part lion, part goat, and part serpent.

Because *of course* the Titans would summon a chimera.

Except...

Trivia squinted, making out *four* heads in the mist. The lion prowled closer, and another head appeared—the serpent. Then the third, which was the goat.

When the fourth one came into view, Trivia's blood chilled. It belonged to a purple-faced demon, who leered at her. A dozen inky black eyes dotted his face like that of a spider.

This was no ordinary chimera. Tentacles extended from its torso. Gryphon wings stretched from its sides.

Four heads. Spider eyes. Several various animal appendages.

This was a mutation. An abomination. A *nightmare.*

"What—What are you?" Trivia breathed, drawing back a step. Her ankle throbbed, and she lifted it slightly, trying to alleviate some of the pain.

"I am Prometheus," said the creature. "And I have a gift for you, little goddess."

His long tentacle stretched forward, wrapped around a limp figure. Trivia's heart lurched at the sight. It was Gaia, and she was unconscious. Silver blood surrounded a wound on her temple.

"I will give her to you," Prometheus said, "if you leave this realm and never return."

Trivia's throat tightened. She couldn't tear her gaze from her mother. Gaia looked so weak. Her skin was wan, her eyes red-rimmed and lined with shadows.

No, Trivia thought, her body numb with dread.

"But, if you don't," Prometheus continued, "I will kill her." The tentacle tightened around Gaia, and her body went rigid.

"Stop," Trivia said quickly, and Prometheus obeyed. Gaia's head lolled slightly as the tentacle loosened its hold.

Trivia needed time. She needed him to believe she was considering his offer.

"Where is Sol?" she demanded.

"The sun god? I do not know. The last I saw, Atlas crushed him with his foot. He is likely dead."

No, no, no...

"I'm not leaving without him!" Trivia snarled. "Give him to me."

Prometheus bared his teeth, revealing fangs as sharp as a shark's teeth. "You reject my gift?"

"If you give me Gaia and Sol, I swear I'll leave. But not without both of them."

The Titans were hiding something. If they were truly as powerful as they claimed, they would have killed her by now. Something was stopping them, and Trivia needed to figure out what it was.

Prometheus exhaled a long sigh before calling into the mist. "Atlas! Where is that wretched sun god you disposed of?"

Trivia closed her eyes. *No. It's not true. Sol is alive.*

A rumble rippled over the earth as Atlas shifted. "He is here," the Titan said before depositing another limp form on the ground between Prometheus and Trivia.

"*Sol!*" Trivia cried, hobbling forward. He, too, was unconscious, his face covered in blood. She sank to her knees next to him, brushing strands of sticky hair away from his face. "What—What have you done to him?"

"He got in my way," Atlas growled.

Trivia leaned closer, pressing her ear to Sol's chest.

There it was—a heartbeat. It was faint, but it was *there*.

Relief spread through Trivia. But she wasn't free yet.

"Leave," Prometheus hissed at her. "As you promised."

Think, think, think, Trivia said to herself. She was injured. Gaia and Sol were unconscious. What could she do?

She was completely alone.

Except...

"How am I to carry them?" Trivia protested. Behind her, where Prometheus couldn't see, she pressed her hand into the earth, calling forth her power. "Can't you provide me with something?"

Prometheus made a guttural sound of annoyance. His serpent tail coiled behind him, and the lion bared its teeth with a warning growl. "You ask for too much, goddess. Now leave before my lion tears out your throat."

"It's a bit unreasonable, don't you think?" Trivia summoned more power. Leaves hissed along the ground, obeying her command. They slithered around Sol and Gaia, knitting together underneath them. "If you want me to leave *immediately,* you should provide me with a way to transport them. Otherwise I could be here for days, and that would go against our agreement." She blinked rapidly, dizziness clouding her mind. She was pushing too far again... but she had to keep going.

A long vine coiled along the ground beside her, creeping forward. She kept it going, on and on...

Find her, she urged the vine. *Find Mona.*

"You try my patience," Prometheus snapped. "This is your last warning, or I'll—"

"Kill me?" Trivia asked. "Well, go ahead. I'm at your mercy. I can't leave without Sol or Gaia, and, to be perfectly frank, I think my leg is broken. So I can't exactly run away from you. It might be best to just kill me."

Prometheus went still, his several eyes narrowing at her with suspicion. "You want me to kill you?"

"Well, I *am* in a lot of pain, so..." Trivia shrugged as if this weren't a big deal at all. "I mean, I *could* just wander this wasteland until I find my sisters. I know Mona is an excellent healer, so she could easily mend my broken bones..."

"No," Prometheus barked. "You swore you would *leave.*"

"I cannot walk," Trivia said slowly, as if she were speaking to someone rather dim-witted. "Why won't you do it? Just kill me, Prometheus. End my suffering. Go ahead."

She held still, waiting. Calling his bluff.

She knew he wouldn't do it.

When Prometheus didn't move, Trivia laughed. "You can't, can you? But *why*? You had no trouble destroying gods the first time."

Something tugged on her vine, and a voice called out in the distance. *Mona's* voice.

Prometheus stiffened. The goat head bleated loudly. "What have you done?" he roared.

"*Now!*" Trivia shouted.

The vine pulled taut, and she grabbed it. With a sharp yank, the vine dragged her along the ground. She, Gaia, and Sol rested on a bed of leaves, and the vines dragged them almost like a sled. The ground was bumpy and rocky, and the leaves provided little protection. Trivia winced and groaned with each sharp jab, then glanced at Gaia and Sol, worried their wounds would worsen from the jolting and bumping.

The ground rumbled, and Atlas roared. Trivia glanced over her shoulder, noticing his massive shape lumbering toward them.

Trivia held her breath, staring in the distance as the vine continued pulling them forward. Surely, they had to be close now. The leaves hissed along the ground, and they sounded so loud to her ears. She knew Atlas would find them.

The thundering steps drew nearer. Trivia grabbed Sol and Gaia's hands, prepared to cling to them if Atlas tried anything...

A shadow slammed into the ground in front of her, making her scream. The vine snapped as Prometheus crept toward her, his gryphon wings spread wide. Gods, how many animal body parts did he possess? He truly *was* an abomination.

Black eyes glittered with malice as he drew closer. "You think you can outsmart me?" he hissed. The lion's maw dripped with saliva as he gazed hungrily at her.

Trivia reached, trying to summon more vines, but she was spent. She had no more power to draw from.

Before Trivia could react, Prometheus's tentacle snatched Gaia, then pulled her toward him.

"No!" Trivia shrieked, hands outstretched as if she could grab Gaia by sheer will power.

"I warned you," Prometheus snarled. His tentacle tightened, and a loud *crack* echoed. Gaia's back bowed, her body going limp.

Trivia's chest hollowed. She gaped in horror at her mother's lifeless form.

No.

No…

Prometheus's tentacle drew back before flinging Gaia into the air. Trivia's scream died in her throat as she watched her mother go flying, her body twisting and distorting before it vanished in the mist.

Trivia slumped to the ground, her body numb. She couldn't think. Couldn't breathe.

"I may not be able to kill you," Prometheus said softly as he closed the distance between them. "But I can make you suffer. And I can start by making you watch as I kill *him*."

The tentacle wrapped around Sol's waist.

"*No!*" Trivia sobbed, lunging as she gripped Sol's chest with both arms, tightening her hold on him.

I will not lose him.

I will not lose anyone else.

The tentacle pulled. Sol slipped from her grasp.

A beam of gold light appeared, burning and brilliant. Trivia gasped, squinting against the intensity of it.

Sol?

But no... She glanced at him, and he was still unconscious.

Then, what—

An echoing battle cry rang out, followed by a crowd of voices. Hurried footsteps drew closer. Jets of light—gold, violet, and green—shot through the air. One of them struck Prometheus's goat head, which bleated loudly before drooping. For a moment, Trivia thought it had died, but... it was *snoring*.

The goat had fallen asleep.

What the hell?

Blinking through tears, Trivia lifted her head as a figure appeared through the mist, wielding a giant sword. With a grunt, he swung and chopped off the serpent's head, making Prometheus scream.

Midas lowered his sword, then met Trivia's gaze. All she could do was stare at him, her mouth hanging open in shock.

"You—You're *here*?" she squeaked.

He grinned. "Sorry it took so long. Some of the gods needed... convincing."

Trivia's wide eyes fixed on the figures who appeared behind him. She recognized some, but not all of them. There was Hypnos, the god of sleep—he must have rendered the goat unconscious. Deimos, Eris, and Morpheus... There were at least a dozen gods, many whom Trivia had never seen before.

Midas knelt by her side, his grim gaze fixed on Sol. He pressed a hand to his nephew's forehead, muttering words in a language Trivia couldn't understand. Gold light shone in the air, and the blood vanished on Sol's head.

Midas waited, then his brow furrowed. "Damn. I was hoping by sealing the wound, he would wake." He shared a regretful look with Trivia. "I'm afraid that's all I can do until we can find a proper healer."

"How did you even get here?" Trivia asked, still in shock. More jets of light burst in the air as the other gods fought with Prometheus. The lion's roar echoed around them.

"I created a portal," Midas said. "It wasn't easy, and I needed Clotho's help."

"*Clotho* is with you?" Trivia asked. "You got the Fates on your side?"

"Well, just one. The other two wouldn't come." He peered around, squinting in the fog. "Where are your sisters?"

"I—I don't know," Trivia said. "I need to get to them. Together, we can merge our powers and defeat the Titans. They're trying to keep us apart."

Midas nodded, extending a hand to help her to her feet. "Say no more. We can keep them busy while you get to your sisters."

"But, Sol—" Trivia cast a worried look at the sun god, who was still unconscious.

"I'll look after him," Midas said solemnly. "You have my word. Now, *go*."

Before Trivia could reply, Midas let out a deep bellow, slashing his sword and cutting off the lion's head. Prometheus screamed with rage and anguish.

"Go!" Midas shouted, striking with his sword again, which the tentacle managed to block.

Trivia cast one last look at Sol, vowing to return to him,

before she hobbled away as fast as her injured leg could carry her.

DESPERATION
PRUE

PRUE'S HEAD WAS A MASS OF MUDDLED CONFUSION. Oceanus had ripped through her, tearing apart her mind and her thoughts, infiltrating without permission. He had warped her senses, twisted her imagination, and painted Cyrus to be the villain.

She had lost all sense of control. All sense of who she was.

Everything she knew had been ripped from her.

And when Oceanus was jerked violently from her mind, the blazing clarity that overcame her was enough to make her ill. Her stomach churned. Her skin pebbled. Her blood chilled. She had no sense of right and wrong. She could only stare in numb horror while Cyrus lovingly stroked her—as if she needed comforting. As if she hadn't been about to impale him and watch the life leave his eyes.

She had been about to murder her husband. And if the

strange pearly ghosts in the sky hadn't stopped Oceanus, she would have done it.

"Prue, darling," Cyrus whispered, still running his fingers through her hair. "Our fight isn't over yet. Stay with me."

Bile climbed up her throat and she swallowed hard, not wanting to vomit all over him. But Goddess, she couldn't do this. The horrifying image of her hovering over Cyrus while he looked at her in terror and regret kept flashing through her mind.

She couldn't escape it. This would haunt her forever.

"Prue." Cyrus withdrew to look at her, his blue eyes intense and fierce. He framed her face with both hands. "You did not kill me. I am still here. What Oceanus did to you was terrible, and he deserves to be punished for it. But *I am still here.*" He took her hand and pressed it to his chest. There, underneath his torn tunic, she could feel the rapid thundering of his heartbeat.

The pulsing rhythm was soothing to her. She closed her eyes, focusing on that familiar pounding.

Thump, thump.

Thump, thump.

She listened to it for several long moments, blotting out everything else. The screams and screeches faded around her. All she felt, all she *knew*, was Cyrus's heartbeat. Real and solid underneath her palm.

She exhaled, long and slow, letting her own pulse match his. When they were synchronized, she opened her eyes, her insides warming at the look of tender affection on his face.

"Thank you," she whispered, pressing a soft kiss to his

lips. "Please don't ever let me do that again. If your life is in danger, you *have* to fight. Even if it's against me."

Cyrus gave her a pained look. "I can't hurt you, Prue. I... *can't.*" His voice was so broken, and she knew how much it ripped him apart to have blood on his hands.

He wasn't always like this. The man she had first met—the arrogant deity who would do anything for power—barely batted an eye at the lives lost on his account.

Goddess, how far he'd come... How much he'd changed...

And she loved him all the more for it.

She brushed a lock of dark hair out of his face and fixed him with a hard stare. "I can handle a few bumps and bruises. I *can't* handle a life without you. Promise me you'll fight, even if it hurts me in the process."

His eyes swam with despair, but her eyebrows lowered, and she glared.

"*Promise,*" she commanded.

His eyes closed, his expression crumpling with regret. "I... promise." The words sounded uncertain and feeble, but she knew it was all she would get from him.

"Prue!" Mona shouted suddenly.

Prue turned to her sister, who was still in Evander's arms. Her trousers were torn and bloodstained, but she had healed the gash there, and the color had returned to her cheeks.

"Listen," Mona urged, raising a hand, her eyes distant.

Prue stilled, her ears straining. Around them, the sirens continued to screech. Shouts echoed, mingling with Oceanus's roars of rage and anguish as he was attacked on two fronts.

Then, she heard it. A loud, echoing cry.

Prue stiffened, then looked at Mona with a frown. "What is that?"

Mona's eyes widened, recognition lighting her features. "It's Trivia!"

"Who is... Wait." Prue's face scrunched up in confusion. "Do you mean Pandora?"

"No. I mean—Well, yes." Mona shook her head quickly. "It's our sister, Prue. She's somewhere close by." Mona stood, scanning the foggy surroundings.

Something hissed nearby, and a shape emerged from the fog, slithering toward them. Prue was on her feet in an instant, her heart racing. Was it a serpent? Had one of the fire witches survived?

But when the shape reached them and halted, Prue found herself frowning again.

It was a vine. A thick, rope-like cord, similar to a liana.

Mona lunged, grabbing the vine and tugging hard. She closed her eyes, and earth magic filled the air. "Trivia!" Mona shouted, her voice echoing in the space around them.

Following her lead, Prue crouched to her side, conjuring her own magic to tug on the vine. It went taut, pulling on something within the mist. The end of the vine coiled next to them, gaining slack the more they tugged.

Prue's magic could sense a powerful presence nearby. But there was so much magic around them that it was hard to tell where it was coming from. The sirens, the strange ghostly spirits, the fallen fire witches, or even Oceanus himself... It was too chaotic to make out a magical signature.

But then, she felt it. It smelled of the sea and palm fronds and *home.*

Prue's heart lurched in her chest. "Mama," she murmured.

Mona's head whipped toward hers, and she inhaled deeply. "I sense it, too!" Her magic tugged harder, dragging more of the vine toward them.

A frantic urgency swept through Prue. Her mother was here. She could *feel* her. So close. So close...

Suddenly the vine snapped. Whatever weight it was carrying vanished, and the broken vine slid across the ground toward Prue and Mona, coming to a halt at their feet.

The two sisters stared at it in numb horror.

"What happened?" Cyrus asked, kneeling to inspect the vine.

"No!" shrieked a voice. It sounded close by, close enough for Prue and Mona to run to.

Prue moved toward the sound, but Cyrus grabbed her wrist.

"Prue..."

She turned to look at him, desperation pulsing through her. "Stay with Evander and the spirits. Keep watch in case Oceanus searches for us."

Cyrus's eyes burned with panic. "You *can't*—"

"I have to," Prue said softly. "It's my mother. My sister. Cyrus, I *have* to. Please let me do this."

His lips spread into a thin line, and then he nodded, releasing her hand. Prue glanced at Mona, who was sharing a passionate kiss with Evander. Goddess, Prue had *never* seen Mona like this with a man before. Their mouths collided, tongues clashing with reckless abandon. Prue's normally shy, reserved sister looked like she was about to devour this man whole, without a thought of who was watching.

When they broke apart, Mona's face was pink, but she looked determined. Without another word, the two sisters sprinted into the mist, heading toward the distant shouting. Prue's legs pumped furiously, driving her farther and faster as she followed the scent of her mother's magic.

She froze when a resonant *crack* echoed. There was something terrifying and final about that sound. It pulsed through her, making her tremble.

And then, the scent of her mother's magic disappeared entirely. She couldn't track it. There was no trace of it at all.

Horror pooled in her gut. *No, no, no...*

"Prue, *look!*" Mona cried from a few paces behind her.

Prue followed Mona's gaze and squinted toward the sky. They were now far enough away from the ghosts to make out slices of pale blue sky, barely visible through the mist. And for a brief moment, Prue caught sight of some kind of creature flying through the air.

No, not flying. *Falling.*

Prue staggered back a few steps, trying to keep the figure in her sights. It pierced through the mist, careening toward them.

"Mona, get ready!" Prue shouted, spreading her arms and conjuring her magic. A canopy of leaves formed above them, creating a net to catch the figure.

Together, they backed up several steps. Then several more. The figure was racing toward them at breakneck speed, and Prue feared they wouldn't catch it.

A heavy weight crashed into the leaves. Prue grunted,

pain flaring up her arms as she struggled to keep the net upright. Beside her, Mona groaned, sinking to one knee from the force of it.

When the figure went still, they carefully lowered the bed of leaves to the ground and rushed forward. Prue's heart tripped over itself at the sight of her *mother* lying in a crumpled heap. Her arms jutted out at odd angles, and there was something horribly wrong with her spine. It was...

"Goddess no," Mona breathed, her eyes filling with tears. "Her spine is broken."

Prue's heart stopped for a full beat.

No.

No.

Gaia wasn't dead. The Mother of Earth was *not dead.* She was too powerful for that.

This couldn't be happening.

"Mona," Prue said, her voice strangled. Goddess, she was truly going to be sick now. She shook her head, struggling to hold on to a semblance of her sanity.

Gaia wasn't dead. If she was, Prue would break, and she wouldn't come back from it. She could not survive another loss. She *couldn't.*

Swallowing down her despair, she hurried to Gaia's side, pressing her fingers into her mother's cool flesh.

It was *too* cold. Not the warm softness of someone living.

Prue sucked in sharp, wheezing breaths. She couldn't get enough *air.* Goddess, she was going to die here, right alongside her mother.

Except...

"Mona," Prue said sharply. "Help me."

"Prue—" Mona choked on a sob.

"Get over here and help me!" Prue shouted.

Mona stumbled forward, sniffing. She wiped her nose, her breath shuddering.

"We can bring her back," Prue said.

"Prue, she's gone," Mona whispered.

"I know that!" Prue snapped. "But we can *bring her back.* This—This isn't over. I sensed her magic just moments ago. It can't have left her body yet."

Not like Lagos, she thought. The Titans had stolen Lagos's magic, using it for themselves.

Magic was part of the soul. Once separated, it was near impossible to reconcile the two.

It was too late for her friend.

But Gaia... she had only *just* died. They could still save her.

Prue knew it. They had to save her. They *had* to.

She glanced at Mona, who was weeping silently at the sight of her mother lying on the ground.

"Mona!" Prue cried. "Help me with this!"

Mona shook her head. "I—I can't. Prue, I've never... I *can't.* I don't know how."

"Come on," Prue said, sinking to her knees next to Gaia. She forced herself to look away from her mother's ashen face, from the bruises on her cheeks and neck. Instead, she focused on her own magic still pulsing inside her.

Gaia's power might have vanished, but Prue's was still here. Her mother had gifted her power to her, and now Prue would use it to bring her back.

"I've done this before," Prue said. "Well... sort of." When

Cyrus had resurrected her, she feared he wouldn't wake up. Gaia had coached her through the process of awakening him.

It had to be similar to bringing someone back to life. Their magic was meant to *create* life, after all.

It was possible. It had to be.

She closed her eyes, sensing the growing power inside her. Her mother's words echoed in her thoughts. *You must breathe your life magic into the soul. I cannot force it from you; it is something you must feel for yourself. Close your eyes and open the doors to your magic. Do not be afraid.*

She took a long, steadying breath. "Open the doors to your magic," she said to Mona. "Sense the force of life within you. It's there; you just have to access it."

She forced her body to relax, despite the tension making her rigid and stiff. Deep breaths washed over her, calming her and relaxing her. She let the magic within her take her away, sweeping her into a gold haze of bliss.

Gold. That was what she saw when her magic was awakened. Gold shimmering light.

"Relax," she urged Mona. "Let your magic take over. Mine looks gold, like witchdust."

Beside her, Mona's breaths grew steadier. In tandem, they breathed together. In and out. In and out.

Silver light glinted, mingling with Prue's gold magic. She gasped, eyes open to find the two tendrils of light coiling next to one another like snakes. Gold and silver. Prue and Mona. The beams of light hovered over Gaia's prone figure, twining together, the glow beckoning to them.

"Goddess," Mona breathed. "It's *beautiful.*"

"We have to breathe life into her soul," Prue said, her eyes fixed on the gold and silver beams. "Try to direct it into her. When I awakened Cyrus, I fed my magic into his mouth."

"His mouth?" Mona sounded alarmed.

Prue nodded. "It will be all right, Mona." She sounded more certain than she felt. "Follow my lead." She finally looked at her mother's face, taking in the shadowed creases of her wrinkles, the sickly pallor of her skin. A knot formed in her throat, but she swallowed it down, forcing the emotions down where they couldn't distract her.

Her magic was light itself, and she trusted it. Her gaze dropped to her mother's mouth, and she *willed* the magic toward it. The tendril of sparkling gold floated toward Gaia, dancing in the air. It circled around her face, highlighting her worn and broken features, before gently prying her lips apart.

Mona's silver light followed suit, flitting closer to Gaia and joining with Prue's power. Together, the sparkling light descended until it funneled directly into Gaia's mouth.

Prue held her breath, waiting. With Cyrus, his eyes had opened immediately.

But Gaia was perfectly still.

Prue grabbed her mother's wrist, clutching Gaia's cold hand in both of hers. "Please, Mama," she whispered. "*Please.*"

Mona's fingers suddenly dug into Prue's arm. Prue turned to find her sister's eyes closed, her face tight with concentration.

"I can... *feel* the magic inside her," Mona said in a

strained voice. "It's searching for an echo of her power. Her soul. It's... trying to heal her. To knit her back together."

Prue's mouth opened in surprise. She tried to sense her own magic, but with it buried inside Gaia, she had lost her connection to it.

Mona had always been better at sensing magic than Prue.

"Can it bring her back?" Prue asked, her voice laced with desperation. Goddess, she wouldn't be able to bear it if this didn't work.

"I—" Mona made a frustrated sound, followed by a soft gasp. "*There*! Yes. I feel it."

Prue's heart lifted, and she squeezed Gaia's hand tighter.

"Come on," Mona urged, her brows drawing together. Sweat trickled down her brow, and Prue had no doubt her sister was mentally coaxing her magic onward. Mona had more experience with healing. If anyone could do this, it was her.

Warmth slowly spread into Gaia's hand. Her fingers twitched in Prue's grasp.

"Holy shit," Prue whispered.

Gaia's face filled with color, and her eyes flew open. She inhaled a deep, rattling breath. Several loud *cracks* echoed as the bones in her body repaired themselves. Her back arched as her spine realigned, and a low, keening moan poured from her lips. Her eyes were wide with confusion and terror until they landed on Prue. Warmth and disbelief struck her face, and she slowly sat up. Her eyes slid to Mona, and she pressed a hand to her chest, her eyes filling with tears.

"My... my darlings," she sobbed.

"*Mama.*" Prue fell into Gaia's open arms, and Mona did

the same. They held one another, all three of them sobbing, their cries broken by relieved laughs. Prue's heart was soaring, her insides weightless. She couldn't stop the tears from flowing down her face. She was sobbing so hard she couldn't even see straight.

So much emotion. The fear in her body dissipated, but she was still so tense, so full of a volatile intensity that she needed to release somehow.

Gaia was alive. Prue and Mona had brought her back.

Their mother was alive. She was *here*.

When Gaia released them, she looked at each of them in turn, her eyes full of love and affection. She glanced to the space next to Mona, then frowned.

"Where is Trivia?"

Mona and Prue exchanged looks. "We don't know," Mona said. "She's close by, though. We heard her—"

Gaia's face grew pale, strikingly similar to how pale she had looked in death. "You must go to her. *Now*."

Prue frowned. "But Mama, you're *here*. You can help us. We can—"

"I cannot," Gaia said, her voice firm. "My mantle has passed on to *you* now. When Trivia returned from the dead, she sealed the prophecy of the three witches. Together, you now hold the key to unlocking the Triple Goddesses' power. And the Titans know this. They are trying to keep you apart, and they will stop at nothing to do it."

"Trivia returned from the dead?" Mona sputtered. "How?"

Gaia rose to her feet, helping Prue and Mona to do the same. "There is no time to explain this, my darlings. But with the power of the Triple Goddess now flowing through you, the Titans are bound by sacred laws and cannot kill you. But they have stolen many souls to fuel their magic. That's how they conjured the sirens. It's how they altered their appearances."

"*Stolen souls?*" Prue asked in horror. "I thought they were using Lagos's death magic."

"They were," Gaia said. "But it wasn't enough to summon the creatures to do their bidding. They needed more."

Mona's face drained of color. "Oh Goddess... The Thanassian Empire."

Gaia nodded gravely. "The Thanassian Empire is no more. The Titans slaughtered all the mortals in the kingdom... and devoured their souls. *That* is what is giving them power. And they won't stop until they've consumed every last soul in the entire realm."

EVERYTHING

MONA

MONA STARED AT HER MOTHER IN HORROR AS HER words sank in.

The mortals of the Thanassian Empire have been slaughtered.

The Titans devoured their souls.

So many lives lost... and for what? Power? Domination? What would the Titans do when there were no souls left to feast on?

They would never be satisfied. Never be content.

Unfettered rage roared within her. The sight of her mother's broken and mangled body had altered Mona, twisting her into something feral and savage.

These Titans had waged war on her people. Her *family*.

And Mona vowed to do everything in her power to destroy them.

Gaia's brilliant blue eyes shifted to Mona's, as if her

mother could sense the rage rippling from her body. Gaia squeezed her hand.

"You are strong enough for this, my darling," she murmured.

Mona swallowed hard, her nostrils flaring and her breaths coming in short spurts. She was so full of energy and chaos that she felt she might explode. She wasn't sure if she wanted to cry or scream... or both.

But she had to do *something*.

Prue was climbing to her feet, wiping tears from her eyes. She looked at Mona expectantly.

Mona faltered, casting a worried look toward Gaia. "I don't want to leave you." There were still so many unspoken words between them. So many things she needed to say.

"You have saved my life," Gaia whispered, her eyes sparkling with tears. "And I will never forget that. End this war, and I swear we will spend an eternity catching up. I vow to withhold nothing from you ever again. You will always get the truth from me. I promise you that."

A knot formed in Mona's throat, and she found it difficult to swallow.

What if you die?

What if I die?

What if all the realms perish?

There was so much that could go wrong. So much that could come between Mona and her mother. What if this was it? What if this was the last time they would see each other?

Gaia leaned closer, her eyes full of intensity and fire. "My daughters are the strongest forces I have ever met. It was foretold that your power could save the realms. *I believe in you.* And I *know* you can do this. This is not goodbye."

The words were spoken with such conviction that Mona's breath hitched. She believed her. The fierce determination in Gaia's gaze left no room for question or argument.

This would end today.

But this was not the end of Mona's story.

After a quick nod, Mona climbed to her feet, standing next to Prue.

"Can you sense her?" Prue asked. "You know Trivia's magic better than I do."

Mona closed her eyes, trusting her earth magic. But as the powers inside her stretched forward, she went perfectly still.

Something was shifting toward them. Something that scuffled in the dirt.

Mona's eyes flew open. "Do you feel that?"

Prue froze, holding her breath. "What is that? A creature?"

Mona inhaled deeply, then uttered a soft gasp. Without warning, she sprinted into the fog with Prue right behind her.

Within seconds, they collided with a tall figure. Mona's arms came around Trivia, clutching her tightly to keep her from falling.

"Trivia! Thank the Goddess!" Mona was laughing with relief, amazed that Trivia had been merely steps away. Her smile faltered when she withdrew and looked over her sister. Cuts and bruises marred her tan skin, and her leg was twisted at an odd angle. Dark shadows lined her eyes, and streaks of dirt and tears stained her cheeks.

"What happened?" Mona breathed, touching Trivia's cheek. Tears spilled from Trivia's eyes, and she shook her head, her lower lip trembling.

"Gaia," Trivia whimpered. "She—She—"

"Gaia is alive," Mona said quickly. "We revived her."

Trivia blinked, then her eyes widened. "Are... are you certain? It isn't some kind of trick from the Titans?"

Mona smiled softly. "Yes, I'm certain."

Trivia closed her eyes, leaning heavily on Mona for support. An exhausted laugh burst from her lips, and she wept some more, sniffling loudly. "Thank the gods. Thank you, Mona." She turned to Prue. "And thank you, Prue."

Prue nodded stiffly, her mouth forming a tight line. Only then did Mona realize that the last time Prue had seen Trivia, the Underworld had been destroyed. Prue's last memory of Trivia had been her treachery.

No wonder she was less than enthused to be reunited with her.

"Can you walk?" Mona asked, glancing at Trivia's leg. "We need to—"

She broke off as the ground shook and cracks split the earth. The three sisters darted out of the way as the fissures widened, forming gaping black holes all around them. With her arm around Trivia to keep her upright, Mona fled from the abyss, dodging more chasms and gaps in the ground. Her foot snagged on one of the cracks, and she was falling toward the ground—

Prue grasped her by the elbow, hauling her upright before

she hit the hard earth. Arm-in-arm, the sisters raced through the mist, seeking shelter from the never-ending earthquake.

But there was no escaping it. The earth continued to break, dissolving into the gaping maw that would devour them completely.

That same fury from earlier swelled in Mona's chest, making her see red.

She had had *enough* of these Titans toying with her. Their reign of death would end *now*.

"We're earth goddesses, dammit," Mona snarled, standing her ground and stomping her foot. "We don't have to put up with this any longer." She knelt to the earth and closed her eyes, digging her fingers into the soil beneath her. The ground hummed and the air sang with energy. Power crackled through her, swift and volatile. Blades of grass sprang from the earth. Lush flowers and leaves surrounded her.

And the earth beneath her remained intact. All around her, the ground fell away, breaking and dissolving into nothingness until all that remained was a yawning abyss.

But Mona held on, her brows knitting together, sweat trickling down her brow. She felt Trivia and Prue clinging to her, huddling close to avoid falling into the pit.

At long last, the earthquake ceased, and the air grew eerily still.

Slowly, Mona opened her eyes and stifled a gasp.

They stood on a single patch of grass. An island amidst a sea of darkness.

And everything in sight had been consumed by the black void of nothingness.

"What—What have they done?" Trivia whispered in horror, her eyes wide. She stared into the distance, and her face paled. "How much is gone? Is—Is *everything* gone?" Panic edged her voice, and Mona knew she was thinking of Gaia. Or Sol. Perhaps both.

She wasn't the only one. Terror cinched Mona's chest, cutting off her breath.

Evander. Cyrus. Gaia. *Everyone* left in the realm... Had the Titans destroyed them all so easily?

Clearing her throat, Mona took a deep breath. "No matter what, we have to put an end to this. We have to believe that those we love are still alive and unharmed. But even if they aren't, it doesn't change what we've been tasked to do."

She exchanged solemn looks with Prue and Trivia. They both looked equally horrified, but a spark of determination lit both their gazes.

They were afraid. But they were ready.

Mona extended her arms, taking her sisters' hands and squeezing hard. The moment their palms met, heat seared through their joined hands, burning Mona straight to the core. She sucked in a sharp breath, hissing at the pain that coursed through her body.

From within the darkness below, something unleashed a deep, bellowing roar.

Mona's blood ran cold, her heart stuttering in her chest. Flames rose up from the pit, warming her flesh and making her skin flush.

"What the hell is that?" Trivia cried.

Prue's grip on Mona's hand tightened. "Summon your magic. *Now!*"

Mona nodded in agreement, closing her eyes to call upon her power. The earth magic inside her rose up, but the beast in the darkness roared again, the sound louder than before. Mona's ears rattled, and her eyes flew open. She couldn't stifle the fear flooding her body, clouding her concentration.

"Mona!" Prue shouted, clearly sensing her hesitation.

With a loud *whoosh*, two large wings raised from within the abyss. They pumped, drawing a massive emerald creature into the air, hovering right in front of them. It was easily as tall as the castle of Elysium, with a long, scaly and serpentine body. It coiled into a twisted shape, its large red eyes fixating on Prue, Mona, and Trivia. Several jagged teeth leered at them, and sparks emitted from its mouth.

"The Colchian dragon," Mona breathed, half awestruck and half consumed with terror. This was the great beast that had guarded the Golden Fleece. The monster so large and powerful that it had to be put to sleep by witches.

And here it was, hovering in front of them, teeth dripping with saliva. It inhaled deeply, the sound loud and rattling...

"*Down!*" Mona screamed, tugging hard on her sisters' arms. They dropped to the ground, barely avoiding getting scorched by the dragon's flames. The top of Mona's head burned, and her back felt singed.

A protective dome appeared around them, shrouding them in tree branches. Mona wasn't sure which of her sisters conjured it, but it, too, was lit up in flames. They screamed, trying to turn away from the flames, but there was nowhere to run. Nowhere to hide.

They were trapped.

Thinking fast, Mona buried herself deeper into the

ground, envisioning a cavern of dirt. Then, she lifted a hand and doused the flamed with rich soil. It smothered the fire, quickly putting it out.

But the dragon had cornered them, and it wouldn't stop there.

"We have to get off this!" Mona cried, looking down at the tiny patch of earth they occupied.

"No, we have to *kill it*!" Trivia shouted, gesturing to the dragon, who was rearing its head, eyes burning with rage. Trivia lifted her hand, conjuring a long, jagged branch. She grasped it tightly, wielding it like a spear.

"Trivia, don't!" Mona shouted.

The dragon breathed fire again. Mona ducked, but Trivia let out a roar, her scream piercing the air. She threw the spear directly into the creature's mouth. Its flames cut off as it made a harsh choking sound. It hacked and wheezed, struggling to free the spear from its throat. The dragon twisted in the air, wings flaring. It flew higher and higher, then soared directly toward the three sisters.

It was going to land right on top of them.

Mona screamed, lifting her hands to summon some kind of magic—*anything* to save them—

A gleaming white figure swooped toward the dragon, slashing something into its back. Black blood spurted, gushing like a waterfall.

Mona peered into the sky, her heart thundering in her chest. Her eyes grew wide.

A muscular man with two large wings and long dark hair was flying through the air, his body translucent and glowing.

As Mona watched him, he slashed his dagger into the beast again, drawing more blood.

The man's gaze shifted to Mona and lingered there, recognition lighting his features.

Her heart stopped for a full beat. Her gaze roved over his wings. She *knew* those wings...

"Typhon," she breathed in wonder.

Several more winged figures appeared, but these weren't ghosts. They were sirens. Some of them carried other figures within their talons. A golden arrow shot through the air, lodging into the dragon's chest. Mona followed the golden glow, finding a dark-haired woman holding a matching gold bow in her arms.

It was Diana, the Goddess of the Hunt.

Mona's jaw dropped as she made out other gods and goddesses, some she didn't recognize, all being carried by sirens. They swarmed the dragon, encircling it and blocking its view of the sisters.

They were distracting the beast. This was their chance to finally end it.

Mona grabbed Prue and Trivia by the arms, then closed her eyes, unleashing all the pent-up power burning within her. Silver light flooded her body, igniting around her. Prue followed suit, her matching gold light rivaling even the power of Diana's bow.

They waited for Trivia, but nothing happened.

Alarmed, Mona opened one eye to see Trivia's face contorted in pain. When she glanced down, Mona realized Trivia's entire leg was scorched black.

"Goddess, *Trivia!*" Mona cried, moving toward her.

Trivia shook her head, biting down on her lip. "Don't. It's fine. We have to end this, right? So let's end it." Her face screwed up in concentration, and a faint amber glow surrounded her hands. Then, she shook her head. "*Dammit. I—I'm sorry. This power is still new. I can't...*" She made a noise of frustration.

"Picture the door to your magic bursting open," Prue said quietly, her eyes fixed on Trivia. "Picture it flowing from you like a rushing river. Nothing holding you back. Nothing hindering you."

Trivia's brows knitted together, and she nodded. Gradually, her expression relaxed, and the amber glow spread around her, deepening in color until it was a vibrant crimson. It burned, coiling like flames as it joined Prue and Mona's powers. Their light converged, together igniting to form a brilliant river of rose gold.

Something jerked violently within Mona's chest, and she let out a loud groan of pain. It sliced through her, cutting deep.

But she refused to let go. This was it. This was what she was meant to do.

"Oh gods," Trivia moaned, falling to her uninjured knee. "I can't—I can't—"

A deep, rumbling laugh echoed nearby, and Mona went rigid. Thundering footsteps sounded, and then a large figure lifted its head from within the abyss, leering with jagged teeth. A single bloody eye blinked at them.

"It's too much for you, isn't it?" he taunted.

"Go to hell, Atlas!" Trivia barked.

Atlas. Mona's blood ran cold. The Titan had transformed himself into a Cyclops.

"No, little goddess," Atlas crooned. "I will reserve that honor for *you.*"

He slammed his fist into the ground at their feet. Prue, Mona, and Trivia went flying. The earth they had been standing on disintegrated, exploding into nothing but dust.

Mona was weightless. Her stomach dropped, and she was falling, falling, falling...

Something swooped in and caught her under the arms. She jerked wildly, biting back a scream. When she gazed upward, she found herself clutched in the talons of a siren. Not just any siren—but the same one she and Prue had healed.

"Strike hard and fast, Earth Goddess," said the siren, still using Evander's voice. "You will only have one moment to do it."

Mona blinked in confusion. "What?"

Screeches echoed around her. She noticed several other sirens carrying figures nearby. Her heart lifted in her chest when she recognized Marina and Romanos. Marina had shifted, though. Her body was large and stony, and atop her head were...

Mona looked away immediately, realizing Marina had transformed into Medusa. She wasn't sure if Medusa's power would work on her, but she didn't want to find out.

Atlas howled in agony. Romanos and Marina must have targeted him. Relief filled Mona's chest. She knew the Gorgon and the death god could handle him or the moment.

"Can you take me to my sisters?" Mona called to the siren as it swooped wide to avoid Atlas's thrashing fists.

"Yes!" the siren called. "But we are weak, Earth Goddess! We cannot hold you for much longer."

"I understand."

The siren's wings beat hard, and Mona could hear it struggle for breath. Sirens were likely not used to carrying anything so heavy for long periods of time.

Mona squinted in the hazy air, trying to deduce where the other sirens were.

Then, she caught sight of Prue's familiar golden light. And there, not much farther, was Trivia's scarlet magic.

"There!" Mona pointed, directing the siren toward her sisters.

The siren flew obediently in that direction, then let out an anguished screech as fire ignited on its left wing. The creature spiraled, trying to right itself, but with only one good wing, it was falling fast.

"Mona!" Prue was screaming. "Mona, *jump!*"

Mona only hesitated for a moment before leaping from the siren's talons. A long vine caught her around the waist, yanking her upward and into Prue's arms.

But the weight was too much for Prue's siren, and it started to sink toward the abyss.

"Trivia, unleash it all!" Mona shrieked. The world was spinning around her, careening as she plummeted to her death.

"What?" Trivia cried. "Mona, no!"

"*Now!*" Mona roared.

An explosion of crimson light ignited like massive fireworks. Mona let loose her own silver power, letting it grow and burn until it merged with Trivia's. Prue followed suit, the gold flowing freely until that same burst of rose gold spun through the sky. Mona stretched her arms wide, feeding everything—every facet of her body, her soul—into her power. It lifted her, letting her rise, giving her flight as she soared higher and higher.

Prue and Trivia were there, arms outstretched, carried by the force of their own power. An endless circle formed as they joined hands, the magic flowing over and over. Never ending. Never ebbing.

Nothing could stop them. Their power continued to funnel within itself, fueling their magic, fueling *them*. Mona could see nothing but the brilliant light of their energy.

The magic of the Triple Goddess.

Around them, roars split the air, making the ground tremble. As the light of their magic burned, so did the Titans' agony. Their screams of anguish shook the realm. Their pain rent the earth in two.

But another scream joined them. Beside Mona, Prue screamed, too. And Mona understood why. That pain—she felt it in her chest, slicing deep. If this much power was enough to destroy the Titans, then surely the burden of carrying such a power was enough to destroy them, too.

Mona gritted her teeth. It didn't matter. Her pain didn't matter. She couldn't stop. This *had* to be done. Their purpose had to be fulfilled.

Trivia was screaming, too. Her hand trembled in Mona's grasp.

"Just a little longer!" she urged them. "You can do this!"

Prue's cries were tainted with sobs. Her body jerked violently beside Mona, who struggled to maintain her grasp on her arm. Hot liquid poured down Mona's palms. Blood. Whether hers or Prue's, she couldn't tell.

Oh Goddess, Mona realized with horror. *This is going to kill us. It will take everything from us to end this...*

She shut her eyes, feeling blood trickle from her nose and ears.

"No," she murmured.

She refused to let this power take her sisters from her. Take anything else from her.

They had given up everything. Their lives. Their souls. They had been born for this purpose, born to die, to give up everything.

But Mona refused. She would let Prue live. She would let Trivia live.

I will be the sacrifice, Mona offered. *I did it once before. And I'll do it again.*

Something sang in the air around them, a haunting melody that strikingly reminded her of the song of her soul. The song she had sung with Evander.

Evander...

She let herself dwell on his beautiful face one last time. Tears burned in her eyes, streaking down her face and mingling with blood.

Forgive me, my love, she thought, knowing this loss would break him.

"Let go!" she screamed at Prue and Trivia.

"Mona, no!" Trivia yelled.

"I've got it!" Mona told her. "I can hold it. This *has* to end. Let go, now!"

Trivia was too weak to object. She released Mona's hand, but Mona kept carrying the power, pushing harder than ever. Her flesh was on fire. Her insides were burning.

"Prue!" Mona wheezed. "Prue, you can let go now!"

"Dammit, Mona!" Prue wailed. "I—I can't—"

"I told you, I've got it! I promise you I can hold it! Now *go!*"

Prue's voice broke on a sob, and then she, too, released her hold on Mona's hand. Something exploded in Mona's chest, bursting within her until she could no longer feel her heart, her organs, her skin... She was nothing and everything all at once. She *was* power itself. Magic. Energy.

She was the earth. She was life.

And Mona gave up everything. Every last drop. Every last piece of herself.

All of it.

Until darkness consumed her.

LIGHT

CYRUS

FROM THE MOMENT PRUE PARTED WAYS WITH HIM, Cyrus's chest cinched tighter and tighter, making it difficult to breathe.

He forced himself to carry on. Prue needed to do this.

And he needed to trust her.

Despite the raging panic mounting within him, the desperation to get his wife back and carry her to safety.

Sirens continued squawking and shrieking, diving left and right alongside the spirits Evander had brought with him. Cyrus still wasn't sure how his brother had not only managed to fulfill his bargain with the Wild Spirits but also *free* them.

Cyrus had certainly underestimated Evander.

From within the mist, a shape barreled forward, colliding with Cyrus and jolting him from his thoughts. Cyrus barked out in pain as he landed hard on his back and elbows, grappling with a hairy mangy creature who seemed to be part canine, part bear. Long, sharp teeth snapped at him as the creature snarled and spat.

Gritting his teeth, Cyrus conjured his lightning, igniting the air. His magic crackled, striking the creature. The beast howled and toppled off Cyrus with a low whine. Cyrus struck again, sending a full blast of his power directly into the creature's chest. A moment later, it fell over, its charred corpse nothing more than a smoking husk.

"What the hell was that thing?" Cyrus growled, wiping dirt from his scraped and bleeding elbows.

"A hellhound," said Evander, who was standing above a similar corpse. He held a sword dripping with black blood, and a long gash ran along his cheek. He exchanged a grim look with Cyrus. "The Titans are drawing out more dark creatures."

"They're desperate," Cyrus said thoughtfully. "They're worried Prue and Mona will succeed." Hope bloomed in his chest, but it was short-lived as a loud and shrill screech pierced the air. It was similar to the sounds the sirens made, but this one was stronger and more guttural.

Cyrus went rigid as another dark shape emerged from the mist, hurtling toward him at breakneck speed. He ducked to avoid another collision, but long claws wrapped around his leg, dragging him in the dirt. His hands flew out, trying to grab something to slow him down, but all he managed to do was peel the flesh away from his palms as they scraped mercilessly on the hardened ground.

His lightning struck out blindly, but he missed the creature. He couldn't even *see* it. He was dangling from one leg, his hair whipping around him as he struggled to detach himself from whatever had grabbed him.

Hot liquid gushed down his leg, spattering his face and burning his eyes. He groaned, crying out when the beast released him and he slammed into the ground. Bloodied cuts stung all over his hands and arms, and he was gasping for breath, his body numb from the pain.

"Harpies," Evander hissed. A slicing wet sound echoed, and Cyrus knew his brother had killed the creature.

"Well, shit," Cyrus muttered, rolling to his side and wincing. "Those are almost worse than the sirens."

Evander gave him a flat look. "Yes, but the sirens are on our side."

Unfortunately, the siren call did not work on creatures like harpies. A harpy, like a siren, had the face of a woman and the body of a bird. But harpies were much larger, their black-feathered forms the size of giant eagles as opposed to the raven-shaped bodies of sirens.

"Do you need my sword?" Evander extended his arm, offering his blood-soaked blade.

Cyrus was about to snap something at him when he noticed the blade was glowing. It was white and gleaming, just like the souls still floating through the air. "Where did you get that?"

Evander's smile had a hint of smugness. "From Typhon. It won't last long, but it should help you if another harpy tries to drag you through the mud."

Cyrus shoved at his brother, who laughed. "What do you mean, *it won't last long*?"

"The Wild Spirits can only make certain things corporeal

for a certain amount of time. Typhon's blade is different because he shared so much energy with me. I think that's why he's still out there." Evander gestured toward the sky where a winged creature streaked past. "The others don't have the energy to keep fighting as long as he can."

Cyrus's blood chilled. "So... they're leaving?"

"They have to, otherwise their souls will disintegrate. They've fought a long time to find peace, and I'm not going to rob them of it."

Cyrus swallowed hard. He, too, had promised freedom to the Wild Spirits. He didn't blame Evander for letting them go. They were lucky the spirits had fought for them this long.

But with the harpies and hellhounds emerging, it was the worst time for them to lose their allies.

"I wouldn't think less of you if you retreated," Evander said, his silver eyes solemn. "You have a kingdom to rule. Your people need you alive so you can look after them."

Cyrus scowled. "I'm not leaving. Not when Prue is out there fighting."

"But you are mortal."

"So are you!" Cyrus snapped. Then, he faltered, noting Evander's silvery eyes. *Was* he mortal?

Evander shrugged, as if he didn't quite know the answer to this, either. "Romanos siphoned my death magic from me, but Typhon's ghost lingered. I released Typhon to the Wild Spirits, which freed them before they could drain me of my immortal blood. I don't possess magic, but... I am not as weak as a mortal." His eyes glinted, and Cyrus imagined he was about to say, *Not as weak as* you.

A roar interrupted them as a hellhound leapt from the

darkness. With one brutal strike of his lightning, Cyrus ignited the creature, setting its body ablaze. When the light faded, it fell to the ground, unmoving.

"So, what you're saying is," Cyrus said, "you're a mutant, and no one is quite sure *what* you are."

Evander chuckled. "Yes. Precisely that."

A deafening *boom* shook the ground. Cracks splintered along the earth. Chunks of hard rock crashed around them as the very ground at their feet began to break apart.

"Shit," Cyrus hissed, backing away to avoid getting sucked into a crevice. But the ground was splitting too quickly. He broke into a sprint, Evander at his side as they tried to outrun the earthquake.

"I really wish… I still had Typhon's… wings right about now!" Evander panted.

Cyrus was too winded to respond, his body straining and throbbing with each frantic stride. Gods, he was so weak. He wouldn't make it.

A burst of gold and silver light ignited in the distance, lighting up the sky. For a moment, Cyrus was so transfixed by it that he almost lost his footing.

"It's Prue and Mona," he gasped, recognizing the beam of Prue's gold magic.

The distraction cost him. His foot connected with something hard, something he couldn't see, and he went sprawling. His arms flew out to break his fall, but he slammed sideways, his head crashing into rocks and debris. Darkness clouded his vision, and he went utterly still.

Muffled voices echoed around him. The world seemed

hazy and foggy. He couldn't make out distinct shapes or sounds. Was he dead? It certainly felt like it.

Smack. Cyrus's head swiveled as Evander slapped him hard across the face.

"Wake up, dammit!" Evander bellowed. The ground continued to rumble around them.

Cyrus gasped, the sound wet and rattling. Blood dribbled from his mouth. He still couldn't clear his damn head. Everything was blurred.

"How many times are you going to trip and fall like an idiot?" Evander asked in exasperation. "Gods, at this rate, you'll be lucky to survive another five minutes."

He was trying to goad Cyrus. Cyrus yearned to respond, to taunt him with his own barb, but only a mangled jumble of sounds escaped him. More blood bubbled from his lips.

"Shit. *Shit.* Cyrus!" Evander's voice sounded closer, as if he were right next to Cyrus's face. Evander grabbed him, clearly trying to rouse him. "Cyrus, can you see?"

"N-No." Cyrus could barely *speak.*

Oh, gods. He was dying. He had to be. *That* was how he would end his pitiful existence—by falling like a damn fool.

"The—The earthquake?" Cyrus rasped, coughing up more blood.

"I think it settled," Evander said, but his voice was uncertain. "For now."

"Why—Why is everything still shaking?"

Evander went deadly quiet at that, and Cyrus knew something was horribly wrong.

"Cyrus—" Evander finally spoke, his voice tinged with horror.

A loud screech sounded, and Evander was ripped from Cyrus's side, his strangled cry fading in the distance.

"Evander!" Cyrus roared. He sat forward, squinting and blinking, trying to clear his head. Gods, he couldn't *see*!

He took several deep breaths, remembering the all-consuming darkness of Tartarus. When he'd traveled those caves with Prue, he had coached her on how to trust her goddess senses instead of her mortal ones.

Cyrus didn't have that power anymore... but he *did* have his mortal senses.

That would have to do.

On wobbly feet, Cyrus stood, arms stretched on either side of him for balance. He could only make out vague shapes—there was a jagged boulder nearby, and the mist still lingered. But everything continued to quake and tremble, as if the earthquake were still going on.

Cyrus clenched his teeth against the pain spiraling through him, making him nauseous. He stopped trying to move and merely stood there, closing his eyes and relying on his other senses.

Evander's voice rang out, but it was far away. *Too* far.

What took him? Cyrus asked himself, ears straining.

Then, he heard it again: that same piercing screech. It was a harpy. It had to be.

Cyrus blindly flexed his arm, reaching forward, then summoned his lightning. It illuminated the space several feet in front of him, enough for him to see the tracks Evander had left when the harpy had dragged him off.

Cyrus moved, his steps clumsy as he hurried after Evander. Occasionally, he stopped to conjure another bolt of lightning to show the way before taking off again.

Evander's voice grew closer. He bellowed with rage, which Cyrus took as a good sign. If Evander was angry, it meant he was still strong enough to fight back.

I'm coming, brother, Cyrus thought.

Another bolt of lightning, and Cyrus froze. *Hundreds* of black shapes flitted in front of him, wings spread and talons extended.

It was an army of harpies.

"Shit," Cyrus whispered.

The harpy had been dragging Evander to its flock. To feed its family.

Cyrus was severely outnumbered.

A loud squawk made him yelp and stumble backward as a harpy appeared before him, wings flapping wildly. The feathers tickled Cyrus's skin.

With a hoarse shout, Cyrus's lightning forked through the sky, exploding into the ground at his feet. The harpy screamed, its body twitching as the electricity jolted through it.

But now every single harpy was facing him, their wings flapping as they raced toward him.

Without hesitating, Cyrus dropped to the ground, covering his head with his hands.

"Evander, take cover!" he bellowed.

Then, with every ounce of strength he still possessed, he rained down lightning on the beasts that swarmed him. Flashes of blinding light burst all around him. Each bolt slammed into the ground with a deafening sound, making his ears rattle. The harpies' cries turned into anguished sounds, drowned out by each crash of thunder. The smell of charred flesh and burnt feathers stung Cyrus's nose.

He kept his head buried, flinching from each strike. He hadn't yet struck himself with his power... but he knew it was a very real possibility. He was not immune to Titan magic. He knew that firsthand.

When the harpies were finally silenced and the air went still once more, Cyrus lifted his head. He could see a bit more clearly now, but everything was still hazy, and the corners of his vision were still dark.

He had likely sustained permanent damage from that fall. But he couldn't dwell on that now.

"Evander?" he called, staggering forward. Dizziness clouded his mind. Gods, he had overexerted himself. He had nothing left.

He needed rest. He needed a healer.

His feet nearly tripped over the hundreds of bird carcasses now littering the ground. While he should have been impressed by the amount of power he'd exerted, all he felt was dread.

Because he was spent. Burnt out. And if even one harpy survived that attack, he was done for. He had nothing left to fight with.

"Evander, dammit, answer me!" Cyrus barked, his voice hoarse. His legs wobbled, and he reluctantly sank to his knees. He couldn't go any further.

A raspy cough made him stiffen, his heart lifting.

"Was that really necessary?" Evander's voice sounded thin.

But he was alive. A relieved smile spread across Cyrus's face. "Thank the gods. You scared the shit out of me."

"I scared *you*? That's hilarious. Thanks for the lightning storm, by the way."

Cyrus's smile only grew. He had never been able to joke with Evander like this before. Cyrus had been too power-hungry, and Evander had been too reserved.

But they were different people now. They had both found their confidence and their purpose.

And, wounded as he was, Cyrus couldn't have been more grateful to be there on that battlefield with his brother.

"Can you walk?" Cyrus asked. "Because I can't. I think I might just collapse here and lose consciousness."

"Cyrus," Evander said, his tone suddenly sharp. "Do you hear that?"

Cyrus froze, straining to listen. Then, he heard it.

The beating of wings. Growing closer, closer, closer…

"Cyrus!" Evander shouted.

A harpy struck Cyrus in the chest, driving him into the ground. Cyrus roared, clawing at the creature, trying to summon a modicum of his power.

But it was completely dried up. He had nothing.

Evander's shouts faded as the harpy's talons tore at Cyrus's flesh. Fabric ripped. Blood spilled. Cyrus managed to elbow the harpy in the face, but it retaliated by thrusting its sharp beak directly into Cyrus's eye.

His scream drowned out everything else as an explosion of pain consumed his body. He fell backward, his head hitting the ground. Hot blood gushed from his eye, and now he was truly blind. He couldn't see at all.

The harpy's weight pressed on him, its putrid breath burning his face. Gods, this was the end. He was about to be devoured by a godsdamned *harpy,* of all things.

I'm sorry, Prue, he thought, his body going limp as he accepted his fate.

A sudden explosion of magic burst in the air, rippling across the ground. The earth beneath him trembled like before, but there were no cracks. No massive crevices.

The harpy's squawks turned into panicked screams, its wings flapping. The heavy weight lifted from Cyrus's chest as the harpy tried to... flee? It was attempting to *escape* from whatever had lit up the sky.

Light burned against Cyrus's good eye, piercing through the dark haze that threatened to drown him. For a brief moment, he made out a brilliant sea of rose gold shimmering light. It filled the air with the scent of jasmine and pine.

"Prue," he whispered.

Darkness took him, dragging him beneath its depths.

SONG

EVANDER

Relief coursed through Evander when he heard Cyrus's frantic voice calling for him. And when his brother was lucid enough to taunt him, that gave Evander hope that perhaps they could both survive this.

Until a harpy, who had somehow survived Cyrus's lightning storm, appeared out of nowhere, tackling Cyrus to the ground.

Evander screamed his name, trying to rise. During the attack, one of the harpies had sliced into Evander's upper thigh, which was bleeding far too quickly. Silver blood gushed and flowed, and when he attempted to stand, it only worsened. He was losing too much blood.

The sound of ripping flesh echoed, mingling with the harpies shrill shrieks.

It was killing Cyrus. It would tear him apart.

"Move, dammit!" Evander growled at himself. He hastily

tore a scrap of fabric, then wrapped it as tightly as he could just below the wound in his thigh. The flow of blood slowed, which was all he needed. He stood again, leg wobbling, then hurried over to Cyrus as quickly as he could.

Before he could reach him, a burst of rose gold light appeared. It was more blinding than Cyrus's lightning. The glistening aura swept through the sky, sending creatures flying and screaming. Their bodies sank to the earth all around Evander with heavy *thunks.*

A deep bellow resonated from the abyss. Anguished cries echoed.

Evander once more buried his face, trying to avoid getting disintegrated like the other creatures. But, somehow, this light did not harm him.

Somehow, the power knew Evander was not its enemy.

"Mona," Evander whispered, closing his eyes as his chest warmed. She had done it. She had unlocked her powers.

The earth trembled. The burning light intensified. Evander's bones rattled as the air pulsed with power. Too much power.

Something vibrated around Evander. His ears prickled, and his skin pebbled. It was a more potent magic than he had ever experienced in all his life. It felt as if the very earth were being cleansed and reborn. The fabric of the universe was being rewritten.

Evander couldn't breathe. The air was too thin. He swallowed hard, trying to suck in gulps of air, but his lungs were straining.

Just when black spots appeared in his vision and he

thought he would lose consciousness, the powerful magic faded. The air stilled once more, and, hesitantly, Evander peered around his hands to survey his surroundings.

Dead hellhounds had fallen alongside the harpies, leaving a broken battlefield of corpses. The harpy that had attacked Cyrus also lay dead.

"Oh, gods," Evander whispered, hurrying to Cyrus's side. He sank to a crouch to inspect the damage. There was blood everywhere. Cyrus's face looked like bloody ribbons. A massive, gaping hole had replaced his left eye. It looked as if the harpy had eaten it.

Bile churned in Evander's gut, but he swallowed down his unease and checked for a heartbeat. He held his breath, praying, *begging* for that pulse.

And there it was. But it was faint.

Cyrus was certainly dying. The power of the Triple Goddess might have spared him, but it hadn't healed him.

Evander searched the skies, wondering if Typhon was still here. But even if he was, what could he do?

Mona, he thought. *Mona can heal him.*

But where was she?

"Help!" Evander bellowed, not caring who heard him. If any creature survived, they might hunt him down. But this was too important. *Cyrus* was too important. "Someone help me!"

Hurried footsteps approached, and Evander stiffened. Was this a friend or a foe?

Several shapes took form, and only then did Evander realize it wasn't one person answering his call—it was many.

Unease wriggled through him. In his condition, he

couldn't fight off multiple assailants *and* keep his brother alive.

Through the fog, two women appeared. One of them had Mona's exact shade of raven hair. She also had the same almond-shaped eyes and stubborn chin.

This had to be Gaia.

Evander went rigid, unsure of how to react to the presence of the earth goddess. He knew Mona had a very strained relationship with her mother.

But... this was far better than facing a Titan or a harpy.

"Please," Evander begged, gesturing to Cyrus. "Can you save him?"

Behind Gaia, another woman appeared. Evander glanced over her briefly before he recognized the dark hair and emerald eyes.

Marina. She, too, was a healer. Surely together, these two goddesses could heal Cyrus.

Gaia knelt by Evander's side, her brow furrowing as she looked over Cyrus's shredded form.

"Please," Evander whispered again. Tears burned in his eyes. Gods above, he couldn't lose Cyrus. He *couldn't.*

Gaia pressed a hand into Cyrus's chest, then closed her eyes. A faint hum pulsed in the air.

"His wounds are severe," she murmured. "But... he is still tethered to this world. His connection to Prudence is holding him here."

A knot formed in Evander's throat. "Can you save him?"

Gaia's brow furrowed, her lips forming a thin line. "I—I cannot heal *everything*. But I will try. Marina, can you assist me?"

Marina obediently joined Gaia's side, her hands emitting an amber glow as she placed them on top of Gaia's. Together, the two witches began chanting in another language. A brilliant white glow engulfed Cyrus's form, and for the third time, Evander shielded his eyes.

After a long moment, the light faded, and Cyrus was no longer covered in blood.

But his eye was still missing.

Evander stared hard at the sight of his brother, still unconscious, but no longer wounded. "His eye," Evander whispered.

Gaia withdrew her hands, then smoothed them on her skirts. "I am sorry. I cannot repair it."

Despair filled Evander's chest, but he nodded. Cyrus was alive. *That* was what mattered.

But he knew in his bones that Cyrus would wake up despising himself.

"Thank you," Evander said in a strained voice. "Both of you." He nodded to each of the goddesses in turn, then frowned. "Are you both all right? The fire witches? Romanos?"

Marina sighed heavily. "Most of the fire witches died in battle. But Romanos still lives. He took down Prometheus himself." Her mouth twitched in the ghost of a smile, but her eyes were haunted. She, too, had seen much death today.

Evander looked at Gaia. "And... Mona?"

Gaia's smile was triumphant. "You saw her magic, I'm sure. She did what she was born to do."

"So, she's all right?"

Gaia's expression dimmed. "I—I do not know. But I can sense the Titans are dead. She has succeeded."

This should have come as a relief to Evander. But it didn't. He hated himself for thinking it, but he would rather let the Titans live than sacrifice Mona's life.

Evander woke with a splitting headache. He groaned, turning over in his cot and blinking in the darkness. Where was he?

He recalled the battle with the Titans, and Marina and Gaia healing Cyrus. He had helped sift through the wreckage and corpses, trying to find those who were injured and still alive.

So many had perished.

He blinked, his brain foggy from sleep and his heart heavy with grief. As his eyes adjusted, he sat up slowly. A faint light filtered in through a gap in the ceiling.

A cavern. He was in the fire witch caves. At some point, he had collapsed from his injuries and been brought here to rest.

He turned, then let out a sharp gasp. *Mona.*

Evander lunged for her, tripping over his cot and sending it toppling. But he didn't care. Mona rested in a cot directly next to him, her eyes closed and her expression peaceful. He took her hand in his, then froze.

Her hand was cold. *Ice* cold.

"Mona?" Evander whispered, shaking her arm.

She didn't move.

"*Mona!*" Evander shouted.

Still nothing.

No, no, no. She wasn't dead. This couldn't be...

Frantic footsteps pounded nearby, and a figure appeared at the mouth of the cave. It was Prue, her curly hair wild and disheveled. Her eyes were red-rimmed, as if she'd been crying. "Is she awake?"

"No," Evander said with a frustrated growl. "Prue, what's happened? Why is she like this?"

"She—She held on to the power of the Triple Goddess for too long." Prue's voice was broken by sobs. "She should have let go sooner. But she forced Trivia and me to leave first, before it destroyed us. And she—she—"

Evander's chest shuddered, and he let out a low, anguished groan. "Gods *dammit*, Mona." He slammed his fist into the hard ground, not caring when pain sliced through him, making his knuckles bleed.

It was just like Mona to sacrifice herself so others could live. She had done it countless times. It had even killed her once.

And now, it seemed, it had killed her a second time.

Anguish choked Evander, cutting off his breaths. His stomach twisted. His chest caved inward. He couldn't *breathe.* He couldn't function.

Not Mona. Please, not Mona.

He hunched over, his body breaking down. He couldn't see or hear anything. Only his rasping breaths. Only his shattered heart.

Not Mona. She cannot die. Please.

A warm hand pressed into his shoulder, and his head snapped up. For a moment, he thought it was her, touching his arm, reassuring him she was here and *alive.*

But it was only Prue, her face streaming with tears.

Evander almost snarled at her to leave. This was *her* fault. If she had only held on longer...

But no. No good would come from such thoughts. Evander knew this. And he was too tired for rage. He had no strength for it.

"She isn't dead, Evander," Prue said softly. "But... we can't get her to wake. Gaia and I have tried everything." She took a shaky breath. "Gaia believes only *you* can bring her back. Just as you did before, in the Underworld."

Evander frowned. It took him a moment to realize Prue was talking about after Mona had died. Her soul had been disconnected from her body, and Evander had found a way to merge them together again.

Through the song of her soul.

Evander scooted closer to Mona, daring to hope that this could work. Still clutching her cool hand in his, he began to sing. His voice was hoarse and trembling, but he didn't care. He sang the melody of her soul, the string of notes that was both haunting and beautiful, lovely and tragic. The song of *Mona.*

Their shared song.

He sang louder, his voice gaining strength. The tune floated through the caves, echoing against the walls. And still he sang. Even when his throat was raw and parched, he continued. He gripped her hand more tightly, drawing it to his chest and *willing* her to answer his call.

He could have sworn one of her fingers twitched. For a moment, it seemed like her hand had warmed, as if the life had returned to her.

But she was still unmoving.

Evander's voice died as he let the melody trail off into nothingness. He drew closer to Mona, a tear sliding down his cheek.

He leaned in to press a kiss to her soft lips...

And her eyes flew open.

Evander's heart slammed against his rib cage as he drew back only a breath, wondering if he'd imagined it.

Then, she gasped. Her chest rose and fell, and she made a choked gagging sound as if something was lodged in her throat. There was something... different about her.

But Evander didn't care. The tears spilled more freely from his eyes as he found himself laughing with relief. "*Mona*," he breathed.

A smile lit her face, and she sat up, her arms coming around him to pull him closer. She smelled the same—like seawater and parchment. *Mona*.

She was here. She was alive.

Prue joined them, sobbing and laughing as well, muttering a string of curses for what Mona had done to her. For several long moments, the three of them held each other, each of them weeping but smiling, clinging to one another to treasure this moment.

When they withdrew, Mona blinked tears from her own eyes, and then Evander realized what was different.

Her eyes. They were no longer the gleaming emerald he was accustomed to.

They were hazel. They had flecks of gold and green in them, but nothing as vibrant as before.

Evander frowned. The only time he had seen someone's eyes change like that had been...

"Goddess above." Prue raised a shaking hand to her mouth as she discovered the same thing. "Mona... you're *mortal.*"

REDEEMED

MONA

FOR DAYS, MONA REMAINED ON THE COT IN THE witch caves, letting her body recover from expending too much energy. Too much magic.

She felt sluggish. Foggy. Incoherent. Everything was duller, her senses muted. She had never before realized just how clear and strong her senses had been before this.

Before she'd lost her immortality.

Evander remained by her side the entire time. He never left, not even for meals. Prue always appeared with a tray of food and sat on the floor next to Mona's cot while she ate. After a day of this, and upon realizing Evander wasn't eating, Mona forced him to take bites of her own food. At first he refused, until Mona threatened to have the witches throw him out of the caves. With that threat looming over him, Evander relented.

They did not speak of the future. He only tended to her present needs, checking in to ensure she was healing properly and there were no infections or wounds that were worsening.

But the unspoken words lingered between them like a dark cloud threatening to unleash a downpour of rain.

What did this mean? Mona was no longer a goddess. She wasn't even sure if she could cast witch spells. She was too afraid to try.

Everything was different now. And for the first time, Mona truly understood how Evander had felt when Romanos had siphoned his death magic. She felt lost. Empty. A presence that had been a part of her was now *gone* forever. That gaping hollowness in her chest might never be filled again.

So while she rested and healed, she waited for that piece of her soul to repair itself so she could feel whole once more.

But it never did.

Around lunchtime on the third day, echoing footsteps signaled Prue's usual delivery of Mona's food. A forced smile immediately spread on Mona's face as she sat up, preparing to put on a brave face for her sister.

She couldn't let Prue know how much it hurt. With Cyrus's injuries and difficulty recovering, Prue had enough on her mind at the moment. She didn't need to worry over Mona, too.

But Mona's smile faltered when she realized it wasn't Prue—it was Gaia.

Her heart lodged itself in her throat. She wasn't sure if she should call her *Mama* or *Gaia.* Neither felt right, so she just uttered a soft, "Hello."

Gaia's eyes were tired, but her smile was full of affection.

Slowly, her gaze shifted to Evander, who was sitting on the cot opposite Mona, his brows lowered.

"May I have a moment alone with my daughter?" she asked.

"No," Evander said at once.

Mona's eyes widened, then darted quickly to Gaia. To her surprise, Gaia smiled.

"Do you think I would harm my own daughter?" she asked coolly.

"Given what she's endured because of you, I'm not so sure," Evander said calmly. "But regardless, I'm not leaving her side."

Mona's eyes closed with a soft sigh, but she couldn't deny the thread of warmth that filled her chest from his conviction.

Slowly, Gaia looked at Mona with raised eyebrows. Mona knew that look well. Gaia was waiting for her daughter to fix this situation. To be *obedient*, as she was known to be.

Mona took a deep breath. "He stays. If you wish to talk, there is nothing you can say that I wouldn't want Evander to hear."

Gaia's chin lifted, her eyes flashing. There was a time when that look might have cowed Mona into submission. For her entire life, she had been the timid and obedient child, the one who studied endlessly, kept to herself, and did everything her mother asked of her.

But that woman was gone. And Mona wasn't sure if she would ever come back.

After a long, tense moment, Gaia smoothed her hands on her skirts and drew closer to Mona's cot. "As you wish." Her voice was stiff, and Mona wondered just how often Gaia's orders had been refused. "I came to see if your magic has returned."

Mona frowned. "No. My goddess magic is gone."

"Not that magic. Your *witch* magic."

Dread coiled in Mona's chest. "I'm... not sure."

Gaia arched an eyebrow. "You aren't sure? The Pomona I knew would be aching with curiosity. She would be itching to cast a spell or perhaps even write one herself."

"The daughter you knew was a lie," Mona said sharply, then clamped her mouth shut. She wasn't sure where the outburst had come from. But she was restless and agitated from being stuck in this cave for three days. Her patience was gone.

Gaia's eyes softened. "You are not a lie, my darling. The goddess you became was nothing but *you*. Just because I deceived you about my identity does not make your growth any less real."

Mona shook her head, her eyes burning with unshed tears. She had to look away before the sight of her mother broke her completely. "I suppose it doesn't matter. I did what I was born to do. What I was *bred* to do."

Gaia stiffened. "I did not conceive you with the intent to wield you as a weapon."

"No, but that's how you raised me, isn't it? All those years, you drilled into my thoughts, my entire *being*, that to serve the witch coven was the highest honor. That was why I sacrificed myself to save Krenia from the Book of Eyes. *You* made me that way. Because you always knew I would be the sacrifice, didn't you?"

Gaia's silence was damning enough. Mona huffed a sigh and dropped her gaze to her hands folded on her lap.

"I—I did not know for sure," Gaia said in a strained voice.

Mona looked up. Gaia often spoke with smooth, assured words. But for the first time, she sounded... *broken.*

Gaia took a shuddering breath. "After Trivia was taken from me, I wasn't sure if the Triple Goddess magic could still be accessed. And with you and Prudence being considered for Maiden of the coven, I thought you two had found a different path..." She trailed off, her face twisting with regret.

Mona flinched. She recalled the day she and Prue had discovered their witch coven required one of them to die so the other could acquire enough power to become the Maiden. She and Prue had both been *so angry.* More lies kept from them. More deception.

That was when they had opened the Book of Eyes. They had hoped to find a spell to merge their powers as the daughters of Janus.

But it had backfired. And then, Mona had died.

"As for the prophecy of the three witches..." Gaia continued. "There were parts of the prophecy that indicated one of you would die when the Triple Goddess powers were unlocked. I prayed it was a mistranslation, that it wasn't true. And when you gave yourself up to the Book of Eyes, I—I shattered. I couldn't even imagine having to watch you die *twice.*"

"Is that why you tried to prevent Prue from bringing me back?" Mona asked quietly. She couldn't stop a tear from rolling down her face.

Gaia offered a sad smile. "Yes... and no. I didn't realize what your soul had gone through. I truly believed that bringing you back would undo your sacrifice and unleash the Book of Eyes once more. I was wrong, and for that, I'm sorry.

"But... I also wanted you to have your rest and your peace. I wanted you to be free. Bringing you back only meant you had to suffer more, and I—I wasn't sure I could bear it."

"It wasn't about *you*, though," Mona said. "It never was. And that was the problem. You did what *you* thought was best. You made the choices *for* us, instead of giving us the truth and allowing us to decide for ourselves."

Gaia nodded. "You are right."

Mona blinked. "I am?"

"I have long since regretted keeping you and Prudence in the dark. There are... *many* things that I regret." Her voice broke again. Her eyes filled with a despair so potent that Mona's heart twisted.

Perhaps she was thinking of Trivia.

Or perhaps she was thinking of Sybil, the woman she loved, whom she had left on Krenia.

"You might not have known me," Gaia said. "But I knew you to your core, Pomona. You *have* grown and changed into someone different, but I knew your soul before you became a goddess. I know how you react to failure. You give up." She gestured to Mona, who was still stretched out on the cot. "You become languid and unresponsive until something new piques your interest, drawing you back to the surface."

Mona's eyes narrowed. "I am not *languid.*"

"Then prove it," Gaia challenged. "Perform a simple healing spell on your body. See if it works."

Mona shook her head. "I can't heal anymore."

"You can with the proper ingredients." Gaia lifted a small sack at her side. "Which I happen to have here with me."

Mona stared at the sack, her heart racing. Her gaze flicked to Evander, who was watching her intently, Hope gleamed in his eyes.

Did he agree with Gaia's assessment? Had Mona *given up*?

"I—I have been through a lot," Mona stammered. "I'm not sure if I'm ready…" She trailed off, unable to pull her gaze away from the sack in Gaia's hand.

Mona knew exactly what was inside. Saffron root. Lavender. Eye of newt. Mugwater. The standard ingredients for a healing elixir. It wasn't quite as powerful as using her goddess powers, but it was still effective. They had used it for many illnesses and injuries in Krenia.

"Just try," Gaia urged. "If it causes you physical pain, we will stop, and you can spend a few more days recovering."

Mona licked her lips, uncertain. Fear wriggled in her gut. Why was she so opposed to this? She took a shaky breath and looked at Evander, whose brow was furrowed.

"What do you think?" she asked him.

Evander glanced from her to Gaia, then back again. "I think," he said quietly, "that the decision is yours. But you have always been in tune with your witch abilities, Mona. It's a part of you. And I think that… casting a spell can remind you of that connection."

Mona swallowed hard. He was right.

But that wasn't what Mona was afraid of.

She was afraid that it *wouldn't* work. That her magic was completely gone. That she wasn't even a witch anymore.

She wasn't sure if she could process that loss. She wasn't strong enough.

Her breathing turned shallow. She couldn't get enough oxygen into her lungs. "If—If—" she broke off, unable to finish, unable to even speak. Her chest constricted, and her throat closed up. She shut her eyes, her head spinning. "If it doesn't work..." She choked on the words, then hunched over, sucking in rattling breaths that did nothing to fill her lungs.

In an instant, Evander was kneeling at her feet, his hands on her knees. "Mona."

His tender voice soothed her, along with that woodsy scent she knew so well. *Her Evander.* He was hers. He was here.

Her eyes opened, locking with his silver ones. She nodded at him, her gaze still pinned on his. Those silvery orbs pulled her in, beckoning her closer. They were beacons guiding her home. She would be lost without them.

"You can do this," Evander murmured. "And if, for some reason, you can't... we will weather that storm together. You are not alone, my love. I am here with you no matter what."

Warmth filled Mona's chest, and her eyes burned. She blinked rapidly to keep herself from crying again.

Evander pressed her hand firmly to his chest. "This heart... is yours. For all eternity."

Her vision blurred with tears, and she sniffed. "And mine is yours," she whispered.

A small smile lit his face, and he sat back on the floor to give her room. He stayed close, as if he knew that withdrawing too far would make her panic again.

Gaia silently approached, removing each item from her sack and placing them onto the cot next to Mona. The last items were a mortar and pestle to mash the ingredients together.

"Do you recall the conditions of the healing spell?" Gaia asked softly.

Mona could almost slip back into the routine of answering her mother's questions. Teacher and student. A witch apprentice learning from the Mother of the witch coven.

"Essence of saffron root. A sprig of lavender. An open heart and mind. An eye of newt. Three droplets of mugwater."

"I have everything here." Gaia gestured to the ingredients spread on the cot. "But the open heart and mind must come from you." Her blue eyes flared with intensity, challenging Mona.

Mona sat up straighter. She took three deep breaths, feeling her chest expand with each inhale. She cleared her mind of all frustrations and worries, all thoughts and concerns.

Open heart. Open mind.

It was just her and the spell. Nothing more.

Silently, she nodded. Gaia watched her expectantly, unmoving. Mona reached for the mortar and pestle, then grabbed the jar of saffron root. Her hands shook at first, but after a moment, she settled into the familiar rhythm of spell-casting. *Grind the root. Add the lavender. Mix together. Crush the newt eye. Add the mug water. Mix again.*

Her hands moved of their own accord, her thoughts emptying. She knew nothing but the task at hand. The mixture became an olive green paste that smelled of witch magic and lush forests.

It smelled like Krenia.

"Good," Gaia said once the paste was finished. "Now, the next step?"

Mona said nothing as she dipped two fingers into the mixture, then smeared it under her tunic over her own chest. It felt cool to the touch, making her shudder. Her eyes closed, and she froze for a moment, suddenly remembering the reality before her.

Her lost powers.

Her wounded body.

The healing spell that might work... but it also might not.

No, she thought, gritting her teeth. *Empty your thoughts. Open heart. Open mind.*

She took three more deep breaths, then continued smearing the salve onto her chest. The coolness seeped into her bones, bringing a tingling awareness throughout her entire body.

"Now, the incantation," Gaia prodded.

Mona inhaled a slow breath, then whispered, "*Sano.*" She pressed her palm flat against her chest, right where her heart was beating. Her fingers were sticky from the paste. "*Hoc vulnus sana.*"

Nagging thoughts crept into her mind, but she pushed them away. The worries and fears within her urged her to fret over the possibility of failure, to overanalyze how long this was taking to produce results.

But she refused to succumb to those thoughts. It was just her and the spell. Nothing more. Sometimes it took a few moments for the magic to work, especially with inexperienced witches. Her mind traveled far away, distancing herself from everything personal about this situation.

A fresh new witch was casting a spell. Her magic was unpracticed and unpredictable. If the magic did not come forth immediately, the witch would need to utter the phrase with more conviction. More surety.

The witch had to believe in her own abilities. Sometimes, that was the most important thing.

Believe, Mona thought. *The magic will work. The conditions are met. The ingredients are here. Believe in the power.*

"*Hoc vulnus sana,*" she said, louder this time. Her voice was firm and confident.

Power brushed against her, whispering along her skin, tickling her flesh. Sudden warmth seeped into her chest, blotting out the cold and spreading throughout her body. It extended from the top of her head to the ends of her toes, filling her with a comforting heat that soothed her aching muscles and throbbing wounds. It knitted the pieces of her heart and soul back together.

A relieved exhale left her, loosening the tightness in her chest. The salve dissolved into her flesh, making its way through her body as the spell did its work.

When the warmth finally left her, she let her eyes flutter open. It was not as earth-shattering as the powerful and instantaneous healing she had performed as a goddess. This was... gentler. More subtle.

In a way, she almost preferred it. It was a delicate presence that needed to be nurtured. It wasn't something that came easily, but it meant that the results felt *earned.*

Mona had no true power within her. But the power she *could* wield had been honed through years of hard work and practice.

She was breathing deeply and fully now, a smile spreading across her face. In front of her, Gaia was beaming, her eyes shining with tears. Evander's gaze bored into hers, full of pride.

That's my Mona, his affectionate gaze seemed to say. He'd had no doubts. No concerns.

He had known from the beginning that she could do it. He had always believed in her.

Always.

Gaia squeezed Mona's shoulder, jolting her from her thoughts. "I am more proud of you than you could ever imagine, Pomona," she said softly. "You have more power than you know, my dear." One by one, she gathered the ingredients and placed them back inside the sack. When she stood, she smiled down at Mona. "I'll return tomorrow with another spell we can try. Will that be all right?"

Mona couldn't stop smiling as tears rolled down her face. She choked on a half laugh, half sob. "Yes. Yes, I would very much like that."

Gaia nodded once, then left the cavern.

Mona felt Evander's gaze burning into hers. Slowly, she

faced him again, and her chest cinched at the desire sparking in those eyes.

"That's always been you, Mona," he said gently. "You've always been a witch first and a goddess second. *This* is who you are." He gestured to her with that same look of pride on his face.

"I—I couldn't have done this without you," Mona said breathlessly. Energy churned through her, restless and volatile. She wanted to leap and scream. She wanted to sprint and laugh.

She wanted *everything*.

Evander's expression sobered, the joy in his face dimming slightly. "Yes, you could have."

Mona's smile faltered. "Evander…"

"You *can* do this without me, Mona."

She shook her head. "Why are you saying this?"

He took a deep breath, then shifted so he was sitting on the cot next to her. "I have to stay in the mortal realm. I made a deal with Typhon and the Wild Spirits. I vowed to help free the other creatures who have been unfairly punished by the gods. Starting with Clotho."

Mona felt the blood drain from her face. "The *Fate*?"

Evander nodded. "It is thanks to her that Typhon was kept alive. I must try to return the favor as best I can."

A hard lump formed in Mona's throat, and she found it difficult to swallow. "So you're leaving?"

Evander frowned. "No, I'm staying. *You're* leaving."

Mona let out a surprised laugh. "What? Where am I going?"

"I—Well—I assumed you would return to the Under-world. With Prue."

Mona's mouth opened and closed. "*I* assumed I would be returning to the Underworld with *you*. But if you must stay in the mortal realm, then I'll stay, too."

Evander's brows furrowed with confusion. "I can't ask you to leave your sister. You two have been through so much."

"You're not asking me at all. I'm telling you, my place is with you."

"But it's *Prue*," he argued. "Prue has *always* come first."

Mona's heart dropped at the devastation on his face. Goddess above, he looked so forlorn and lost. Had he truly believed she had chosen Prue over him?

Her gut twisted with the realization that she *had.* Every time, Prue had come first. Mona had given up her memories of Evander in order to rescue Prue from the Underworld. She had stayed by Prue's side when the Titans had closed in, knowing it would result in her capture. And she had chosen to stay with the witches and fight with Prue instead of returning to the Undead Wilds with Evander.

Realization struck Mona like a bolt of lightning. She had urged Evander to rediscover himself, to find a purpose worth living for, something *besides* her...

But she needed to find herself, too. She needed to find who she was without Prue. Without Gaia.

And only now did she realize that, for the first time in her life, she *wasn't* worried about her sister. Her thoughts were free of all worries or concerns for Prue. Mona had been over-come with self-pity and sorrow over her own losses.

But she hadn't thought of Prue at all.

Mona's ultimate sacrifice had guaranteed Prue's safety. Mona had given up everything for her sister.

And she was finished. Finished with the sacrifices, with the loss. She was finished with worrying over someone who was already being looked after.

Prue would be fine. She would thrive as Queen of the Underworld alongside her powerful husband.

Mona took a deep breath and leaned closer, framing Evander's face with her hands. She forced him to meet her gaze. His eyes were still filled with that broken confusion mingled with desperation.

"Not anymore," Mona said softly. "Prue has Cyrus. And even if she didn't, she is strong enough to take care of herself. I've given up my entire life for this cause. For my sister. For my mother. It's time for me to live for myself. And *I choose* a life with you, Evander. If you'll have me."

Evander's mouth fell open, his face slack with shock. Clearly, this was the last thing he'd expected her to say.

Mona pressed the flat of her palm against his cheek, her thumb tracing circles along his chin. "Freeing Clotho will not be easy. I think you'll need a clever witch by your side to help you. Don't you agree?"

Evander huffed, but she wasn't sure if it was an inhale or a breathy chuckle. "I—I don't know what to say."

"Say yes," Mona urged. "Say you'll have me."

"Oh gods, Mona, *of course* I'll have you. I'll have every piece of you that you're willing to give." In a swift motion, he gathered her in his arms and lifted her against him, settling her on his lap. Mona yelped, then laughed in surprise, wrapping her legs around him and draping her arms over his shoulders. She let her fingers tangle in his black and silver hair, then pressed her forehead to his.

"I love you, Evander. My soul belongs to *you*. I'm—I'm so sorry I caused you to doubt that. But I will spend the rest of my mortal life proving to you how much I love you."

Evander's hands slid along her waist, bunching up her tunic until his long fingers brushed her bare skin. She suppressed a shiver of pleasure from the tenderness of his touch.

"Perhaps we will both have to spend our lives worshipping one another," he mused, tilting his head at her. His eyes had a predatory glint that made her toes curl. "To prove how we feel."

Mona's mouth went dry. Her heart raced as she gazed at him, her eyes dropping to his lips.

He leaned in, angling his head so their mouths aligned. His lips brushed against hers, the softest of touches. Jolts of awareness spiked through her body until she couldn't take it anymore. She closed the distance between them, drawing his mouth to hers.

A noise of pleasure rumbled in his throat as her lips roved over his. He tasted deliciously warm. He tasted like *home.* The kiss started off slow and exploratory, but as their mouths moved hungrily together, it became something urgent and desperate. His tongue slid between her lips, tasting her thoroughly. She welcomed it with her own, their tongues clashing with brutal intensity. Her legs tightened around him, feeling his hardness pressing against her thighs.

Goddess, she wanted him. It had been so long since she'd claimed his body. Since he'd claimed *her*.

Evander's hands snaked up her back, and then he eased her backward until she lay on the cot. He pinned her there with his body, hips grinding against hers. She writhed, rubbing against his arousal until he growled in her mouth. She bit down on his lower lip, savoring the strangled sound of his groan. Her hands fumbled with his trousers, and he tugged at hers in turn. After some shifting, they managed to remove them both.

Mona's hand wrapped around his cock, and he jerked against her with a low gasp. She squeezed, and he moved his mouth lower to bite hard on her shoulder.

Mona cried out, arching backward, delighting in how the pain from his bite sizzled through her veins like lightning. Goddess, he made her *feel* so much.

And she wanted to feel it all.

She spread her legs, her feet digging into his back. His fingers glided along her center, teasing her. Taunting her.

"Now," she commanded in a strained voice. She was in no mood for games. She had to have him *now* or she might die all over again.

His mouth curled into a smirk, his eyes wild and crazed. Right now, he was her feral beast. Even without Typhon, he was still volatile and unhinged.

And she loved him for it.

With a single powerful thrust, he buried himself inside her, making her moan loudly. He filled her with such completion, such perfection, that she wanted to preserve this moment, to memorize it and capture it forever. Her legs spread even wider as he pushed harder, making her see stars.

"Goddess, Evander," she gasped when he withdrew and plunged into her once more. She lifted her hips, allowing him to drive into her harder. Deeper. *Faster.*

His pace became wild. Punishing. The cot creaked beneath them, far too feeble to withstand their violent movements.

But neither of them cared. Evander was pounding into her mercilessly, and the rage of her pleasure was mounting more and more until she thought she would drown in it.

"More," she urged him, her voice barely more than a breath. "*More.*"

Evander grunted something unintelligible, grabbing one of her legs and hitching it upward so he could slam into her again. The angle of his cock driving into her made her dizzy with delight. She cried out again, sweat pouring down her neck. With his other hand, Evander tugged her tunic to the side and massaged her breast, capturing a nipple between his fingers and pinching.

Mona's climax washed over her like a tidal wave, burying her. Drowning her. Obliterating her entirely. She continued to meet his thrusts with her own, chasing her climax over the edge, drawing every ounce of pleasure from her body.

Evander's breaths became more hoarse. He groaned and growled, the sounds animalistic and manic.

Crack.

The legs of the cot snapped in two, and with a jolt, the two fell in a heap on its broken remains.

Mona gasped, clinging to Evander's arms, her eyes wide.

But he was lost in his passion, his eyes closed and his face covered in a sheen of sweat.

"Are—Are you hurt?" he rasped.

"No," she said. "Don't stop, Evander."

He groaned, thrusting deeper. Her thighs spread, her legs tightening around him. Her fingernails dug into the flesh of his arms. She leaned in and kissed him, her tongue roving over his lips.

With a violent shudder, he spilled into her, his body convulsing with his own climax. Her hips rolled, coaxing out every last drop from him.

"I'm yours, Evander," she whispered as he leaned his sweaty head on her shoulder. They were both gasping for breath, their bodies tangled and sweaty. The broken cot was in pieces beneath them, but they didn't care. "For all eternity, my soul is yours."

Evander kissed her forehead. "For all eternity," he echoed.

REIGN

PRUE

"I HAVE DONE WHAT I CAN TO HEAL HIM," MARINA said to Prue, her voice quiet so as not to disturb Cyrus, who was sleeping. "He will wake when his body is ready. But he has been through an ordeal. And his eye cannot be repaired."

Prue took a shuddering breath and clutched her chest, then nodded. "I—I understand. Thank you, Marina."

Marina nodded, then strode for the tunnels, stopping when Prue called after her.

"Marina? Is—Is the coven going to be all right?"

Marina slowly turned to face her, her expression grim. "We lost a lot of witches. And the coven has no leader with Farah—" She broke off, her eyes tightening.

With Farah dead.

Prue's insides twisted with grief as Marina cleared her throat. "Vivian and I will remain here while we get the coven in order. But it's likely the witches will never recover from this tragedy."

Prue's heart constricted from those words. *Never recover.* As she watched Marina disappear in the tunnels, Prue wondered how many others would *never recover* from this.

Mona would never recover her goddess magic.

Cyrus would never recover from losing his eye.

Marina and Vivian would never recover from losing their sister.

Prue would never recover from losing Lagos.

Even though the Titans had been defeated, they had *still* managed to take so much from everyone.

A hoarse cough echoed behind her, and Prue stiffened. She whirled, finding Cyrus shifting in the bedroll. He groaned, cursing under his breath.

In a flash, Prue was by his side, her fingers wrapping around his arm. "I'm here, Cyrus."

He had been in and out of consciousness for days. At times, he seemed lucid, speaking to her as if he knew she was there. But he had only been talking in his sleep.

Prue assumed this was the same, until his one eye fixed on her, and a frown creased his features.

"Prue?" His voice was cracked and dry.

Prue hastily lifted a canteen to his lips. He greedily gulped down the water, pausing to gasp as it dribbled down his chin. He coughed again, and she set the canteen down, taking his hand in hers.

"Why... why are you so... *blurry*?" he squinted his good eye, then tilted his head as if to use his other eye.

He froze.

Prue held perfectly still, waiting for him to acknowledge it. She recalled the last time he had woken up to find his body significantly altered. Upon realizing he was mortal, he lashed out at her, blaming *her* for his situation.

He had claimed that death would have been preferable.

She braced herself for a similar outburst, holding her breath. Her resolve hardened, and she determined not to hold it against him.

He's been through an ordeal, she reminded herself. *Do not take it personally. He still loves you, even if he will claim otherwise.*

Slowly, Cyrus lifted his free hand to touch the black hole where his eye had once been. When he reached it, his hand shook, and he sucked in a sharp gasp.

"I—I've lost my eye, haven't I?" His voice was hollow and dejected.

Prue swallowed. "Yes. Marina says she—she is unable to repair it."

Cyrus's mouth pressed into a thin line, and he nodded once. "Well... damn."

Prue blinked. She hadn't expected that. She cleared her throat. "Are you—Does it hurt?"

Cyrus shook his head. "Only when I try to squint. It... feels like it's still there, though. Like there's something dark hovering in my vision, blocking things from view."

Prue's heart clenched with sympathy. With the loss of her ear, she felt a similar blocking sensation on that side of her head, making all sounds a bit more muffled. But Cyrus had already been through so much. Her fingers tightened around his. "I thought I'd lost you," she said in a broken whisper.

Cyrus's one blue eye fixed on hers, and it burned with regret. "I'm sorry for frightening you."

Prue's expression crumpled, her eyes filling with tears. She leaned closer to him, prepared to burrow her face in his chest, then stopped. He was still healing. What if her touching him brought him more pain?

"Come here," he urged, his arms wrapping around her. She nestled into his side, and he stiffened.

"Shit, I'm sorry." She tried to pull away, but he dragged her back to him.

"Don't you dare," he muttered, stroking her dark hair and pressing a kiss to her temple.

For a moment, they lay there together, his fingers idly weaving through her curls. She kept her ear on his chest, feeling the comforting rhythm of his heartbeat. Each pulse seemed to resonate within him.

Alive.

Alive.

Cyrus is alive.

"Maybe... Maybe Gaia can create a *new* eye for you," Prue mused, tracing circles along his chest.

Cyrus's chuckle rumbled against her. "It's all right, Prue. I can live without my eye."

Her brows furrowed, and she sat up to look at him. His expression was so... *calm.* How was he handling this so well?

"You aren't upset?" she asked.

He took a deep breath, turning his head to gaze absently at the cavern wall. After a long moment, he said thoughtfully, "No."

Prue's lips parted in surprise.

"I thought I would die," Cyrus explained. "*Truly* die. It wasn't like when I brought you back from the dead. This time, it wasn't my choice. And I was fighting harder than I'd ever fought before. Your face appeared in my mind, and I was... filled with regret for all the days we wouldn't share together. All the moments wasted. The life we could have had... just gone." His eye turned glassy with looming tears. "When I lost consciousness, I expected to awaken as a lost soul in the rivers of the Underworld. I knew I would see you again, but it wouldn't be the same."

His fingers intertwined with hers, and he brought her palm to his lips. Her blood heated when his mouth brushed against the back of her hand.

"I'm just grateful to be here with you now," he whispered against her skin. "For however long it lasts."

"You say that like this is temporary," Prue said with a frown.

Cyrus arched an eyebrow. "Isn't it? Your people need you."

"*Our* people need us. *Both* of us."

Cyrus sighed. "They have no use for a crippled king."

Rage roared within Prue, and she drew back to fix him with a withering glare. "Don't you dare insult my husband like that. You think since you've lost an eye that that makes you any less of a king? Does the loss of my ear make me any less of a queen? We were both wounded in a battle fought *for our people.* Your injury makes you a war hero, Cyrus. Not an invalid."

"I have made so many mistakes, Prue," he said in a shaky voice. "So many lives lost because of me. I can't—I can't—" He broke off with a shuddering breath.

"You are learning," Prue said gently. "And so am I. We

can learn how to be King and Queen *together.* I'll be with you. Always, Cyrus."

Cyrus stared at her, his eye filled with wonder and awe. "How? How, after all this time, are you still here by my side? How did I manage to snare such a perfect goddess like you as my wife?"

Prue snorted, then smirked at him. "I believe it had something to do with pomegranate seeds and a spell gone wrong."

He tugged her so she lay against him once more. "There was nothing *wrong* about it, darling."

She turned her head to gaze at him. His eye sparkled with delight as he leaned in to kiss her. His lips were soft and tentative, almost as if he were... afraid.

Her hands framed his face, drawing him closer as her tongue glided along his. She refused to let him be gentle with her. She caught his lower lip between her teeth, and he let out a low groan.

"You're mine," she whispered. "I don't care if you've lost an eye or an arm or both your legs. Don't you dare forget that *you are mine,* Cyrus."

He was panting, staring down at her in surprise and longing. "I—I'm not the same anymore, Prue. Things will be different."

She kissed him again, hard and unyielding. "Good," she said. "Life would be quite boring if things stayed the same, wouldn't you agree?"

Amusement gleamed in his eye, and the hint of a smile spread across his face. "You are a marvel, wife."

"As are you, husband."

His arms came around her, clutching her waist. She straddled him, hovering over him so she could kiss him endlessly. She planned to explore every part of his body, every facet of his being. It didn't matter how this battle had altered or changed him.

He was hers.

And she was his.

Now and forever.

HOME
TRIVIA

Trivia paced the length of the narrow tunnel, wringing her hands together over and over. Anxiety and worry wriggled through her, making her stomach knot and swirl with nausea.

Gods, she was so nervous.

A figure appeared in the cave entrance, and Trivia stilled, her eyes going wide.

Midas offered her a small smile. "They're here."

Trivia swallowed and nodded. "Good. Good. Is he..." She trailed off, unable to ask the question.

"Sol is leading the council, yes," Midas said. "I'll be by his side."

"Good," she said again, breathlessly.

Midas paused. "He's asking for you."

Trivia went rigid, her heart slamming against her ribcage. "*What?*"

Midas chuckled. "You're acting like I just announced that a hydra has claimed the throne of Elysium."

Trivia was too stunned to reply.

"Trivia," Midas said, his tone gentler as he drew closer to her. "He wants you as part of this council."

She was shaking her head, backing slowly away from Midas, although there was little room. Her back immediately met the earthen wall behind her. "I don't belong in there." She gestured to the vast cavern behind Midas. "Not after what I've done."

"Hell, if *I* can be a part of this after what *I've* done, then so can you. Get in there, Trivia."

All she could do was keep shaking her head.

Midas drew closer, his brows lowering. "If I have to haul you over my shoulder, I will. But I'd wager that wouldn't make a good impression on the others."

Trivia fixed him with a loathsome scowl. "Bastard."

Midas chuckled again, then offered her his arm. "Shall we?"

"Don't pretend like this makes you a gentleman," she said, but she still looped her arm through his.

"Of course it doesn't. I'm just doing this to keep you from fainting and collapsing into a pitiful heap on the ground."

Trivia rolled her eyes, but her mouth twitched into a smile. He was teasing her, but she knew he was doing it to make her feel better. To make her feel *normal*.

For a brief moment, it was working.

Then, she stepped into the massive cavern and took in the gods and goddesses seated in a circle around the hearth.

Her heart dropped to her stomach.

Twelve figures sat there, watching her expectantly. Some she recognized—Sol, of course, his eyes gleaming as he gazed at her; Marina, her back rigid in her seat, looking as regal as ever; Cyrus, still managing to appear fierce and intimidating, even while wearing an eye patch; Hypnos, with his dark skin and shock of white hair; Diana, her chestnut hair gleaming and her bow and quiver strapped to her back; Gaia, blue eyes sparking with pride; Deimos, the god of terror, whose thin and wiry frame barely took up the space of his seat; dark-haired Eris, the goddess of conflict, her crimson eyes flashing; and Morpheus, Hypnos's son, the god of dreams, with tawny skin and bronze eyes that fixed on Trivia with curiosity.

The other three deities were people Trivia had never seen before: a man and two women. They looked at her with part curiosity, part suspicion.

Unease coiled in Trivia's chest, but she let Midas lead her to the seat next to Sol. She sank into it and clasped her hands together on her lap. Midas took the seat on Sol's other side.

Sol looked at Trivia, but she couldn't bring herself to meet his gaze. Even her bones seemed to quiver with trepidation. Her gaze snapped to Deimos as she briefly wondered if he was using his influence on her.

He offered an amused smirk, as if he could *sense* her fear. He probably could.

"I want to personally thank all of you for assisting us in battle," Sol began, his voice strong and full of a confidence that Trivia envied. "We couldn't have defeated the Titans without you."

A few of the deities murmured their agreement before Sol spoke again.

"There is obviously a lot of cleaning up to be done among the three realms. But I think, first and foremost, we must select a ruler for Elysium. From there, he—or she—can rebuild and guide the souls to their final resting place. I don't want to repeat the pattern we established before, of a power-hungry monarch who rules with no restraint. *This council*"— he gestured to the circle—"will be the deciding force of Elysium, should a conflict arise. But whoever is the ruler will make the bulk of the decisions." He paused, eyeing each person in the circle "So... any volunteers?"

Silence met his words. Gaia's brows knitted together in clear displeasure. Cyrus lifted his chin, his lips curling into a cold smile.

Deimos spoke first, his voice thin and reedy. "I vote for Midas. We wouldn't even be here if it weren't for him. He convinced us to fight."

Hypnos and Morpheus nodded their agreement.

Midas shifted uncomfortably in his chair. "I have served my time as a king in the mortal realm. I don't wish to do it again." He cocked his head, eyeing Sol with scrutiny. "But my nephew would make a *fine* king."

Sol stiffened, his eyes widening. "What?"

"He trained directly under Apollo," Midas went on. "He knows the duties associated with the crown. And he can fuel the sun of Elysium as well."

"It was his magic that helped rebuild it," Gaia offered.

Eris and Diana murmured their agreement, although judging by the way Eris was eyeing Sol up and down, Trivia would wager her thoughts were less on his king-like qualities and more on his proclivities in the bedroom.

The thought sent a spark of fury shooting through her, and she was speaking without realizing it. "We could not have defeated the Titans without him. He charged fearlessly into battle, even before realizing we had allies on our side." She reached out her hand and took his, squeezing his fingers.

Sol was staring, wide-eyed, at the circle of deities, his face paling. "I—I don't—That's *not* why I gathered everyone. I am just conducting the meeting. That's all."

"Do you accept the nomination?" Midas asked. "Or will you refuse the honor?"

Sol's brows lowered as he glared at Midas. "It's inappropriate. I was too close to Apollo. Aren't you worried I was working alongside him?"

"He murdered your mother," Deimos said softly. "I don't think any of us believe you sided with Apollo."

A solemn silence filled the room.

Then, Marina spoke. "You were the only god from Elysium to willingly fight alongside the witches. When all hope seemed lost and victory seemed hopeless, you were there, fighting with us. The rest of you arrived later, for which we are grateful. But only Sol was there from the beginning."

A few of the deities looked uncomfortable at this, and Trivia wondered just how much pleading had been required to convince them to fight.

Sol was squeezing Trivia's hand now, too. When she looked at him, she found his gaze already fixed on her, filled with warmth and passion. A faint scar gleamed from the lamplight, tracing a line from his eyebrow to the corner of his mouth. Courtesy of Prometheus.

"I would not be here at all," Sol said softly, "were it not for Trivia."

Trivia's heart stuttered in her chest. Sol's eyes were still locked on her as if they were the only ones in the room. He spoke with such reverence, such tenderness, that she could almost believe they were alone.

Until Hypnos spoke up. "Wasn't this the woman who brought down Elysium?"

A few others murmured in agreement.

Sol opened his mouth to speak, but Trivia touched his knee to stop him. With a trembling breath, she said, "Yes. That was me. I was under Pandora's influence, but my choices were my own. I know I cannot undo what I did, but I am deeply sorrowful for the pain I have caused."

"I believe Trivia more than paid her dues by willingly giving herself up to Pandora's box in order to save Elysium," said Midas, his voice full of pride and a touch of irritation.

Gasps echoed around them. Diana straightened in her seat. "You destroyed Elysium... and then sacrificed yourself to save it?"

Trivia swallowed hard. "Um, yes. Well... I mean, I gave myself up to save Gaia and Sol so they could continue to rebuild the wards of Elysium."

"And then she united with my other two daughters to unleash the power of the Triple Goddess," Gaia said. The affection in her voice made Trivia's heart lift. "She defeated the Titans."

"I had help," Trivia argued. "It wasn't *just* me. My sisters—"

"She also willingly accepted the punishment for her crimes," Marina said. "My sisters and I sentenced her to rebuild Elysium alongside Gaia and Sol. Trivia agreed to this. She has paid for her grievances. Sacrificing herself to Pandora's box was not a requirement. I would say she has *more* than redeemed herself for her past actions."

Trivia's heart was twisting and tightening inside her. She wasn't sure if it was excitement or dread that filled her. Her pulse was racing. Good gods, this couldn't be happening. Were these people... *praising* her? She was torn between shame and gratitude. She didn't deserve it, and yet... she was touched that people were acknowledging the lengths she had gone to to atone for her sins.

"I will gladly accept the nomination to become Elysium's king," Sol said. "So long as Trivia can reign by my side as queen."

Trivia's head whipped toward him, her eyes widening. And he *winked* at her. As if this were all some joke.

"Trivia, do you accept this?" Midas asked.

Trivia's mouth opened and closed. Gods above, what could she say to this? Did she even *want* to be queen?

Sol watched her, his eyes softening with an unspoken question.

You can say no, his expression seemed to say. *You have the choice.*

But in that moment, Trivia realized she would do *anything* to be with him. They had been given a second chance. And a third and a fourth...

They could finally be together.

And right then and there, she realized she would do it—she would become queen—so long as she could be by his side.

How long had she been plotting her revenge, angry at how the gods had treated her? How long had she spouted on about the despicable actions of those like Apollo?

This was her chance to change it all. To bring justice and freedom to the lesser gods and goddesses like herself. To change the realm for the better.

Strength and resolve swelled in her chest, and she found herself nodding. "Y-Yes. I accept."

"Fabulous." Midas clapped his hands together with a grin. "Are there any other nominations?"

"I *would* nominate myself," came Cyrus's drawl, "if I weren't already King of the Underworld."

Several deities grumbled in annoyance.

"I nominate Gaia," said Morpheus in his deep voice. "She was once our queen alongside Apollo before she was wrongfully banished."

But Gaia was shaking her head. "I must refuse the nomination. I am not meant to be queen. I am meant to lead my coven of witches. As soon as our council is adjourned, I will be returning to my home in Krenia."

Trivia's chest tightened with dread. Gaia was... *leaving*?

But as Gaia met her gaze then, a mixture of sadness and joy filled those blue eyes. She was eager to return home. From what Trivia knew, there was a lover who awaited her.

And Gaia had suffered enough. She deserved to live happily with the one she loved most.

Trivia found herself smiling, and she nodded to her mother.

"Can I nominate myself?" Eris asked with a light laugh. Beside her, Diana rolled her eyes.

"Ah yes, the Goddess of Chaos as our ruler," Deimos said in a flat voice. "No cause for concern there."

"*Conflict*," Eris said with a sniff. "Chaos is a nasty word. Far more disorderly."

"Are there any other *legitimate* nominations?" Midas asked, his voice rising over Eris's.

Silence met his words. A few of the deities exchanged looks in the circle, but none spoke up.

"Are there any *opposed* to Sol and Trivia as our king and queen?" Midas asked.

Trivia's heart stopped for a full beat as she gazed around the circle with wide eyes. She wasn't sure what she was most afraid of—objections, or acquiescence.

Would she become queen?

Or would she be rejected, as she had her entire life?

A tense silence filled the space. Her chest cinched tighter, tighter, *tighter*...

"Very well then." Midas was beaming. "All hail Sol and Trivia, the new King and Queen of Elysium."

Oh my gods, Trivia thought, shock rippling over her. *Is this really happening?*

Sol turned to look at her, eyebrows raised. A taunting smirk pulled at his lips, but his eyes were earnest as they bored into hers.

He was waiting for her to react. And she *could* say no. It

wasn't too late. She could claim she'd changed her mind. She could say she wasn't ready.

But... she *was* ready. She had brushed with death far too many times. She had been ripped away from Sol, fearing she would never get to live her life with him.

This was her chance to make things right. To start anew.

She took a deep, steadying breath, then smiled at the man who held her heart, whose soul was forever entwined with hers.

One by one, the deities slid from their seats to take a knee before their new king and queen. Midas and Cyrus wore amused expressions, as if this whole ordeal were hilarious to them. Gaia's eyes were shining with tears as she knelt, her head bowed in reverence.

Sol helped Trivia to her feet as they stood, hands clasped in unity to acknowledge the role they would play in rebuilding the realms.

King and Queen of Elysium.

Trivia found herself grinning broadly, all knots loosening in her chest. This was right. This was perfection.

She looked at Sol, whose eyes burned with intensity.

This—right here, with Sol—was *home.*

EPILOGUE
GAIA

The chilled autumn air nipped at Gaia's arms, and she rubbed them, gazing expectantly toward the garden pathway that led to the cobbled road. Behind her, Sybil's arms came around her, and a soft kiss pressed to her cheek.

"You worry too much, Polly," Sybil murmured.

Gaia let her eyes close, relishing the feel of her lover's warm embrace. Goddess, she had missed this. The briny sea air, the whispering wind, the chill of autumn nightfall at Samhain...

It was so familiar, and yet, she had never expected to experience it again. She fully intended to die, whether by Trivia's hand or by the Titans'.

But here she was with the woman she loved. A blessing she did not deserve.

"I wish I could wait for them at the docks," Gaia murmured.

"You're needed *here*," Sybil protested. "And, I must admit, you're doing a terrible job. I need more willow sprigs."

Gaia sighed, falling back on her knees to sift through Sybil's thriving garden. She found the discarded willow sprigs that had been abandoned as she had once more thought of her daughters, worrying they wouldn't make it.

But Prudence, Pomona, and Trivia had promised to be here. Gaia knew they would come.

A coil of powerful magic curled in the air, and Gaia stiffened, her head lifting as she gazed down the path. After a few moments, three figures appeared, and a wide smile split across her face.

In a flash, Gaia was on her feet, rushing down the path and throwing herself into the waiting arms of her three daughters. Prudence and Pomona hugged her back immediately, squeezing tightly. But Trivia held back. She touched Gaia's arm, but she remained distant, the twist of her lips betraying her discomfort.

Displays of affection among family members was still foreign to her.

My fault, Gaia thought. *It's my fault she's like this. My fault she didn't grow up with a mother to love her.*

Swallowing down her grief and regret, Gaia parted from Prudence and Pomona, then embraced Trivia fully, crushing her against her chest.

Trivia yelped slightly, her arms flailing before she hesitantly grasped Gaia in return.

"You are loved," Gaia whispered in her ear. "My daughter, you are so very loved. Never forget that."

When Gaia pulled away, Trivia's eyes were moist, and she sniffed. "Um. Well. It's good to see you, Mother."

Mother.

It wasn't *Mama,* but it was better than calling Gaia by her given name.

Gaia smiled, taking in her daughters' appearances. Prudence's face was glowing, her lavender eyes bright. Her usual curly mane of hair was slightly puffy from the humid air. Pomona was more altered. Her face was a bit paler, and her eyes seemed so strange now that they were hazel instead of emerald.

But the small smile on her face and the shrewd look in her gaze was all Pomona. She was still Gaia's daughter, even if she was mortal.

Then, there was Trivia. She wore a golden gown with a sleeve over one shoulder, and a laurel crown atop her head. She looked every bit the Queen of Elysium.

"My darling daughters," Gaia said thickly, struggling to keep the tears at bay. "I am so grateful you've come."

"Sybil!" Pomona cried, darting around Gaia to embrace her stepmother. Prudence followed suit, the two girls clinging to the woman who had helped raise them. Sybil's beautiful face was just as glowing, as if she, too, possessed goddess blood. Her smile was wide, lighting up her features.

Sybil might not have birthed the two girls, but she loved them as her own. It was one of the many things Gaia adored about her.

"Are we too late?" Pomona asked, looking at Gaia with a small frown.

"Not at all." Gaia scooped up the basket of herbs she'd

been collecting, then jerked her head in the direction of the path. "We were just heading to the square."

They walked down the cobbled path, Prudence chattering about the affairs of the Underworld. A council of demons was helping her and Cyrus rule. Some of the gods in Elysium were unhappy with this, but from what Gaia gathered, it was working quite well.

Certainly better than when Aidoneus had been in charge.

A few villagers passed by, nodding politely at Gaia. One or two smiled broadly at Prudence and Pomona, easily recognizing them, even after all this time.

This was still the girls' home. Even if their hearts were now elsewhere, in Gaia's eyes, the three of them would always belong here.

Trivia's brows were furrowed as she took in everything, her eyes roving over the swaying palm trees and the thatch-roofed homes. This was her first time on Krenia.

"Have you been to a Samhain ceremony before?" Gaia asked her.

Trivia blinked, then met her gaze. "No. I never had the chance."

Because of how I was raised.

The unspoken words hung between them, but there was no guilt or accusation. Just the truth.

It was something Trivia might never heal from. And something Gaia might never forgive herself for.

Gaia took Trivia's hand in hers. "It is something to behold. You'll see."

They reached the town square where a circle of chanting witches stood hand-in-hand as they muttered the words of the spell. Already, the air was thick and potent with the presence of spirits. The veil was its thinnest at dusk. Once the sun fully set, the echoes of the ancestors would cross over to greet them.

Sybil inserted herself into the circle, grasping hands with her fellow witches and joining in the chanting. But Gaia and her daughters stood on the outskirts, not wanting to intrude.

This was a sacred ceremony, fueled by the magic of witches. With this much power between the four of them, Gaia feared it might alter the spell circle. She didn't want to risk damaging the veil or the spirits.

"Do you feel it?" Gaia asked Trivia.

Trivia nodded, her wide eyes fixed on the witches. She looked so young. So innocent. In this moment, Gaia could envision her as a little girl experiencing this for the first time.

"What are they saying?" Trivia whispered in awe.

"The words translate to, *Open. Receive our gift. Commune with us.*"

"What gift have they offered?"

Gaia gestured to the altar resting in the middle of the witches where a slaughtered goat lay, its fresh blood gleaming on the stone.

Trivia shuddered. "Lovely."

"It's the way of the witches," Gaia said with a shrug. "If it hadn't been sacrificed, it would have been eaten with the meal."

Trivia snorted at that.

Then, she suddenly froze. A keening wail pierced the air, echoing around the square. The townsfolk gasped as several other whispers and murmurs resonated from the witches' spell.

Gaia loved this part for many reasons. For one, it was always awe-inspiring to see how the spirits communicated with them. For another, she loved watching the reactions of the villagers who possessed no magic. The people's eyes were wide and full of wonder. Some were only children, clearly experiencing their first Samhain ritual.

"Prue," murmured a voice.

Prudence went rigid and uttered a soft gasp.

Gaia looked around, searching for the source of the voice, but she couldn't see anyone.

"I am always here with you, Prue," said the voice.

Tears glistened in Prudence's eyes, and she pressed a hand to her heart. "And I am always with you, Lagos."

Gaia's throat tightened. She had not known Lagos, but from what she had heard, he had been a fierce ally of Prudence's from the beginning. And she would always think fondly of him for that.

A shimmering form appeared in front of them, this one taking the shape of a woman with long hair. "Your coven is beautiful," the woman said, her voice deep and firm.

Pomona's breath hitched, and she covered her mouth with her hand. "Farah?"

"Do not mourn me," Farah said. "I have died a warrior's death, and for that I will be honored."

"And so she is," Trivia said softly. "I have met her in Elysium. She has found peace."

Pomona let out a shuddering sob, tears streaming down her face. All around the square, spirits were visiting their loved ones. There was not a dry eye in the space. Even the chanting witches were weeping from the power emanating around them.

"I am glad to see you so content, dear one," said a voice in Gaia's ear. Her eyes closed as she relished the sound of her old friend, Hestia.

"I am glad, too," Gaia whispered.

She leaned her head on Pomona's shoulder, then took Prudence and Trivia's hands in hers. "This is true beauty right here," she told her daughters. "To experience the purest form of witch magic guiding these spirits to us in a celestial reunion—alongside the people I love most in the world." She caught Sybil's eye from across the square. Sybil's gaze seemed to burn into hers with the intensity of a raging inferno.

Gaia's heart was full. And as her daughters expressed their agreement with her sentiment, she realized there was nothing more perfect than this.

Home.

Family.

And the thriving beauty of earth magic.

NOTE TO THE READER

Thank you so much for reading! I greatly appreciate you taking the time.

If you would be so kind, please leave a review to let others know what you thought of the book!

ACKNOWLEDGMENTS

I honestly cannot believe this series has come to an end! It is so surreal, and sometimes, I'm devastated that it's over.

But at the same time, I'm in love with these characters and how their stories ended. I never knew when the series began just how much the characters would grow and transform, or how much they would work their way into my heart.

There are so many people I have to thank for helping me write the ending to this saga.

My amazing beta readers: Jenni, Tori, Melissa, and Kari. Your helpful critiques helped me improve my writing and make the story the best it can be.

My incredible ARC team for your early reading and supportive reviews. Thank you for being so excited to dive back in to the Ivy & Bone world!

art_jake, for the beautiful art you created for the reversible dust jacket.

To all my Kickstarter backers: a huge thank you for your pledges! Without you, the amazing special editions for this series never would have been created. Thank you so much for your support.

And, most importantly, thank you Alex, Colin, Ellie, and Isabel. You are the greatest joys of my life. Thank you for standing by me through it all.

ABOUT THE AUTHOR

R.L. Perez is an author, wife, mother, reader, writer, and graphic designer. She lives in Florida with her husband and three children. On a regular basis, she can usually be found napping, reading, feverishly writing, revising, or watching an abundance of Netflix. More than anything, she loves spending time with her family. Her greatest joys are her two kids, nature, literature, and chocolate.

Subscribe to her newsletter for new releases, promotions, giveaways, and book recommendations! Get a FREE eBook when you sign up at subscribe.rlperez.com.

www.ingramcontent.com/pod-product-compliance
Lightning Source LLC
Chambersburg PA
CBHW021228190726

48289CB00005B/1229